Tynedale

Jean Simpson

© Jean Simpson,2005

First published in 2005.

Printed and bound by
Lintons Printers,
Crook, County Durham
Tel: 01388 762197

ISBN: 0-9539714-1-4

Robinsonwalton Publications
31 Wells Green, Barton DL10 6NH.

This book is dedicated to Roger
and each member of our delightful family.

AUTHOR'S NOTE

Although trying to capture the spirit of the age in the Northern Region, for the ease of the reader I have written largely in a modern idiom, and telescoped some geographical and historical facts for the sake of the story.

All the characters in this book are purely imaginary.

Chapter 1

Joanna cast a worried eye towards her husband, Richard, exhausted from coughing and slumped beside the choking fire of their meagre dwelling. With a sigh she picked up their sleeping baby strapped to the wooden board, and, nudging aside the cowhide, quickly stepped outside. A blast of bitterly cold wind pierced her homespun cloak and threatened to take the baby's breath away. Nothing daunted, she hugged her child protectively in its shawl, and toiled uphill to the large stone-built farmhouse, which she entered with hushed reverence. Only the crackling logs on the hearth cheered the sombre scene. She eagerly peeped at the other baby, sleeping in a cradle by the fire, whom she had herself lovingly wrapped in her bands that afternoon, and she smiled as she saw her, in full health, concentrating on sleeping, her sweet innocence unaware of the developing drama surrounding her.

Joanna looked towards John, but in his anguish he was oblivious to her. He was sitting on a cracket, beside the bed of his dying wife, Margaret, with his young, already gnarled hands tightly gripping his head. His thoughts were tortured as no one else would ever know. He had loved his wife from childhood when her fresh beauty had captured him irrevocably. Every hair of her head was infinitely precious to him and his heart had swelled with happiness at her very presence. He recalled the time when she had to go away to work at Woodall's residence, when he had wanted her terribly, in silence, like the earth yearns for sun and rain.

When she returned he instinctively guessed her trouble, and had readily married her, and cherished her, and enjoyed seven months of her bright sunny chatter and loveliness. He had worshipped her like an untouchable goddess, and that was how she appeared to him now. He sensed that her time was near, without being told by old Nancy, who sat mute in the corner. The silent numbness of overwhelming distress hung like a cloud over the room. In these circumstances, words, the greatest deceivers anyway, were absolutely unutterable.

John ffarbrigge recollected the day when she came back. He had just finished sowing the field and was preparing to make his weary way homewards. When he screwed his eyes against the setting sun his heart leapt as he recognised the

1

familiar figure hurrying towards him. He rushed to enclose her in his strong arms. Weeping, she looked into his eyes with smothered sobs. "John, I couldn't help ......", and a swift intuition told him what she was trying to say. Never failing, and in absolute trust, he had drawn her closer to him, their souls had spindled together, and they had been allowed for a short time to be again complete.

Soon it would be all gone. In despair he searched his mind for the bright spark that had been her. The only way he could keep her essence was to shut it up in his heart, isolated, and forever his, and he vowed that he would never allow any word to defile its sanctity, not even her name. He slowly raised his head. Every single object in the room lacked substance against his tremendous loss. Why her cooking pot? Why the herbs that she had hung from the ceiling? Why old Nancy? Why the silly horseshoe over the door, nailed there in defiance of the fairies who might steal the good woman in the straw? His mind was floating away from bitter reality.

John noticed that Joanna had arrived only because she had disturbed the bony, bedraggled dog which immediately slunk over to the bed intending to lick its mistress's face. He roughly brushed the whimpering creature aside, to prevent it crossing the dying woman, an act which, according to the old tradition, would result in the animal's death.

Joanna built up the fire with fern and furze to warm the baby's tail clouts. Patient old Nancy, who had been sitting in a dark corner waiting to finish her task, slowly and painfully rose, and examined the body that had thwarted all her efforts. Eyes watched her intently, and without a word she shook her head. It was all over. The hard fight had been fought, and Margaret was with the angels. Now she could only dispose of the bloodstained wrappings and prepare the body for burial. Joanna clutched the dead mother's baby tightly in her arms and, half sobbing, whispered to Nancy: "Early babies are always a danger to the mother. Nature isn't ready for it. It's amazing the baby survived.....and poor John," she sympathised, as her voice faded away.

Nancy nodded, her thoughts deep and unspoken. Handing the baby over to John, Joanna carefully took the white wedding dress from the big chest and gave it to the old woman who gently dressed the deceased in white, like one who had retained her virginity. Only John knew that it had been prised rather than freely given, and wrenched from her at such a high price. The dress and the dead woman's pale skin contrasted sharply with her magnificent black hair, arranged around her face in beautiful tresses. Nancy had noticed the brown birthmark on the young mother's breast and remembered a similar one on the new baby. She was always fascinated by the never-ceasing rhythmic continuity of the generations. She wondered if life and death had any more meaning than the constantly turning wheel of the mill race? Were we just insignificant drops in the hands of the Maker, even the most precious of us crazily swept in circles, and then casually cast aside?

As she went about her task she reassured herself by chanting absent-mindedly: "Death shall be the beginning of everlasting joy .....". She broke off with a deep sigh and then resumed: "In sorrow thou shalt bring forth children and thy desire shall be to thy husband and he shall rule over thee."

John cradled the baby affectionately in his arms, reluctantly wresting his gaze from the still beauty of his dead wife to the last precious gift which she had left him. As he bonded with her baby, he vowed silently: "With all my strength I'll look after you forever, and ever." This resolution relaxed him, and the baby slumbered peacefully, as if blissfully aware of the good man's promise.

Unnoticed, Joanna picked up her little girl, Isabel, who was crying, and, remembering her own ailing husband, quietly left the house. The dog followed her.

Such were the sad events at Hackford, a small rural community in Tynedale, Northumberland, in the year of our Lord, 1646.

Chapter 2

Eighteen years had passed, eighteen years in which John had never mentioned, and still could not mention, his first wife's name; eighteen years of the stark reality of a patient, determined fight for survival. John had married the widowed Joanna, and he had found consolation in her sweet nature.They had enjoyed watching their two daughters grow strong together, happy in the convenience of their parents' union, which was not complicated by sentimental demands and grudges, but based on the harsh necessity of creating a comfortable existence. Sweet childhood memories, fleeting glimpses of the past, were gathered and retained preciously in their hearts. The steady rhythmic beat of life, throbbing for ever on an apparent upward track, sometimes stony, sometimes steep, was in reality flat and continued so. However, as happiness is finite for everyone, whatever the circumstances, they were blissfully content in their wild and remote valley like caged princesses, preserved from outside threat.

John's daughter, Elizabeth, had become a young woman of eloquent beauty, tall and slim with sparkling green eyes, even features, haughty clear-cut eyebrows, long eyelashes, and well-formed rosy lips, her flowing auburn tresses reaching down to a graceful waist. Her smile would thaw even the severest demeanour, so that she charmed the whole neighbourhood. She was quick-witted, and from early childhood had been the great favourite of Canon Ritschell who, on his frequent visits from Hexham, had found Elizabeth a willing pupil in learning the elements of reading and writing. When she was happy, which was most of the time, she would sing the songs that Joanna had taught her, and John, working in the fields, loved to hear her sweet voice soaring as she busied herself with the daily chores.

Her dark-haired stepsister, Isabel, was plain and less clever, but she too was attractive, not least because of her ready smile, cheerfulness and warm personality. Her solid frame suggested dependability. The two girls were entirely different; yet they had remained loyal and inseparable companions. Elizabeth was a free spirit, bold, full of energy and a desire for knowledge. Joanna's daughter, Isabel, was soft and malleable, responsive to the needs of others, but cautious. Many years they had explored the moors together and were frequent visitors at the homesteads within easy reach of their own farm. Yet their attitudes were completely different, no more than in their relationship with the old crone, Nancy, who lived in the far part of the moor.

She had attended both of their own births, and had been generally sought after in the valley, but now she was a gibbering, twisted old woman, living in an turf-walled house at the edge of the common, forever muttering angrily at her cruel fate as she staggered painfully across the moor. Elizabeth was a frequent visitor to her abode, which was a crude hut without proper windows. The floor was covered with well-trodden pads of heather, rushes and coarse grasses, concealing the bare earth. The rickety door swung on hinges of plaited willow, leaving wide gaps through which the wind would often whistle with a merciless chill. The walls of turf, timber, and rocks supported the thick thatch of branches and twigs which were tightly bound together with heather and straw.

Her fire occupied the middle of the space, occasionally flaring with a precious flame, but all the while belching acrid smoke, which escaped mainly through a hole in the roof, and partly by the door. Her bed was straw-covered, arranged on rough wooden boards, framed to form a shallow box to allow her to crawl in to the small compartment where she slept, snuggling up in the warmth of its heather-packed recess, her head resting on a humble pillow of wild bird feathers. Everywhere there were bunches of herbs, hanging up to dry, and pots of carefully prepared potions, all arrayed on rickety shelves. A vessel for cooking the occasional rabbit, a washing tub, and a wooden pail, completed the meagre inventory.

Sad in her isolation, she was avoided as a witch, blamed for misfortunes, then forgotten. Even the sympathetic Joanna was influenced by the scorn directed at the old woman. "Do you know she turns into a hare and races across the moor? Have you heard her voice piercing the night? Old William says...", and so on. Elizabeth, however, her only true friend, was fascinated by her rural skills, and often helped her as she scoured the hedgerows and ditches for herbs to make her strange concoctions, which neighbours secretly sought, as stealthy as they were critical. Elizabeth's enquiring mind absorbed knowledge of her recipes, which the most desperate craved in their need. She soon knew which herbs to collect and which to avoid like the plague. She quickly learned how to make draughts, salves, and soaps, and delighted in experimenting on the farm animals' sores and cuts.

As the wind hurtles across the moor, flattening the tall grasses in its headlong race, so old Nancy's bold spirit sped, defying her infirm body. Elizabeth marvelled at her, yet, in contrast, others saw her only as a half-forbidden gesticulating wretch, her wiry but weakening frame silhouetted against the sky as she battled against the elements. She had forgotten how to straighten, and painfully curled up more and more in a vain search for comfort, strangely bending in the very foetal curl which had been such a symbolic part of her ministrations. People saw only the drooping mouth with its broken foul-smelling teeth, and her unkempt grey hair poking out from below her crumpled hat. As she muttered execrations, her mouth twisted with contempt, hiding the desperate spirit in need of succour and love, yet unable, and too proud to show it. Her sole pleasure was when she sought the doubtful warmth of her rough bed at night.

Elizabeth quietly observed all this, and her neighbours' attitudes, and was appalled. "Senseless gossips deserve rubbish to chew over," she thought. Her independence of mind forbade her to bray, miaow, bellow or squawk with the mob. Fascinated by a compulsive tendency to observe appearance and reality, rather than to mould others, she was rendered vulnerable. Her anger sometimes erupted in blind defiance of feelings with which she could not associate. How many times had she taunted them with concocted claims that: "Yes, she had herself consorted with the witch and had danced at night on the moor." Alas, she had not yet learnt that those who do not go with the herd are picked out as victims, and she did not realise that in such rebellion she was courting danger. Inherited traits of lineage might be safe and attractive in one protected by wealth and power, but could spell doom for those who ought to follow only one order, that of obedience to the common weal. Too poor and weak to fight a cause, and with the ignorance of youth, she was the helpless play-thing of Fate.

However, all this was briefly submerged in the general excitement at Hackford. A wedding was in the air, with new life and new beginnings. Isabel ffarbrigge was to be married to Cuthbert Teasdale from the neighbouring farm. The wheel was turning.

Chapter 3

Such a hurry and a scurry on the wedding morn.
Such a blushing, squealing, hushing
That could e'er be borne.

The bridegroom left early, in a cart creaking and groaning as it swayed under its heavy load of parents, relatives and friends. The bride followed later in an even fuller waggon, and the air rang with care-free laughter all the way to Hexham. The sunny day grew warm as the scene transformed into pure Northumbrian beauty. On the moor the heather still spread in a sea of purple and green; in the valley the birdcherry was blossoming profusely, and the still air was sweet with the fragrance of the flowers, attended by the drowsy humming of the bees.

Hours later, across the hills and valleys, the sun shimmered on the grasses, and all eyes at Hackford turned to the north to see the wedding party return. The first distant sign of their arrival was the younger men leaping in great excitement from the waggons and then racing nearly a mile to see who was the first to reach the bridal home. The bridegroom's brother, John Teasdale, a powerful, long-legged lad, easily outstripped the others, and sat at the back door, red-faced and panting, waiting for the rest to catch up. By ancient custom he had won the right to demand the garter from the bride.

"Come on, where've you been?" he demanded of the slower runners as they came in. " I thowt you'd been taken with the ague, or grown wooden legs."

His friends, variously snorting and heaving for breath, could only grin wordlessly. They gladly slumped against the grey stone walls of the farmhouse, young Robsons alongside Wrays, Hutchinsons with Armstrongs, Pattersons with Johnsons, all sweating and thirsty with the heat, and swatting away the clouds of flies. They did not have long to wait for the bridal party. As the track rose, and dipped, and rose again between the brees and gullies, the slow-moving nuptial procession disappeared into the hollows and re-emerged, gradually coming nearer and nearer. Even the patient old horses, bedecked in their rosettes, and roused by the excited voices, seemed to join in the spirit of the day and heaved with a special flowing strength. So the wedding guests, tossing and jolting in the gaily decorated farm carts, returned joyously from the abbey at Hexham, and the waiting crowd of neighbours, young and old, peered and pointed with increasing restlessness as the crunching wheels slowly ate up the distance. Eventually the waggons turned off the main valley track and headed down towards the farm and the babbling voices of the wedding party grew louder. Children ran to greet the bridal couple who sat in pride of place on the leading cart.

"Hello, Mistress Teasdale! You do look pretty," one cried.

"Isabel! Isabel! I'll take your flowers inside," insisted another.

"Look out, Cuthbert, you're one of the ffarbrigge family now. You'll have to mind your manners!"

Cuthbert proudly helped his bride down from the cart and they were besieged with kisses and handshakes from their neighbours as they made their way towards the cool interior of Hackford farmhouse. The house, clean as a new pin, was strewn with rushes, herbs and rosemary, and gaily decorated with garlands over every beam and lintel. Cuthbert good-naturedly tousled his brother's hair as the couple approached the doorway, and, in a state of exhilaration, congratulated him: "You rogue! So you won the garter again!"

Cuthbert lifted up Isabel and kissed her before pausing in front of John, indicating that he should unfasten the garter below her knee. John deftly seized his chance and brandished it in high glee, the company cheering and chuckling at his antics. A shower of wheat grains pattered over the couple, promising fertility, as, amid raucous laughter, the happy bridegroom whisked the bride effortlessly over the threshold. The bridal pair were followed closely by the two sets of parents, relaxed and joking together in the company of old acquaintances. The closeness was apparent as their clans had been intermarried through the generations. In hard times and danger, not so many years ago, their bonding had been essential for survival.

"Mind her head!" came the chorus.

"I hope you have as many as Alice Tucker!" cried old William Robson.

"And how many did she have?" croaked Robert Mason, grinning mischievously as he predicted the answer.

"Twenty!" came the chorus from several onlookers.

"Phew! Give over," said Cuthbert, blushing.

They crowded inside the farmhouse where a large feast had been prepared. There, sitting by the fire, was John ffarbrigge's younger brother, Anthony, a prosperous widower, who loved family occasions, and was newly arrived from

Newcastle for the wedding feast. He was fond of his nieces and relished the joy of this new union. Small, rotund and jovial, in contrast to his tall wiry brother, he had left the farm to become a merchant, and by honest endeavour he had prospered. Smiling by the fireside, his fat red face glowed with happiness. He was out to enjoy the festivities, and his expansive personality infected all around him, with his tapping foot and encouraging mien. In his excitement he was constantly rubbing his large nose round and round with the palm of his hand, and his whole body rippled with laughter, which, once started, was impossible to suppress.

Cuthbert lowered Isabel to the floor with an extravagant grunt of feigned thankfulness. Anthony rose to greet them, smiling broadly.

"You've had a beautiful day for your wedding. That's surely an omen for a long and happy life together. Good health to you both!"

His sharp eye dwelt on his niece, Isabel. She wore nothing richer than a white nightgown with its edging of lace around the bosom, and on her head was a cap, lined with homespun green material and tied with matching ribbons, over which a little straw hat was perched cheekily. Her borrowed wedding ring adorned her thumb which she held out with pride for all to see.

"We're back, Uncle Anthony. We're back at last!" she smiled, almost bursting with joy as she held her hands out towards him.

"This is indeed a blessed day," said Anthony, noticing the fresh bloom of her skin and the thickening waistline. "You look so pretty, my dear, but I expect you're tired and hot after the long journey. Sit yourselves down and tell me all about the ceremony."

"Oh", replied Cuthbert, glad to rest beside him on a little cracket, with his knees spread wide. " It was the same as all weddin's - quiet, solemn and movin', especially for us. Canon Ritschell said some nice things about marriage, and there's not a parson to touch him for deep meanin'."

Cuthbert's attention was diverted to the throng of neighbours who were pressing indoors to join the feast, leaving their children skipping and chasing all the way down to the burn, and there was much shaking of hands and wishing of good fortune, everyone enjoying the welcome respite from work. The older women bustled round with slices of meat pie, pasties, scones, cakes and tankards of strong sweet bride-ale which everyone quaffed gratefully. Anthony's eyes turned to Elizabeth, who had picked up the Northumbrian pipes and was earnestly examining the instrument on her lap, as if she desired to improve its design. She turned it this way and that and plied the piper with a string of questions. He was making the most of his time, being well into his second helping of meat and alc, and through a full mouth dealt with the interrogation as best he could.

"This arm squeezes the bag to supply continuous wind, and my fingers control the reeds for the tune. All the time I'm playing I have to keep my eyes on the dancers to set a proper pace. Sometimes I have fun, quickening them up, but I need to take care not to overwork the elders," he winked.

With the musician's permission, as was the custom, Elizabeth rescued the bride's garter from John Teasdale and carefully tied it to the pipes. By now the piper, had ensconced himself in the corner, and, full of concentration, busied himself with a vigorous filling of the wind-bag, his arm pumping against his side. It was the work of seconds to tune up, and it was not long before the roof and rafters really did dirl. The guests responded with an infectious animation and soon feet were tapping, shoulders dipping and hands clapping. Some of the young people wanted to dance and tripped out of the door. Andrew Patterson flew after the pretty Mary Armstrong and they were the first to form the line. "I love weddings, don't you?" said Andrew, looking deep into her eyes. Mary blushed and looked down as she took his hands, unable to reply but looking pleased.

Behind his elation Anthony studied Elizabeth thoughtfully. He felt a deep concern for her, because he knew that she would be most affected by her sister's marriage. He recognised that the sisters had been inseparable all their lives, and things would never be the same again. However, he reflected, who knows the inner recesses of anyone's mind, let alone Elizabeth's?

In fact Elizabeth was having the time of her life, the celebrations being a welcome change from the normal farm routine. She was not in the slightest jealous of Isabel, because she knew that, if she had wanted, she could have easily been in the same position, but life proved to be so exciting that being tied in matrimony was well down her list of priorities.

There were soon more people outside than inside the farmhouse and the piper sauntered out without a pause in his music. The bridal party followed and as Elizabeth caught up with her sister she gave her a reassuring squeeze round the waist and teased Cuthbert with her cajoling banter.

"I suppose we'll have to put up with you all the time, now! You'd better behave yourself, lad, or you'll be out in the pig sty."

Cuthbert only grinned more widely. "Anything to keep the peace, my dearest sister."

Then the dance separated them as new partners came face to face along the line, moving to the piper's tune. Eventually, as the weather was congenial, even the elders moved into the open air, swelling in numbers all the time as whole families from neighbouring farms joined the celebrations. There was a large flat area outside the farmhouse, conveniently skirted with trees, below which the slope dropped gently to a small burn.

The clear waters of the stream winked and gurgled as they rushed between the stones on their eager way to the River Tyne. The children gathered on each bank, splashing and arguing. The boys were keen to build a dam, wading barefoot into the middle, while the girls sat down to watch and shout advice on which gaps should be plugged, intent on keeping their dresses clean.

Above them the local fiddler, who had waited his turn patiently, now came to the fore, and with great vigour struck up a jaunty tune. The bridal couple led off across the grass with gusto, followed by their friends, arms outstretched and knees raised high. Reel succeeded reel as the throng threw themselves into the spirit of the well-loved music of the traditional northern dances. As the piper joined the fiddler, the air vibrated with the strains of familiar melodies, bringing back poignant memories for many of the guests.

Elizabeth danced in the lines continuously and she was so full of energy that it showed in her own special way. Each step was an explosive upward hop as she bounced and bounded from the turf, her back stiffly upright, and her knees rising higher than anyone's. The dancers laughed as they grabbed their partners and reformed the swirling lines. The elders pointed and clapped in time with the tune, regretting that they could not join in, and remembering their own youthful capers of years ago.

Cousin Thomas, a tall, lithe young man with a beguiling smile, pounced on his neighbour, a heavily-built woman who, despite her reluctance, was dragged into the dance.

"Come on, everyone says that you were a good dancer in your time."

"No, no. I can't manage it now," she protested. However, it was to no avail, and, flattered at first, she puffed and panted as she tried to keep up the pace and was all smiles until she was swung too vigorously and was flung skidding out of line, just managing to grasp the branch of a tree which prevented her plunging headlong down towards the burn. Turning several shades of purple she gasped as she tried to recover her breath. Thomas stood at a distance for a while, looking somewhat alarmed. Concerned mothers nudged his subsequent partners warily as he approached them but he did not falter before seizing them and whirling them off, down this line, and round that circle. Drops of perspiration ran down the fiddler's face as he called on all his musical memories to play a series of the most bewitching tunes.

Breathless at last, Elizabeth escaped from the tumult. She spied her beloved Uncle Anthony, resting happily under a tree, and joined him, sitting on a convenient stone. "Well, Uncle, are you enjoying yourself?"

"Of course, bonny lass. It's one of the happiest days of my life. I expect it'll be your turn next. Which poor man have you got your eyes on?" he quizzed, his eyes twinkling as he surveyed the company.

"Bah," Elizabeth spat out explosively.

After a pause he queried: "Why don't you try your luck in the town? The choice there is much greater. Will you please an old man by coming to stay with me in Newcastle? I get lonely by myself."

Elizabeth thought for a moment, considering the idea.

" That would be exciting. Yes, yes! Of course I'll come. I've never been to Newcastle, and I'd love to see that wonderful house of yours." She kissed him lovingly on the cheek.

At this point, seeing Elizabeth's excitement, Isabel approached. "What are you two concocting?" she demanded.

"Oh, Isabel! I'm going to Newcastle, to stay with Uncle Anthony," then added teasingly, as she looked at Anthony with one of her most engaging smiles, "and run that big house for him."

"Who said anything about that?" retorted Anthony, staring at her with a mixture of feigned alarm and amusement. "I've enough servants to take care of everything."

"Well, cousin Thomas will have to go with you. He can keep an eye on you," Isabel jested, pulling Elizabeth's chin.

" I'd love Thomas to go with me. Uncle, can Thomas come as well?" she pressed.

"Yes, he can be your escort and guide, because I shall be too busy to be with you much of the time," replied Anthony, rubbing his nose.

"Isabel, will you ask him if he wants to go. Now, this minute?" pleaded Elizabeth eagerly, as she preened herself, thinking of being accompanied by the tall, fair, and amiable Thomas, her companion on so many childhood romps.

Isabel spotted the handsome, blue-eyed Thomas, laughing and joking in the midst of a bevy of local beauties, but nevertheless vigorously beckoned him to join them. Excusing himself, he strode over, asking: "Now what's happening?"

Uncle Anthony said: "I'd like you and Elizabeth to come to stay with me in Newcastle for a while."

Without a second thought Thomas readily assented: "Of course. Newcastle, London, anywhere. It's all the same to me." He bowed his head politely to his uncle and smiled at the two women, then he was off to the dancing once more.

Filled with the exhilaration of the wedding, Elizabeth felt anything was possible, and she was relishing such an adventure. Anthony, on the other hand, glowed inwardly, because his kind nature revelled in solving a problem which, unbeknown to him, did not really exist. He beamed with delight at his own supposed intuition.

Infected by her excitement, a crowd of children encircled Elizabeth, eagerly clamouring for games. She quickly responded, threatening in a loud voice: "You all know what I am - I can be a mouse, a hare, a fox, anything I like! I dance like a witch on the moor!" and she pretended to pounce on them one by one, and chased them, screaming, through the trees. Anthony shook his head and his face grew serious.

There was something different about her. Women should be far more compliant. Who would have her, he bewailed to himself, shaking his head. Any casual watcher would be wondering at him as he muttered to himself, grimacing in tune with his thoughts. Anthony remembered how often in church Elizabeth had been the leader of the restless young miscreants who, bored by the tedium of the service, had attracted the stewards' disapproval. The more stern their glances as they patrolled pompously down the aisles, the more explosive the giggles of the young people, led by his erring niece. He continued shaking his head. All Joanna's fault! She had not chastised and whipped them enough. Everyone knew that a hazel stick regularly whacked across the back did wonders for a rebellious nature! Then there was that interfering old priest, Canon Ritschell. Had he stretched the girl too far?

He shuddered. All of us have wickedness and kindness in varying proportions. Wicked thoughts can spread from one to another like an uncontrollable disease, exploring every cranny of human consciousness. Such thoughts were teasing, taunting, tempting and downright dangerous. Everyone needed to safeguard against them, in the strength of prayer, because they could linger in some people, to their eternal damnation. His face relaxed and, with a shrug, he reassured himself that kindness was the stronger force, gently spreading like the ripples from a stone cast into the water. Rising stiffly and nursing his aching joints, his thoughts happily switched to the present and, shivering in the cooler air, he was encouraged indoors.

Even when the shadows lengthened and dusk descended, the dancing continued, with crowds of moths fluttering around the lanterns which had been brought out to decorate the trees. The music-makers had several lengthy rests, but nevertheless the tunes gradually became less animated. The exhausted revellers sat down to finish off the bride-ale, before they eventually dispersed to their own homes in the greatest good humour. Leaning against the doorpost, Anthony watched his brother and Joanna saying farewell to the departing neighbours, and was amused by the sight of the tired-out little ones, some already sound asleep, their tousled heads bobbing up and down on strong shoulders as they were carried back to their own cottages.

All that remained was for Cuthbert's close friends to whisk him off to be undressed, and with raucous laughter, led by brother John, they escorted him upstairs to the bridal bed, where they found his blushing new wife surrounded by mother, bridesmaids and friends. The bride's stockings were thrown backwards to the girls, amid screams of delight. Elizabeth grabbed them both with great dexterity and, as the two sisters' eyes fixed on each other, Isabel raised her eyebrows. So the happy day ended and, the majority being in a pleasant frame of mind for slumber, retired to bed, contented. However, in the shadows down by the stream, Andrew Patterson and Mary Armstrong still lingered awhile, dreaming up plans strictly of their own.

Chapter 4

It was a warm June afternoon when, utterly weary and choked with dust, they came to a high hill overlooking Newcastle. The horse was pulled up and the waggon slowly creaked to a halt. Enthused by his new role as guide to the town, Thomas threw off his fatigue, and jumped off while the old carter clumsily helped Elizabeth down.

Elizabeth said: "Thank you for bringing us here safely."

The carter simply nodded and remounted his cart. "I'll see that your boxes get to Anthony's house. Furyee, ah ha!" he encouraged the tired horse, and he was off and away into the town.

Rejuvenated, Thomas turned round with glee and, pointing expansively with his arm, said proudly, " I asked Charlie to drop us here because I wanted you to see the best view of Newcastle before we go through the town walls. You can see the shippin' lyin' down there.

It's a good way from the sea and this must be one of the safest harbours in the land. The River Tyne is always crowded, full of colliers and the foreign ships runnin' up from Tinmouth. There's a stronghold where it enters the sea. Do you see all the little carriages? There's oxen and pairs of horses takin' the coals from the pits to the keel boats. They row them or pole them down to the ships, only four men to a boat. When the tide's in, the coal is lifted into the colliers, which sail to Billingsgate in London. The tide's in now, and they're usin' it. Look at the clouds of dust risin' from their shovels. I bet they're sweatin' down there, and smothered in coal dust. And see up there, on the Gateshead side, all those little coal pits."

Thomas's enthusiasm was communicated to his companion. Elizabeth held her breath with excitement, but at length whispered with distaste : "What an awful smell!"

"Why aye, lass, it's the air full of sulphur comin' from the coal smoke - but you'll get used to it. A brave and bonny place is Newcastle. Like London they say. Let's go down," continued Thomas, " and we'll find the Westgate. It's the best gate for us."

As they walked towards the town Thomas announced: " I've been here often enough but there's nothin' like seein' Newcastle for the first time. It's very special and I love sharin' the new sights with you, Elizabeth. Keep your eyes open."

They approached the Westgate, which was a massive brick building, with double gates under an arch. Inside, Elizabeth was astounded by the noise, the air being filled with a heady mixture of vibrant activity. Barrows crashed and bumped over the potholes, horses' hooves clanged in competition with ill-lubricated axles, and all this was overlapped by the raucous warnings of barrowmen and carters and the mournful strains of a drunken piper, playing out of time and tune. The overwhelming cacophony was different from the quiet everyday life of the open Northumbrian countryside, and titillating beyond measure.

Thomas ushered the wide-eyed Elizabeth down to the quayside where there was even more activity. It was very crowded and dirty, full of seamen, food sellers and sail menders, streams of people spilling from every tiny alley, with the whole quay running off at great length along the river bank. Great hoists swung to and fro as unloading went on. There were timber boats from Scandinavia, ships bringing small quantities of highly prized silks from Asia, spices from India, rarities from the Americas and the produce of both the distant Indies. The pair were now close to the colliers which were lining up along the jetties to be loaded with coal bound for London and east coast towns. In front of the warehouses, offices, and taverns lay casks of liquor and of water, sacks of flour, barrels of salted meat and biscuit, rolls of sail-cloth, tar, brushes and ropes, all ready to go on board. People were hurrying to and fro in great haste, orders being shouted out continually and the new arrivals could hardly move for being jostled.

Many steps ran down to the water and they saw a fleet of keels waiting up-river to receive the shiny black coals from the riverside staithes, in sharp contrast to the clouds of snow-white flakes billowing out from the salt works further down river. Up above was the grim grey castle, with its prison, overlooking the busyness of the crowded Sandgate. The striking appearance of the bridge over to Gateshead inspired Elizabeth with awe. The great piers supporting the high and broad arches looked imposing, and the houses built on them were like huge ramparts. She shuddered as she scrutinised its northernmost stone tower.

"Is that where the cut-purses are kept?" she whispered timidly.

Thomas nodded, savouring her reaction. She continued to stare in wonder.

After a while Thomas urged: "I'm hungry. Let's go and find Anthony's house."

They reluctantly climbed the hill away from the quayside and Elizabeth stared with admiration as they toiled up the handsome wide street and gazed up at the high buildings with their steeply pitched roofs and mass of tiny windows.

"Like London," Thomas interposed, although he had never been out of Northumberland! The chinking of the iron-clad wheels on the cobbles and granite sets gave them ample warning to jump out of the way of the carts and carriages of all shapes and sizes that were filling the street. The horses going downhill were assisted by their carters who walked in the lead, straining to hold them back. Those hauling laboriously up the slope were similarly guided by their drivers on foot, sweating and panting, and crying "Howay then! Giddy up!"

A fine stream of water sped down a channel in the cobbled street, diverting at one point into a large cistern before careering down the hill towards the river.

"We'll wash our faces here, and look decent," said Thomas, laughing at Elizabeth's hot and dusty face, and he bent over to lave his own face and neck. Thus refreshed, they turned into a narrow chare which reeked of dung, and along which they stepped gingerly in the deep shadows. The sun's rays rarely entered the innermost recesses, shadowed by the gable-tops which almost touched each other. Elizabeth held up her dress with both hands, and tried not to breathe. As they penetrated further into the depths of the tenements, a putrid smell issued from the middens situated at the bottom of the stairs of each of the closely-packed houses. They fought off the flies which buzzed in hundreds round their heads, feeling increasingly confined as the passage grew even narrower. Then, as they advanced, their ears were assailed by strange screeching voices, rising in volume as they approached, and becoming distinctly unpleasant.

"What a bob's-a-dyin' they're makin'," whispered Thomas nervously.

Elizabeth mused: "Are they out of the madhouse?"

A female voice screamed: "Ye're a pox-ridden bitch!"

An even harsher voice retorted: "How can ye say that, with your pitted face? I cannot stand ye!"

As they approached, Thomas shouted: "Whisht, you old crones!" A sudden silence ensued. The two hags, dressed in filthy rags, checked their abuse of each other and turned their pale and bony faces to survey the new arrivals. Blocking the passage they slowly looked them up and down, down and up, their mouths curling up with distaste at the strangers' presence.

"Shut your gob and keep it shut!" eventually snapped the older woman, glaring at Thomas with her hands on her hips.

"You're a hoity-toity fellow!" screamed the other crone, and, welcoming the further opportunity to abuse, made a sneering aside to her companion: "A proper grand cock-a-ride-a-roosie we have here."

Backing up her friend the other affirmed: "We divvent want any more daft folks here. We've got enough of our own."

Hostilities started were now in full swing. The hags had viewed Elizabeth closely. Her country beauty, lack of pocks, and defiant air, were just too much to bear. It was Elizabeth's trim dress, fashioned by Joanna's loving hands, which annoyed them most. Though simple and stained with travelling, it fitted her perfectly and was transformed by her trim figure into something special. Elizabeth and Thomas were taken aback by the ferocity of their reception, and remained silent. Suppressing nervous giggles they skirted the two women in the narrow passage, and hurried out of the dark alley into the warm sunshine, casting anxious looks behind them as the angry abusive voices gradually receded.

However, the local women, like disturbed wasps, continued their scornful buzzing: "Ye can hear by their talk that they come from Tynedale. They cannot even speak right, never mind make sense. They cannot say an `r' and there's always trouble when they come. Such a fighty lot."

The other replied: "Aye, there'll be trouble with them. They can't even say 'trouble'," and she mimicked the Northumbrian "r", nearly making herself physically sick in the process. Meanwhile the objects of their execrations had emerged into a wider road running to left and right with a terrace of larger houses, whose doors and stables indicated a more prosperous set of inhabitants. Thomas immediately recognised Anthony ffarbrigge's house.

"Here it is. This is where Uncle Anthony lives. I hope he's at home."

Having climbed the steps he energetically pulled the bell-handle beside the substantial double doors. While they were waiting they stepped back to admire the handsome three-storied red brick house. Elizabeth, with raised eyebrows, exchanged enquiring looks with her cousin.

"Who would have thought that Uncle Anthony lived in such a magnificent house as this?" asked Elizabeth, wide-eyed.

"Aye, it's marvellous what trade can do for a man. I only wish his wife had lived to share it with him. They say Uncle Anthony took it very badly when she died so young of the pox."

Eventually, after two pulls, the latch was secretly lifted by a rope from the apartment above, and, unaware of this, they crept rather mystified into the peace of the large hall. Elizabeth gazed with wonderment around the interior, which easily surpassed anything she had seen before. As her eyes slowly surveyed the room they dwelt on the sandstone fireplace with its magnificent overmantel of

Flemish design, accommodating a polished iron fireplace with tongs and rake.

A long oak table held an array of pewter candlesticks, surrounded by drinking pots, plates and goblets. Four substantial iron lanterns hung from the walls and Elizabeth was intrigued by the unfamiliar sight of a pair of virginals on one of the tables. They hardly had time to take it all in before Uncle Anthony ponderously descended the stairs, his arms wide open, and Elizabeth was quickly encircled in his warm embrace.

"Welcome to the toon!" he boomed. "Welcome Thomas. Good lad. You've brought her safe and sound! We knew you were on your way because old Charlie has already delivered your boxes."

The new arrivals felt pangs of hunger as their nostrils savoured the delicious odours emanating from the open kitchen door below the stairs. The sound of pots and pans being moved in the kitchen, and the chink of pewter plates reinforced their anticipation. Thomas felt his mouth watering as he smiled at his host.

Always anxious to please, their uncle promised them an interesting evening: "You'll be ravenous but the food is nearly ready. Some of my cronies are joining us for a meal this evening. They're good fun even though they are perhaps old for the likes of you, but they're full of stories, so pray make ready in your rooms and try to be downstairs as the company arrives. I'll take you up myself. We've got everything prepared."

Chapter 5

The travellers immediately felt at home in this warm friendly environment. Anthony's geniality and good will were well known in the family, from his frequent visits to Tynedale, and Elizabeth, especially, was brimming over with the fascination of these sophisticated surroundings and the promise of new companions. Their boxes had been installed in their bedrooms, and Elizabeth was delighted to find a washing bowl, an urn of water and even a mirror provided. The four-poster bed looked soft and inviting with its gorgeous feather pillow, and alongside it stood a small table with a candlestick. She peered from the tall window into the street below, where the carts trundled slowly by, carrying diverse loads, among which hay, potatoes, kindling, coals, and hides could most easily be seen.

When Elizabeth had changed from her travelling clothes and was enjoying preening herself in front of the mirror, Thomas's knock on the door summoned her to dinner and they made their way to the top of the stairs which rose from the end of the hall.

Thomas waxed enthusiastic: "God be praised! I never thowt it would be like this."

They could feel the heat rising from the roaring fire below, and could hear Anthony, who was ensconced in a comfortable oak elbow chair, talking animatedly to his four friends. Curious, but both a little diffident, Elizabeth and Thomas paused a while to eavesdrop on the conversation below. They could just distinguish little snatches of the talk and heard Uncle Anthony saying: "The best defence of Newcastle was put up at the Pilgrim Street Gate by the Joiners' Company. They were stout fellows, mark you, and even the tough Scots praised them."

Another guest was saying: "What about the Newcastle Whitecoats battling in White Sike Close at Marston Moor? If Colonel Hugh Frazer's dragoons hadn't blasted a gap in our infantry we would have won the battle for the king. The brave Whitecoats died where they stood, fighting to the last man. A high price to pay, and a bitter defeat for the royal army."

An excited high-pitched voice interposed: "It was unfortunate for the king's men that, as the Roundheads were charging them, the useless Duke of Newcastle was wandering off to his coach hard by, and calling for a pipe of tobacco. Then what did he do? Why, he fled to the continent because he could not endure the laughter of the court. Bah!"

It was the beautiful vision of Elizabeth, effortlessly floating down the stairs like a Greek goddess, which brought a sudden silence to the company. There was a shuffling of feet as they all rose. Everyone stared at her lovely form, and warmed to her captivating smile, but one guest in particular was so transported by her that he became white and shocked at her sudden appearance. He was transfixed. She bore such a close resemblance to his late beloved mother that he could scarcely believe his eyes and felt quite giddy. Her confident grace, her look of lively curiosity, the tilt of her head, the magnificent auburn hair, and overall, her melting warmth, charmed him with memories of times long forgotten, and he spent much of the evening gazing at her in silent tribute.

Anthony, immensely proud of his young visitors, introduced Thomas and Elizabeth to his company of friends. "Gentlemen, here are my visitors from Tynedale: Elizabeth ffarbrigge, my niece, and her cousin, Thomas Hubbach."

Turning to the young people, he described his old friends. "Our worthy Mayor, Henry Woodall; the barber surgeon, Mr. Nicholas Liddle; Captain Christopher Roxby; and Mr. Francis Hall, our scrivener."

They all nodded approval. As the meal had been delayed, the guests were shown without further ceremony to their places at the long oak table which ran down the centre of the hall. Two matching oak chairs stood at each end, and forms ran along the sides. Anthony stopped at the middle and, stooping awkwardly, showed Elizabeth and Thomas the long deep carving which ran along the rail below the table-top. With pride he ran his fingers along the date 1659 and the initials CF. "This is the mark of your cousin, Charles - the best cabinet maker in Newcastle. But this is nothing compared with the magnificent staircase at Nunburn Hall which he supervised himself."

"What about Richard Farrington?" his portly friend Liddle remonstrated, with a smile in his eye, as he winked at the young visitors.

" Bah! He's nothing but a brogler, a clay joiner, and a dirt dauber." Anthony grinned at Liddle and went on: "But don't tell his father I said so, 'cos he's nothing but a bothing, throating fellow, himself. The whole family are thorough braggarts." He laughed, but unconvincingly, since he knew that the Farringtons were indeed the biggest and best cabinet makers in Newcastle. Pausing, Anthony raised his eyebrows at his old friend and then, unabashed, continued to show Elizabeth the fine details of the massive table's six heavily carved legs.

"The secret of this design, with legs so thick, curved and bulbous, is to stop mice running up to the table-top. It's not just beautiful, but useful at the same time."

The wide-eyed Thomas gasped: "It's just like London here. What grand furniture!"

Elizabeth was seated at the top of the table opposite to her Uncle Anthony. Although the guests were considerably older than herself, she was intensely curious about them and spent a considerable time quietly scrutinising their faces and noticing their gestures. She gradually concluded that their company was most genial, and their collective wisdom intrigued her. On her left was a serious yet friendly gentleman, the Mayor of Newcastle, Henry Woodall, tall, lean, clean-shaven and sharp-featured. His natural hair was auburn, revealed by bushy eyebrows, but his long curled wig was black and he seemed uncomfortable with it, because his restless hands constantly tossed stray ringlets over his shoulders. However, as the night wore on, Elizabeth noticed that he began to wriggle distractedly on his seat, like one ill at ease, and he appeared pale and unwell, his piercing blue eyes forever dwelling on her. She could not understand why he spoke to her so hesitantly, and at times it made her feel very uncomfortable.

As a consequence, much of her attention was fixed on the other side of the table where sat Uncle Anthony's teasing friend, a corpulent and hearty barber surgeon. The pinched-faced scrivener sat beside Thomas, midway along the table on Elizabeth's right. His presence was marked by his persistent laughter, a high pitched "Hee, hee, hee," sounding like a whinnying horse. From Anthony's right hand side came the deep sound of the voice of the burly ship's captain, Roxby, with his trim white beard and weather-beaten face, testifying to his years at sea. He was one of a family of mariners who had been well known in Newcastle for many years. Opposite him sat Thomas, spaced at a good distance from his host.

In spite of the long journey, Elizabeth, fortified by the excellent food, somehow found the energy to radiate good will. A large variety of fare was offered at the table and the overall smell was delicious as she surveyed it with relish - a whole salmon cooked fresh from the Tyne, a crisp fat roast capon, a large rabbit, brought in from the countryside and stewed to an exquisite tenderness, and fresh vegetables and sweetmeats, with preserved gooseberries and plums. Although Elizabeth had enjoyed the best possible childhood at Hackford, she felt suddenly liberated and stimulated. This was her first experience of the company of educated townspeople, who sounded so different from the Tynedalers and whose knowledge of the outside world was so extensive. At the same time she was strangely relaxed and contented in these new surroundings. Uncle Anthony made an amusing picture at the other end of the table, looking small and rotund in his huge chair, and just able to peer rather comically over a well-filled plate. Nevertheless, he managed to dominate the proceedings in his good-natured way.

Elizabeth smiled as she noticed Thomas, looking slightly alarmed at being interrogated by the pinch-faced scrivener, red and sharp of nose, who was sitting next to him. He was asking him in a high-pitched voice: "By your accent, Thomas, you're from the North, but you're not one of those rascally, thieving, plundering Scots, are ye? Even the young lads are a century old in mischief and villainy."

Blushing, Thomas hastily assured him that he came from Tynedale, from a hard-working farming family. "We've had enough trouble ourselves from the reivers. We still talk about the time in about 1587 when my family had to flee from a Scottish attack on Haydon Bridge. They captured my great-grandfather on that occasion and a bonny price we had to pay to get him back. That year the harvest was bad and the family had little enough to eat anyway."

The scrivener was eager for more detail and fixed his eyes on Thomas. "Did they treat him brutally? I've heard that they beat and tortured their prisoners with hot irons."

Thomas warmed to his companion's enthusiasm, nodding vigorously: "Yes, it's true.They fettered their prisoners naked and tied them to the trees in chains. In summer they were eaten by midges and were perishin' cold in winter. Apparently my poor great-grandfather returned in a terrible state. Man, he never recovered, and was always watchin' the far hills in case they came back. It's been quiet now for years but I don't trust them even now."

The scrivener nodded silently as Thomas continued: "Mind you, there are some awful women here in Newcastle, worse than Scottish dogs. We met two of them in the nearby chare this afternoon on the way up from the quayside. They were shoutin' and bawlin' their heads off. I thowt we'd arrived in Hell."

"Shh! I know who that would be. Be careful." The scrivener took a quick look at Anthony, assuring himself that he was preoccupied in deep conversation with Captain Roxby, and then continued confiding in Thomas through tight lips.

"Jane Bilton, Charles ffarbrigge's mother-in-law, so different from her daughter, and a great embarrassment to the rest of the family. She's mad, that woman, and her friend makes her even worse. They're proper alley cats," he said, shaking his head. "The two of them need a strong arm to deal with them but truly they are both pitiable souls, widows as a result of the Scots' invasion. I can't help feeling sorry for them. Their husbands were both good cabinet makers, and died in defence of the gate, leaving these two almost destitute.

Anthony frequently has to help them just to stay alive. They make good watch-dogs but sometimes they go too far, and somebody soon will have to teach them a lesson. Don't tell Anthony, because he wouldn't approve, but I've been chewing over an idea for a long time. Thomas, are you willing to help me, for a bit of fun?" he said, lowering his voice even further.

"What's in your mind Francis? Count me in, as long as it's harmless, and good for a laugh," replied Thomas with a grin.

"I'll explain later," whispered the scrivener. "It's kinder than a housewife's scold anyway," he said, eyeing Anthony discreetly.

After that, with shared agreement on common enemies, the two conspirators relaxed into a casual friendship and chortled the night away. The pinch-faced scrivener belied his stern looks and he was good fun, thought Thomas. However, a casual observer might have wondered if the display of easy confidence the scrivener exercised abroad perhaps contrasted with the iron rule of discipline which he may have been suffering at home.

Meanwhile, as his head peered over the top of the table, Uncle Anthony smiled encouragement to his niece. Well-trained willing servants continued to bring a delightful array of victuals to the table and the conversation was punctuated periodically with peals of laughter, both high-pitched and low and hearty, as if orchestrated. After the meal they sought the comfort of the fire and enjoyed all manner of sweet dishes.

"Try these candied fruits," said Anthony to the scrivener, who had been eyeing his favourite gingerbread on the other side of the fireplace. Sweet wafers were passed round with the chinking pewter jugs of malmsey. Elizabeth, for the second time in her life, enjoyed the companionship of a kindred spirit, Nicholas Liddle, the barber surgeon, who moved his chair nearer to her to question her closely on precious country remedies.

Remembering what she had learned at Hackford, Elizabeth could be heard telling him: "Nancy, an old friend of mine, who lives out on the moor, believes that tormentil gets rid of worms, and she always recommends the ashes of a burnt snail if you have a spot on the eye. Within three days it will be gone," she assured him with great conviction.

Liddle nodded his head and an amused smile danced on his lips. "I didn't know that, but it sounds good." Soon in spite of himself he found he was treating her almost as an equal. She was not like a lass. She was...... as a man, and her interest sparked his own. He found himself giving her his most treasured recipes.

"Best remedy I've tried recently is Watered Hemp - freshly prepared from dried leaves - best for headache, and for fever. Hemp's beneficial in all its parts

- the seed for a jaundice, which is accompanied by fever, readily opening the passages of the gall. Mix the pressed fresh root with a little oil and butter and it's good for burns, and the seed mixed with milk for coughs."

Looking over to the captain he continued: " Captain Roxby has brought me back some Indian hemp from his latest voyage. I'll try it, but it's best left alone - gives a sensation of pleasure - as such it's no good. The book of Proverbs unceasingly reminds us of the important difference between happiness and pleasure."

Strange to say it was Woodall who interjected. "But happiness is a condition; pleasure is a feeling. Being solely drawn to pleasure is a frailty, but you cannot be in thrall to happiness."

"It's best to take a quiet joy in simple things," resumed the barber surgeon soothingly. "True happiness comes when your mind is fixed on another object, the best happiness coming by the way."

Meanwhile, the captain turned in their direction when his name was mentioned. The sea was his life and had been for generations of his family. He knew his land-bound friends would hang on his every word and he loved it. His sparkling blue eyes brightened as, with a faraway look he recollected: "There are lands and peoples beyond our wildest expectations out in the East, you know, and plants of which we can only dream."

Nodding his head, the Mayor came more fully into the conversation. " We ought to be encouraging our trade abroad. There's plenty to exchange out there. Our East India Company ought to be selling English cloth in Asia. We in turn need more spices, quilts and hangings from India. Expanding trade is this kingdom's best way to prosperity. That is why I have sent my younger son to Barbados in the West Indies," he said proudly. " He's always pressing me for more servants to be sent to develop the land on our sugar plantation, but in any case there are shiploads of stout slaves from Africa which are always available."

Addressing Thomas, he continued: "In London, apothecaries are recommending a new drink, called tea, and they all chew tobacco to ward off the plague." Thomas nodded thoughtfully in response, pleased to find himself chosen to be associated with his precious London.

Anthony asked: "What's the Dutch East India Company doing now? Do they still work out of Batavia?"

The captain, with a penetrating look, and slightly lowering his voice, confided: "The Governor General is actually prepared to make losses on voyages, encouraging new explorations. The tropical spice cargoes are so cheap and so easily carried in their original state that he knows that the gains are going to be handsome."

The Mayor's ears pricked up and his eyes gleamed as he nodded knowingly: "Yes. They're shrewd, the Dutch. He'll send out ships to discover new lands and peoples, with the idea of developing trading opportunities, like they've done in the West Indies. They didn't yield up the Spice Island of Palo Run as promised in the Dutch treaty, you know, and even our Royal Fishery Company haven't been able to keep their herring busses from the English coast."

Encouraged, the captain continued: "A Dutch seaman I know sailed with a captain called Abel Tasman, and he says that there are islands beyond belief out there. They're looking for the Gold and Silver Islands but other islands are absolutely bewildering - they are found, and then they suddenly disappear. You must have heard a few years ago about the Smoking Island, near Sumbawa, which smelt so dreadful?" The rest nodded their heads wisely, though not perhaps confidently.

"Well, according to hearsay, it suddenly disappeared - poof, as if by magic."

They were all very impressed, and for a moment silence reigned. Point made, the captain sat back, beaming with great satisfaction.

"How strange," Elizabeth eventually exclaimed, beginning to feel sleepily detached.

The mayor interposed with great passion: "The Dutch commerce should be destroyed. We are fools to tolerate them. They are dependent on the merchant convoys for their sustenance at home. If we attacked them nearer home the Dutch wouldn't win and we couldn't lose. With them out of the way, our trade with the New World would be absolutely secure with fortunes for us to win. If we don't act now," he warned, his eyes embracing the whole company, "Those greedy upstarts will be attacking us in our own country. We've already tried to exclude them from the British colonies, but is it working? We've struggled against their power in America and Africa without success. The declaration of war against them in March hasn't frightened them. They're still acting like demons and looking for any chance to seize our ships."

The captain shook his head. " It's not as easy as you think. There are rumours that the navy is in a bad state because of shortage of money. Ships cannot be paid off, repairs are too costly, and just this summer the rope-makers staged a mass walk-out because they had not been paid."

In truth, however fascinating the conversation had been, Elizabeth was becoming increasingly drowsy, following her journey, and with the combined effects of the extended meal and the heat of the fire, her eyes became heavy and her head drooped wearily.

"I'm afraid I shall have to retire," she confessed reluctantly.

The barber surgeon was sympathetic. Elated with the enthusiasm of a successful evening, and the effects of the ale, he suggested: "Tomorrow you can come to the Barber's Hall, and I'll show you a few surprises. But will you be able to bear it?"

Uncle Anthony raised his eyebrows. Would his niece accept this challenge?

Suddenly revived, Elizabeth retorted without hesitation: "Of course I can. As well as any."

Anthony's heart swelled with pride. His lovely girl had taken up the gauntlet, but did she know what she was letting herself in for? He looked triumphantly towards his portly friend who said: "We'll see you tomorrow then. Your uncle knows where we abide."

The Mayor rose quickly, anxious to intercept her before she reached the stairs, and urgently asked: "Where do you come from, Elizabeth?"

"The most wonderful place in the world - Tynedale. The people are strong in body and spirit, the moors are as wild as I am, and the air pure and healthy," replied Elizabeth proudly.

He looked on her lovingly and sagely nodded his head.

As she said goodnight to the company and wearily climbed the stairs no eye lingered on her longer, or with more fondness, than that of the Mayor of Newcastle.

So ended the travellers' first night in Newcastle as they gratefully collapsed into their comfortable beds, too tired to be bothered by the strange noises of the creaky old house and the street below. As they sank into a deep and dreamless sleep, all thoughts of Hackford were temporarily put aside.

Chapter 6

Elizabeth woke to the sudden sound of a horn. It was the town drover calling for the cows to be brought out so that he could drive them to graze on the Town Moor. She peeped out of the pale blue bed curtains, which had once been magnificent, but now were a little faded and tattered, altogether understandable in the house of a bachelor. The room was well-ordered and comfortable, with dark wooden panelling. A lattice of hand-sized diamond shaped panes, some warped, bubbled and greenish, bent the early morning sun into wonderful rainbows, which reflected across all parts of the room.

Longing for fresh air she rose quickly to open the window with a flourish, and enjoyed the wide view of the street, which was alive with those who seemed to be on urgent business. Hardly able to wait to join the throng she wondered that she could sleep so long amid the vivid sounds. A pack of hungry dogs of many sizes barked defiantly, startled by the hoarse cries of the vendors advertising their wares, which in their turn competed with the high pitched screams of groups of excited children. Dressing hastily, Elizabeth rushed down to breakfast, to find Thomas already there.

"Uncle Anthony has gone out on business but he said that if we followed these directions we would easily find the way to Charles's house and the surgeon's place."

"I'm looking forward to meeting cousin Charles and his family, and also to seeing what mysterious tricks the barber surgeon can perform in his lair," replied Elizabeth lowering her voice with eager anticipation.

Without unnecessary delay, the two young people hurried out to discover "the toon." In the headlong rush of their enthusiasm they nearly tumbled over the poor mop-squeezer. She was busy cleaning the outside steps with wet sand, already looking a little weary, but forcing a smile as she smartly moved aside for them.

Their first obligation was a courtesy visit to cousin Charles, who lived in the neighbouring street of St. John's Chare. Crossing the wide yard, they could hear the staccato tapping of the mallets of the apprentices and joiners, intent on fashioning the beautiful furniture of which Anthony ffarbrigge was so proud.

They found Charles, busy in his large workshop below the living quarters. Dark-haired and stocky, he was taller than his father, with powerful arms below his rolled-up shirt sleeves. On their entry he immediately put down his plane, brushed the shavings from his apron and edged past the neatly stacked planks of wood, arms outstretched and eager to greet them.

"You will be cousins Elizabeth and Thomas from Tynedale?" he smiled. "My father said that you would be coming to see us, and I'm delighted to meet you. Please let me show you the workshop and then I'll take you upstairs to meet my wife, Barbara. Just mind your eyes amid the chips flying up from the chisels."

"I've already admired the beautiful table at your father's house and I envy Uncle Anthony. Our furniture at home is very plain and simple by comparison," replied Elizabeth.

Having shaken hands with Charles in his vigorous way, Thomas approached the nearest bench: "The tools are so cleverly made and so sharp that I would love to try my hand."

When he saw that Charles pursed his lips uneasily Thomas hastily added: "But I know that it takes years of training to fashion such excellent furniture, so I may as well forget it. After all, God did make me a farmer."

Deliberately diverting his attention, Charles pointed out: "You'll be interested to know that these mahogany boards came all the way from the American Indies as ballast. Aren't they beautiful? Come into the back and see our inlaying work. Our chief craftsman is Roger Vipoint, who comes from France. He has made inlay his speciality, and is teaching our apprentices. We were lucky to get him because of the restrictions on foreign craftsmen."

As they approached, the Frenchman nodded and Charles patted him on the shoulder. The visitors carefully scrutinized the clever workmanship, the like of which they had never seen before, and were amazed at the quality of the inlaying. The craftsman beamed, perfectly understanding their favourable reaction, and spoke to them flamboyantly.

"Monsieur, Mademoiselle, I am enchanted to meet ze family of Monsieur ffarbrigge. We are trying to encourage ze craft of ze wood inlay. Zese are tools of my own from La France. And zese are designs of mine. As you can see, I prefer ze flowers and ze tracery."

"Roger, I've never seen anythin' so beautiful in my life. It's so clever," gasped Thomas as he eyed the tools and the workmanship. "But who can afford to buy all this furniture?"

Charles replied : " Oh, there are plenty of rich merchants and big coal owners in Newcastle, who value good quality furniture. You should see the insides of their homes. The fronts may look small, but, behind, the rooms are spacious and full of treasures. Many are keen to buy the Frenchman's work and we can't supply enough of it. Some of the inlaying involves several kinds of wood - there's cherry, holly, ash, beech and box, here," he said, as he ran his fingers lovingly over the latest intricacies.

Charles ushered Thomas towards the stairs while Elizabeth still tarried at the back of the workshop, feasting her eyes on the workmanship. He confided to Thomas: "I must take you upstairs now to see Barbara, because shortly I have to go to a meeting of the Joiners' Company at Pilgrim Street Gate." He looked flushed and full of tension, and was speaking quickly.

"I happen to be Steward this year and there was merry hell to play at the last meeting because a troublemaker called Joseph Thompson was pleased to tell everybody that I'd broken my oath, and read the secret orders of the company to my wife."

"That was unfortunate," commiserated Thomas.

"When you meet Barbara you will see that she is naturally quiet. She never sees many people, so I couldn't believe how the tale had been spread. When Thompson said that, I was speechless and couldn't stand the fellow's impudence so I gave him a hard thrust on the breast and walked out."

"You did well. It was no more than he deserved," laughed Thomas.

"Aye, but the laugh is on me. Violence between the brethren is not tolerated, so now I'll have to pay a fine, half to the fund for the Tyne bridge, and half to the Joiners' Company. Women! Can you ever trust them?" said Charles shaking his head and becoming confidential. "You can imagine how I behaved when I came home. I was so angry with Barbara, I regretted it afterwards. I spat out the food that she had ready for me, and I felt like killing her. She still says that she hadn't talked to anybody, so I have a suspicion that it was her mother, Jane Billton, who coaxed something out of her, and, once that odious woman has any news, it's spread all round the toon."

"Oh, it's that woman again," said Thomas shaking his head.

"So you've met her already?" Charles looked surprised, and Thomas nodded.

" Anyway, now I'll have to turn up and face the brethren. Luckily I have some close friends among them, but it's a very awkward situation which I'm not looking forward to. I know Richard Farrington is another who will be after my hide today. He's not suited because I've got the Frenchman. Now I must go and face them. I'm sorry to have to leave you so soon. But come upstairs now, and meet Barbara." He put his arm round Thomas's shoulder.

Elizabeth caught them up and sensed that Charles was upset about something as he escorted them upstairs to the large living room where his wife was waiting. On entering the room she was appalled at the state of the house but did not let her eyes stray too far because the whole place was untidy and in a distressed condition, in sharp contrast with the elegant furniture that was being produced downstairs.

Charles introduced them to Barbara who gave them a friendly but weak smile. She had once been beautiful, Elizabeth guessed, but now she was obviously in a sad decline. Her face was deathly white, apart from some ugly bruise marks on her cheek. Her hair was untended and her dress worn and dishevelled. Her conversation, interspersed with nervous apologetic laughter, was interrupted at times by uncontrollable coughing, and a baby cried feebly in the cradle beside her chair. However, she hardly had the energy to rock him off to sleep.

Elizabeth's heart went out to her as she approached the cradle to look at the little boy. She smoothed down the covers to peep at the little one and what she saw, alas, was a very sickly baby. Her brow furrowed, and she bit her lip, realising that he would have a hard struggle to survive.

Charles took no interest in his son and Barbara seemed to cower before his gaze.

"I shall have to be away now and see what they've got to say," he announced apprehensively as he discarded his apron and took up his coat and hat.

Barbara tried to get up but a coughing fit overwhelmed her and she sat down abruptly.

Thomas hastily suggested: "I'll leave the women to chat by themselves while I enjoy a further spell in the workshop."

"Well, don't touch anything you shouldn't, or distract the workmen too much. The work is held up already and I've got troubles enough. One slip, and a valuable piece of furniture can be ruined," warned Charles.

The two men descended, and while Charles set off briskly to attend his meeting, Thomas walked with care round the benches, ankle deep in shavings and wood chips, fascinated by the work in progress and the infinite care displayed by the craftsmen. It was not long before he discovered the painful price that the apprentices were paying for the maintenance of the high standard of craftsmanship. For even minor mistakes there was a heavy cuff on the head and there were constant taunts of "Lousy rogue" and "Lazy bastard" and other abuse in spite of the fact that the lads were very willing and appeared to show complete obedience. Thomas winced for them at each blow.

31

Upstairs the two new friends had just begun to feel at ease with each other when their chat was suddenly interrupted. The door burst open and a rough-featured woman entered, grumbling: "I've got plenty of work to do but I'll take the baby for the afternoon. Nobody can say I don't help."

She paused, glaring at Elizabeth. "Humph! You again!" Elizabeth was surprised and much alarmed to recognise her as one of the two unwelcome acquaintances of the day before. She was even more startled when she realised that she was Barbara's mother. The offer to look after the child was made with poor grace but Barbara appeared relieved to accept it. The baby was roughly plucked out of the cot and the grandmother hurried out without another word. Barbara relaxed slightly when they were alone and went on as if nothing had happened.

"How do you find Newcastle then? I understand it's your first visit and Charles' father was so happy that you were coming."

"Oh, it's wonderful here," replied Elizabeth. "A complete change from Hackford. I find the crowds and noise so different from the peace of the valleys. I can't say I like the smells of the town, but I suppose it's just a matter of getting used to them. The castle and the churches, the Town Wall, and even the offices of the merchants of Newcastle are magnificent."

" And what of the riverside?" asked Barbara.

" It was fascinating to watch the ships and keels along the quayside when we first arrived, with hundreds of men swarming around like insects. I recken there is much money to be made from mining, manufacturing and trade. We admired Uncle Anthony's house too, and felt that Charles was so lucky to have grown up in such a fine place. Uncle Anthony must have worked hard to pay for it, but all his life he has been bounding with energy. He is a favourite visitor at the farm, you know, though we don't see him often enough. When he last visited he thoroughly enjoyed himself at Isabel's wedding."

"Yes, he couldn't stop talking about it and I wish we could have come. I would love to go into the country sometime. The smoky air here catches my throat and makes me cough," she said, looking rather tired. "It's so hard when you haven't got the strength to keep control of your own house, and the baby is ailing. Charles gets so angry these days, Elizabeth, and I don't know what to do. I have no one to confide in."

As she said this she was fighting to keep back the tears and her voice quavered.

Elizabeth looked at her, full of concern.

"Barbara, I think you should use the free time you have to rest. I have loved talking to you but I would so much like to come back on another day when it is more convenient."

Besides, Elizabeth was eager to take up the invitation of her surgeon friend of the previous evening, so she excused herself, promising to return soon. Once the earnest Thomas had been dragged away from the workshop, the two explorers picked their way again through the unfamiliar streets.

"I wonder how Charles is managing at the Joiners' meeting?" said Thomas.

"I have a feeling that he can well look after himself," Elizabeth assured him. "Leave all your sympathy for Barbara."

They came to a small shady square nearby, where the women had gathered, chatting animatedly while they washed clothes. As the two passed by, an ominous silence fell over the busy company. At first they wondered if they were responsible, remembering their recent   experience of the alleys. However, a quick sidelong glance assured Elizabeth that it was a dark towering shadow that had stilled the conversation. It was indeed Barbara's mother again, with a basket under one arm and the baby crying feebly on the other. Elizabeth and Thomas tried to shrink into obscurity while some weaker members of the community were visibly blanching. With beaky nose outstretched, brows low, and eyes spitefully narrowed, she spat out her words like venom, screeching: "Why should an auld wife like me have to look after this ailin' bairn? It's a poor housewife that cannot manage her own hoose. She's a worthless lazy slut."

One brave soul protested: "Auld legs can have tough muscles." To which came the sneering reply: "With a brashy tongue like yours, ye'll not last lang."

Elizabeth and Thomas were quickly out of earshot, but Elizabeth was still disturbed and doubly vowed that she would do everything she could to help her cousin's wife and baby. Why else were we on this earth, but to make it a better place?

Five minutes later they had found the barber surgeon's hall, a substantial brick building, in front of which lay a pretty walled garden, full of sweet smelling herbs, flowers and buzzing insects. Eagerly they climbed up the steps to the heavy oak door, which was already open, and entered a large room where they found Elizabeth's companion of the night before, in his shirt sleeves and wearing an apron. He was exceedingly surprised to see them, because his invitation had been more casually given than received.

"I've urgent business to perform today, which doesn't require spectators," he said abruptly, panic showing in his eyes. However, he recovered at once from his embarrassment and genuinely welcomed them to his rooms, with the guilty feeling that he had been both rash and foolish to issue the invitation which had seemed so plausible on the previous evening. He was standing at a strong table placed in the centre of seats and benches so that, when needed, students could easily see his demonstrations on the dissecting of bodies.

His grisly old apron, brown and stained, was tied by tapes round his back, and he was flourishing a sharp but dirty knife. On the table was a body, which he was preparing to dissect, and which was beginning to smell, and attract flies. He feared that Elizabeth would be horrified, as Thomas was in fact, retiring to the window to seek a pleasanter diversion. However, Elizabeth drew closer, absent-mindedly brushing aside the flies from her face, beside herself with curiosity, and almost ready to take up the blade herself. The barber surgeon eyed her apologetically, explaining how they had obtained the cadaver. He had been hanged for stealing.

Being reluctant to abandon his work, the surgeon skilfully and with great deliberation showed Elizabeth the body's sinews as he peeled away the skin. Elizabeth had never in her life seen anything so interesting, and the time flew. For his part, Thomas was engrossed for a long time in peering at a child playing with some extremely interesting stones in the street beyond the gate, all the time wishing that he was back in Charles' workshop. At intervals the surgeon sneaked a sidelong look at Elizabeth, restraining a mischievous smile, because he could hardly believe that she was still there.

Eventually he broke off to straighten his back, and took her into an adjoining room, lined with shelves full of jars with preserved body parts, and mysterious containers. She was alarmed to see that there was a complete stuffed man, standing in an upright position in the corner. The toughened skin was like leather. "This rascal was a notorious felon, robbing decent people along the roads outside Newcastle, and killing mercilessly. This is his righteous end. In the next world he has hellfire to face," said the barber surgeon dismissively.

Elizabeth shivered. To make her feel more at ease he pointed to a small table and suggested: "Let's have some cold meat. It's delicious," and he made to cut some slices off the joint with his dissecting knife, having carefully rubbed it and his hands on his grubby apron.

Elizabeth said: "No thanks. Sorry, but we have no appetite at the moment."

Motioning to Thomas, and nodding towards the door, she thanked the barber surgeon:

"What an interesting morning we've had! I'd like to come again, some time."

"Come any time you like. I'll be here."

Thomas had shot out of the door at the first opportunity and stood in the street breathing deeply and almost ready to vomit. When Elizabeth joined him he was muttering: "I've never had such a queer morning in my life. What a strange warped fellow Mr. Liddle is! If surgeons are like that here, what are they like in London?"

As they picked their way back to Uncle Anthony's they came upon a boy sitting at the corner of the street, keeping guard over a chicken with its leg tied to a stick.

He eagerly pounced on them: " Come on. Have a go! For a small wager if you throw this mallet and kill the chicken, you can tak' it hyem." The panic-stricken creature fluttered wildly on its string. Elizabeth eyed it ruefully. "Come on, Thomas. You can do it," she encouraged and she marched confidently ahead, followed in a few minutes by Thomas. He carried the prize under his arm. He was already recovered and anticipating his next meal with obvious relish.

Chapter 7

Late one evening, gathered round a table near a dingy window on the first floor of the alley tenement which was the humble abode of Jane Bilton, a group of four ragged women sat round a rush light. Their grubby tattered clothes and frowzy hair spoke of a casual approach to cleanliness, and their lack-lustre eyes betrayed a low level of intellect and energy. They leaned forward on the bare table, supporting their chins with their elbows, and listened to Jane. She felt in complete control of her audience as they hung on her every word.

"Everythin' is goin' wrong in this town at the moment. Do you know that the food supplies are runnin' short? I've heard that if it grows much worse the keelmen are threatenin' to storm the granaries. Precious little we have to eat now. What's it going to be like soon?"

She gradually became further embittered. "There are bad signs every day. Did you see the flashes in the sky last night? Some poor souls have been terrified by strange sights in the heavens. They have seen witches ridin' up to the moon on flamin' broomsticks. You know what that always means."

The group shuddered. She lowered her voice to a whisper, looking furtively from side to side. "Evil is spreadin' and the wrath of God is at hand," she predicted, her eyes flashing, her arms flung out wide and her fists tightly closed.

The listeners felt their hair standing on end, and cold shivers raced up their scantily-clad backs. They knew that the devil was never far away, always willing to catch them unawares. Poverty and hunger had weakened them. Their dull existence had worn down their mental faculties so that they were a prey for every insidious rumour. They were frightened because they were convinced that Jane was always right. The very fear that had gripped the women persuaded them into complete agreement as they grumbled among themselves, worrying about their precarious situation.

"Something will have to be done now. We can't stand any more trouble. What can we do ourselves? There's no hope of us marryin' again, with all the men lost in the Civil War. We'll have to shift for ourselves."

Such were the hapless wretches' mutterings.

Jane focussed their anxiety and boldly proposed a course of action. "We need all the hungry people to march on the Guildhall and you must bring out everybody we know. We'll meet tomorrow at ten o'clock at the end of the Tyne bridge. Don't forget to bring all the folks in your street."

Their agitation made them determined to take action the next day, and, as they hobbled downstairs one after another, they could hardly wait to launch their complaints before the civic authorities. Having seen them out of the tenement, Jane and her friend lingered on in the dim light. They were desperately lonely and reluctant to part from each other. Then, from the silent gloom of the alley, they were astonished to hear an unearthly voice reverberating along the chare.

"You remember me, Jane?" the voice wailed. "Jack, your long-lost husband. I loved you truly once and cared for you with all my strength."

"Well, that can't possibly be Jack," Jane thought, gulping down the acid in her gullet which threatened to undermine her resolution. The tremulous voice continued to waver eerily as it echoed through the darkness. A less intrepid person would have been absolutely petrified, but, puzzled, Jane whispered: "Who can it be?" as she peered at her friend by the flickering light. Her companion, whose eyes were popping and whose spine was suffering from icy quivers, did not reply. Her mind was already full of demons, ghosts and witches. Jane had warned them that evil was abroad, and this voice confirmed her fears.

It continued: "Jane, you have not been a good woman. Follow me to the Pilgrim Street Gate where I will have something to help you."

Her trusty friend's nerve snapped and she smartly took to her heels, leaving Jane alone in the dark alley. She was speechless and dry-mouthed, and had never replied to a ghost in her life.

"How do you address it?" she wondered. "If I get angry with it, what will it do?" She was by now more worried by protocol than frightened by Jack's voice.

The ghost was rising to the occasion. "Come, come, come," it cried, the voice fading away into the distance, drawing her ever onwards.

In her dull life this was too good and rare an opportunity to miss. Forever inquisitive, she clutched the meagre light and followed the voice, as it drew her through several narrow streets towards the Pilgrim Street Gate. It was there that she knew her husband had died with so many other gallant men, defending the town against the Scots. The pathetic flame flickered in the draughts circulating in the alleys and was finally extinguished, leaving her in impenetrable blackness. Although there were no stars or moonlight to show the way Jane was unabashed. She slowed to a groping walk, heading towards the sound of the voice.

"Captain George Errington requires the widow of the stout soldier, Bilton, to come to the gate," was the order as she approached the towering town wall. "Wait on the outside of the gate, and I will deal with you." The voice had become increasingly authoritative.

Jane dutifully did as she was told, feeling her way through the gateway and miraculously finding her destination despite the total darkness. Standing obediently in an unaccustomed silence at the Pilgrim Street Gate, she thought she could detect the sound of steps in the building and maybe a far distant snigger. A more earthly high pitched voice from above suddenly shouted: "Prepare for your reward." Straightway a deluge of soot descended on her.

She screamed, she cursed with indignation, she punched out wildly, she coughed, she choked, she spluttered, and she fought the soft black enemy, but she was covered from head to foot. Soot was in her hair, her mouth, her ears, her nose, everywhere. Whatever she did, she could not escape being smothered. She was unaware of the fleeting footsteps and stifled giggles which were gradually fading away. However, the disturbed gatekeeper came running down the stairs. He had never heard such execrations from a woman. His lamp revealed her pitiable state and the sight of her sooty figure, with two white eyes peering from the blackness, somewhat alarmed him. He stood well back.

" What's happenin' here? Who are you?" he enquired.

"I'm Jane Bilton, and I've been tricked into comin' here by a voice. And some devil's dumped a load of soot all over me. Can you help me? Have you a brush or a wet clout? I'm chokin'," Jane sobbed.

"Look, there's a trough of water here. I'll guide you to it. I'll find a cloth you can use. But dust off as much as you can before you wash," the gatekeeper advised, thankfully disappearing inside his sturdy tower. Jane recklessly discarded her outer clothes in the dark and shook them vigorously, then felt her way to the tub of water, shivering with cold, fright, and anger. She started washing her hands, face, neck and hair with great vigour, muttering curses all the time. The gatekeeper returned with a cloth and some new woollen clothes, and handed them to her in the light of his lamp, sympathising with her dreadful predicament.

He stuttered: "Two gentlemen left these .... in case ...er.... in case anyone ever .... needed them." Shivering, she dressed herself, and as she poked her beaky nose towards him, it collided with his. The poor man recoiled.

" That water was cold, and not very clean. It stinks. I hope it wasn't filled with piss to whiten the clothes. Did you have anythin' to do with this vile sooty trick?" she hissed through her teeth.

"Definitely not," asserted the alarmed gatekeeper. "But I know who will have to clean it all up at first light."

Jane carried on threateningly: "When I find out who's done this, they'll be pleadin' to be sent to Hell."

"I don't blame you," replied the keeper, trembling at the force of her passion.

As she shuffled along the dark streets on her way home she felt three crown coins in the pocket of her new coat. Although the money somewhat mollified her, she was determined to raise the whole neighbourhood, and howled, complained to herself, and screamed with anger as she stumbled through the blackness of the narrow alleys. Those hearing such unexpected eruptions shrank in their beds and prayed for deliverance. The event was much discussed in the town next morning and further added to the rumours that witches were abroad in the night.

Indeed: "The way of the wicked is as darkness, they know not at what they stumble."   (Proverbs)

Chapter 8

One hot July evening when there was hardly enough air to breathe and they were sitting in the coolness of the hall, Anthony warned Elizabeth that he and Charles had been called upon to travel to Stockton on urgent business.

"The corn harvest was very poor last summer so food is running short here, and there's an ugly mood building up among the hungry people. Time is running out and we will have to shift to see what we can glean further south." He looked more perturbed than she had ever seen him before.

"Would you mind looking after the house in my absence?" he asked her, almost apologetically. "I would be grateful if you would also keep an eye on Charles' wife and the baby? I saw them yesterday and they are both off colour. Barbara is seized with a sharp pain in the back, perhaps owing to her coughing spasms, so if you could help her we'd be grateful, but don't let it become too much of a burden to you."

Elizabeth replied proudly: "I'd love to be mistress of the house for a while. I'll enjoy managing it for you as long as it takes, and I promise to go and see Barbara as soon as possible."

Anthony warned: "Watch out for twisted-faced Jane, Barbara's mother. She's been a bit subdued recently, but there's a touch of the devil in her. Charles was almost expelled from the Joiners' Company and I'm sure it was because of her poking that long nose of hers into their private affairs. I'm told that even when she was young she was a right beaky girl - very strange - knew everyone's business, but as sly as a fox about herself. Many times I have watched her, staring fixedly in front of her, absolutely out of this world, narrowing her eyes and screwing up her face as if she was thinking evil thoughts. She is always plotting and planning against somebody. She's a vixen. Her happiness has rested in creating trouble since she became a widow in the siege. You're too open for her, Elizabeth. Such innocence gives the trouble-makers easy pickings. Anyway, be careful. I'm sure you'll manage alright, and I'll be back as soon as I can. It won't take long."

The following morning Uncle Anthony and Charles were off early, leaving Elizabeth in charge, with the trusty Thomas to help her. At first the servants seemed to be testing her reliability, but Elizabeth was a quick learner. Even the kitchen scullion, a scallywag of a boy of whom Elizabeth was very fond, asked her cheekily: "How d'you clean these pots, Miss?" in a whining sing-song tone. Her sharp reply: "Scour them with sand," seemed to satisfy him and he continued obediently, although his smarting fingers were already red and sore with the work.

Elizabeth soon tired of all these tormenting questions. When one of the maids came down in a great flurry, complaining: "There's bugs in the tester," she impatiently retorted: "Fumigate the room with a pound of roll-brimstone, and add some Indian pepper. Take the bedstead to bits, and paint it with arsenic." The maid was crestfallen, for it was more than she had expected.

Having passed these household tests, from then on everything ran smoothly for Elizabeth, which was just as well, because, when she went to visit Barbara a strange calm greeted her. She stopped short in the yard and listened for the sounds of the joinery tools. There was only silence. The doors were closed and as she opened them she found the place deserted. There seemed to be no workmen or apprentices about. From this eerie scene she mounted the stairs to the living quarters only to find that the household was in a terrible state. The only domestic servant was absent and unwashed dishes lay on the table.

"Barbara! Are you there? It's Elizabeth!" she called.

Barbara's mother came out of the bedroom, looking really presentable for once, in what seemed like a new garment, but agitated to a high degree. She addressed Elizabeth with great deference and this time in an ingratiating tone, speaking unusually quickly.

" Thank goodness you've come. You know all about everythin', and I'm sure I'm a poor useless body." By now she was close to the door. "Barbara and the baby are a bit unwell, and I just have to pop out to see to somethin'. I'll be back as soon as I'm ready. You haven't much to do."

And with that she was gone!

When Elizabeth approached the bed she was shocked to see that mother and baby were infected with some kind of fever. Now she understood why all the people of the household had fled the premises. She called out of the window to a likely lad who was passing: "Do you know Anthony ffarbrigge's house?" He nodded brightly.

"Can you take a message to Thomas Hubbach who resides there and tell him that Elizabeth is detained, looking after Barbara ffarbrigge and her baby. No-one is to come anywhere near because I think they have the fever. I'll drop down a coin for your trouble."

The lad looked at the coin but he was afraid of the contagion and did not move. He shuffled from foot to foot, looking up and looking down. He dearly wanted the money.

Elizabeth urged him to action. "Take it. You'll not be infected. I've only just arrived here."

"All right, then. Tell me the message again and I'll run round to ffarbrigge's."

She repeated the warning and he eagerly picked up the treasure and was off down the road. As the lad disappeared from sight at the end of the chare she prayed that the message would be safely delivered and turned back into the chaotic room in despair.

She was afraid for herself but what could she do? She could not leave them now, and her faithful Uncle Anthony had specially asked that she look after them. She hoped that soon Charles would be back to help but she sensed that Jane Bilton would be of little assistance. In the meantime she would feed and nurse them.

For the next three days she ministered to her patients willingly, tirelessly, and without any thought for her own safety, sleeping from time to time in a chair near their bedside. They had both been semi-conscious when she arrived, and Barbara occasionally raved incoherently, but on the fourth day Elizabeth noticed small sores on Barbara's face, and by the sixth day her whole face was covered in a very horrid manner. It was then that she realised the bitter truth that they were infected with smallpox. Elizabeth felt trapped and she prayed fervently that the cow-pox which she had already experienced on the farm might save her. Milk-maids rarely caught smallpox anyway, she consoled herself.

As she was dozing by the bedside she was suddenly awoken by small pebbles being thrown at the window. She was relieved to find that it was the young lad with a message from Thomas. "Thomas has promised to come round to see you today," he shouted, pronouncing his words very clearly.

Elizabeth was alarmed. "Tell him that there is smallpox here and he must on no account come anywhere near. It will just add to my worries, though I should welcome some food left on the doorstep. Off you go straightaway and warn him."

In the following days, nothing she could do, or think of, could save her patients from their inevitable fate. She tried unsuccessfully to feed the mother and baby, and had discovered in the house all the available cures for smallpox - cordial julep, pectoral syrup, gargles, oil of almonds, and purges - but in their condition they were too weak to resist the infection. She was herself almost helpless with exhaustion. No matter how carefully she bathed and soothed the sores, the bred venom increased, and the infection spread to their hands and even to the soles of their feet. Death struck quickly despite Elizabeth's weary but sustained efforts, the baby dying one day before Barbara. In the end she could only seek help for the burials.

She had already begun fumigating the house with a mixture of pitches and frankincense when Barbara's mother arrived, responding at last to Elizabeth's urgent messages.

"I'm not channerin'. Right poorly I've been. Couldn't put one foot in front of the other." She approached the bed and saw the terrible disease-ravaged faces of her daughter and grandchild. In fright she began pulling her hair and screaming: "What have you done with them? They weren't very ill when I left!"

Sitting huddled in a chair, looking tired and drawn, Elizabeth was too exhausted to react. She could hardly speak. "I did my best. Perhaps I could have done more, but I was so tired."

Jane exploded, screeching in a high-pitched voice: "You wretch! I know the likes of you. You killed them. Yes, you did. You did it deliberately. I'll see you burn in Hell. You said you could have looked after them better. You said it yourself. I knew that there would be trouble when I first saw you. You haven't heard the last of this."

Her long ugly pointed nose was directed towards Elizabeth and her blazing eyes were narrowed in rage and hatred born of guilt. With that, she stormed out. However, floating with tiredness and unable to think straight, Elizabeth did not feel too upset at Jane's attitude, knowing her reputation, and she was pitifully unaware of the dangers closing in around her. She had been isolated in the last few days and had not heard about the increasing unrest among the hungry people. The march from the bridge to the Guildhall had been an ugly affair, with stones flung wildly, and many windows broken along the route. The noisy crowd had to be fed with a reason for their troubles, and they had to relieve their ills with a scapegoat. Their leaders had drawn up a petition to the common council, blaming their ill fortunes on the evil deeds of witches. The corporation, eager to pacify the mob's wildest excesses, had agreed to send two representatives to Scotland to bring back the witch-finder. The delegation was expected to return this very day but, because of her confinement, Elizabeth had heard nothing of these developments.

Feeling obliged to remain at Charles' house to see to the funerals, she was engrossed in making the final arrangements and had consulted the Joiners' Company for advice on the customary procession from house to church. However, she was surprised to hear the approach of the town's bellman, the ringing becoming louder and louder as he announced: "Those good people who have cause to complain against any woman for a witch bring her out forthwith to be tried." He had already collected four poor gibbering wretches, who were manacled and stumbled along behind him and his assistants.

Leaning out of the open window to satisfy her curiosity, Elizabeth felt a stab of alarm as she saw Jane and the bosom friend with whom she was always arguing, now striding arm in arm along the street, almost in step, and with a viciously determined look on their faces. When they reached the bellman they both screeched in absolute agreement: "In there! There's a witch. She's nae canny. Get her!"

The bellman halted outside, and then Elizabeth could hear his slow heavy footsteps as he climbed the stairs. Without the courtesy of a knock, a rough-looking, thickset man burst through the door. Elizabeth was speechless with fright, finding herself face to face with a very stern-looking official, unlike anyone she had ever met, the cold stare and the deep creases round his mouth emphasising his severe demeanour. He was somewhat taken aback when he saw Elizabeth's youthful figure, but nevertheless fixed her with his steely eyes and warned her icily: "Come quietly, and none of your cantrips! Your accusers are outside. Hurry up!"

Elizabeth felt utterly helpless and could only remain silent. As a heavy hand, thrust into her back, roughly ushered her down the stairs, she was bewildered at finding herself in such a dire situation. All she had ever done was to care for her sick relatives. She was quickly manacled and pushed ignominiously into line. Jane and her crony watched in the street, glowing with evil satisfaction when Elizabeth shamefacedly joined the ragged band of old and withered wretches, herself dishevelled by the duties she had recently been undertaking. Abandoned by good fortune themselves, the triumphant crones took a malicious delight in at last being in control. They had brought down the brightest butterfly that they had ever seen. Their satisfaction was boundless, and they showed it.

"That will teach her to be so clever!" Jane whispered maliciously to her friend.

"Not for long I reckon," her companion smirked wickedly, displaying her almost toothless gums.

Chapter 9

Elizabeth was dragged through the streets, accompanied eventually by fifteen other poor victims of gossip, who were taken to the castle and incarcerated in the dungeon. They were harshly directed inside by an evil-smelling, foul-mouthed gaoler, who leered as he predicted:

"You'll be no trouble here. Half of you will be carried out with the spotted fever! Not many survive in this place!" His bitter laugh reverberated around the prison walls which were already closing in on her and stifling her spirits.

She stumbled through the filth underfoot to the doubtful safety of a far corner of the damp and airless dungeon and sat down dejectedly, her head clasped painfully between her hands. She could not conceive how evil were the minds of Jane and her crony, and they were so contemptible that she could not summon up the energy even to feel anger against them. Encircled by loving care all her life, she felt bewildered, alone in the world for the first time, and hopelessly rejected.

The reek of the place made her feel like vomiting, and through lack of food in the preceding days she felt faint. She looked around at her pathetic jailed companions. What if they were indeed witches? A more hideous array of despised humanity could not be conceived. Their grey sunken cheeks and wrinkled skin revealed deprivation and old age. She was frightened, and sick with apprehension. There was no succour either inside or out of the prison: no escape. An enraged mob without was chanting: "Burn them, burn them, burn them!" Was everyone in Newcastle mad? None of her loved ones could possibly know that she was here. Feeling hopelessly trapped and distanced from reality, she beat her head frantically against the cold damp stone wall, grazing her brow. With tiny rivulets of blood trickling down her face and wild green eyes bright and staring, she looked crazed. From the safety of being cosseted and protected, as she recalled the happy days at Hackford, she was now in the depths of despair, finding herself in the foulest situation that could be imagined.

Sleep was fitful in the prison, if not impossible. There were desperate fights over the small quantities of food which were allocated to the prisoners and they were all very hungry. Elizabeth was pestered constantly by one pathetic creature, old, shrivelled up, and bewildered, who seemed actually to be enjoying her own incarceration. At least she was given some food here, and she was noticed, so she preened herself, wallowing in this new-found attention and companionship. She often approached Elizabeth, eagerly enquiring "What can you do? I can fly to the moon. Where's my cat? Have you got a broomstick?"

Elizabeth weakly replied: "Don't ask me, because I must be the silliest person on this earth."

Pointing to a rat on the other side of the cell, she would say: "Look, your cat's over there . Better get after it." And so, using such ploys, she gained what little peace was possible, and the old woman circulated round the dungeon, sometimes pushed and jostled, but thankful for any attention that was coming.

Each day fresh captives were thrown into the prison and at last, after a terrible week in their miserable, bedraggled state, the unfortunate women welcomed being taken out of the stench to the Guildhall to be tried. By then even those that were of sound mind had given up all hope, and were numb with apprehension and despair. On the quayside there was a crowd, shouting, jeering and laughing hysterically. It was the worst nightmare that Elizabeth could have endured. There were grinning strawmen outside, with wisps of straw in their shoes, indicating that they were willing to bear false witness. However, they were not really needed, as there were plenty of misguided souls inside the Guildhall, ready to exercise their imaginations.

By the time Elizabeth reached the hall of justice she looked a completely different person, almost unrecognisable from her former self. Her once fine complexion was pale, stained with dirt and blood, her beautiful auburn hair was now tattered and dishevelled, and her body was pitifully emaciated, her shoulders bowed and her eyes dulled with the hopelessness of her situation.

The motley array of wretched women was led in a staggering line into the impressive Guildhall. Heads down, they shuffled across the marble floor, not seeing the magnificence of the long and lofty courtroom with its carved hammer-beamed roof. There were windows on the south side, and on the north an arched gallery, extending the whole length of the hall, which was full of leering excited spectators, out for entertainment.

"Here they come, the filthy witches, the dregs of the town! Let's see if their evil spells can save them from their punishment," shouted a man in the front row.

"Nothing can save them!" came another shout. "Look at the state we've got into with their dirty tricks. Hanging's too easy for them!"

Although they rarely raised their eyes, the accused were conscious of the oppressive atmosphere of hate surrounding them. As they filed towards the front, the witchfinder, surrounded by local worthies, could hardly stifle a cruel sneer as he awaited them. The Scot, a tall sparely built man of fifty years or so, had a sinister appearance with his small beady eyes, which squinted ferociously as he surveyed the company, scarcely hiding a vicious excitement. His unkempt black hair spiked out from behind his large ears, emphasizing the jerky words he uttered. He wore a coarse dark homespun suit which contrasted with his white neckerchief, worn specially for the solemn proceedings and giving him a doubtful dignity.

With his harsh Scottish accent he harangued his audience, now easily receptive to his authority. "Your witches are not only those who persecute and confound their victims, but appear to be learned men and women, healers, and those who indulge in strange practices in administering to the sick. These last are the most dangerous because they seem to spread blessings, when they are in reality servants of the devil. They all deserve to die." His hearers shuddered to hear such revelations, but were diverted by the spectacle of the stumbling procession of accused women.

Elizabeth thought she could hear Thomas saying piteously: "A pox of God, a plague of God," but as her ears were singing, she could not be sure, and, in any case, she was past caring. In front of her was the sorry deluded creature whom she had befriended in prison. Alas, this woman was in her element in the courtroom, declaring her powers in a croaky voice, and interrupting the whole proceedings with nervous laughter. "Aye, I have been well-known in these parts for my seven cats. They roam the streets, doin' my messages. Nothin' goes on in Newcastle that I don't know about." She nodded enthusiastically as she looked around her and upwards to the gallery, expecting admiration.

The audience greeted this with long moans of "Oo-oo-oo-oo", as they nudged each other and exchanged gleeful glances. It was more fun than they had expected! The old woman waxed enthusiastic: "Who tells Jack Preece, the highwayman, when the rich merchant is carryin' home his gold? Hee-hee-hee!. The answer is, my cats! Who brings the storms when the colliers set out for London? Who damned the King and Oliver Cromwell? Me, and only me, of course," she declaimed dramatically, pointing a bony twisted finger towards herself. At last she turned on the witch-finder, looked closely into his face, and after a moment's silence, predicted emphatically in an accent which had become distinctly Scottish: "In your ain country ye will be hanged and a hundred witches will be waiting to escort ye tae Hell."

Holding up her shaking fist, and nodding her head, she repeated the prophesy: "Ye will. Of that I weel ken." There was a baffled silence throughout the hall and all eyes centred on the witchfinder. He stiffened, stood staring at her, and seemed filled with a sudden fear of her premonition. The deluded old soul rambled on further, creating an interesting diversion for the onlookers, and in the end she was easily convicted.

Last of all it was Elizabeth's turn, she stood in front of her accusers, stupefied. Jane Bilton, now exercising an unaccustomed restrained eloquence, which her cunning mind calculated would produce approval in the court, accused Elizabeth of giving noxious substances to her precious daughter and grandchild, causing their deaths.

"I trusted those poor innocent souls to her for a few hours and when I came back they had perished in a hideous way. I can't guess what she gave them, but it killed them. The terrrible sight of them will always be with me. My lovely daughter and her baby, gone in a flash," she wept.

Another demonic harridan shouted: " She tormented my two sisters." Then, rising to the drama with enthusiasm, she described how : "They saw her sittin' on a throne at the bottom of their bed, arrayed in purple and scarlet, with her eyes pulsatin' with light. She held a goblet in her hand from which she spread abominations. Behind her stood four blind beasts with mighty horns. She commanded the ferocious creatures to drag my sisters to a bottomless pit from which a great smoke issued. They were only saved by heavenly angels sweepin' down with golden trumpets. The witch, the throne, the beasts and the bottomless pit vanished in an instant, leaving my sisters gibberin' with fear."

There was temporarily a hushed silence as everyone tried to work out the implications. Taking advantage of this, the newly-arrived barber surgeon took the opportunity to intervene. Though slightly out of breath his voice boomed out impressively, reaching to every part of the hall.

"I grant that some unfortunate souls have been taken over by the devil.... though this is beyond my own experience...... I would, in God's name, caution you all to be careful in naming a witch.... both because accusations be many.... and because the manifestations of natural diseases are surprising to such as have no knowledge of medicine."

Perhaps most of the crowd did not really understand him, or did not want to understand him. They were like hungry wolves, eager for blood and the general hubbub was soon renewed, his words being largely disregarded. This was definitely not the time for such a rational debate and his arguments fell on stony ground, while the witchfinder was intent on doing his job, remembering his twenty shillings for each witch, and his other allowances.

"I know witches!" he insisted, through clenched teeth, already pricked to the heart by the fatal prediction of Elizabeth's ragged predecessor.

Referring to Elizabeth, the Deputy Governor of Newcastle firmly protested: "Surely this young and goodlike woman need not be tried."

By this time, Woodall, the Mayor, was standing by his side, looking equally agitated as he recognised Elizabeth and was obviously appalled by what had happened. However, in spite of all the pleas, Elizabeth was subjected to the witch test like the rest.

The witchfinder, exploiting the drama associated with his present power, flamboyantly whipped up her dress in sight of all, and put her clothes over her head, by which fright and shame all the blood flowed from below her waist. The Mayor was shocked, not so much by this violation, as by the brown birthmark on her breast. The sight sharply jolted his mind, kindling long-forgotten memories. At the same moment he was speechless with horror at the present situation, stunned by remorse, and feelings of abject impotence. In a flash he could see all before him - the selfish arrogance of his youth, his irresponsibility - and this contrition centred powerfully on Elizabeth.

The witchfinder quickly pressed a pin into Elizabeth's thigh. Letting her clothes fall, and not even looking at her, he continued with the entertainment, walking away from her and asking with a flourish: " Hae ye aught o' mine that disna bleed?"

Amazed and confused, and, living her own private nightmare, she made no reply. The witchfinder put his hand up inside her clothes and pulled out the pin. No blood. She was immediately set aside as guilty.

Mayor Woodall and the Deputy Governor hastily consulted each other and urgently asked for the test to be repeated. The Mayor approached the witchfinder with his back to the concourse, concealing a glint in his hand. Impatiently the witchfinder began again. By this time the circulation of blood had been partially restored, and owing to the new flow of blood, or perhaps to other considerations, the Scot was obliged to pronounce: "She is nae a child of the Deil." His disappointment in failing to produce another witch for the hangings was evident in the deflated tone of his voice.

Jane and her crony were indignant with rage. "She is the devil's creature; she is not fit to live," Jane screamed in protest. "Where is the justice in this? She is the worst of the lot."

Her friend snarled oaths and the two wicked cronies threshed around in anger and could hardly contain themselves. If the furies of Hell had been released, they could not have been more threatening. They had been thwarted and their disappointment was voiced in a shrill volume of angry tirades. The roof rang with their caterwauling, but it was too late. Guards were soon clearing the hall, and the mob, realising that their fun here was over, trudged out, eager to head for the next spectacle on the Town Moor where the guilty women would soon be dangling. Meanwhile the witch-finder, once he had been paid, donned a hat and a long coat, pulled his collar up high, and sneaked out through the back entrance. The road to Scotland beckoned.

Thomas was able to fight his way to the front in the face of the dispersing crowd, and eventually joined a dazed Mayor and barber surgeon, both kneeling near the collapsed body of Elizabeth. Woodall, with large beads of sweat glistening on his face, turned to his friend Liddle.

"God a-mercy! Who would have believed the horror we have just witnessed?"

Liddle replied: "The last half hour has been worse than purgatory. I thought that there was no hope."

"Let us look to her and get her to safety," urged Woodall.

Half-fainting, Elizabeth was quickly raised by loving arms. She barely realised that it was the ever-faithful Thomas who carried her through a door leading to the Maison Dieu which adjoined the Guildhall. By the time they arrived there she was senseless.

Chapter 10

The Maison Dieu was a haven of peace after the hate-filled cauldron of the crowded courtroom. Two women leaned over Elizabeth and their gentle hands tended to her needs. Her dirty clothes were expertly removed and her person cleaned and tidied, as much as was possible in the circumstances. By the time she was restored to partial cleanliness Thomas had returned from Anthony's house with fresh clothing for her. When she was fully dressed, Mayor Woodall and the barber surgeon looked down on Elizabeth sympathetically. They withdrew to an alcove, and an earnest, hushed conversation took place.

"She must be taken away from Newcastle," said Woodall, the tension in his voice apparent, and his eyes wild with fright, the overall impression being one of a powerful man who for once had lost control.

"The mob are restless and will be on the look-out. Even now I fear for her safety. In any case, her ordeal has made her ill, and she needs rest and careful nursing."

"Anthony ffarbrigge and his son are out in the countryside, searching for spare supplies of corn, so we can't ask them for help," replied Liddle. "Can we smuggle her out to her home at Hackford in a waggon?"

"Yes. But Hackford cannot provide the nursing and comforts which will be essential if she is to recover from this ordeal," insisted Woodall. "She must go to Nunburn where we can supply all of these."

Liddle was startled by this suggestion. "I'll call in Thomas Hubbach. He must be consulted as the only relative at hand."

Thomas offered no objection to the Mayor's plan, and volunteered to accompany Elizabeth on the journey. "I cannot leave her alone in this state. I solemnly promised John and Joanna that I would look after her."

"Thank you, Thomas," said a grateful Woodall. "I'll send a man for a covered waggon. There will have to be two riders to escort it, and you must stay in the waggon with her. I'll send word to Nunburn to warn them to prepare some rooms."

A capacious waggon eventually appeared at a side entrance, in a street now empty of its crowds, and Elizabeth was carried out and laid on a palliasse of straw, which had been specially loaded into the bottom. Woodall and the barber surgeon watched as she was made as comfortable as possible. The anxious Thomas took up his seat near her head.

It was twilight when the waggon slowly trundled out of Newcastle, the occupants having far different feelings from those experienced when they first entered the "Cock o' the North", a few short weeks ago. They were accompanied by two strong-looking horsemen, wearing sheathed swords. Beyond the Westgate, Thomas heard the driver shout to the horsemen: "Have you seen the ring round the moon tonight?"

One of them replied: "Aye. A bad sign for us."

Thomas prepared himself. "There'll be a big storm coming before the night is finished," he thought, and, within the hour, black storm clouds surged up across the sullen sky, and heavy rain began to fall as they journeyed along the road to the north of the River Tyne. The rain penetrated the waggon as it jolted and swayed alarmingly through the water-filled wheel-ruts. As they pursued their long and tedious way, the riders and horses were increasingly spattered with mud, and in their discomfort never a word was spoken between them and the driver of the waggon. Shying only once when they were alarmed by a loud crash of thunder, the horses slithered on as occasional flashes of lightning illuminated the hedges and the track, which glistened like a river.

Elizabeth had only a fitful sleep, waking up from time to time, moaning with terror. Thomas soothed her as much as he could, but was himself shattered and helpless.

"You're all right now," he murmured. "Just rest, and try to sleep. We'll soon be at our journey's end."

The rain eventually stopped and the moon emerged from a cloud as they passed north of Corbridge on the old Roman road. Thomas was now more able to relax as he recognised familiar slopes and summits. Mile slowly succeeded mile, with Elizabeth at last sound asleep on her bed of straw. At a fork in the road the driver swung the horses northwards, and in ten minutes they were crossing a bridge over a channel brimming with a torrent of storm water. Now Thomas was in new territory, and his eyes swept both sides of the track. The clouds were breaking up and the moon was lighting the undulating landscape.The waggon climbed a low hill and he saw the darkened outline of a village on its lower slopes. He thought he heard the driver mutter: "God-a-mercy. Humshaugh at last!"

A few more miles of the stony road, now rising, then falling, gave way to a track through woodland, and cottages appeared on both sides. Thomas sensed that they were near journey's end, and quickened into alertness. He stared intently at every new shape, listening for any word from the riders. At length he could not resist climbing out to sit alongside the driver.

"Where are we?" he demanded wearily.

"We're just about to enter Nunburn Hall estate, thank the Lord," the man replied. "It's been a terrible night, which I wouldn't like to go through again. I'm so cold and wet and hungry. But how is the lady? Is she still sleeping?"

"Yes, God bless her. The sooner we're inside the better for all of us," said Thomas fervently.

At length they came upon a substantial wall with tall gates, which opened on to a sweeping drive through parkland, bordered on each side by long lines of well-clipped egg-shaped yew trees. One of the escorting horsemen spurred his mount and galloped ahead to warn of their arrival. As the waggon eventually slowed down, Thomas realised from the shouts of their protectors that they had reached their destination and peering ahead he was overwhelmed at the sight of the building. In the bright moonlight he could appreciate the large size of the Woodall mansion.

Crunching across the pale gravel of the courtyard, the waggon drew up at the foot of the steps leading to the entrance. Thomas gazed thankfully at the long grey stone building towering above them, low trees and bushes obscuring its base. Impressive double oak doors welcomed visitors to the central part of the building. In the moonlight Thomas could distinguish the ridge of the roof which carried ornate chimney stacks, as did the gabled offshoots flanking each side of the main building. Lights could be seen in several of the upstairs rooms and across the courtyard in the stables.

Soon friendly Northumbrian voices were heard from the main doors. Two women with white aprons ran down the steps, followed by a tall, dark-haired man dressed in a simple woollen suit, leather waistcoat and gaiters, who took several steps in his stride.

"Move her to the back so that I can lift her. Be very careful," said the man. "That's it."

His strong steady arms gently lifted the unconscious Elizabeth out of the waggon, and he easily bore her up the steps into the building. As Thomas followed them uncertainly into the hall, he was conscious of the stout defences that had safely protected the Woodall family for generations, now encircling them in its all-embracing grasp, and he felt relieved of his burden. As Elizabeth was carefully carried across the great candle-lit hall she was unaware of the magnificence of her surroundings with the deeply carved oak staircase rising in the corner in three flights around a broad well in the centre. The sturdy newel posts were surmounted by carved vases of fruit and the massive hand-rail was embellished with a bold egg-and-dart pattern. Each panel of the balustrade was decorated with acanthus scrolls, while the walls of the staircase were lined with impressive family portraits.

From the landing a tapestried passage led to a series of rooms on the first floor, and Elizabeth was carried to the largest bedroom at the centre of the house, whose balcony and tall windows overlooked the front garden. Grass stretched away from the back of the house, sloping gently up into the distance. The moonlight warped the shadows of the topiary bushes, which in long and regular lines pointed towards ornamental gates which were half-way up the slope.

The bedroom was luxuriously furnished with thick curtains of rich red cloth, and a tapestry covered the bedroom door. The curtains of the canopy bed were full and neatly folded, made of scarlet silk thickened with extra baize linings. The tall man laid down his unconscious burden on the smooth white bedsheets.

"Is there any more I can do, Mistress Grant?" he asked quietly.

"No, thank you, Robert," she replied. "I'll see that she gets some rest, poor thing."

Elizabeth lay where she had been placed, oblivious to the surrounding opulence, and was still in a deep and troubled sleep.

Meanwhile, downstairs, Thomas sank down thankfully on a long high-backed bench beside a cheery log fire in the spacious hall. At last he was free from his responsibility, although in truth this made him feel useless and excluded. Up till then he had kept his composure, but the full horror of the most hideous day of his life began to reassert itself. His body shook from head to foot as he recalled the evil of the trial witnesses. Control was impossible. A concerned maid-servant offered him a jug of burnt ale which he sipped as well as his trembling hands would permit.

To calm himself he tried to take in his surroundings and strained to see the portraits that were displayed on the panelled walls around the hall. Alas, there was a further shock to his system when his eyes came to rest on a full-length portrait of Elizabeth. Her auburn tresses trailed in curls round her lovely face and the engaging green eyes seemed to be for him alone. She was wearing a dress of the most exquisite blue material, and she looked very confident and regal, but manifestly lacking Elizabeth's natural warmth. Thinking that he was dreaming, he rubbed his eyes, and made an effort to compose himself as he heard a further commotion coming from the courtyard, indicating new arrivals.

Thomas shivered with more than just the cool draught from the door but he was thankful to hear voices that he recognised. Anxious and travel-stained, in came his Aunt Joanna, Uncle John, and Uncle Anthony, all looking bewildered, and Thomas's manly face nearly collapsed into tears at the sight of their familiar loving faces. They embraced him, and John asked anxiously: "Thomas, what on earth has been happenin'? Charlie, the carter, called on us, very upset, and gave us a terrible account of the troubles in Newcastle. We just couldn't believe it. Where is Elizabeth? Is she alright?"

A footman brought chairs for the latest arrivals and they shuffled closer to face Thomas, eager for his news. Thomas, on account of his shaking, found it very difficult to talk sensibly, and could hardly recount the lurid events of the day. At length, heaving with emotion, he stumbled tearfully through the whole heart-chilling story from start to finish. His astounded listeners hung on his every word. They found it difficult to absorb the accumulated details of the horrors perpetrated on their lovely daughter.

Bending forward, and holding his head, Uncle Anthony winced. "Charles and I were devastated when we heard that the pox had struck again, this time at Barbara and the baby. Charles remains at home to look after the business. I blame myself for inviting you and Elizabeth to stay with me at such an inauspicious time, and then abandoning you in such haste. You were a hero to go through all that and bring her to safety. And thank God for my old friend Woodall's kindness!"

Taking Thomas kindly by the shoulder, John explained: "We heard from the carter that Newcastle had been purged of witches, and that Jane Bilton, a well-known trouble-maker, had accused Elizabeth of witchcraft, and had her arrested and imprisoned as a witch, so of course we set off at once for Anthony's house in Newcastle. As soon as we arrived there we found that Mr. Woodall had left a message for Anthony and Charles to say that Elizabeth had been freed, and that the pair of you had been diverted to Nunburn Hall."

They were interrupted by a trim and obviously inquisitive maid who had nimbly brought in victuals. She departed with her curiosity unsatisfied since nobody spoke. The newcomers rested beside Thomas, welcoming the warmth of the fire, but overawed by the surroundings. After a while John's eyes alighted on the portrait resembling Elizabeth. He too stared at it long and thoughtfully, and seemed to be transported.

"A strange likeness, don't you think?" queried the troubled Thomas leaning towards him.

John nodded but remained silent. Fears clutched at his heart and in his head a distant drum was already beating. Uncle Anthony was not slow to follow their gaze and began to understand the implications of something that had puzzled him for years.

Mistress Grant bustled in from the kitchen. Seeing Joanna's eyes straying to the staircase she asked: "Would you like to go upstairs and see your daughter? I'll bring you something to eat up there."

Joanna turned towards her husband. "I'll go up now, John. You stay here." She hurried up the grand staircase after Mistress Grant, frightened to the core and quite stunned by everything around her.

Thomas, still trembling, blurted out to Anthony: "I'm sorry that we had to leave your house so quickly, but there was no choice, what with the illness at Charles' house, and ...."

Anthony dismissed this kindly: "Don't think of it, lad. Charles will be in charge now. I'm only too glad that you took the course you did. We're lucky it wasn't worse. Newcastle can be a dangerous place when tempers are inflamed."

At this point Uncle Anthony rose to greet Henry Woodall himself who had arrived at the Hall in great agitation, issuing orders to the servants before he had even reached the door. He was wet and mud-stained, looking tired and drawn, yet it was obvious that he was possessed of a tense energy. Anthony conversed privately with him for a few moments, then led him towards the two men by the fire.

"This is my brother, John, Elizabeth's father, from Hackford. His wife, Joanna, is upstairs, attending to her and, of course, this is Thomas."

With only a fleeting look of welcome towards Thomas, Woodall brusquely took John's arm and ushered him into the adjoining study. He sat down at the substantial table, and indicated the seat opposite him. John marvelled at the room, the like of which he had never seen before, rich in furniture and fabrics, with chairs and cushions upholstered in a sumptuous cloth of red damask woven with intricate gold patterns. For a few moments there remained a silence between the two mud-spattered men, in which each was able to collect his own thoughts.

Their eyes met but John's gaze never wavered. Shuffling nervously in his seat and adjusting his short riding wig, Woodall cautioned John with a pained urgency in his voice.

"This mess must be settled immediately, for the good of all parties concerned."

He paused and gulped before he went on, suffering the intensity of John's piercing stare.

"I want you to answer me truthfully, as it is of the greatest importance. Are you Elizabeth's natural father?"

John was taken aback by such directness. His lips tightened and he could feel an immense tension building up across his heart. He had kept his first wife's secret for years and did not feel like revealing it to a stranger. However, as he slowly reasoned, this was the house where she had come to look after Woodall's children all those years ago, when the mistress of the house was ill. The portrait. The striking likeness. Elizabeth's spirit. It all fitted into place. The recent danger. He had never known such paralysing fear.

His jaw clenched and his tightening knuckles whitened at the realisation. Without compunction he could have struck down this despicable and selfish stranger sitting in front of him. This man who had ruined his life. This man who owned so much, yet whose selfishness had robbed him of his most precious first love. His mind raced and struggled, fighting for control over his emotions. Then suddenly, his brain calmed and, with an immense effort of will, he dismissed these useless and unworthy thoughts. He realised equally that, for Elizabeth's sake, this was no time for silence.

Just then a maid appeared, bearing two tankards of ale.

"Mistress Grant thought you would need refreshment, Sir."

Woodall did not appreciate the interruption and glowered at her in his agitation, but thanked her absentmindedly. It seemed to take an age before she had set them down and left the room. The men drank, deep in their own thoughts, and John, now more poised, was able to speak quite firmly.

"No, I must admit I am not her natural father. I was happily married to her mother for a few months, but she died in childbed. In time Joanna and I were wed and brought Elizabeth up as our very own child. She was treated with every lovin' care, and we adore her."

Trembling in his heart but still intent on his purpose, Woodall summoned all his courage and responded, his embarrassment causing his voice to rise.

"I have reason to believe that she is of my lineage, and I therefore suggest the only possible solution in the circumstances. My wife blessed me with two sons to preserve the family line. I hardly ever see them and I admit I am a desperately lonely man now, so I propose to you that Elizabeth should be my ward. If she accepts, it will bring her safely within the bosom of her family and I will be able to secure her future happiness and prosperity. I know of many possible relationships which will be to her advantage. For me life will be more complete. What have you to say?" he asked curtly, expecting a life's work to be abandoned in a moment.

John was out of his depth in every way. He felt desolate at the thought of losing the precious daughter whom he had raised tenderly for so many years. Yet he was only too aware of his position as a poor yeoman, and he felt overwhelmed by the magnificence of his surroundings, and totally inadequate in the present circumstances. He could not even begin to understand what had happened in Newcastle, which made him suspicious of the world beyond Hackford. He was wild with the apprehension of what might have happened, having seen the hideous sight of the witches being led away to the Town Moor in the death carts.

He looked down at his cracked, toil-worn hands, and thought long and hard. His memories raced back across the years to that picture of fleeting bliss when Margaret had returned to him and they had come together again. He sensed once more the same heady feeling as their souls had spindled together on that far-off happy day. Now his mind cleared, and he suddenly felt as if his life had taken a new turning. He had done all he could for Elizabeth, but now she was beyond his sphere of understanding. She was someone different, and in truth he had always been a little in awe of her, not able to relate to her fully - not like his simple and faithful Joanna.

He realised that he had never given his second wife the devotion that she had deserved, but she had not complained even once. It was time now to bid farewell to the secret past that had haunted him and in that moment he felt liberated, as if a heavy burden had dropped from his shoulders and the paralysing tension had eased. He suddenly saw with clarity how life for them would be different from that day onwards. Although he loved Elizabeth dearly, and would miss her badly, he realised it was now time to give her up, for her own sake, to her real father.

Woodall brought him out of his reverie with a sharp jolt: "Well, what do you think?"

Clearing his throat, and controlling the emotion that was again threatening to overwhelm him, John straightened his back, and agreed.

"Yes, that seems the only solution in this troubled world. I am aware of no reason why this arrangement cannot take place, if Elizabeth wishes it."

Woodall heaved a sigh of relief and, coming to the other side of the table, he patted John on the shoulder. "She was a happy and confident woman until this late disaster. You and your wife have done a fine job of raising her. I shall be eternally grateful to you, and you will be welcome at any time in my house, while she can stay with you as long as she wishes. However, at the proper time, we will have to see if she herself agrees to this arrangement."

Thus reconciled, the two men held each other by the right arms, with tears in their eyes, each trying to address the past in his own particular way, and each marvelling at the fate that had brought them together into this strange situation from such vastly different directions.

Finally, John lowered his head and said simply with sad resignation: " I give her into your safe keeping."

Chapter 11

Elizabeth lay unconscious in a troubled sleep for a further three days, with her stepmother constantly by her bedside. Joanna had plenty of time to be bewildered at the magnificence of these new surroundings and often stood at the window, marvelling at the view, but despairing of Elizabeth's eventual return to health and lamenting the state of her beautiful hair, which had been left so long untended. Events had followed one another so rapidly that she could not understand anything that had happened, not even why they were here in this splendid Hall. Without a word of explanation and unable to meet her eyes, John had returned to the farm where he was desperately needed and she had sensed his pain and had worried about his withdrawn look. However, she had not probed with further questions. She felt instinctively that she must talk to Elizabeth, to bring her back to life, so her voice droned on endlessly, in her native Northumbrian burr, relating everything that had happened at Hackford since Elizabeth had left.

"One mornin' poor Nancy was found up on the moor. She'd died a few days earlier and we laid her to rest in Hexham churchyard. Mind you, some miserable people chuntered on about that. You know the sort. But Canon Ritschell had always appreciated her worth and her kindness to the sick, and he was sympathetic, as you would expect. But now there's no-one to collect the herbs and make the salves and potions. All that precious knowledge has died with her, and everyone is desperate for remedies. Complaints that old Nancy could cure easily are now keepin' folks abed and seem beyond mendin'. I wish we'd talked to her more and could remember the herbs she used."

"Isabel and Cuthbert are so happy in their new home.They've done well and they're enlargin' their house.We've helped them with the buildin' work, of course. Now they have taken on a pig and a few geese. They've raised some decent crops and, considerin' the weather, we've had enough to eat."

She continued to relate matters which she had gone through the day before, and the day before that, and then she recollected: " That reminds me, I'll have to be back at Hackford soon, because Isabel needs me. In a few weeks she'll be getten her bed, and needin' us all. She's expectin' a baby."

Joanna's voice quavered as she felt a thrill of expectancy run through her whole body, cheering her troubled spirit. Almost at the same time she thought that she saw Elizabeth's eyelids flicker slightly. When Mayor Woodall next visited she was happy to report what had happened, and this indeed marked the beginning of Elizabeth's recovery.

The next morning Elizabeth woke up wide-eyed from her deep sleep. She looked around her, slowly taking in her new surroundings with great astonishment. She had never before seen such a strange beautiful room and she took her mother's hand and hung on to it with a panicky grip. She felt a gnawing sensation in her stomach. Dazed, she asked: "Are we in heaven, mother?"

Joanna whispered reassuringly: "You're in the country now, in Mayor Woodall's house. He's been so good to us all. Uncle Anthony and Thomas are still staying here. But you must be very hungry. I'll ask for some potage from the kitchen."

As news of Elizabeth's recovery spread through the house, nobody could dissuade Uncle Anthony from visiting her immediately. Bursting into the bedroom he exclaimed: "At last, you're with us again, lass. We have been so worried about you, and we thought you would never wake up." He sat down beside her, lovingly feasting his eyes on her improved condition.

Their host joined the happy circle, his face beaming, and, with tears in his eyes, he assured Elizabeth that she could remain in his home as long as she desired. How much of these kind words she understood was far from clear.

By now the food had arrived and Joanna carefully spooned it into Elizabeth's mouth, popping in soaked bread at regular intervals.

Pausing, Elizabeth suddenly asked in a weak voice: "Have I been ill? Did I take the smallpox?" In a panic she hastily felt all over her face for pockmarks.

"Cousin Barbara and the baby died of smallpox, you know," she said sadly, looking at Joanna. Believing her to be wandering, and not knowing how much she remembered, Mayor Woodall said: "You have been suffering from a terrible fever and you must have as much rest and quiet as you can."

"Yes, yes, yes," said Joanna, patting her gently, and looking knowingly over Elizabeth towards their benefactor. In truth Elizabeth's mind had completely obliterated the memory of her ordeal. However, she turned to Joanna and asked: "Is Isabel really going to have a baby?"

Joanna hugged her, laughing. "Of course she is."

Uncle Anthony protested: "I didn't even know that, but it's good news."

He sat for a while, thinking of the baby, and watching Joanna feeding her daughter. At last, putting his hands on his knees, he rallied.

"However, now that Elizabeth has recovered, I'll have to leave you. I have to see to urgent business in Newcastle. Thomas has already gone on a mission for me and I promised that I'd catch him up today."

"I, too, will have to return home as soon as Elizabeth is well enough to travel. It'll be harvest time before we know where we are," said Joanna uncertainly, putting her arm around Elizabeth's shoulders. "The important thing is that she is safe and recoverin'. Don't worry, we'll soon have her home again."

The Mayor interposed quickly: "I have arranged with John that she is to stay here."

Joanna was shocked, and in her silence looked distinctly disturbed. Elizabeth was unresponsive.

Chapter 12

With the Mayor's plan confirmed, inevitably the wheel was ready to spin, and it was not long before Elizabeth was her old irrepressible self. After Joanna and Uncle Anthony had left, she was often left alone during the succeeding weeks when Mayor Woodall was obliged to spend long and frequent absences in Newcastle, but she settled down in her new home very well and felt that she would be lucky to stay there for the rest of her life. With the wise Mistress Grant in charge, she found herself plunged into many domestic duties, and in the ensuing weeks she visited many of the farms on the estate, where the tenants and their families soon became charmed by her friendly personality. She felt more at home when Thomas returned from Newcastle, and was given a position at Nunburn Hall, helping the steward, with whom he lodged at the Dower House.

Unlike the majority of young ladies of her newly acquired station, Elizabeth pursued her interest in the animals on the estate, frequently visiting the stables to check on the welfare of the horses. One day she saw the steward, Robert Carr, returning to Nunburn, leading a young black stallion up the drive behind his own horse. Even from a distance she admired the magnificent beast. Its flowing tail and graceful high-stepping movements intrigued her.

She quickly made her way to greet them at the stables. The head groom, Will Thompson, was out first.

"What have we got here?" he demanded, his face a picture of mixed astonishment and delight.

"You'd never guess where Mr. Woodall bought this handful. He's come up from Derbyshire. I met the agent at Corbridge and collected the horse this morning. Mind, I'd better warn you that the fellow who delivered him wondered if Mr. Woodall realised what he had bought. This one has a mean streak, and they were glad to be rid of him."

As if comprehending the description, the stallion chose at this point to snort and half-rear.

Will jumped back in trepidation. Normally a carefree joker, his face became serious. He bent down to pluck a piece of straw from the yard and began to chew it nervously. Then he closed in and took the rein from the steward.

"This villain won't get the better of me, Mr. Carr. I've met hard cases before but, man, I must admit, never as powerful-looking as him."

By this time Elizabeth had reached them and the steward called out to her.

"Stay well back. He might kick sideways. We've heard he's dangerous."

Elizabeth viewed the horse from where she stood.

"He's certainly a beauty. Is he going to stay here?"

The steward replied: "Yes. I think the master knows somebody in the Duke of Newcastle's estate in Derbyshire, and the stallion could have been recommended for breeding. Perhaps he intends to start a new strain in Northumberland with his own stud. I hope he hasn't taken on too much. The Duke of Newcastle never gives up a good horse."

The groom screwed up his eyes. "I heard at Hexham market that there's just been a horse fair at Lee Gap down in Yorkshire. Perhaps the agent bought him there."

Elizabeth scrutinised the beast. She had always taken a deep interest in horses at Hackford, but they had merely been trained for the plough, cart-work, and short journeys such as John made to Hexham. None of them had been described as mean, or even high-spirited. But this animal had eyes that looked everywhere, as if possessing an unusual intelligence. He had a restless energy, and a wariness about him. His nostrils flared. Besides there was a fascination in thinking that he must have been close to the charismatic Duchess of Newcastle. Edmund had told her about the flight of the Newcastles to the continent in Cromwell's time and how their lands had in due course been restored. The Duchess was well-known for her fine clothes, poetry and writings, while the Duke kept wonderful riding stables, teaching horsemanship to the court of Charles II.

The beast was intriguing. Elizabeth felt that she could almost touch these famous people through him. His shoulders were deeper and lay further into his back than in any horse she had seen, and the prominent muscles of his rear legs gave his quarters the impression of great strength and power.

"If he has come all the way from Derbyshire he must be tired. Let's give him food and water."

Approaching the horse slowly from the side she stroked his withers for a while. Then she allowed him to smell the back of her outstretched hand. He snorted again but was much pacified. She darted to the stables and returned with two apples.

The steward spoke quietly but firmly: "Watch out. He might rear at any minute, and he's a powerful creature. You could be sent reelin', or worse."

However, danger was irrelevant to her. The stallion came forward, attracted by the smell of the apples. She, too, was drawn to him as to a lodestone rock. She stood her ground calmly and offered him an apple on her extended flat hand. He took the delicious offering and in a couple of bites it was all gone and he was looking for the other. But in that moment Elizabeth had noticed something wrong.

She said: "Look! Something has injured his mouth. And can you see those cuts on his flank? Did you see the painful way in which he's eaten that apple. This is the only tale he can tell us. What have they been doing to you, old lad? We'll have to get this mended."

The steward and the groom looked at each other in surprise. They were not used to having any interference.

"Righto," said the steward. "We'll get him into the stall and see if he likes our sweet Northumbrian hay and water."

They took the horse away from her and Elizabeth, buoyed by her interim success, followed them.

"I hope he'll remember the smell of me tomorrow, because I'll need to treat his sore mouth and cuts."

True to her word, Elizabeth went down to the stables early next morning. She had prepared certain well-tried salves for the horse, but spoke to Will Thompson first.

"He hasn't kicked the doors down yet, then?"

"No. He seems to have had a good night. But, man, about half an hour ago he gave the side of the stall an almighty kick. Be very careful as you go in. We've left the next stall empty so you can reach him from there."

Elizabeth tried the lure of an apple once more and the horse gobbled it up, enabling her to smooth ointment on to the cuts and bruises.

"He's had enough for one day. Let him rest a while. If you put little Merrilegs in the stall beside him, he might settle better."

"You needn't worry about him. He'll not take any more harm here," Will promised.

However, though the horse's condition improved, it did take a long time for him to settle in his new surroundings. Elizabeth recognised in the horse a kindred spirit and over the following weeks spent hours stroking his head, making him feel comfortable with her as he explored her with his nose. She talked lovingly to him.

"I love you, Periculo. You're safe here. We'll all look after you. Relax then. Good times are ahead."

Will, hearing this, commented: "Man, that's a funny name for a horse. Where did you get that?"

"Never mind."

Will turned to his other duties, shaking his head. The ways of women were strange and this woman was stranger than any.

Thanks to the efforts of Elizabeth and the grooms, the horse's condition improved rapidly and Periculo's black coat was worked up to perfection, gleaming in the sunlight. Woman and beast were eventually as one and could sense each other's every mood. With every confidence she insisted on riding him and would not be gainsaid. Neither the steward nor the grooms had either the authority or the inclination to oppose her and soon she became a familiar sight accompanying Thomas around the estate on the prancing horse.

One day she and Thomas were making their leisurely way down to the farrier's at Humshaugh when Thomas grew serious.

"Are you truly happy here, Elizabeth? One reason I am staying on is because Joanna wishes me to keep an eye on you. How do you get on with Mr. Woodall?"

When Elizabeth was silent he went on: "Wouldn't you be better off back at Hackford in your old familiar life?"

A cloud came over Elizabeth's face as loyalties began to bite deep, and Thomas felt sorry that he had opened up the wound. Tears came to her eyes and she was unable to reply. She quickly changed the subject to their present business, but afterwards doubts about the uncertainty and strangeness of her position began to fester in her mind.

However, her new equine friendship eased her thoughts, and there was only one occasion when she was given a fright. They had been riding along the banks of the North Tyne when they came upon a sandy strand and the horse became excited. He suddenly reared up, almost straight and seemed to be attempting to shake Elizabeth off his back with great violence. She felt out of control and frightened and hung on to his neck for dear life, using all her strength and agility. He came down and then reared up again on his powerful back legs. This time Elizabeth was prepared and was better able to keep her seat. She realised that there was a rhythm in all his motions as he jumped forward twice on his hind legs. Again his front legs pounded the ground and he reared and danced for a third time. The horse was telling her, in the only way he knew, something about his previous life that she had so longed to know, and he was sharing his prowess with her.

When she returned to the stables they both enjoyed cavorting for the wide-eyed grooms who had never seen anything like it before. The horse seemed to thrill to their approval and backed proudly, then he carefully went down on his knees without unseating Eizabeth. She laughed hysterically and the horse shook his head and the men at the stables clapped their hands with enthusiasm. Life was fun with these new arrivals!

Chapter 13

And so it was that as Woodall returned home from Newcastle one day he rested his eyes on the beautiful vision of Elizabeth riding towards him at great speed on his new stallion, expertly pulling up and wheeling round the yew trees to join him. His first words were full of concern: "Wouldn't a quiet nag be more suitable for a woman?"

"Perhaps, but who wants to be deadly dull? Besides, this horse needs extending," replied Elizabeth pertly. Woodall looked down ruefully at his own modest mount.

He admired her skill in controlling the horse and noticed how it responded quickly to her every wish, reminding him of a performance of horsemanship he had once watched in the arena. He would not be surprised if with a bit of training she could get it to do anything. The next day he would have a word with the steward to see what had been going on in his absence.

Robert Carr was distinctly reticent in describing the recent history of the Barbary stallion. Shaking his head he gradually recounted the story.

"We had trouble in settling him in at first, but we did have some help."

"You don't mean Elizabeth?"

"Well, yes. We couldn't keep her away, Sir."

"I appreciate that, but don't you think it's madness to put a woman in control of that kind of horse?"

"But Periculo is like a lamb with her."

"What? Periculo! Do you know what that name means?"

"Yes. And Elizabeth is well aware of what she is doing. You should see her with him. He wants to please, and I am convinced that she is safe with him."

As a consequence of this meeting and much introspection during the afternoon, Woodall made up his mind. That evening, looking across the dinner table, he said briefly: "Elizabeth, I am very happy to give you the Barbary horse for your own use."

Elizabeth was astonished and sat quiet for a moment, then her face flushed with happiness.

"This is the most precious gift I have ever received," she said slowly. "I should not accept it, but I adore him and am truly thankful because I know how scarce even ordinary horses have been since the war."

In spite of being excited about such generosity, Elizabeth was restrained during the rest of the meal. She was already feeling somewhat uncomfortable in her privileged position at the hall and it was the very gift of this splendid horse, which was far above the level of ordinary hospitality, that brought everything to a head.

Over the weeks she and the Mayor had grown closer together, and Elizabeth was gradually becoming very fond of him. It was obvious that Woodall himself revelled in the new companionship. The barber surgeon had sent Elizabeth a rare copy of Lyte's Herbals and they had been feeling a special togetherness as Woodall helped her to read it that evening. She sadly wondered how long she would be able to continue this happy and relaxed life at the great Hall.

"All these books fascinate me, but I shall have to leave sometime. Your kindness is overwhelming and indeed an embarrassment," Elizabeth blurted out.

The Mayor tried to take hold of her hand but just managed to grasp the tip of her finger. "You can stay here until I have closed my extreme day," he said, smiling mischievously.

Elizabeth protested at such a sad thought, feeling awkward. "But I have no right. Your son will be returning, and what will he think?"

The Mayor paused for a moment, and, looking up at the biblical story depicted on the plaster relief over the fireplace, he confided: " Solomon in all his glory is not as happy as I am. Yet his wisdom is shown here. See the two women and the disputed baby. And here is his servant, ready with the sword to divide the child between them."

He looked steadily at Elizabeth with great affection. "John and I didn't have that problem. We settled it man to man."

Elizabeth was slow to absorb his meaning. She stared at the relief and then gradually turned towards him.

"I knew you were someone special and I could feel it in the unity of our minds. I love John so much, too, but it was never the same. I do feel that you are my real father!"

"Haven't you noticed your striking resemblance to my mother's portrait?"

"Yes. I have gazed at it often. But I couldn't presume to think that I was connected in any way."

"When your mother came to the Hall to look after Lancelot and Alexander, my wife had been so affected by childbirth that she rarely left her couch and was unwilling to walk even as far as the gardens, which had always been her pride and joy. She never fully recovered and that is why I have only two sons. I am under an obligation to your dead mother and the circumstances of your birth to take care of you. To regularise our relationship, I propose that you are my ward, if you are willing."

His tired eyes looked at her intently with a poignancy that melted her heart and she nodded, yet she was still deeply aware of John and his unselfish devotion towards her over her whole life.

Now that the situation had been explained, Elizabeth, with tears in her eyes, put her arms round his shoulders, and, for the first time, kissed him again and again.

"Thank you. Thank you. At last I feel at peace with myself - at home, with you and the prospect of two half-brothers that I never knew existed."

Her father confessed: "Old eyes can look back at the self-centred attitudes of youth, and bitterly regret the past, but I couldn't regret you. You are just sheer perfection and I am so proud of you, Elizabeth. I can hardly contain my pleasure, because you fill my home with delight. We are so at one that Newcastle no longer has the same attraction. My sons, too, are my pride and joy, but I don't feel the same with them. My eldest, Lancelot, is sensible and will manage the estate well when I am gone, but he has always been coldly calculating, and distant from me. My younger son, Alexander, is endeavouring to make his fortune in Barbados, but he is adventurous, and looks for present frivolities instead of long-term stability. His mother's family were like that and they were always up to the eyes in financial troubles. Alexander himself doesn't seem to realise that there are plenty of people willing to take your money if you are a fool to fate. I have good reports from certain contacts in the West Indies, but although I love him dearly, I am not sure that he will succeed, and I worry about him constantly. I just don't know how far to back his judgement."

Elizabeth put her hand on his, reassuringly. "I'm convinced that everything will turn out alright in the end. I will smooth your path as much as I can, and share all your joys and sorrows. I am most indebted to you for your concern for me. But what of John and Joanna? They have been so good to me, and I love them too."

"Yes, of course. I am aware that they are fine people, and the bonds are strong. There's no doubt that you should visit Hackford soon because they will be longing to see you."

Elizabeth replied: "Well, I was hoping to go when my sister's baby is due."

Now that the air was cleared with the exchange of these family confidences, father and daughter relaxed. As they retired for the night they both felt more contented as the promise of building on their new relationship stirred and reassured their hearts.

Chapter 14

In November the weather was unseasonably good and Elizabeth was able to ride with a groom from Nunburn Hall to Hackford for the first time. When she walked through the door of her old home she found Isabel was lying in the bedplace, contentedly overlooking a cradle.

She squealed with delight as they embraced:

"How good to see you, Elizabeth! You've missed the birth of the baby by only two days.....but it's a boy.., " she cried out triumphantly, "And he's to be called John, after our father. You will be a godparent, won't you?"

All this came out in joyous gushes, as she felt released from the trauma of childbirth. "Isn't he the most beautiful baby?.......and just like Cuthbert ...... I'd been working in the fields and he was born almost as soon as I came back into the house .... Mother was the only one there, and you can imagine how surprised Cuthbert was when he returned."

Cuthbert, who had been ravenously devouring his meal at the table, scrambled to his feet and managed a broad smile: "She's been like this ever since the baby was born. We can't stop her talking, day or night. Joanna has pushed me into the other bed to get some sleep."

" I should think she has," said Elizabeth. "Let me peep at the little one."

She quietly stepped over to the cradle, and, peeling back the coverlet with great care, saw the most beautiful baby that could be imagined, making little snuffling noises and all the time intent on forming sucking motions with his mouth.

Joanna came bustling in and kissed her. "It's so good to see you, Elizabeth. You look well. I've just been out to feed the pig. It's hard to concentrate on our normal work here because we're all taken up with this little one."

"Sounds as if all the women in this house are equally excited," laughed Elizabeth, looking at Cuthbert, who nodded.

"Well, I'm here to help," said Elizabeth, piling more food on his trencher and being greeted with another grateful nod.

Cuthbert said persuasively: " Come and tell me what it's like, living at the hall like a lady. We often think about you. What a stroke of good fortune for you! We could hardly believe it. What a difference you must find, coming back here."

Isabel protested: "She has come to see me and the baby. She wants to sit beside me."

Joanna warned: "Stop acting like children.You are parents now."

Elizabeth chose to sit beside Isabel, and smoothed her hair affectionately as she looked round the room. Surveying the familiar fireplace with its large stone lintel, and staring at the ceiling with its heavy wooden beams, all strong memories from childhood, she felt that there was a strangeness about their very familiarity which she could not understand. At Nunburn there were none of the homely smells from the animals, no pots and trenchers lying on benches, no bedding being aired, no casual clumps of soil inside the entrance. Now she lived in a double world, her mind flitting between the two scenes. Fate was moving her from the old to the new and the great wheel was indeed turning.

Her reverie was interrupted when John walked through the door. He was thrilled to see his two daughters together again and kissed them both.

"Well, what do you think of the little 'un?" he asked as he sat down at the table beside Cuthbert. Joanna put his food on the trencher immediately, and as they came close together Elizabeth sensed that they were different now. There was a touching tenderness between them, which she had never seen before, and, which in a strange way, threatened to exclude her. This was a totally new experience and there were others besides. Inexplicably, although they were obviously idyllically happy together, she felt an unbounded pity towards them all, which was very painful.

As the evening wore on, and she listened to the family talk, she could appreciate the difficulty they had in achieving even limited ambitions. She was moved as she realised their great happiness in small acquisitions, and even felt sorry for them in the love they felt towards each other. The pain in her breast was confusing and unpleasant. She bit the inside of her cheek. She still loved them dearly, but it was becoming increasingly difficult to relate to their lives. Her horizons had expanded, and truly now her life lay beyond Hackford.

She recognised that they seemed to be more in awe of her, and John was more distant, more involved in this close circle of family relationships, which were increasing with Isabel's marriage. All their talk, however, was of mean objectives, all hope limited, any material progress almost impossible. Their situation was more brittle than they could possibly know, and yet their happiness was so complete. She shivered as she wondered if she herself might be deluded.

However attractive her new surroundings might be, there were new snares and pitfalls of which she might be unaware. Were these new acquaintances as sincere as the simple, happy, and genuine community in which she had been raised? Where, indeed, did she belong? Perhaps all hope lay in a critical balance between the two, which only she herself could create.

She felt safe here, but it was not enough for her, because she was fascinated by her new life. However, as she stayed longer at Hackford, she became increasingly used to the less comfortable lifestyle, and yet still felt redundant, apart from the time spent caring for the baby. However, towards the end of her visit a circumstance occurred which suddenly plunged the whole house into an unusual emergency, and gave Elizabeth a sense of purpose in life.

One afternoon John came rushing into the kitchen in great agitation, describing an accident to the husbandman.

"There's a sorry sight in the farmyard. George was lookin' after the bull in the byre when the devilish beast suddenly turned on him. The animal's always been so quiet and it's never been vicious before, but it pushed him to the ground, stamped on him and gored him badly in the thigh. They're bringin' him in. Get the table cleared, quick!"

White with shock, and moaning, George was carried into the farmhouse, his trousers torn and his leg bleeding profusely. Everyone was aghast at such a shocking sight, and all was thrown into confusion. Elizabeth felt protective towards Isabel, in her fragile state, forced to witness this new crisis. Yet she had to take the initiative in tending to him, immediately recollecting the barber surgeon's dexterity as he had peeled away the sinews from the cadaver's body, and she knew exactly how to clean and tend the wound.

"Bring me a pad of those late marigold petals and comfrey leaves to make into a poultice. That should stem the flow of blood and keep the wound free from poison, and then we can try henbane or hemlock to reduce the pain," she directed. She cleaned the wound and wrapped the pad in place with a tight bandage. Joanna held George's head and pressed him back when he groaned with pain. John fetched a palliasse of straw and Elizabeth spent the whole evening attending and comforting him.

Next morning, when she was sure that he could be moved, he was taken back to his own house on a stretcher. Elizabeth followed him there and sat beside him constantly, mopping his brow as he sweated with a fever, and administering Joanna's meagre supply of medicines. Mary, his wife, had been in great shock when they had first brought him in, and was very angry that he had taken such a chance with the bull. The neighbours who came to visit George tried to mollify her.

"You never know when these devils are going to turn on you. He couldn't help it," insisted one of the stretcher bearers. Mary, however, still showed signs of being unconvinced.

He went on: "We'd been killing the animals ready to salt down for the winter and the bull must have got himself agitated by the smell of blood."

"Look you can't tell me anything about bulls. I've known them all my life. They need an iron ring through the nose, and a very short lead, if they are to be handled," she snapped. "A stone pen with a strong gate between you and him, that's what you want. They're not pets!"

Thankfully it took only a few days before George's leg began to heal, the fever vanished, and the patient was eating and drinking normally. With this improvement Mary felt more capable of attending to him, and soon he could not be restrained from staggering around the farm kitchen with the aid of a stick and getting in everyone's way.

"How we miss old Nancy!" lamented Joanna over the meal-table one evening, and it was at the mention of that name that Elizabeth realised in a flash what her mission in life must be. Old Nancy, in reality, had been a respectable pillar of the community, if somewhat unappreciated. Like her, she must also look after the sick and injured, providing medicines where none existed. It was obvious that in an emergency she herself could cope with a calm concentration which others could not summon. At Nunburn Hall she had every opportunity to grow herbs, and could obtain all the unusual remedies that she would ever need through her connections in Newcastle. She would learn more of medical matters from the barber surgeon and her combined knowledge of the countryside and sympathy for country people gave her the opportunity to be useful at Nunburn Hall. These thoughts made her feel more contented, yet, in the back of her mind, there were still some lingering doubts, dark compulsive shadows that would not leave her, rendering her strangely uneasy. Indeed was it her past nightmares that were preparing to surface?

When she was ready to travel back to Nunburn Hall a message was sent for one of the grooms to accompany her. After a final visit to George, who was very thankful and improving tremendously, and a last lingering look at the baby, who was happy and thriving, they set off along the country track to her new home, accompanied by everyone's best wishes. She was proud to ride the beautiful black stallion that her father had entrusted to her, and firmly controlled the friskiness which resulted from his days of freedom in the Hackford meadows.

As soon as she arrived she sought out her father, who was writing in the library, and she was shocked by his distraught appearance.

"Elizabeth! How relieved I am to see you," he burst out. Then, in great agitation: "There is bad news from the plantation in Barbados. Alexander is very sick with a fever, and I fear for his survival. I have been obliged to send Thomas out there, with another four of my servants, to look after our interests. They've started off for London already."

Elizabeth was shocked at the news. "What! To Barbados! I wish I'd been here to say goodbye to Thomas when he was beginning such a long journey. If I'd only known ...."

Her father reassured her: "Yes. The party has left for London in one of my colliers, and my agent will arrange for them to sail to Barbados as soon as possible. Depending on the weather, it will take several weeks to reach the island. He promised to write us a letter as soon as he has news."

"Write? I hope he can," replied Elizabeth, puzzled. "There are so many dangers, especially in London. What if he is seized by the press gang?"

"Don't worry. He'll be all right. He's a stout fellow, and he has four of my strongest men with him. Nothing will harm him," her father insisted, somewhat optimistically.

That evening, when Elizabeth retired to her room, she took out a small package which Joanna had pushed into her hand when she left. Unwrapping the material, which she recognised as her own well-worn neckerchief, she found a wooden pestle and bowl. Then she recollected Joanna's words in the haste of her departure: "I think she wanted you to have these." Her eyes filled with bitter tears as she mourned the ill-judged old woman who had been her mentor, and realised how much she had loved Nancy. She would put her gift to good use and the old woman's time on this earth would not have been altogether wasted.

Chapter 15

Towards the end of March, a letter from Cambridge arrived at Nunburn Hall. It contained the exciting news that the students were to be sent home immediately due to the threat of an outbreak of plague spreading out from London, and Lancelot would soon be on the road north.

His father eagerly anticipated Lancelot's return, and the whole household was busy with preparations for his arrival. A look-out was stationed at the gates of the estate to give the first warning of his coming. When the great day eventually came, Lancelot arrived on horseback, accompanied by his friend, Edmund, a fellow Cambridge student, who was with him at St. John's College. Since he lived further north he was to interrupt his journey to enjoy a rest at Nunburn Hall.

A fine rain had just stopped falling as the staff faced each other in two long lines down the front steps. At the top was Mistress Grant, brimming over with tears. The two riders were sombrely dressed in long black coats, black hats and breeches, all soaked with the rain. Nevertheless they dismounted athletically. Lancelot, tall, dark-haired and elegantly straight-backed, ran quickly up the steps, smiling and calling greetings, as the servants welcomed the return of the heir with gracious bows and deep curtsies. After being embraced by his father, unabashed, and full of confidence, he was intrigued to see Elizabeth at the entrance of the hall, and stopped dead. She was equally affected.

Turning back, he asked his father in a whisper: "Who is this charming young lady?"

Woodall looked slightly embarassed. "I'll explain later."

Shaking hands with Edmund he said: "Welcome Edmund. You can stay here as long as you wish."

"Thank you very much, Sir. I am so tired after that long journey that I am in need of a rest," replied Edmund, his eyes also resting on Elizabeth. Mistress Grant, laying a lingering hand on Lancelot's shoulder, urged the travellers indoors, where a cosy fire and warm food awaited them. The servants ran in to their various posts, while questions buzzed backwards and forwards between father and son as they entered the hall. Lancelot again did not disguise his eagerness and whispered. "Who is that beautiful vision of delight?"

Responding to his quizzical look, his father took Lancelot into the study and explained the situation with regard to Elizabeth. His son's reaction at first was: "How many more will we have to accommodate? It seems you have been dashed careless, father."

His father ignored this, and began to acquaint him with all of Elizabeth's good qualities. However, when he warned him of the accusations against Elizabeth in Newcastle an alarmed Lancelot retorted: "Father, have you gone absolutely mad? You might have brought into the house another version of Elizabeth Evans.You've heard of her - Canterbury Bess, who used to lure unfortunate men away to be killed by her accomplice?"

His father went red with anger. "I've never heard such a ridiculous suggestion. She has been raised in a good God-fearing family, and she was the victim of malice."

"Well, if you are convinced that she is, in fact, my half-sister, I will accept her, but as to her worthiness, I will have to make my own decisions and act accordingly. You are getting rather old, father, and I see we will have to look after you. Now, tell me about my wandering brother, who has given you so many worries. I've been sick with apprehension since I heard your news."

Lancelot was pleased with the information that someone had been dispatched to look after their interests when Woodall informed him that Thomas Hubbach had been sent out to Barbados.

"I can't pretend that Thomas is skilled in business, but he is an honest fellow, stout and loyal, and I felt that he could be trusted to look after your brother. Alexander always seems to be unlucky. However, time will tell."

"I'm sorry to hear of his illness, father, but I don't altogether blame luck for some of the calamities he has fallen into."

" Now you must sit down and eat," Woodall said, disguising his dismay. "I shall bring you up to date with business during the rest of this week. But where is our young friend, Edmund?"

Before they reached the door, Lancelot turned towards his father with a smile. "By the way, according to our ancient and traditional ordeal by examinations, designed to test our knowledge of Euclid, both Edmund and I have been successful, and we are now scholars."

His father shook his hand vigorously. "Well done, Lancelot. Your mother would have been so proud of you! Let's go and find Elizabeth to tell her the good news."

They searched everywhere in the house but she could not be found. Eventually they came out to the garden terrace, and there they discovered Elizabeth and the dark-haired Edmund, taking a turn around the gardens, in deep conversation and oblivious to the cold and dampness. As they approached, Elizabeth's face shone with wonder as she pointed to the beautiful rainbow that had appeared after the rain and Edmund was heard to be dismissing it with: "Isaac Newton solved all that with his work on prisms, which showed that the rays of light are split up."

Elizabeth looked crestfallen. Nature's beauty was being reduced to a chain of mathematical reasoning. Could the scholars leave none of God's beautiful wonders alone?

Seeing his host approach Edmund explained: "I am just escorting your ward round the garden and enjoying again the bracing air of the north."

"If Elizabeth wishes to walk in the garden, I am perfectly capable of taking her," insisted Woodall grudgingly, regretting his rather hasty offer of hospitality, and almost immediately his present pettiness.

They retired indoors as dark clouds brought the threat of more rain, and Lancelot and Edmund took their places at the dining table.

"Your father's ward is very charming," said Edmund eventually. "It's strange that you never mentioned her before."

"She is a closely guarded family secret. You've seen how father docsn't let anyone have even a whiff of her," replied the diplomatic Lancelot, smiling. "Come on upstairs. I'll show you to your room."

In the next few days Elizabeth spent a great deal of time with Edmund under the ever-watchful eyes of her father, listening eagerly to tales of student life at Cambridge and the new ideas that were circulating in those learned circles. She found it very difficult to understand some of the concepts. As they continued their long conversations in the warmth of the parlour, Edmund waxed enthusiastic as he explained some of the new theories of the universe.

"The movement of the planets in the heavens as they orbit the sun is in elliptical, rather than in circular paths."

This confounded and almost frightened Elizabeth. Her green eyes opened wide as Edmund continued.

"Man has great power over all living things," he pontificated.

"Then why is he so helpless in the face of natural calamities?" asked Elizabeth.

"Men are often the object of human wickedness and divine displeasure. Just as women are inferior to men, and suffer the pangs and dangers of childbirth, as a result of the control that Eve used on Adam."

Elizabeth grimaced, but Edmund, carried away by his own eloquence, pressed his point: "Some of our scholars do experiments to show that the earth has special powers to attract objects. In fact they believe it is alive. My own idea is that the stars and the earth itself have their own particular intellect from the very beginning of time and are capable of renewing themselves."

Elizabeth retorted: "How can anyone dream up anything as peculiar as that? I don't know what Canon Ritschell would think about it. Don't you fear hell fire, saying such things? These ideas are beyond belief. When I dig the earth it doesn't sound as if it hurts. If it was living it would cry out. I can't believe all this. I didn't think people at Cambridge were so strange. I shall have to warn Canon Ritschell. His sons are studying at Oxford."

" I should add that one of the greatest brains in our college calculated that the earth began on November 5th, 4000 B.C. at precisely 18 minutes past 1 o'clock. Others disagree, of course - our own eighth century historian, the Venerable Bede, at Jarrow, placed the creation at a date of 3952 BC."

Elizabeth was aghast and becoming increasingly confused. Eager to change the subject, she enquired: "Tell me news of the court and what the ladies are wearing."

Edmund replied wearily: "I have no idea. Studying at Cambridge does not involve excursions to London, let alone to the king's court. Have you had any experience of the Royal Family?"

Already relishing the subject, and wishing to appear knowledgeable herself, Elizabeth took on an air of sagacity. " I know it was as far back as 13th of May, 1646, in the year when I was born, that King Charles' father was brought back a prisoner to Newcastle, but people are still talking about it. Uncle Anthony was there, and remembers the line of muskets and pikes, which stretched from Gateshead all along the streets to Major George Anderson's residence, where the king was to stay."

She took a quick look at Edmund, who could not take his eyes from her. He appeared to be transported by her stimulating conversation, so she continued: "He was greeted with bonfires, and it was deafening to hear the guns exploding, trumpets sounding, drums beating and bells ringing. They say three hundred horsemen guarded him. Later Uncle Anthony watched him playing at golf on the Shield Field, without the walls."

Elizabeth's voice grew harsh: "The dastardly Scots received the price of the king in thirty-six covered waggons. What was worse, my uncle was appalled to hear a Scottish minister preaching arrogantly before the king. After accusing him to his face, he quoted the 52nd Psalm: 'Why dost thou, tyrant, boast thyself, thy wicked words to praise?' At this his majesty rose and called for Psalm 56: 'Have mercy, Lord, on me, I pray, for men would me devour'."

Another swift look at Edmund assured her that he was still listening, and he appeared interested. She went on: "The sympathetic congregation, moved by his humiliation, showed more respect for the king than for the minister and sang the king's request. Poor man, he was later executed so horribly, and yet they say that he bore it with great dignity. Everyone says his son is handsome - different from Oliver Cromwell, who was positively ugly. It's all very interesting to me. Sorry, I have gone on too long," apologised Elizabeth, coming to a sudden stop.

Edmund shook himself out of his reverie and laughed, "No. I could listen to you all day. In any case, the more facts I have about the royal family the better. Now that I have finished at Cambridge I wish to find a favourable appointment in London, the king being very generous, and there are fortunes to be made there for the asking. At any rate, as a second son, I'll have to make my own way and a beautiful woman at my side would be a great asset."

His companion shuddered as his eyes rested on her. She had already heard about the ways of the court.

One evening she confided her thoughts to her father. "I begin to wonder at Edmund's sanity. He has such queer ideas about nature and the stars, and describes the earth as a living being, while at the same time he knows nothing about the wonders of everyday living things like insects, plants and trees."

"Yet he is considered to be very clever, learned in the classics and mathematics," rejoined Woodall. "He has studied many obscure books and was well esteemed by his tutors at Cambridge. There is still a great deal to be learnt about our world and I have heard Edmund talk with enthusiasm about joining the Royal Society in London, which furthers our knowledge by exploration. I should have thought that you would be very interested in such ideas. I have been watching you both very closely and thought you were forming a mutual attachment through shared interests. I am sorry you do not care for him, because I take him for an honest young man and, as a friend of Lancelot, we must wish him well. Please treat him with toleration. He will be leaving us soon and we must continue to make him feel welcome."

"Of course," said Elizabeth.

Woodall did not mention Elizabeth's reservations about Edmund to Lancelot when he was settled with him in the library later that evening. He was anxious to discover Lancelot's attitude to his new half-sister.

"How are you getting on with Elizabeth?" he asked.

"At first I was very suspicious of her, thinking that she had tricked you into believing that she was your daughter. Now I am prepared to believe your conclusions and appreciate her quick wit and her personality so much, that frankly, I am willing to accept her for herself, and am not too bothered about any other considerations. She has an open nature, is concerned beyond her own interests, and has an intellect which can absorb as much as is put before her. I feel that she is an asset to the family, and, with some direction in social graces, will earn respect wherever she goes."

Woodall was pleased. "How is she passing her days when I am away?" he asked.

" She visits the cottagers frequently, administers to them devotedly, and they seem to respect her advice, and welcome her visits," said Lancelot. "Even the children run to her when we call at the farms, and she knows all their names, which is more than I do."

"How are the Barbados families faring? Does she console them?"

"Those are the very people who love her most," replied Lancelot animatedly. "She keeps telling them that her cousin Thomas has gone to Barbados, and that his kindness and energy will take care of the men. She is very convincing and even I am beginning to believe it. I often wish that she wasn't my half-sister because she would be a valuable asset to the estate."

"I am gratified to hear this news. I don't think that even a man could be more influential. She does have an uncanny charm about her and Anthony ffarbrigge told me that in the Hackford area she is loved above all others," commented Woodall.

"I must tell you this," said Lancelot. "One day I overheard her giving precise details to Robert Carr concerning the new herb garden which she is planning. She knew every plant by name and which grew best together. Poor Robert was quite overwhelmed by her erudition and authority, and could only nod his head and dutifully write down her orders. I was very amused."

"Yes, she does have an intimate knowledge of the plant world. When I was helping her to study Lyte's Herbals I was impressed by the speed at which she remembered even the Latin names and the characteristics of plants. Nicholas Liddle, I know, is frequently recounting the story at dinner and laughing at the way she joined him at an anatomy session. He was dreading her fainting at any moment, like some of his students who are regularly carried out, but as he dissected the body she was wanting to know more, and more."

Lancelot pulled a face. "This is indeed an unusual ability. She will be very useful at salting time," he joked. "Seriously, I should like to expand her talents in a different direction. In some circles she might appear to lack polish and, to prevent her being fair game for the mischievous, we will have to enlist someone to help. I thought that Aunt Caroline would be perfect to explain to Elizabeth how to behave in polite society, how to dance, how to talk, and how to acquire the accomplishments of young ladies. I expect that her country style of dancing will be more energetic than dignified, and her topics of conversation rustic rather than sophisticated, but she is so beautiful that she must have a mile start on her rivals."

Woodall agreed. "You must arrange a great ball at Nunburn. This will give us a good reason for polishing her range of social achievements and I'm sure Caroline will make a splendid tutor as she is the kindest and most tactful person I know."

As he retired to bed, Woodall felt that everything was going well and that he could only congratulate himself on discovering Elizabeth. He chuckled inwardly at her views on Edmund because he had similar thoughts himself and resented that young man's effrontery in making advances towards her. His own hopes led in a different direction.

Next morning an urgent and somewhat peevish letter from Edmund's mother called her son home, and with great reluctance he was obliged to leave Nunburn. Elizabeth looked on this as a welcome development, but said nothing. At first she had regarded him with great wonder and admired him immensely but now she was beginning to compare him unfavourably with other men in her life, and was finding him lacking in charity, in strength of mind, and in constitution.

Chapter 16

One afternoon Woodall came back from Newcastle in great glee and immediately sought out Elizabeth and Lancelot who were reading quietly in the drawing room. He burst out: "At long last a letter has been delivered from Thomas in Barbados. He asked a local priest to write it for him and it's a complete account of his adventures after leaving Newcastle." They were both eager to hear the news and their father read it out aloud.

"Woodall Plantation, Barbados.

To Mr. Woodall at Nunburn Hall, Northumberland.

With the letters of introduction we easily found the collier to convey us to London in the convoy, and it was our good fortune that the sea was remarkably calm. It was a strange coincidence that Jane Bilton, of all people in Newcastle, had hidden herself on the ship, because she wished to seek her fortune in London. We had set sail before she was discovered, and when she saw me her allusions to Tynedale and myself were barely civil. We were well on our way to London when a chance ill-judged remark of mine, referring to soot, rendered her completely crazy. At first I thought it amusing, but she was furious beyond belief. In fact, she tried to injure me, pursuing me around the ship with a large roundy of coal, which was silly, as her position on board was very doubtful. This the captain could not tolerate and he ordered that she be rowed ashore in a small boat near Grimsby.

As she left the collier she was still using fierce gestures, standing up in the rocking boat, screaming at me, and threatening all the fires of Hell both on me, and on all the ship's company. The sailors were vastly entertained and responded with appropriate hand signals of their own. The last words I heard her shout were: "The Day of Judgement is at hand! Armageddon is nigh!" I felt really sorry for her, and I pray that she is safe, for I wish her no harm.

Apart from this, our voyage was without any trouble. The Dutch ships did not interfere, although at first they followed us along the coast at a distance, so we sailed on to London with growing anticipation. However, on arrival, we were considerably alarmed when we found that plague had broken out, and everything was in confusion. Almost everyone we met was chewing tobacco, and there were scenes of great distress, with plague houses marked by red crosses on the doors and the words "Lord, have mercy upon us," as we were told.

In truth, London was a very miserable place. The court, the clergy, and the government had fled for safety to the countryside, and only the sturdy noncomformists lingered on to preach and administer to the sick. We saw men parading down the streets ringing handbells and carrying long red sticks. They were searching everywhere for corpses to carry off for burial and we learnt from them to put cloths over our faces to preserve ourselves from the tainted air. The continual tolling of church bells made us miserable and the sight of the crows and ravens searching the shallow graves with their greedy beaks was sickening to us. Contrary to my expectations, London was in the depths of despair! I wished to be many miles away from it.

We found a lodging house, but it was ill kept and the smell was dreadful. We were offered the choice between a dank, stuffy cellar, almost without light, and an attic with a low roof and tiny slits of windows, so we gladly chose the latter. Sleeping five to a bed, we were disturbed during the hours of darkness by an alarming crashing sound and the next morning we found that a house nearby had suddenly collapsed. Luckily there appeared to be no one inside but there was no means of verifying it, except through our landlady.

The good woman, who was expecting her husband home from the sea, was terrified by the thought of catching the plague and described the symptoms to us vividly, dreading the sweet smell in the nose that presaged its onset and the suppurating boils underarm which erupt so savagely and with such great pain. Warning us seemed to provide her with a strange sort of relief from her worry but filled us with the utmost anxiety. She would have wished to leave London, but was afraid of her home being looted, and in any case did not want to take to the open road alone.

We passed several graveyards, full to bursting, from which issued a most pungent unhealthy stench. Bodies were being buried together in common graves, which were only covered when full. In the case of some churches the ground had been raised by as much as one yard. There were no cats and dogs roaming the streets and we were told that a mass slaughter had been ordered. The most horrendous vision was the mad naked prophets, pacing through the streets, pleading for repentance before we were all damned.

We viewed some impressive buildings and took a boat to Westminster where we saw the inspiring sight of the magnificent abbey with its noble tombs of kings and nobility, admiring the rare workmanship in wrought iron, stone, marble and brass. We all said a fervent prayer for salvation before the king's chair. We also visited the notorious Tower with its cannons, ships and armour, but due to the infection we were still fearful and eager to leave London as soon as possible. Besides, prices were very high and famine was killing more people than the plague.

We speedily made our way in a few days to Lyme Regis on the south coast, where we were fortunate enough to find a small ship ready to sail to Barbados. Through all of this, the stout fellows that you commissioned to help me were extremely diligent in their support and kept the party's spirits high with their good-natured banter. After a tiring six week voyage, driven in the later stages by the steady north east trade winds, we reached the island of Barbados safely and without incident. Armed with your letter to Thomas Rutter, I began to search out your business interests in pursuance of which he was extremely helpful.

I missed Alexander by some weeks. I understand that many residents, sorry for his poor health, had personally supervised him on board ship, providing him with nourishment for the voyage, when they were surprised by officials who opposed his departure on the grounds of debts. However, the situation was resolved when his friends clubbed together and offered money. They were conscious that his lack of experience had led him into bad bargains when he first came to the island. I am sorry I missed him as he would have been able to clear up many problems.

Before he could pay for his passage Alexander sold the four servants he took out with him - William Askew, Edward Buckham, John Dinning, and Uriah Pattinson - to an adjoining plantation. He had expressly wished that this should not be generally known on the estate at home.

Barbados is understood to have the best climate in all the West Indies because the rising sun brings in cool sea breezes. Although it is hot and damp these keep the climate agreeable, so the island produces abundance of fruits and vegetables. You would be amused to see us sitting cross-legged on the ground, with our grass plates full of oranges, thirst-quenching drinks made from the huge lemons and limes, baked bananas and tasty sweet potatoes. The cassava beer is excellent, but our men prefer to devour the Barbados pineapple with great relish. All we lack is meat. However, I am most interested in searching out the best trading products which grow well here, such as ginger and pepper, to supplement the sugar and cotton that we already produce.

I will have to be on my guard because the local rum is very strong and the settlers' hospitality is excessive. Returning from the Sunday service last week, I came upon the most horrific sight. A drunken man had collapsed in the road and had been badly mauled by land crabs as he lay unconscious.

I have found the land which you bought for Alexander, and it appears to be very fertile, but in great need of cultivation. When the men were removed, leaving only the African slaves, Thomas Rutter made financial arrangements for another planter to keep an eye on it, so that the crops would not go to waste. Half of your hundred acres is now under crops, mainly sugar cane. As for the rest it will take about five to ten servants to clear the land ready for the growth of additional crops, such as tobacco, cotton and indigo.

They say that Africa can provide slaves by the millions, as long as we wish. However, some say they are sorely treated on most plantations and are regarded like animals. Since I have found them extremely helpful, both on our own land and when visiting neighbouring plantations, I believe that such ill treatment is unnecessary. However, the planters give them only sufficient food to keep them working and if they fall sick they are doomed. In some places the slaves are said to be secretly mutinous but there is brutal punishment for those who do not obey orders, which is intended to keep them subdued. The Dutch are bringing in more slaves from the Gulf of Guinea every month, so I am driven to wonder if their numbers will soon exceed those of the British people.

You will be pleased to learn that our navy continues to control the seas but we dread the avarice of the French in seizing British islands, and we are hampered by the Dutch having most of the sea trade, both in fetching slaves and taking out the produce of Barbados.

We are in sore need of tradesmen, their tools and, indeed, all agricultural implements. Our homes are simple shelters, open to the air and alive with insects, and it is exhausting to rest, let alone to work. However, the men have kept in good spirits and attend church with me on Sundays, but they miss their families and their homes. We hope that some arrangement can be made to buy back those former Nunburn men to work alongside us on the plantation here. I have visited them and they are in dire need of our help.

As you can understand, there are many trading opportunities here, especially if merchants take on the African trade. However, men and money are essential as the plantations grow.

I send my best wishes to everyone at home and hope that my good cousin, Elizabeth, is much improved.

Your obedient servant

Thomas Hubbach."

Lancelot had listened to the letter very thoughtfully as his father had read it to the end.

"I believe that you chose a good man in Thomas Hubbach. He sounds intelligent and resourceful. The information in that letter is most useful, and gives us the background on which to base our future plans."

Elizabeth was pleased to hear this praise of her cousin but frowned as Lancelot went on:

"Yet his attitude will have to be harder if he wishes to make himself a successful man of business."

"What do you mean?" asked Elizabeth.

"Well, his attitude to the slaves is incorrect. Everyone knows that somebody has to pay the penalty for success, and the slaves have nothing to lose anyway. He'll have to learn that our risks are great, and failure is always close at hand. You have seen how Alexander seems to have yielded to the pressures without putting up a struggle."

Elizabeth was taken aback.

"But what about the men that were sent out with Alexander?" she asked. "Surely they will have to be bought back, so that Thomas has enough workers? I have been visiting their families, and, although father looks after them, these men are badly missed at home. I cannot bear to think of their being sold like slaves."

Lancelot replied curtly: " If it is known that they have been sold, it will be bad for the reputation of the estate, and the morale of our workers at home will take a hard knock."

"Even so, we know the truth. Don't you think that we have a Christian duty to restore them to their former position?"

As Lancelot realised the full extent of the mismanagement in the West Indies he showed signs of increasing impatience. His face clouded and he gritted his teeth.

"We have so many duties that they become intertwined. To unravel them we are going to have to examine some fundamental principles."

Their father said: "We need to think hard about this. Now Elizabeth, leave business to the men. Lancelot has many more important things to consider."

As she was summarily dismissed, Elizabeth was shocked to the core. Never in her life had she heard such callous attitudes expressed and she felt upset and rejected.

Seeing her reaction, and in order to change the subject, her father enquired: "Who is this Jane Bilton, the strange lady who becomes so agitated at the mention of soot?"

Growing more circumspect, Elizabeth admitted only a distant connection with her.

"I can't imagine why she should be like that. I knew her only slightly in Newcastle."

Her father smiled. He remembered the scene at the Guildhall, the horror of which Elizabeth had apparently forgotten, which, of course, was all to the good.

In truth, Elizabeth's thoughts were with the men in Barbados. She knew that, come what may, she must send a letter to Thomas privately, to see if she could do something for these poor souls, marooned far away from home, even if it risked Lancelot's displeasure. How this was to be done would need a great deal of thought. Leave business to the men indeed!

Chapter 17

The days at Nunburn Hall passed very pleasantly now that they had the company of Lancelot, and Henry Woodall was more relaxed as he was freed from some of his domestic responsibilities. Elizabeth devoted much time to her herb garden and continued to discuss its progress, not so much with the gardeners, as with the steward, Robert Carr. He welcomed her proposals, because no one had given any attention to the grounds for many years, and he had a countryman's attachment to natural medicines. He was a tall, handsome, strongly-built fellow, with jet black hair, and Elizabeth was fascinated with the way it formed deep waves across his head and fell forward over his brow. Nothing was too much trouble for him and she felt that she trusted him enough to talk to him freely. He seemed so sympathetic towards her, and above all, kind. His strong muscular frame reminded her of John, and his air of authority was reassuring. Besides, she liked the way he looked at her.

One day, after visiting the cottagers, she pleaded with him: "What can we do for the men who are left out in Barbados? Is there any means of having them released from their new contract, or even to bring them back to their families?"

"Alas, I have no great authority here. I just do as I am bid. I expect it is beyond us to get involved. Servants and women have very little say here and, alas, the only thing that counts in this world is money, of which I am rather short. My poor father suffered an early death when he supported the wrong side in the Civil Wars and was badly wounded fighting with the Duke of Newcastle at the battle of Marston Moor. After that my life changed completely."

"I am very sorry, Robert. What happened?"

"Indeed those were bad times for Roman Catholics. We were deprived of our horses and had to have a licence to travel more than five miles from home. My parents refused to receive the sacrament in a church of the Protestant religion and celebrated mass in our small chapel, in defiance of the law. That meant that they were regarded as enemies of the state, and it was then that the Roundheads were instructed to plunder the house. I remember that even our bread had to be buried in the soil to conceal it from them. Thank goodness the buildings were not slighted or there would have been nothing left. It was decided by interfering strangers that one fifth of the family's estate would remain with my mother, of which one half was mine if I accepted a Protestant education."

"So you went with Lancelot and Alexander to the Grammar School at Hexham?"

"Yes. But all these worries were bad for my parents' health, and, when they died, Henry Woodall was very kind. In such times a trusted friend was without price. Lancelot and I were brought up together as children, and educated together, and we have remained firm friends ever since. I admire both Lancelot and his father tremendously, and I'm grateful to them for providing a place on their estate for me, which I shall never forget."

Elizabeth listened to this tragic story sympathetically and was touched by Robert's appreciation of her father's generosity.

"Where were your family estates?" asked Elizabeth.

"Just a little further north," replied Robert vaguely.

"Well, you'll just have to get them back again," declared Elizabeth.

Robert looked at her in alarm. "Many people have regained their property since King Charles was restored but it is not easy, and I am careful not to show any resentment as it could break valued friendships," he replied firmly. He pressed his heel into the soil, twisting it back and forth in half circles. "I do feel sympathy with our former tenants, but at the moment I am powerless."

Unaware of the full significance of this, Elizabeth remained thoughtful for a while as she realised that she too, surrounded by such affluence, was equally penniless. Her mind raced ahead to her present problems. She did not dare to press Lancelot for money, as he had warned her not to get involved. The only person she could possibly ask, with any chance of success, was her Uncle Anthony, and even in his case it might be wise not to explain the reason. Sometimes she sensed that he did not always agree with her and an excuse would be more sensible. Yet it was impossible for her to forget the unhappy state of the families that she was visiting. She could not just ignore them, because she knew that the men had been reluctant to go and the women were desolate. She must do something.

However, even these worries were diverted as preparations for the ball were imminent. An urgent, almost desperate, message for help was sent to Woodall's sister, Aunt Caroline, a widow who lived on a small estate a few miles away. She was much amused at the male panic that had set in, and was so invigorated by her new role that she did not mind the lack of tact with which she had been summoned. She was a no-nonsense, let's-get-on-with-life sort of person, neat and tidy by social obligation, but not greatly interested in herself or her own appearance. She came promptly as soon as she was invited. She had heard of Elizabeth's presence and of Lancelot's return and she was intensely curious to see them both. Bustling into the hall, where she had her first sight of Elizabeth, she stood back with admiration and said: "How lovely to have such a beautiful girl in the family! What can you do to help?"

Elizabeth opened her mouth, and, finding not a single thought in her head, shut it again quickly. As Elizabeth followed her to her bedroom on the upper corridor, Aunt Caroline suggested enthusiastically: "You can deliver my messages."

From Aunt Caroline it was made to sound such a great treat that Elizabeth felt proud to be of service. Plans followed in no time and soon a complete survey of the house was being taken, with Elizabeth trailing behind her, finding it difficult to keep up. Older than her brother, Aunt Caroline had happy memories of her home in the good old days and was very thrilled to restore life to the Hall as she remembered it. She accepted the new arrangements at the Hall, not asking any questions, nor offering any advice beyond the task in hand. Yet an interested observer would easily be able to detect that nothing escaped her scrutiny. Her twinkling eyes, full of good nature, informed a brain with great organising power, as acute as her brother's.

Elizabeth was a quick learner and an enthusiastic helper, and the older woman was a kindly soul, helping Elizabeth tactfully in every way. Aunt Caroline's sole preoccupation was with the preparations for the ball. The bemused concern lingering around her lips was always ready to burst into a broad smile as she guided the servants in their tasks. She used Elizabeth to convey her instructions to the staff. Every nook and cranny of Nunburn Hall was thoroughly cleaned and even the housekeeper, Mistress Grant, did not mind her interference because it was so well intentioned.

Elizabeth and her aunt spent most of their time dressed in loose and comfortable Indian gowns, shouting instructions to the staff, as they watched the menservants, high on long ladders, using bellows to blow off the dust from the delicate stucco, and carefully removing a maze of half-seen cobwebs with their dusters. Aunt Caroline despaired of the floors! The maids were everywhere with their hard long-handled brushes, polishing vigorously as she urged: "Harder, harder, more herbs." As a result the wooden planks gradually took on the fine brown richness of the original natural timber .

Eventually the portraits came to her attention, and she peered at them closely, standing half way up the stairs. "How could my brother have let these priceless pictures reach such a dirty, disgraceful condition?" she said to the housekeeper, who was awaiting her instructions.

"Well, I just do what I'm told," Mistress Grant replied defensively, pursing her lips. This, together with the tightening of the muscles in her face, and hands clasped primly in front of her, were the only signs of disapproval that could be detected in her. She was confident that her value to the household was appreciated by all. She was a small erect woman of some forty summers, possessed of a boundless energy. Her long greying hair, neatly gathered in a ribbon, and her even features, gave her a quiet dignity. Although she said little, her grey-brown eyes flashed with intelligence, and she was held in great respect by both the family and servants. Her authority was based on long years of service to the Woodalls from an early age. She could joke with the grooms so that they enjoyed their duties, and she could take the maids to task without undermining their confidence. She knew herself that it was due to her steady influence at the hub of domestic affairs that Nunburn was such a happy place.

Aunt Caroline was all too aware of this and sought quickly to reassure her. "I know you do, and a very good job you've done, Mistress Grant, considering all the work you have, and without any proper directions from anybody over all these years."

Continuing to scrutinise the portraits and not in the slightest daunted, she insisted: "I think we're going to have to take these down and clean them with a mixture of vitriol and borax, and then varnish them with nut and linseed oil, but we'll have to choose the most careful servants. It will take a delicate touch."

The weeks went by and Elizabeth and Aunt Caroline beamed inwardly as they saw the house being transformed, little by little. Meanwhile samples of new silks were ordered from Newcastle, and the old lady was in her element, planning everything down to the smallest detail. She showed the materials to Elizabeth, spreading them delicately along the dining table.

"You will look wonderful in this beautiful deepest blue sarsenet which will set off your lovely auburn hair, and this style will suit your figure," she urged enthusiastically.

"But I will look exactly like the portrait of your mother."

"Yes," replied Aunt Caroline.

Elizabeth just gave in.

When the seamstresses arrived for the first fitting, Elizabeth was thrilled to view herself in the long mirror in her bedroom, trying on the most beautiful dress that she had ever seen in her life, although it had not as yet been fully decorated.

"I feel I don't deserve to own a gown as wonderful as this," she murmured as her hands explored the material.

"Of course you do, you silly goose. Every young girl has a special dress for her first ball," cried Aunt Caroline. Elizabeth raised her eyebrows.

The older woman stepped back, surveying her with great pride and squeezed her affectionately. "I wish that I had had a daughter like you," she whispered, "So like my lovely mother!"

The seamstresses had been patiently waiting, pleased with the success of the dress which had taken them many weary hours to stitch. They knew themselves that their deft hands had fashioned a gown that fitted her figure exquisitely, and they departed for Newcastle wearing satisfied smiles. Caroline had thanked them profusely, and they promised faithfully to return the finished dress before the ball.

Elizabeth and Aunt Caroline exulted as they saw the continuing improvements. The whole house began to smell fragrant and looked bright and shining. Creaking doors now opened silently, windows allowed full daylight to shine in, and the ancestral portraits glistened in their full glory. Henry Woodall and Lancelot, after years of loneliness, were now looking forward to being again the social centre of the neighbourhood, although they had sometimes displayed impatience with the many and varied upsets to their routine.

No more than when their peace was disturbed by the surprise arrival on their doorstep of a slim excitable Frenchman, clutching a large black bag and almost dancing on the step.

" Monsieur Anzony ffarbreedge has sent me 'ere to teach ees niece ze dance. I am coming from La France and can instruct in ze latest dances from ze court of our noble King Louis."

With these important credentials, he was immediately admitted to the Hall with every courtesy! From then onwards there was no peace for Elizabeth and Lancelot. Morning and afternoon their instructor's squeaky voice insisted on nothing but perfection as they practised the new dances to achieve complete synchronisation. He produced sheet upon sheet of new tunes for the local musicians from his most capacious black bag and rehearsed them thoroughly without respite.

Before they began the first practice Aunt Caroline whispered in Elizabeth's ear: "Remember, finger tips. If you get too close, lace and buttons will become snagged, and, above all, remember to take small steps to avoid treading on your dress."

Elizabeth was apprehensive when she began, but a smile from Lancelot left her reassured, and under his calming influence her hands and knees stopped trembling. At first the musicians were far from helpful because they were not themselves familiar with the music, and were a little afraid of the dancing master's quick temper. His impatient voice could be heard: "Eyes level, bend boze ze knees, bend and rise, oop two, oop five, seex. Look at your partnaire."

The two dancers often relieved the tension by exchanging amused glances and the maids passing through took a great delight in snatching a sly look at the spectacle. A busybody, namely Dolly, enjoyed relaying the news of progress to the anxious kitchen: "She'll never learn the steps, and the Frenchman is almost bursting."

Mistress Grant grimaced, and even she was seized with the growing tension, chewing her lips as she vigorously chopped the vegetables.

The little dancing master, his long waxed moustache twitching in exasperation, emphasised, in English which was not improving with his temper: "You veel 'ave to lead off ze commencement of ze boll, and you must verk 'ard. Ze steps are tres difficile. Even ze dancers of ze magnifique cour de la France practees 'ard, 'ard, 'ard." Some days he was wringing his hands in desperation.

At first Elizabeth despaired of learning the complicated steps and attendant gyrations, and worried in case she let down Lancelot and the family, but as time went on she slowly began to master the footwork, the bowing, and the turning and twisting of the head. Eventually Aunt Caroline judged that their standard was sufficiently high and their excitable master was summarily dismissed, with profuse thanks, back to Newcastle.

Elizabeth was happier as she wrote out the invitations in the beautiful script that Canon Ritschell had taught her. When the acceptances began to arrive, she was delighted that some friends were coming from Newcastle, including her erstwhile dinner companions, the barber surgeon, the scrivener, and Uncle Anthony, of course. John and Joanna had been invited but they had declined. Elizabeth sadly wondered if they realised themselves that they would be out of place in every way. Edmund, too, had eagerly accepted the invitation and was bringing his mother.

Woodall had longed for the return of his younger son, but, as often happens, two days before the event, in the middle of these tiring preparations, when everything was in confusion and he was temporarily out of mind, Alexander startled everyone with his sudden appearance. Late in the afternoon, Elizabeth was passing through the hall, when she heard a commotion at the front door. She was surprised to see a strange figure striding confidently into their clean hall in heavily mud-caked riding boots, casting a mud-splattered cloak on the floor, to reveal a disgusting array of dirty lace, velvet and silk underneath. He shouted gruffly to the footmen. Figures peered out of several doors, and a bewildered Woodall appeared at the sound of the voices. Elated, he flung his arms round his exhausted son. "This is Alexander," he announced proudly to Elizabeth, and to Alexander: "This is Elizabeth, your half-sister."

It was definitely not the right moment to receive this news. Alexander stood back, astounded, and surveyed Elizabeth.

"I can't believe it," he said bluntly, displaying a disgust which added greatly to Elizabeth's discomfort. His father's face changed.

By then Aunt Caroline had joined them, and Alexander addressed her rather brusquely: "And you're here too? What's happening? Who's dead?"

Keeping her equanimity, she responded haughtily: "I'm helping to arrange the ball."

"Ball! We're not having a ball when I've just arrived back home! I can't be bothered with a lot of people. What rotten luck! We never have balls. Why now? Is it because of her?" he pointed to Elizabeth accusingly.

"No, your brother has been away from home for a long time at St. John's and now needs to meet our neighbours. He'll be intending to settle down soon and I wish him to be married into a northern family. It is a chance for him to meet the local people, and Elizabeth may find someone to suit her too," said his father, almost apologetically.

"And where do I fit into all this? Surely the prodigal son deserves some fuss?" Alexander whined.

"Your turn will come. But try to look pleasant and see the better side of things," Woodall retorted.

By now they were all settled in front of the hearth in the hall, and Alexander was already divesting himself of his tattered boots. Elizabeth carefully scrutinised her new half-brother and did not like what she saw. He was fair-haired, short and stocky, with prickly stubble on his chin. He had blackened, broken teeth and his devious wandering eyes, bloodshot and threatening, were incapable of looking anyone straight in the eye. His skin was tinged with yellow as a result of his illness, and further criss-crossed with ugly red veins. His finger nails were ridged and repulsive. His general appearance was dirty and tousled, beyond the effects of his long journey.

Elizabeth marvelled at how he could be so unlike Lancelot.

Aunt Caroline rose to order food from the kitchen as her brother explained: " We have already sent someone out to Barbados to help you, but your ships must have crossed on the high seas. You seem to have taken a long time to arrive here. Where have you been?"

"I stayed in Bristol for a few weeks after the voyage because I was exhausted, and a lot of money it cost me. I had to come home urgently," replied Alexander.

"Have you been completely alone? I thought I sent out four servants to help you. What happened to them?" queried his father, carefully scrutinising his son's face.

At this point the food arrived and Alexander, avoiding the question, ate greedily, munching loudly and scowling at the maids as he grabbed extras. The servants remained straight-faced, apparently disinterested, but they were desperate to hear news of their relations and were reluctant to retire when bidden.

Alexander continued unabated: "I needed a hundred servants to work that plantation. Those you sent weren't very good. Lazy bones. They refused to come home with me. Loved the West Indian weather. Couldn't stand the thought of coming back to the cold North Sea winds. And I can't blame them. I'm already thinking of going back myself, but I need some money to make a success of it out there. I've been desperate to produce good crops but it's back-breaking work, and I have had no encouragement from a single person. You would not believe what little help I've had. There are a lot of old Royalists living out there but they seem to have forgotten their origins," complained Alexander.

"What shall we tell the families of our men in Barbados who are patiently waiting for them to come home?" enquired Elizabeth, suppressing her anger at Alexander's lies.

Alexander picked his teeth with a dirty fingerrnail.

"Just tell them to forget all about that scum. They're settled out there quite happily without them. Have taken up with other wenches, anyway," he lied, as his eyes searched idly round the room. He seemed to resent Elizabeth's question.

All through this Elizabeth and their father were looking regretfully at each other. They both sensed that there was trouble ahead and neither of them knew quite how to begin to tackle it. Elizabeth believed confidently that what Thomas had said would be right and her father thought he knew exactly how Alexander would have been spending his time in Bristol. Gaming and whores, no doubt! How was he to deal with this wayward son? Nevertheless Alexander was his own child and would have to be supported in the best possible way. However, Fate was probably against him. He remembered that he had already warned Elizabeth about the wildness and lack of commonsense among the family of Alexander's mother, so that she would not be altogether surprised. They were always fonder of horses than people, and favoured food and wine before study. Perhaps the lad could not help himself.

In spite of all his son's faults, Woodall's face was continuing to beam, savouring his unexpected return, and he anxiously took him up to his old bedroom, fussing over him and ignoring his petulance. The more attention Alexander received, the more ill-tempered he became, but all his father had ever wanted was his son back, safe and sound, and he rejoiced. When Lancelot returned home he immediately joined them upstairs, and greeted his brother with outstretched arms, saying: "Alexander! What a relief it is to see you safely home."

His greeting was returned with a scowl, which Lancelot received with the greatest composure, because as of old, he expected such a reaction. Alexander barely spoke to him and with great amusement resumed his old particular brand of fun. He took his brother for a fool with whom he could trifle with no fear of retaliation. He knew that Lancelot valued family relationships more than he himself was ever capable of, and he loved experimenting with him. It gave him a tremendous sense of power over the bewildered Lancelot, constantly bringing their relationship to an aggravating crisis. Lancelot was so different from his brother that he could not understand the latter's coarseness and cantankerous attitude. He was too clever to argue with irrationality and dismissed the irritations as he would those of a child.

However, happy times were near and there were only two days left before the ball, with plenty of pleasant things to think about, so the time passed quickly, and no one had any time to consider Alexander's ill temper. Although Elizabeth gently probed, Aunt Caroline would not be drawn on Alexander's questionable ancestry. Owing to his habits, he was easily absorbed into the household, spending most of his time alone in his room, imbibing.

Chapter 18

On a warm evening the shadows were beginning to lengthen as the guests arrived for the ball at Nunburn Hall. The grooms were kept busy outside as they looked after the multitude of horses, coachmen and conveyances which arrived in the courtyard and smartly liveried footmen smiled a welcome from the steps. Woodall introduced Elizabeth and Lancelot whose pleasing manner and handsome appearance made the visitors sense that this ball was no ordinary affair. In they swept, young and old alike, dressed in their most extravagant finery, and the great hall was soon filled with colour, laughter and music. Many interested mothers looked round with wonder as they ushered their precious daughters into the mansion that had so long been a mystery to them. Woodall shook hands with landowners, lawyers, military men, and other pillars of county society, and was introduced to their families.

Elizabeth was thankful for taking Aunt Caroline's advice as she waited at the side of the hall with Lancelot. She revelled in her dress of luxurious Indian silk whose folded and quilted bodice had been recently finished off in Newcastle with the most eye-catching embroidery and jewels. She was conscious that her gown and head-dress twinkled bewitchingly in the light of a myriad of candles. Her stiff corset encouraged her to stand up straight and revealed a very appealing bosom, now heaving with apprehension. She remembered her close resemblance to her grandmother and felt more confident in the memory of that lady's self-assurance in the portrait.

Even so, when the time to start the ball came close, her knees trembled, but she kept her mind powerfully focussed and a dignified Lancelot led her proudly into the centre of the hall amid a hushed expectancy. All eyes were turned on them as they waited for the music to begin. They followed the tunes in complete harmony, their movements quick and precise in the twist of their heads as they bowed to each other and circled. With an unruffled gaze, each in turn took the initiative in the circling movements, and they achieved the difficult tension between the music and the dance steps with studied expertise, but too soon it was at an end and they were finally bowing and curtseying to each other. Their father and Aunt Caroline were brimming over with pride, and the dancers gazed at each other with mutual approval. Alas, it must be admitted that Alexander's vulgar eyes, too, had scrutinised Elizabeth throughout the dance, and, when it had finished, his upper lip remained curled up in a sneer.

At every opportunity, Edmund was also most attentive to Elizabeth, whose startling beauty he found quite hypnotic, and his mother watched them with fascinated concentration. After a short time, wearying of his company and reckoning him weak and spindly, she fled alone to the terrace to enjoy some fresh air. Looking down over the ballustrade, she could just discern the figure of Robert Carr, the steward, who was keeping a wary eye on the outside proceedings.

She bent over and whispered: "For a thousand reasons I would rather be down there with you."

Not knowing whether he had heard, she fled back, blushing, into the hall, which was brimming with merriment. Lancelot was dancing with his umpteenth partner and was clearly enjoying the music and the female adoration. Elizabeth skirted the throng deftly and purposefully. She knew that this was the best time to contact her Uncle Anthony concerning the buying back of the men in Barbados. She found him easily enough, following the high-pitched laughter of his friend the scrivener, and smiled as she came upon him in deep conversation with his two Newcastle friends, exalting over the recent naval victory against their old enemy, the Dutch.

"The sea battle at Lowestoft in May sent the Dutch fleeing, and, with Admiral Opdana killed, we've taught them a lesson they won't forget, hee, hee, hee," gloated the scrivener, graduating to his customary treble.

In the wake of this Elizabeth was greeted enthusiastically, exchanging pleasantries and happy to renew their acquaintance. However, it was not long before she was able to detach Uncle Anthony from them.

"Well, did our friend from the court of King Louis do a good job?" she asked eagerly.

"You did him great credit, as I knew you would," Uncle Anthony beamed.

"I am sorry to have to ask you unexpectedly for another favour, but I need some money urgently. Could you arrange to send it on to Thomas in Barbados as soon as you can?" she whispered earnestly.

"I trust you enough to know that it must be something important. Of course you needn't even tell me what it is all about," he returned, temporarily enjoying the conspiracy.

She whispered the amount in his ear, and he started, aghast at what he had heard.

"I am sorry to have to ask you for so much," she apologised, looking at him in dismay.

He nodded, bemused. It was later that he would find himself worrying about the mystery with which he had become so closely involved.

"Thank you, thank you, you'll never know how relieved I am. I knew I could rely on you. I'll give you a covering letter to send to Thomas, by way of the London office," said Elizabeth, as she kissed him on the cheek. It reminded her of the wedding and happy days at Hackford, and she asked him if he had visited John and Joanna recently.

"Yes, Isabel's baby is in fine fettle, a proper little smiler, and so strong that he is already standing up. They were thirsting for news of you, so you'll have to visit them soon," said Uncle Anthony.

Elizabeth nodded.

"And how is Charles faring?"

"I'm relieved to say that he has survived all his woes and is still a valued member of the Joiners' Company. He is throwing himself into his work and is coming to grips with his new situation. The suddenness of his bereavement was a blessing in a way, ensuring that he didn't have to watch his little family die, as you did. We all feared that they were weak and ready to catch some dreadful disease, but it was unfortunate that it had to happen just when you were in charge. However, I assure you that Charles always speaks well of you."

At this point her father came over to them.

"You must meet Edmund's mother. She has been asking after you." Elizabeth got up wearily and so the conversation, which Elizabeth felt was the most important of the evening, ended somewhat abruptly.

There was Edmund, standing deferentially behind his mother's chair, grinning sheepishly. A particular emotion made her stomach churn. She could have slapped him on the face for his silliness. She had not wanted to have any dealings with them, and was irritated by the presumption of this woman she did not know, and indeed did not wish to know. Her father introduced her.

"Here is my beautiful ward, Elizabeth, who has brightened my days at Nunburn since her arrival," he announced proudly. Elizabeth was inspected closely by the most disagreeable woman she could have imagined. The eyes were as cold as ice, and she looked down her nose imperiously, with a conviction about herself which totally belied her looks. Her jaw and teeth stuck out in front like those of a horse, as if she was about to whinny at any moment.

To Elizabeth she did indeed seem to whinny, and she prevented herself from laughing in her face when she enquired: "I presume you come from a distance. Where is your father's seat?"

"He has land in Barbados and is going to be very rich soon," Elizabeth announced, casting a mischievous look at her father. "Let's dance, Edmund. You look so bored here. I can't bear to see you like this," and with that she led Edmund away, leaving her father and his mother looking at each other, somewhat shaken. Before she left them she thought she detected a flash of carefully concealed amusement on her father's face because, in fact, he had never liked Edmund's mother. The lady, however, was affronted.

The dancing went on till late, by which time Alexander had been escorted to his bedroom, having drunk so heavily that his head was spinning. Lancelot, however, remained quite sober, and, having met most of the guests, seemed to have settled on a very pretty young lady, Anne Shafto, the richest heiress in the room. They had enjoyed several dances together and stood side by side, chatting. He was looking different from his usual composed self with a flush of boyish enthusiasm heightening the colour in his cheeks. His bright eyes flashed with an intent purpose, and a smile of delight revealed his mood. Both their fathers had drawn together and were grinning over the couple with obvious approval, thinking of the rich acres that would be joined together if they had their way.

Elizabeth was tired and decided to retire for the evening. She crossed the hall to where Aunt Caroline was sitting with Uncle Anthony, who was regaling her with some amusing story and they were laughing convulsively together.

As she passed, Elizabeth smiled and said: "What a wonderful night we have had, and it is all due to your planning, Aunt Caroline."

The old lady beamed with satisfaction and Uncle Anthony amiably nodded his head, a somewhat thoughtful look lingering on his countenance as he watched Elizabeth's back disappearing.

As the guests chattered their way to the door, Elizabeth paused to view the departure of all these painted, pouting creatures. She wondered .....and wondered ..... and again wondered. They were so unlike her Uncle Anthony, who always displayed a joviality beyond immediate self interest.

She climbed wearily up the stairs to her bedroom and sat down on the bed, slowly removing the shoes from her aching feet. Almost immediately muffled sounds in the passage outside came to her ears. Someone was stumbling along, trailing against the wall and as the door burst open, she was shocked to see Alexander, supporting himself against the door post and leering at her.

"I've never seen such a beautiful wench as you, and you've got spirit. I've watched you all night. It'll be fun to take you!" With a drunken lurch he came towards her and she jumped up in alarm, darting to the door of the balcony.

"I'm your step-sister, Alexander," she protested.

"If you believe that, you'll believe anything," he slobbered. "I know you're my father's whore. Come on, why not admit it? Why are you in my mother's bedroom?"

Elizabeth did not know what to reply. She was shocked and frightened because she knew he was much stronger and even her sturdy frame would not have the power to resist him. As he approached her, she tried to open the door so that she could back onto the balcony, in a vain effort to escape. However, he lunged at her before she could open it and seized her round the shoulders, trying to kiss her roughly on the lips. With a tremendous effort she wrenched herself loose to escape from his drunken grasp and fetid breath, fleeing towards the door and almost colliding with Mistress Grant who was standing quietly in the doorway, looking very severe. Alexander staggered sideways and fell heavily across a chair.

"There's nothing here for you, Alexander. I suggest you find your own bed," she said firmly, confident in displaying an authority built up on memories of his childhood.

Robert Carr, who had been keeping watch outside, had suddenly appeared in the passage and was eager to assist Alexander, exchanging a knowing look with the housekeeper.

"Yes, I was right, Robert. She's too attractive and she needs somebody to look after her."

"Well, I know how to look after this worthless lump," replied Robert, and his strong arms easily swung Alexander over his shoulder and roughly carried the stupefied drunkard out of the room.

It was now that the value of Mistress Grant in the household could be appreciated. She took the trembling Elizabeth in her arms to calm her and a mist of sadness crossed her face as she reminisced.

"There, there, it won't happen again. Alexander was always a stupid boy who was never kept in his place. When he was young he ran wild with no one to chastise him, because the master was always away, looking after his business interests in Newcastle, and Alexander never took to his studies like Lancelot. Yet he's not as bad as he looks. We'll get one of the servants to put a good sneck and bolt on the door tomorrow and I'll warn the master about Mr. Alexander so that he won't give you any more trouble."

Not completely reassured herself, she feared family history repeating itself in an even more deadly way. After carefully removing Elizabeth's beautiful dress she embraced her like a child and tucked her up in bed, smoothing the coverlet with expert hands and staying with her until the soothing mantle of sleep had overtaken the living nightmare.

So the night of the ball had ended unexpectedly. All the work and worry evaporated as nothing, and there had been a hideous finale. However, come what may, Elizabeth always seemed to have a circle of friends ready to protect her.

Chapter 19

Life after the ball was not so exciting. The old routine was established again but Elizabeth had the persistent worry that she had been dangerously exceeding her expected role in the household. It was regrettable, because she had grown very fond of Lancelot, and there was complete harmony and respect between them. Lancelot was quite different from both his father and his brother. He was more refined and imaginative and looked for the good in people. He was sharp-witted and had a sense of humour in line with her own, whereas her father seemed a little coarse and humourless at times.

She imagined that she had presumed on her special relationship in the inner circle, but she could not help herself, and felt a compulsion beyond her control to help the men stranded in far-off Barbados. Each passing week she longed to hear news from Thomas, but, when it came, it was not as she had imagined it would be.

She had been collecting herbs in the garden when she was summoned by Lancelot to the library. He was red-faced and pacing round the room, unable to contain his anger. When Elizabeth entered he snatched up a paper from his desk and launched into a savage tirade.

"I have just received this letter from a clerk in our London office and I can't believe what he has told me. He says that you have arranged for money to be sent out to free the servants that Alexander sold into slavery as a first stage in their return home. Is this true?"

A short pause ensued, in which Elizabeth was vainly searching for excuses. Still glaring, Lancelot continued: "Have you any idea what it would do to our position on the estate if it became known that Alexander had sold these men into slavery to pay for his ticket home? I might not approve of what my brother does, but at least I can limit the damage he causes. Why am I constantly surrounded by idiots? Even the sensible ones are buffoons. What do you think you have done, to put the welfare of four men before the good of the estate?" He broke off and there was a menacing silence in the room.

"Do you have any idea of the care it takes to preserve our heritage? What do you imagine it was like for father, weathering the Civil Wars, and the years under Cromwell? Everyone was on a tightrope, but for all our sakes he managed to survive. The bad weather we have recently endured is crippling the rents and you must know that we are in the middle of a countrywide financial depression. Elizabeth, I thought you had more sense. We have accepted you readily into our family and you have betrayed our trust. And for what? You don't even know these ignorant peasants."

Lancelot spat out the words violently, beside himself with anger.

"I don't know how you can think such thoughts. It sounds so evil," replied Elizabeth.

"Well, you must know better than anyone, since you've been on trial as a witch!" snapped Lancelot, without thinking. Sensing her reaction, he immediately regretted what he had said, and motioned with his hands to calm her down.

Elizabeth stood speechless for a long time, the blood draining from her face. Her head was swimming, and she took hold of the desk to steady herself. The blackness that she had sensed, lingering in the depths of her mind, suddenly lifted and she saw it all clearly. The dungeon and its filth. She was in the Guildhall again. She had been taken out of the prison and there was the terrible face of the witch-finder in front of her. He was interfering with her clothing and she was mortified with shame. Everyone was there. Her father. The barber surgeon. The baying mob. She gripped her head tightly. She could not stand it any longer and screamed hysterically. Shaking herself horribly, as if she wanted to dissociate herself from her body, of which now she loathed every sinew, she continued screaming until her voice was hoarse. Lancelot had not envisaged this reaction and turned white with panic.

The whole household was raised. Aunt Caroline came down the stairs, still clutching her embroidery. Even a dishevelled Alexander appeared, full of concern, followed by Mistress Grant and three maids. When Elizabeth's father hastened into the room he found Alexander trying to enfold her in his arms, but she was violently resisting him. At last, when she heard her father's voice speaking to her soothingly, her fright gradually subsided and she turned to him, distressed and still avoiding Alexander. Woodall signalled for the domestics to resume their work, and asked his family to sit down.

Elizabeth, hair dishevelled and arms tightly crossed in front of her, was at last able to speak, through her sobs.

"I remember now. You saved my life. I remember it all. You and the barber surgeon looked after me. That is why I first came here, and you have loved me and cared for me ever since then. In my dreadful hour of need you were all there for me. Oh, Lancelot, I'm sorry to give you so much trouble in exchange for your overwhelming kindness. I am wayward, and interfere in other people's lives more than I should."

Aunt Caroline held her gently round the shoulders.

"Never mind," said her father. "We all of us make the most dreadful mistakes," looking at Lancelot accusingly, and rolling his eyes to the ceiling.

Lancelot shrugged in response, and launched into an immediate apology.

"I am deeply ashamed. I was so angry with you, that I couldn't contain myself. I wouldn't have hurt you for the world. But Elizabeth, women shouldn't interfere as you have done."

He went towards her, and, taking her in his arms, smoothed her hair, a look of pain enveloping his face. At last, he straightened up and looked at the others. After a moment's recollection he said: " Now, when you are all here, this is a suitable moment to tell you. I intend to marry Anne Shafto of Eglingham and I would not expect even her to interfere in business matters, in spite of all her wealth and family connections."

Looking earnestly towards his father, he announced: " Father, we must have a long talk. We should make new provisions for the future, so that we can live in harmony with one another. I'm sure my future wife will fit in well with this household, but our affairs will have to be carefully planned and discussed at great length. Lawyers must be consulted and our finances will have to be settled to everyone's satisfaction. We will have to live peaceably together and the family will only gain strength through using everyone's individual talents. Elizabeth, we really appreciate your worth, and we will find a solution that suits everybody, but first father and I need a little peace to work at it."

His father was moved by the news of the forthcoming marriage, and relieved that at last there would be the chance of an heir, and a future for the estate.

"Elizabeth, it might be best for you to go to Hackford for a few weeks, while we settle our business," he suggested.

Elizabeth had by now recovered enough to ponder on what she had done although she was shattered by the turn of events and felt very contrite. She could not be certain how angry Lancelot really remained and she was very worried about the permanence of her privileged position in the household, which up to now she had so easily taken for granted. She was to be supplanted by a new female, mistress of Nunburn, who might not even like her! How foolish she had been to antagonise Lancelot! Yet she felt that she would have always been impelled to act without regard for herself, no matter what. Agonisingly, she wondered if she could have contrived to rescue the Barbados men in a different way, without betraying her trust and then her father would not have expelled her to where she had come from. How silly she had been!

Plunged into misery she took refuge in the garden which was fresh with the exquisite smell of the flowers. She traced her finger round and round a stone sundial in an effort to compose herself. She looked fondly at the garden, at the grey walls, and at the surrounding landscape that she adored and from which she was soon going to be parted. How Fate played tricks with her! She wished she had not made such an exhibition of herself in front of everyone, contrasting badly with Aunt Caroline's example of composure. The shocking recollection of her trial had devastated her, but now, although still feeling weak, she had almost recovered herself. She reckoned that if she could weather the terrible storm which she had experienced in Newcastle, surely this one, too, would blow over her head. Seeking the comfort of the herb garden, which was now planted and growing well, she picked up a sprig of lavender and inhaled its essence long and deeply, enjoying its soothing fragrance. Surprised by a deep voice behind her, she started.

"So you remembered at last. I thought you were never going to recover properly."

Elizabeth turned round and came face to face with Robert Carr, the steward.

"Your screaming disturbed all the neighbourhood," he said accusingly.

She looked embarrassed. "How do you know what happened?" she asked rather hoarsely.

"There's nothing that goes on here that the servants don't know about and Mistress Grant is very concerned about you, to the point of keeping a constant guard over you. She fondly remembers your mother, when she first came to Nunburn Hall, and regrets that she didn't take some of the wise advice that was often given to her. Your mother, in her innocence, revelled in attracting the attention which came so easily in her direction, and then didn't know how to control her employer's advances. She must have been like you, headstrong, to the point of getting out of her depth."

"How dare you mention my poor dead mother! She paid very dearly for her time here. I am perfectly capable of looking after myself and I feel that everybody in this world is very, very horrid," protested Elizabeth, making a weak attempt at stamping her foot.

"Yes, Elizabeth, I'm sure you're right," Robert agreed wearily.

"Just think of those beautiful children on the farms, growing up without a father! How can anybody sleep in their beds with such a tragedy happening on their own estate! I can't stand men! All they think about is land, money and marrying rich heiresses!"

"Yes, Elizabeth, I'm sure you're right," continued Robert, beginning to turn red.

As she talked, she paced up and down angrily between the lines of herbs, always coming back to Robert. She looked at him warily.

"And, another thing, which unfortunate heiress is going to have to put up with the hapless Alexander? Do we warn her beforehand what he's like?" expostulated Elizabeth.

"Yes, Elizabeth, I'm sure you're just the one to do it," he laughed sceptically. His huge frame towered over her as he drew close. By now he was exasperated.

"Do you have any idea of the problems you have created for us? I suggest that you keep to your herbs. For your thousand reasons, I am looking for a quiet and happy life, and I do not wish it to be spoilt by a wayward woman. When you first arrived at the Hall, and I carried you upstairs I sensed then that you were trouble, but I was immediately attracted to you. You were so weak and helpless, and I had felt the warmth of your young body in my grasp. In the following days I hung round the Hall, longing to hear daily reports about you."

Looking down at her tenderly, he admitted: "I would be prepared to look after you for the rest of my life, but not if you are silly. I won't be able to tolerate it. Men can work out their problems without all these female excesses."

Elizabeth looked into his eyes, and her body melted inside her. Here was a strong man she could respect and love. She had found her match, and, in any case, she had learnt her own lessons.

Her composure was beginning to return. "I overlook all of your faults except one," she teased, pouting her lips in her own inimitable fashion.

"What's that?" said Robert tersely, his anger giving way to curiosity.

Elizabeth smiled enigmatically, and said slowly and seductively: "That's for me to know and you to find out."

" I shall need time to solve that conundrum, so in the meantime off you go to Hackford, and leave others to sort out the problems," he said dismissively.

With that, not trusting himself, because he knew the time was not opportune, he turned on his heel and walked briskly away from her in the direction of the stables, which somewhat disappointed Elizabeth, who had been hoping for something different. She shrugged her shoulders. Her heart was beating fast, yet curiously she felt much calmer. Her mood had suddenly changed and she felt much better after talking to Robert. The inner fear that had plagued her was now almost gone, and she was no longer worried about her position at the Hall. She was encircled in the love of her new and old families, and surely even Lancelot still appreciated her in spite of her high-handedness. And now there was Robert!

She sensed that Robert cared for her. All her hopes and ambitions were now centred on him. The future lay before her, bright and rosy, and she had no fears. She relaxed as the certainty grew in her that Robert loved her. If she contained her emotions, remained pleasant, and did not antagonise him, he would be all that she had ever wanted, and her life would be rich and full. What had Uncle Anthony once said? "Love spreads out around us like a stone thrown into the water, casting ripples on the surface." Their whole lives would be supported by love and understanding, to the benefit of everyone around. What a lovely thought to cherish!

And what had Canon Ritschell told her? "Amor vincit omnia. Love conquers all." Women might be expected to be meek and mild, but did that really happen in life? Everyone ought to have a stake in their own well-being and she was determined to take a firm grip. What about Queen Elizabeth and Bess of Hardwick? She had heard about them and they had managed their own lives brilliantly. She knew that there were instincts in her that had to be satisfied, and were irrepressible. Life was not worth living if you could not make the world a better place - daily, weekly, yearly, lifelong.

With lightened steps she made her way back to the Hall. She would soon be off to Hackford.... and she would enjoy it!

Chapter 20

Pausing at Hexham on her way back to the Devil's Water, Elizabeth temporarily excused the groom, while she visited Hexham Abbey to thank God for her good fortune in finding Robert. She stood in the vast empty nave and thought of the many times that she had worshipped fervently at this very spot. She would hang on to those happy years which were so different from what promised to be her new life ahead. Then she knelt to pray. Her prayers were calm and deep.

As she raised her head she saw from the corner of her eye the robed figure of Canon Ritschell, descending the wide stone steps leading from the upstairs dormitory.

"I saw you from the watching chamber. I wondered if you were seeking sanctuary in the frithstol," he teased. "But what brings you to the church?" he asked with great concern. He spoke in that attractive mid-European accent, which had softened so many hearts, particularly on the distaff side of the family.

"I have been sent back because I have been interfering too much in other people's affairs," Elizabeth replied shamefacedly. The wise old man smiled and lowered his head.

She continued: "Lancelot and his father are settling the new arrangements at the Hall, ready for his marriage. He is to marry Anne Shafto of Eglingham. You may know of the family. I am very fond of Lancelot. He is so different from one of his Cambridge friends, Edmund. Do you know what heathen ideas are nurtured at Oxford and Cambridge? They are saying that the earth and stars have lives and minds of their own. How can they believe such invented tales? I fear for your sons."

She took his arm and looked at him earnestly.

"Don't worry, Elizabeth, there are more things in Heaven and Earth than we are capable of dreaming of."

"Yet some of our dreams are well-based and wholesome. For my part I am very much taken with Robert Carr, the steward at the Hall," confessed Elizabeth.

"Would he be a wise man to take you on?" he chuckled.

Elizabeth blushed, but chose to ignore his remark. She had known him too long to expect anything other than good humour.

Taking a more serious tone, Canon Ritschell recalled the past. "You could do worse. I can remember his parents from the old times and they were a fine God-fearing Roman Catholic couple. Very straight and very loyal. I felt extremely sorry for them when their estates were sequestered by Cromwell's bigotted petty tyrants. They were one of the few families round here who suffered so badly. The revenue from such estates in the North was diverted to pay off the debts to the Scots, which came to something like two hundred and twenty thousand pounds. A huge sum. If his parents had lived, I think that by now the estate would have been restored."

"I told Robert that he should regain his lands," said Elizabeth.

The clergyman looked disturbed. "Elizabeth, when will you learn to mind your own business? It is often best to let sleeping dogs lie. I have always felt great sympathy for the Carrs because their case was very like my own, when, because of another tyrant, I was forced to leave my family's estates in Bohemia and we lost everything we had. God willing, I sincerely hope that some happiness will come to you in view of all the recent troubles," and with that he crossed himself.

Elizabeth nodded solemnly.

"I promise to be more careful, but, remember, fortune always favours the brave," she joked with a toss of her head as she took her leave, and escaped further questioning by seeking the fresh air. Canon Ritschell watched her as she walked through the graveyard and shook his head with amusement as she disappeared in the direction of the crowded market place and Priestpopple Street. Before seeking the groom she had a mind to tarry while she wandered round the stalls. She recollected her lively childhood, when she used to chase up and down with Isabel, and have all the stallholders shouting at them. With a sudden leap of her heart she caught sight of the familiar figure of John on the other side of the market. How tall and erect he looked! She spent some time in simply enjoying the sight of him, then, slowly walking up behind him, cheekily tapped him on the shoulder.

"What are you doing out alone, fine sir?"

He turned, and his face flooded with love at the surprise of seeing her. "Oh, Elizabeth, you're a sight for sore eyes. We've just been talking about you. How are you? Any news?"

Holding his arms, Elizabeth stretched up and kissed him on the cheek. " I can't tell you here. I'll hitch my horse to the waggon and I'll explain on the way

112

home."

John quickly finished his business, the groom was dismissed and the old waggon lurched off on the familiar track to Hackford, with Elizabeth's horse trailing behind on a tether, looking somewhat baffled by his inferior position, and chomping at the bit.

Elizabeth told John part of the story of her indiscretion, and he nodded gravely without making any comment. When he heard of the forthcoming marriage of Lancelot he earnestly suggested that she would be welcome to come home whenever she wanted.

"Joanna misses you terribly, and I do a bit," laughed John. Elizabeth snuggled up to his arm as she had when she was a child.

By the time they were within sight of Hackford they were both content in each other's company and comfortable in their easy relationship. Elizabeth sighed: "New friendships might be fascinating, but whereas they are joined by silver threads, old relationships are bound by wonderful anchors of gold."

She squeezed John's arm tightly and looked up at him. She was so unbelievably happy, still close to John, lulled by the familiar clippety-clop of the horses' hooves. Nothing could be better, and life was sheer perfection. She saw it all with a clarity which had never blessed her before.

John was flattered by what she had just said, but somewhat embarrassed, and relieved it by encouraging the horse homewards with a light whip. And so, wishing the journey would never end, they made their leisurely way back to Hackford.

As soon as Joanna saw them, she dashed to check the cooking pot, and Elizabeth followed her to talk by the fire. "Uncle Anthony gave me news of you when he came to the ball. I was disappointed that you didn't come. You would have enjoyed yourselves," said Elizabeth.

Joanna did not respond so Elizabeth did not pursue the subject.

"We haven't seen much of Anthony recently. I think he met a woman at the ball, but I don't really know," replied John, chuckling mischievously.

"We've been very busy here," said Joanna, making excuses, "and, besides, I had nothing to wear."

In truth her mind was taken up with the preparations for the harvest supper and she could not even conceive of herself attending a ball. Elizabeth, however, persisted.

"A dress would never be a problem. You'd have been the belle of the ball, no matter what, and surely you'd have been the nicest people there."

Again Joanna did not respond so Elizabeth asked: "But how is George Dodds these days? Has he had any more fights with the bull?"

John was sitting near the window, mending a whip, trying to hold one thong between his teeth. "Oh, he's in fine fettle. Speaks very well of you. Eager to see you. He'll be back soon from the fields if you want to see for yourself," John said through his half-closed teeth.

"Yes, I've been wondering about him. I think I'll go down now, if you don't mind," suggested Elizabeth.

"That's a good idea," replied Joanna, hoping to catch up on some necessary chores. "But call at Isabel's first and see what a good job they've made with their new place."

Wrapping her shawl round her as she felt the unaccustomed cool breeze blowing down from the wide waste of the moor, Elizabeth crossed the meadow to where Isabel and Cuthbert had settled. After Isabel's joyous welcome she relished the tour of the new cottage and admired the ingenuity of some of Cuthbert's handiwork. Having parted reluctantly from baby John she followed the well-trodden path to the nearest farm at Lilswood and, giving a quick knock on the old cracked door, lifted the sneck to let herself into the Dodds' cottage.

There was George's wife, Mary, a buxom young mother, preparing the evening meal at the pot over the fire. A healthy-looking three year-old was playing with stones on the earth floor, and a baby about one year old was sitting up in the cradle watching him, cooing and gooing happily, and sucking his thumb with great gusto.

"Oh, Elizabeth! What a surprise! We haven't seen you for ages," said Mary, smiling. "Sit down by the fire, while I finish making the meal. The whole family have been out in the fields all day, gathering in the hay, and a bonny time I've had keeping an eye on these two."

"You look very tired," observed Elizabeth.

"Well, it's not so much tired, as I've felt a strange heaviness since the baby was born, and it gets worse as the day goes on. Right nuisance it is, after just two children. I've a cousin who had it after ten. There's a long way for me to go yet," she sighed.

"Keep feeding the baby as long as you can and that will give you time. Don't even stop when he starts bringing you the cracket to sit in front of the fire," laughed Elizabeth. "I'm sure it will gradually get better," she lied, suspecting from her own knowledge that the road for Mary would inevitably lead literally downwards.

It was not long before George appeared and he was delighted to see Elizabeth. "So you're back again in the calf-yard? You can't stay away, I think. Which is just as well, because, thanks to you, I'm as fit as a fiddle." She smiled.

"You've been longer than usual tonight," complained Mary.

"Oh, I've been goin' around the farms."

"Why?" asked his wife.

George just shook his head, looking slightly annoyed.

"I've just put that fine horse of yours out in the meadow. He's a beauty. I put the best horse we have around here in the next field to keep him company so he shouldn't feel too lonely," he laughed.

"How do you like the little uns?" he continued, quickly changing the subject and picking up the eldest, and holding him squealing in the air. "They're in good fettle. We'll just need a few more and we'll not be worried about old age catchin' us out."

Elizabeth and Mary exchanged knowing looks.

By then George was down on his hunkers, making funny faces and blabbing endearing noises at the baby in the cradle.

"John said he would be cuttin' tomorrow," said George. "Will you be there? It's always fun after the harvest is over."

"If you've any energy left," laughed Mary.

"Aye, we'll all be endin' up at John's house as usual, so make sure you're still here," urged George. Elizabeth nodded.

By this time she could tell that their meal was almost ready, and recollected that she too would be expected to be back home shortly. Pausing at the doorway she made a little game of saying goodbye to the children, who responded in a very cheerful manner, then made her way home. At every step she was reminded of her childhood. She lingered on the hillside, breathing deeply the familiar fragrances and enjoying the clear honey-sweet air which she had missed so much on her brief visit to Newcastle. With the evening now becoming slightly chilled, her mind seemed to be as clear as crystal and her senses heightened. The setting sun cast a golden glow over the countryside, tingeing every tree, bush and building, before sinking to the distant horizon, deep red.

Elizabeth admired the views of the rolling moorland in the distance and remembered in detail every gushing little stream and rolling hillock of purple heather. She looked up at the waxing disc of the harvest moon appearing in the eastern sky and thought of Robert. Was he too gazing at the same moon somewhere? Was he thinking of her? She shuddered as she became aware again of the cooling air and she wrapped her cloak tightly around her and hurried homewards.

"I hope you're going to have a harvest supper, because George is looking forward to it," warned Elizabeth, as she came through the door.

"Wouldn't be allowed to miss it," said John. "It's the best time of the year. Almost better than a wedding, except for the couple, of course," he said, pinching Joanna mischievously.

Joanna looked at him with feigned anger and said firmly. "Can't you see that I'm busy?"

Chapter 21

The next morning was typical of harvest time. There was a welcome serenity in the cloudless sky and an undisturbed silence across the fields of mature corn. In contrast, the looming tension of the annual harvest, with its race against the weather, and its back-breaking activity, was welcomed alike by everyone, from the bronzed old timer summoning up his waning strength to be useful, to the lively young ones, bursting with surplus energy, which they were so eager to release.

Bright and early, the workers mustered outside the farmhouse, bonding together with cheerfulness and gratitude for the prospect of a good crop. The day was perfect. "Look at this," said Peter Hall, "You couldn't have better weather. I've been showing our Cuthbert and Samuel how to sharpen a scythe."

Francis Miller, another neighbour, chuckled : "Our William can sharpen a scythe, but I can't allow young Thomas near it. He'd cut his fingers off if I did. You'll remember old Jonathan Ridley."

The sun rose higher, drying off the overnight moisture on the corn, with the promise of a warm day. The workers trooped energetically along the track to the first field, scythes on their shoulders, like soldiers intent on battle. The women and children followed in strung-out groups.

"Watch what you're doing with the baby!" cried Mary Dodds to her neighbour's son. "He's not meant to be carried upside down."

The golden corn stretched out before them. John took up the central position in the line of reapers, and without delay they began their task with a will. The rasping voice of an alarmed corncrake carried across the field, its rusty red wings catching the eye as it cleared the hedge.

The corn fell rapidly, under the concentrated slish-slash of the levelled scythes. After a time, the melody of happy voices gradually faded into the well-worn web of gossip and the half-forgotten memories of gruesome tales as they enjoyed the company of their neighbours, more accustomed to ploughing alone or eating a cold dinner on their own under the hedge.

Elizabeth had happily joined the throng of women and children, gathering and stooking the sheaves of corn, and was working near Isabel, helping her to keep an eye on the baby. As the rhythm of the scythes accelerated, the corn fell at a tremendous rate and the field was being devoured and stooked methodically. Every now and then some small frightened animal made a bolt for it and with a squeal sought the refuge of the surrounding countryside, too fast for the small boys who gave chase. A number of the children scattered in this manner took to gathering and stuffing their mouths with blackberries till they were recalled to their tasks behind the reapers. In time the fast initial pace set by the men slowed, conversation faded, and a calm discipline kept the cutting to a steady regularity. The stooks of corn accumulated in neat rows across the field, and by midday everyone was tired and ready for Joanna's meal, taken in the welcome shade of the hedgerow.

The reapers sank down gratefully wherever they could find a convenient spot to rest, and Elizabeth gave out the girdle cakes, whose cheese linings were much appreciated.

"These brantins are the best since last harvest," piped old William, munching contentedly.

"Yes, there's nothing anywhere like Hackford cooking," agreed Elizabeth, extracting the dirt from her long finger-nails.

After they had finished the meal the men resharpened their scythes, but the young ones gathered round William, hoping he would tell one of his ancient tales. "Stories! Stories! Stories!" they clamoured.

Meanwhile, George had gone alone to the meadow to check on the horses before it was dark. He congratulated himself as he watched the mare, with her tail still bandaged up with a dirty cloth, urinating and backing towards the fence. With his head arched high the stallion took a run and easily jumped the fence. Approaching the mare cautiously from the side, he touched noses, eliciting squeals from the mare. As the stallion worked his way back along her side with his nose, sniffing, nipping and nudging, the mare gradually swung her quarters towards him. George laughed as he noticed the mare's top lip raised and left them together, predicting: "You'll have a good harvest too, boy, and I for one can't wait to see it."

In the corn-field William, teller of the mysterious and forbidding traditional tales, mist-wrapped in folk memory, looked modestly reluctant as was his wont. However, having despatched his last mouthful and taken a much-needed swig of ale for his dry throat, he set his back comfortably against the nearest stook. He looked, felt, and enjoyed the part of an ancient country sage who had a deep awareness of the colour and power of words. Rubbing his whiskers with the back of his hand and swinging his steely eyes round the bevy of children

118

surrounding him, he started out very confidentially in a low voice.

"Once upon a time, in that field over there, a wench breaks her sickle and has to go home for another. A hare appears before her and turns round to watch her, twitchin' its long ears to and fro, to and fro. Ready for a good supper, she hurls her broken sickle at the hare, which suddenly darts across the field as if pursued by Satan.

On her return, at the very same place, she sees what appears to be exactly the very same hare , twitchin' its ears to and fro in the same manner .... to and fro......... Still hungry she aims her fresh sickle and strikes the animal on the head. Crack ! The girl is terrified when, instead of falling, it launches itself upon her, with malice, scratching her face with its sharp claws.

Hearing her screams, three men working nearby come to the girl's rescue, but the wily old hare deftly escapes through their fingers and vanishes through the hedge."

All the listeners sighed. "Did they ever find out what it was?" asked the young pop-eyed Eleanor Bell. She had heard the same story many times over the years, and wanted to believe every word.

"All the villagers were wondering what had happened, and had different ideas, but they agreed on one thing. They had noticed that a lonely old woman bore on her cheek a new ugly cut. Because of this everyone thought that she consorted with the devil. When she realised these accusations were being levelled at her, she cursed and blasphemed. After that the milk and butter went sour in the churn, cattle and sheep fell ill and died, and the corn turned black and withered. Her neighbours threatened to put her in a flaming tar barrel."

"What happened to her in the end?" asked another tense listener.

"She was avoided by her neighbours, which made her ready to die," pronounced old William.

"Just like old Nancy," suggested little Frances Hall, her face covered with blackberry juice. "Not at all," said Elizabeth loudly. "Nancy was a very clever woman, and looked after us all, don't forget. Now it's time to tell the story of the baby which was left in the field," she suggested. "Who's going to tell this one?"

Several heads dropped before Elizabeth chose Isabel, who smiled shyly. "First I'll have to check the babies." She reassured herself that her own child and Mary's were safe and fast asleep by the nearest stook of corn.

"Right! Now I can start. One year, at harvest time, a child was carried to the fields by his mother and laid to sleep near the hedge. The mother worked very hard for a long time. When she eventually went back to see the bairn and peered under the coverlet, she was horrified by the hideous vision that she encountered. Instead of the beautiful baby that she had left with its healthy pink cheeks, there was a disgustin' mass of evil, starin' at her, alert, and preparin' to greet its new parents with a wicked grin, nursin' the prospect of drivin' them to exhaustion."

"It was the work of the fairies," whispered Barbara Walker, a rapt listener. Isabel shuddered like everyone else and looked anxiously towards the babies' cots. With spines tingling, the girls were thinking over the tale but the boys were not bothered at all. They were up and away, and were fighting furiously around the field.

In a whisper, old Martha Robson also offered advice with an air of mystery: "Watch out for the tops o' stooks where there are delicious morsels o' 'fairy butter', there to lead the young astray. Beware!"

More shudders. Many of the grown-ups crossed themselves.

Stories over, it was back to work on the second field of corn, and the reapers set out again with a will to advance the harvest. At last the noisy cawing of home-bound crows was now joined by the approaching strains of a squeaking fiddle. The little boys rushed to meet the musician who walked in front of Joanna.

"Here she is !" she proclaimed, with an air of triumph, as she held high the kirn dolly which had been made the night before. There was a general roar of approval. The dolly, almost the size of herself, and fixed to the top of a long pole, had a cotton cap, and a white rustic smock, trimmed with coloured ribbons and top knots.

The workers thankfully laid down their tools, and made a dancing circle round the last reapers. The young were contending in earnest for the last cut of corn. However much their hands hurt and their wrists smarted from the sharp straw, a few keen souls battled on to the last. George had cunningly concealed the last patch of corn under an untied stook and, with a secret nudge, gave Elizabeth the chance of cutting it, the sign of a marriage in the offing.

Realising what had happened, the outraged contenders murmured their disappointment. "It's not fair," they complained.

"Get away. Anythin's fair in love, war or matin'," laughed George, nudging Elizabeth.

However, quickly reconciled, they all drew together to hear the rhyme recited by old William.

> "Blest be our labours bravely borne,
> For Master John's corn's truly shorn,

And we will have a reward tonight,
Of tasty ale, sparkling and bright,
And a kirn! a kirn! ahoa!"

There was a thrilling crescendo at the end, when everyone shouted in unison. Adam Thompson, who did not join in, had his ears pulled. "It's bad luck not to join in!" his father told him, looking very annoyed.. Meanwhile, the shout had been taken up by labourers from the adjoining farms and sounded and resounded across the valley.

The evening drew on and as the air grew cooler a procession formed, with the fiddler at the front, followed by the corn baby on its pole. As champion of the day, Elizabeth walked closely behind, bearing over her arm the neatly plaited trophy of her good fortune. On arriving home the reapers burst forth in another round of cheers, and Elizabeth gave the last cut into the hands of the grateful John. The fiddler took up his stance, and a harvest dance began before the door, with John and Joanna smiling approvingly. During the dance Joanna gave out kirn gifts of new caps which were conferred ceremonially on worthy maidens and received with much blushing and smiles. At last, the dancers dispersed to their cottages to prepare themselves for the evening's entertainment at Hackford.

Indoors, Elizabeth was very busy, She was seeing to the kirn cream which had to be stopped before it was ready to break into butter. She could hear the guests arriving, but was too busy to come out of the pantry. There were screams of delight as one guest after another arrived. When George came in he was hardly recognisable, dressed as a woman, and his arrival was greeted with roars of approving laughter. With the next round of applause Elizabeth peeped out of the door to see another guest staggering in as best he could, coiled from top to toe in straw ropes. Others were covered in animal skins in order to hide their identity. They looked grotesque as they danced with their bushy ox-tails dangling almost to the ground and swishing cheekily. Some carousers, covered in rough cloth, thought they had succeeded in remaining unrecognised to the very end.

Although Elizabeth had worked hard all day and could not join the party at once because she was looking after the kirn cream, she was nevertheless contented. She showed it as she emerged triumphantly from the pantry and placed the first bowl of the sweet mixture on the table with great pride. She had added to it some sugar, which she had brought from Nunburn. Everyone crowded round the communal bowl with dipping fingers and it disappeared so quickly that in minutes she had to fetch another.

Joanna's delicious food sustained the party-goers throughout the traditional stories, songs and dances, everyone waiting for the 'dance of dances', being the cushion dance, with its haunting minor key. George was the most enthusiastic of the throng, whirling round all the young girls in turn with tremendous energy, yet safely supporting them with his strong arms. His wife Mary cradled the sleeping baby, enjoying the happy celebrations which were the height of her year. George teased her: "Oh, you're like an auld wife now - can't stand the pace!". She pulled a face good naturedly.

Sitting beside her was old William, again in demand, singing the well-loved songs of yesteryear. The precious music, emerging from the mists of time, fascinated the audience, conscious of an inborn folk memory which they cherished and with which they felt completely at home. The lilting tunes rang out, repeating themselves at a higher level, with everyone joining in the refrains. Certain young lads who were not enthusiastic, were in general persuaded by their fathers, with cuffs on the ear. However, the singer was in his element, pouring out the favourite melodies with an intensity and sincerity born of dedicated commitment, often singing with closed eyes as he concentrated on the notes. Aware of the future, when he himself would be unable to be the centre of the feast, he often persuaded some younger reluctant singer to join in, and deliberately sang softly, to give the other an opportunity to excel. And in that way he knew that the age-old continuity would be preserved.

His finale was "The Twa Corbies" and its heart-rending lines:

"O'er his cold banes when they are bare,

The wind sall blaw for evermair."

This drew the usual sobs and sighs from the audience.

All this was watched over by the corn baby, which had been placed in the corner of the room, well out of the way of the spitting fire. Sometimes she was taken over by one of the more energetic dancers and carried proudly through the lively throng, while unheeded, and pervading the whole house, was the overwhelming smell of the byres and stables nearby, pungent and embracing, and completely familiar to the party-goers.

At length, it was time for the guests, tired and leg-weary, to disperse to their various abodes. However, for one joker, Ralph Atkinson, the night was still young. Wrapped up in some coarse cloth from head to foot, he lay in wait for the revellers at a bridge where everyone knew there were ghosts. It was a swampy place where wild-fire was often sighted in autumn, which was probably the origin of the superstition. He had just taken up his position in the darkness when, on the other side of the bridge, he saw what he thought was a real ghost.

The ghost chanted:

"You come to fright, I come to fright,

As long as you're here, I'll stay all night."

At this Ralph collapsed and quite swooned away. Other returning revellers were astonished to find him lying flat on the ground. Nothing daunted, they guessed his identity before they had even removed his costume, and he was carried home to sleep off what everyone thought was his drunken stupor. The next day he was to be heard protesting that he had seen a real ghost, but people only smiled and shook their heads.

At the ffarbrigge farmhouse, Elizabeth was busy clearing up after the party and her whole body ached, as she continued stoically. It would be another busy day tomorrow because the families would be gleaning the last fragments of the corn for themselves, and on the following day the children would enjoy the treat of rich cake made from the fresh flour. She must start the kirn ready for them.

Her thoughts went back to the ball at Nunburn Hall. There had not been the same homely satisfaction there. The exhilaration had not been so intense, and the people did not seem so genuine, not suffering the rural hardship and deprivation which heighten the senses. True happiness did indeed come by the way. The self-centred Nunburn guests had been more interested in the empty quest of impressing each other. But, alas, all her hopes were with Robert, and she longed to be back with him. Perhaps he would come for her one day soon, when everything had been settled. Whatever that meant! She wondered what he had been doing tonight and she wanted to share her own happiness with him for ever.

Retiring to her own special alcove in the kitchen, she suddenly recollected, to her pleasant surprise, that she had promised to look after baby John, who was snuggled up and fast asleep in her bed, a joy to behold! Isabel and Cuthbert had left him for her safe-keeping when they returned home, saving his tender lungs from the night air. She cuddled up to him, smelling his warmth, and enjoying the relaxing sound of his regular breathing. How twice blessed she was! In the future lay only happiness. Of that she was confident and she would not allow even a smidgeon of regret to colour her thoughts. Everything lay in being useful.

Chapter 22

At Nunburn Hall life had not been so cosy. Lancelot and his father had been poring over the problems relating to the settlement of the estate prior to his marriage. Long tiresome hours had been spent discussing all the possibilities available to them, and agreement had required many compromises. Woodall's three children, his sister, and various people close to the family had to be considered, and in addition his business and agricultural interests were unusually widespread. Eventually they sought the advice of Nicholas Hawden, a wise and experienced lawyer from Newcastle, and a day was set aside when Lancelot and Alexander would be available to consult with him so that the final settlement could be put into words.

For a time Lancelot had been avoiding Alexander, as far as was possible while living in the same house, because at every suitable opportunity, his brother had been probing into the projected family arrangements, and in truth there was as yet nothing to report. The day soon dawned, however, when all was to be revealed, and Alexander would know his fate. He was eagerly watching from an upper window when he saw in the distance the unfamiliar figure of the Newcastle lawyer riding slowly up the drive on an old nag. "Looks like a decrepit old fellow. Will his advice be worth following, or is he too stupid?" he sneered to himself.

Dressing quickly and not very carefully, he ran down the stairs to the study, but before he could open the door he heard voices inside talking about him. His father was saying: "I'm sorry to say that, like all younger sons, Alexander has always been a problem, but at least I haven't got a large brood of offspring."

"Well, thank God for that!" his son thought to himself. "Competition just makes things more complicated."

He was not going to let this strange lawyer get the better of him, and, being replete with ale, he was ready for him. He burst through the door aggressively, assured that he would get his own way, seeing nothing past his own needs and greed. He was buoyed up by a habitual conviction that he was always right and he could never make a mistake.

Startled by this sudden intrusion the older men turned to face him. The lawyer stood up to greet him.

"I'm Nicholas Hawden from Newcastle. How do you do?"

He held out his hand, but Alexander chose to ignore him and perched himself on a chair which he had reversed so that he was sitting astride it, poking his head cheekily over the back and feeding his arrogance with foolish conceit. The lawyer cleared his throat. He was beginning to appreciate the problems that had been explained to him. Woodall called a maid to summon Lancelot so that the proposed arrangements could be aired.

Hawden's conversation with Mayor Woodall resumed rather awkwardly. "The land that has been left in trust to your sister Caroline will be useful to pass on again in trust to Alexander. If it is worked with reasonable care, it will support him until his death."

At this Alexander exploded with irritation. "I know what that means! You must think I am a dotard! It means that it will never be mine to do with as I like. What if I don't want to be bothered with silly peasants scratching a living? I am used to Barbados, a well-organised plantation, and crops that grow richly in a wonderful climate. I don't want to be a slave to this dreadful weather and have nothing of my own. I deserve better than that. My mother told me that her family was very prosperous and successful, and, as my father has only two sons, surely some money can be found for me. All I long for is to go to London. That's where all the riches are to be made. I just need a proper start and I'm sure I could be successful."

The lawyer shrank inwardly, cleared his throat and looked at Woodall, pleading for support, which was not forthcoming. "I understand that you have a half-sister, Elizabeth, who will also have to be provided for."

Alexander's face twisted with fury and again he burst out, turning a deep shade of crimson.

"That whore is not to be included, too!" Turning to his father he snarled: "And what about all the auburn-haired brats that are seen round the cottages who are turning up in the second generation. Are they also in the happy band? You have been well versed in exercising your rights as seigneur."

There was a deathly silence and the veins on Woodall's temples throbbed convulsively, his fists clenched, as he struggled for self-control. There was too much at stake to descend to the ale-house coarseness of Alexander's rhetoric, and he could imagine what it would be like if this conversation were repeated in Newcastle. He would be a laughing stock, and his civic dignity would be compromised. He realised that no kind of settlement would compensate for Alexander's headlong recklessness and ignorance. Any investment made for him would quickly vanish, and the family fortunes would be depleted.

Lancelot, by now on the staircase, heard the raised voices and hurried to the study. He had dreaded this day coming and was not surprised at the uproar, but when he saw Alexander's distorted face he knew that his worst fears had materialised. He laid his hand on Alexander's arm. He felt very angry, but knew that anger was the wrong emotion to contribute to the present conversation. All he could try was a cool logical argument to soothe inflamed tempers. Yet he knew that no amount of love, consideration or help ever had any effect on Alexander, whose selfish optimism and lack of foresight ensured that disaster was always lurking in his wake. With sadness he saw that he would have to keep his distance after this, or his brother would bring them both down.

"All my life I've never had a chance to succeed. Nobody has ever cared for me or helped me in the slightest way," complained Alexander.

"Do you realise that as the second son you have no rights? Father and I are trying to help you, as we always have," came Lancelot's emphatic response.

"Mother told me that there would be ample provision for me out of her family estates," retorted Alexander.

"Your mother was very ill towards the end of her life, and had no idea of financial matters," snapped his father. "Indeed I did not want to burden her with the sadness of them. The truth is that if your grandfather had not been preoccupied with gambling, we would have been very rich indeed. Most of their wealth was frittered away and there was very little left to pass on, rendering our marriage settlement almost worthless. It is only through careful financial deals and the wisdom and restraint of Lancelot that we have survived."

"There you go again," butted in Alexander. "Lancelot has always been your favourite son, and I have been second best. And now there is Elizabeth. I can see how you look at her. You think more of her than of me."

His father did not know what to say and stared helplessly first at Lancelot and then at Hawden, while Alexander's attention seemed to be temporarily centred on the progress of a fly which was dancing up and down the window pane. Lancelot moved to the window in despair and directed his gaze across the garden. Was it all worth it? He had tried to care for his father since he had left Cambridge, and had lightened his burden as much as possible, but he was incapable of dealing with the emotional Alexander in any sensible way. His brother's road led to irrationality and there was nothing that he or anybody else could do.

The lawyer cleared his throat and dared to broach the difficult part of the business.

"Now we come to the question of the previous estate of the family of Robert Carr. I understand it was bought very cheaply in the time of the sequestrations with the intention of selling it back to his parents at a convenient time. However their early deaths delayed this plan. Now your father wishes to make amends, and it is proposed that an agreement be signed with the said Robert Carr, in which he promises to pay back the agreed debt over a number of years in exchange for the revenues due from his tenure of the land. This seems a sensible arrangement in view of the fact that the young man has developed the experience to run an estate competently."

"Now we're giving away lands to strangers! I could have managed this estate quite happily. Has everyone gone mad in this house?" Alexander interposed impatiently.

"The honour of our father is at stake in this matter, and I fully agree with these arrangements concerning Robert," said Lancelot with determination.

The lawyer, leaving a decent pause in case of another outburst from Alexander, continued: "As for Elizabeth, it is expected that she will make a good marriage, so her circumstances will be under revision in the future. A dowry of two hundred pounds is available for her on her marriage and in addition she will have an interest of an accumulating eight per cent on the capital. That is a summary of our intentions." Fearing further confrontation with Alexander, the lawyer kept his eyes down on his papers.

A stony silence fell over the company. At last Alexander realised that he was defeated. He leapt clumsily to his feet and the chair he had straddled was sent flying. He turned on his heel and stormed out of the room, in a volley of bitter complaints and blasphemies.

As Lancelot picked up the chair, carefully inspecting it for damage, the lawyer turned to Woodall who appeared dumbfounded: "I hope that your troubles have been resolved for a time, and I shall be very pleased to help you with the final arrangements and any marriage settlements."

With that the momentous visit was terminated.

Chapter 23

Early next morning Robert Carr was summoned to the Hall. His home, the Woodall's Dower House, which had formerly been an ancient defensive bastle, stood near a clump of elm trees within sight of and at a convenient distance from the Hall. The Carr family had lived there, depending on the generosity of the Woodalls, ever since they had lost their estate and had been unable to maintain their former home. Robert's plight had been sympathetically handled by the Woodalls, and his position as steward had given him security and respect in the neighbourhood. After the deaths of his father and mother he had worked conscientiously for his employer and now held a trusted place in the family's establishment. The tenants who remembered his parents always doffed their caps to him and called him 'young master'. Yet he still found himself socially in the gap between gentry and common people, which occasionally caused him misgivings, but his many duties rarely allowed him to feel melancholy. In any case, the arrival into his life of the lovely Elizabeth flushed his soul with a glow of inner delight, and gave him a new confidence and a sense of purpose, tinged with a tantalising uncertainty.

He eased himself into a clean shirt left for him by the indefatigable Mistress Grant, and gave his boots and gaiters a vigorous polishing before crossing to the Hall to report his survey of the harvest. He had been warned that his employers had some important news to disclose to him, and if he had not been given an inkling of something better, he might have been very worried. Lancelot was studying a book when Robert entered the hall and, after a brief exchange of greetings, he continued to do so, while his father stood at the window maintaining an expressionless face. However, Lancelot eventually snapped the book shut and his eyes twinkled.

"Robert, we have news of great importance for you."

He tried to keep a straight face but found it very difficult. Robert looked from one to the other, intrigued. Then, relaxed and beaming, Mayor Woodall approached him with outstretched arms and gave him a warm hug.

"You know how we have always held you and your parents in high regard, and valued your hard work on our behalf. Well, Lancelot and I have decided to restore to your good self the former estates of the Carr family which were taken over by us in the bad times. We had always intended to do it and we think that the circumstances of Lancelot's intended marriage and all the complications which it will entail, make this a suitable time to begin the negotiations. The full arrangements and the terms of our agreement can be explained later."

Robert, though taken aback, was not slow to show his appreciation of their generosity.

"Thank you, Sir. I cannot begin to tell you how delighted I am with this news. When the time arrives, the restitution of the old lands will give me a new life, one full of promise, and I shall be eternally grateful to you. Our families have been close for generations and I trust that this will continue. I hope to repay the confidence you have shown in me."

Lancelot poured wine into glasses and proposed a toast: "To our continued friendship and the prosperity of both estates!" The glasses chinked together amicably.

When he saw Robert's sincere gratitude, Woodall suggested with a smile: "All that you lack now is a good wife." He carefully studied Robert's reaction but the diplomatic young steward was shrewdly inscrutable. His only response was a slight pursing of the lips.

Recognising Robert's embarrassment, Lancelot shrugged his shoulders. "Now back to your work," he reminded his friend, laughing. " You are still our steward until the agreements are finally completed."

Robert's first port of call, however, was to visit the kitchen to see Mistress Grant. As soon as he entered the room she dismissed the kitchen maid and he ran towards her, embraced her with great enthusiasm and lifted her off the floor.

"You were right, you were right, you were right," he chanted in her ear, as he whirled her lightly round the kitchen.

"Oh, put me down before I'm dizzy, lad," she cried.

"I can't think how you are so well informed about the affairs of this house."

She bent towards him and with some hesitation confessed: "Well, I'll tell you a secret, since it might help you in your new position. Running underneath the buttery and kitchen the cellars extend as far as the study and you can hear quite clearly what is said upstairs because of certain large cracks in the floor boards. I have known it for years, but I restrict the staff from going down. I was unable to resist warning you of your unexpected good fortune and so you have found out my little secret. Make sure you keep it to yourself," she warned him brusquely. "But tell me, what do you propose to do now?"

" I know well what you are after, but mind your own business, woman!" Robert chided mischievously. "You're not going to be delving under my floor boards! Your curiosity will have to bide its time. Now I have work to do."

With that he took his leave of a somewhat disappointed Mistress Grant. She knew that her cherished young man was a tease and a torment, but was confident that he would tell her his plans in due course.

When he reached the stables Robert paused for a moment to watch the grooms feeding the horses. Periculo's stall was still empty, and the sight gave him a pang of regret at Elizabeth's absence. Every day he steadfastly pursued his routine with a kind of fierce desperation in order to forget that he pined for her, and his firmly set jaws gave no indication of the longing within him. He concentrated on the men's friendly banter as they worked.

Will Thompson approached him.

"I'd better warn you about one of the wheels on this cart, Mr. Carr. The spokes are coming loose and we'll need it soon for fetching in the corn."

"Is it so bad?" asked Robert.

"Well Sir, I wouldn't like to risk it when it's bearing a full load."

"Aye, it would cowp over," added Thomas Jewett, another of the grooms, remembering his uncle, who had been flat on his back for fully two years following the capsize of a corn waggon. The third groom, George Madgen, showed Robert the offending wheel.

"It's served its term, Sir. Shall we take it off?"

"Yes," agreed Robert. "Can you take it to the wheelwright's in Humshaugh today? Put it on the flat cart and we'll give Merrilegs a run-out."

When his own mount was saddled, Robert rode out to the fields where the corn reapers were sweating at their work under a brilliant sun.

"Fine morning, Mr. Carr," called John Green, a grizzled old man who had worked on the Home Farm since he was a boy. " Another two weeks of sunny weather like this, and we will be celebrating."

"Good morning lads," returned Robert good-humouredly. "It certainly is good harvest weather, but we'll be lucky if it stays like this. Perhaps two weeks won't be long enough. But I am pleased to see that the corn looks in good condition this year."

The reapers gratefully leaned on their scythes and mopped their brows. Old John was bothered over something else. "We're short of a man, Sir. Ralph Stokoe is still off work with a bad gash across his hand, and I can't see him being back till after harvest. Broad Field usually takes three days to cut, but we'll be struggling to do that this year."

"Don't worry, John," said Robert kindly. "Miss Elizabeth will be back soon, and she may be able to cure him."

"Aye, she might," returned John. "I've great faith in that lass and her medicines, but till then we'll just have to cross our fingers for him, poor soul. Let's hope the red streak up his arm doesn't spread. That's always a bad sign!"

Robert appreciated that Elizabeth had already made her mark on the estate and, as he skirted another two fields of barley, rejoiced over how her presence had been thoroughly beneficial. To some extent her cheerful influence had made up for the loss of the men who had been sent to Barbados. The morale of the cottagers remained high and he was sure that the Woodalls were going to profit from a good yield from their farms. As generous employers and progressive farmers, they deserved it.

He turned his horse towards the farms which had formerly belonged to generations of the Carr family, and, as he approached the first of them, Hunter's Gap Farm, there were tears in his eyes as he remembered how unhappy his father had been when he lost the estate. He wished that he could have told him of the present outcome, but in a strange way he did feel a sense of communion with his dead parents. He dismounted and dug his fingers into the rich loam, firmly grasping a fistful, and savoured its wonderful earthy smell before allowing it to crumble back to the ground. The field of oats fluttered in the light breeze and the sun cast a golden light across the landscape, enriching crops, pasture and woodland and filtering right into his very being. Dare he think of Elizabeth sharing the joy of his good fortune? Would her impetuosity spoil the dream? Might he indeed be safer with a meeker soul? Yet her bright personality was the feature he loved most about her, and he had to admit that he adored her. For the benefit of future generations he vowed that he would make doubly sure that these lands were never lost to his family again.

He swung easily back into the saddle and rode along the well-loved tracks that he had known since his boyhood. As he passed the men at work they paused to wave their arms and take a well-earned breather. Some pastures were empty, grazed short over the summer, while others held flocks of sheep, the spring lambs now partly fattened and almost ready for the butcher. Robert promised himself that he would improve the strain of stock, perhaps with more meat on them, or a better quality of fleece. He had heard of the prize rams being used in some parts of the country but had no experience of selective breeding. In the slack period of winter he would spend time investigating this. There were also faint rumours at the market of farms down south which had introduced turnips and special clover on which to feed animals over the winter. This needed discussing with Lancelot. Then he remembered the good news of the morning. His heart swelled with pride as he planned his own bright future for the estate.

The larks soared over his head, shrilling with a joy in tune with his mood, as he proceeded to Woodedge Farm. Everything reflected his own happiness and the whole world was bliss. He admired the way the fields sloped up gently to the dark woods, which climbed the low hill overlooking the beautiful river plains to the east. From the higher ground he could see the workers busy at the reaping and stooking, and the occasional flash as the sun caught the scythe blades. At the next turning in the road he was thrilled at the sight of his ancestral home, its grey stone blending with the browns and greens of the woods behind it. He reached the narrow farm cottages partly hidden by isolated oak trees, and separated from their cow byres by a stony road, on which stood an empty cart, resting on its shafts. Two infants played under the cart, and Robert could hear their squawks of laughter as he rode up. These were the children of James Graham, one of the men who had gone to Barbados.

"Hello, Tom!" he called. "Is your mother about?"

"Hello, Mr. Carr," came the reply. "Yes, she's baking the bread. Just go in."

As he dismounted, a dark-haired woman appeared at the door of the second cottage, her hands covered in flour. "Good morning, Sir," she said politely. "Is there any news?"

"Good day, Mrs.Graham. No news - if you mean from Barbados. You are in the middle of your work, I see. Please don't interrupt your baking for me."

"That's all right. I'm just making some rye bread for the old folks next door."

"I only came up to see my parents' old house. It may be needed one of these days, but it is in sore need of restoration before it is habitable."

"Bless you, yes," Agnes Graham replied. "It's good for nothing at present except as a home for rats and mice, so it'll be a long slow job."

"I'll make a note of the first changes that are required, and send men here to clear it up a little. I thought I'd better warn you, but it will be during the cold weather that these things will come to pass, when I have some spare men."

An old couple had now appeared at the front door of the first cottage. Robert turned to talk to them. "Good day, Samuel, and Alice. How are your pains, Samuel?"

"Hello, young Master Robert. I'm not too bad. The warm weather gives me a bit of respite. It's the cold that makes it worse," replied Samuel Dinning. "We were just talkin' about our John, out in Barbados. We wish he was back. There are so many little jobs here that I can't do now. But is there anything we can do for you?"

"Yes, there is. That little herb garden in front of my parents' house needs a little raking out, if and when you are able? There are plans to renovate the place, but I don't know how soon the work will start."

Alice smiled at Robert. "It would be comfortin' to see the old house restored. I remember you playin' in that garden when you were a little un and tryin' to feed the cows on wild flowers. You were the lad that kept treadin' in the cow plats, much to your mother's annoyance. But this end of the farm would take on a new life if the place was lived in. I just hope that you can return to it yourself."

Robert only chuckled in reply.

Beyond the farm cottages it was a short walk to the small manor house that was Woodedge, a place which in the past he had so often avoided. Even from a distance the property appeared dilapidated, and the garden overgrown with briars and nettles. He noticed with amusement that a flock of crows were in possession, cawing loudly as they exchanged places on the roof ridge. Their nests protruded from every chimney pot. However, the roof seemed to be in one piece, and the grey stone walls as good as ever. The door on the entrance porch had rotted down one side, and its hinges were solid with rust. As he pushed it open there was a tremendous crack as the rotten side disintegrated and he had to squeeze through the gap he had created. The latch on the inner door opened easily, leading him into the familiar screens passage which led on the right to the old kitchen and buttery, and on the left through the tall oak screen into the Great Hall itself, where the whole family used to feast on special days.

This was where they had enjoyed wonderful celebrations at Christmas in the good old days before Cromwell's miserable embargoes. Thank goodness that era was over, thought Robert. The high open roof, stained with the smoke of generations of feasting, gave him such pleasure and nostalgic feelings that he remained staring at it for some time. The timbers of the roof looked sound and might need very little attention. The stone floor, with its pattern of intersecting squares and hexagons, half hidden by a fine mantle of dust and dead flies, appeared to be undisturbed, and the clack of Robert's footsteps was the only sound which echoed through the house.

The oriel room, with its great window extending into the front garden, was still separated from the hall by a wooden screen. Robert recalled one particular magical evening, when he stood on its curving seat in great glee, watching for the first time the large flakes of snow silently falling at dusk and blanketing the herb garden. Here, where the family had eaten most of their meals, in private, away from the gaze of the servants, were thick cobwebs hanging from every beam and every corner. Nearby, an oak door gave access to the tiny private chapel where he remembered his mother, on her knees, praying at least three times a day.

The great parlour, next door, was a sunny room, and had been the main sitting room twenty-odd years ago. Now it smelt musty. Its walls were blackened with dampness, and the wooden panels had swollen with moisture and become detached from the wall, nourishing large fungi. He was confident, however, that Elizabeth would be able to bring back the room to its former splendour and restore further happy memories of his childhood home.

Before he proceeded he felt a strong compulsion to investigate the priesthole. The knowledge of it had been passed on to him before his father's death but he had never had the opportunity of testing it. He approached the fireside and, putting his fingers behind the panelling to the right of the fireplace, pressed hard. The panel began to creak and, with a little pressure, it moved slightly and with a great effort he slid it open and was able to squeeze into the secret room behind. In the dim light he could see a crucifix standing in an aperture. Then, as his eyes grew accustomed, he could make out a chair and what appeared to be a bale of material. Was it damask? His foot caught something which chinked with a metallic sound and he stooped to pick up what was revealed as a silver goblet. A crucifix and a chalice, both of silver, lay under the chair.

Robert realised that all of these treasures must have been hastily concealed when the commissioners came to clear the house. Religious objects would have been condemned and destroyed by those heavy-handed vandals. His mind flew back to his parents, particularly to his mother, who had been devoted to the church and its teachings. He gently replaced the items, cobwebs catching his mouth as he bent low. Straightening up, a sudden pang of youthful imagination made him fearful of being incarcerated in the old house by mistake, so he quickly squeezed out, and with a sigh of relief pushed the panelling shut.

Through the next door lay the little parlour, in which his father had kept his books, now all vanished. This room, he thought, looked in better shape than the others, but the ceiling plaster was damp and disfigured, and probably needed replacing completely. He struggled to clamber up what was left of the wooden staircase to reach the three bedrooms above, and he gasped as one of his boots plunged right through a decaying tread that had seemed solid enough. As downstairs, all the furniture had gone, but on the end of the wall of the great bed chamber an elaborate plasterwork displayed a surprisingly intact royal coat of arms. This had demonstrated the Carr family's loyalty to the old king, a loyalty which had cost them most of what they possessed. A great shudder ran down Robert's spine at the sad memory of what had transpired in those dramatic times.

There was a tiny room leading off the main bedroom, in which he remembered a cradle had been stored. Alas, it had remained empty because he never had a brother or sister to occupy it. He returned to his own room, which overlooked the large neglected courtyard at the back, and poked his foot into the debris on the floor. He thought he saw the tip of something familiar and bent down to investigate. He was intrigued to discover that it was the small wooden horse that he had played with as a child, buried for all these years, only to reappear as if by magic on this special day. He put it into his pocket, cherishing it as his special good luck token and meaning to give it to Elizabeth for safekeeping. It would be a memory of this day to keep for future generations, to remind everyone of the time when there was the first promise of the family estates being restored.

Satisfied with his cursory inspection, he stumbled awkwardly down the wreckage of the stairs and again stood in the great hall for a while, considering its possibilities. In addition to the occasional sound of the scampering rats and mice, he became aware of a presence, a barely discernible figure in the semi-darkness at the entrance to the hall. It was a decrepit old man leaning heavily on a stick and Robert saw that it was Christopher Charlton, Agnes Graham's father, who had been the family carpenter and wheelwright for many years.

"Good to see you," Robert boomed. "What can I do for you?"

"The word got round that you are intending to open up the old Manor. I would be pleased to help you all I can, for the sake of your parents, and the many kindnesses that they showed to me."

His voice was very weak and faltering and as soon as Robert drew close to him he could see how painful any movement was to the old fellow.

"Yes, I remember you, Christopher, and what a valued craftsman you were. How I used to get in your way! But you were always very patient. If you think that you can help you are very welcome, but I think it is time for the younger ones to take their turn. Perhaps you will help us with your advice."

He pointed to the hall screen and admired the beautiful carving, stroking it with his fingers. However, when he touched the old wood it began to crumble into sawdust. Christopher looked alarmed. "Never mind," said Robert, patting his old shoulder, "I will ask Lawrence Johnson to carve some more. He'll quickly sort it out. Let's go out into the bright sunshine. It's too cold and damp in here for both of us."

Robert was touched by the old man's offer, and, as he closed the broken door behind him as best he could, he noticed that there were more cottagers and children outside. Agnes Graham, with flour still dropping from her hands and a substantial smudge on her cheek, was discussing the momentous piece of news with the three women from the other cottages, Jane Dinning, Mary Purvis and Anne Henderson, and Robert was happy that he had lifted their spirits in this small way. He chatted briefly again, before mounting his horse and riding back to Nunburn.

Chapter 24

The next day Lancelot sent for Robert. "I have discussed the Barbados situation with my father and we are persuaded that the best course now is to send out the men's wives and children. With any luck they might like it there, and bring up their families to make the plantation a success. If sugar continues to be a profitable venture, and if they are treated decently by Thomas, which I am sure will be the case, since he has a natural inclination that way, this move may prove advantageous. Can you find out what their feelings are on this matter?"

"That's a great comfort to know," said Robert. "Despite the practical difficulties and the dangers of the journey I believe that the wives will be eager to join their menfolk, but it will take somebody like Elizabeth to talk to them first. Is she likely to be back in the near future?"

"One of the grooms has been sent to bring her back today."

"Oh! I could have done it."

"No. You are needed here. It is better to send a groom to escort her," insisted his employer.

With that, the interview was ended and Robert made his way home, unhappy that a chance to accompany Elizabeth had been lost and musing on the speed with which all their circumstances had changed. He had always felt uneasy over his present inability to control his own destiny when previously, even as a child, he had enjoyed a privileged position. Yet now he was closer to the men whose manual labour created the wealth of the estate and was better able to understand their feelings. Maybe he was a wiser man for it. Thankfully he was rapidly moving towards independence and soon would be his own master.

As he swung open the door of the Dower House he resolved to be patient, to be resolutely devoted to Elizabeth, come what may. Many obstacles had lain in the way of their union because of the unusual circumstances of her birth and his own disestablishment. It was the Woodalls alone who held the key to their future happiness and he hoped that his high standing with the Mayor and his long-standing friendship with Lancelot would prove sufficient to allow his devotion to Elizabeth to ripen into marriage. Much might hang upon Woodall's view of Elizabeth's future. At present she seemed to be out of favour because of her impetuosity, but he felt sure that he could help to guide her undoubted intelligence and energy into more acceptable channels. At least he would see her before the day was out.

He changed into another shirt, donned a soft brown leather hat to keep off the sun, and, after a refreshing draught of ale, he remounted his horse to ride to the village three miles away where his immediate concern was to consult the carpenter about the renovation procedures for Woodedge Manor. The corn fields drifted by as the sturdy mount plodded along the stony track, the rider studying the distant southern horizon beyond the River Tyne, the direction from which he knew Elizabeth would be returning.

To his surprise another horseman appeared, coming from the opposite direction, and halted in order to have a word with Robert.

"Good morning, Sir," the stranger said, doffing his hat. "Can you direct me more closely to the Woodalls' residence. I've been told that it is not much further."

Though the words were plain enough, his south-country accent was strange to Robert.

"You're in luck. I have just come from Nunburn. I am Mr. Woodall's steward, Robert Carr. You are now about fifteen minutes riding from the Hall. May I enquire your business there?"

"My message is for the owner of the Nunburn Hall estate, Mr. Alexander Woodall. I am not at liberty to divulge the nature of the message to anyone but the landowner."

"Landowner!" exclaimed Robert. "But the estate is owned by Alexander's father, Mr. Henry Woodall, Mayor of Newcastle."

"Be that as it may, my orders are to seek Mr. Alexander Woodall and deliver a legal document into his very own hand," returned the visitor.

Robert's heart sank. Alexander had always been an unruly youth, and now it seemed that he was in trouble with the law. "I shall ride back with you. This errand of mine can wait." Turning his horse towards Nunburn, he engaged in conversation with the unwelcome visitor, establishing that he had come from London on behalf of a gentleman from Bristol, but little else.

This skeletal information made him sick to the stomach, fearing lest Alexander had gone beyond the pale in his behaviour at Bristol. There must be a substantial reason to bring a messenger from London to seek legal redress, if that was what it involved. Robert's head declined to his chest. Any upset to the family he served could only be prejudicial to the whole little community. This was proving to be a bad day.

He quickly conveyed his companion to the front entrance, where a footman greeted him. Robert made his way round the side of the house to the kitchen, to warn Mistress Grant of this new development. She sat him down at the table with a drink, and then quickly disappeared.

Meanwhile the stranger had been ushered into the hall and his cloak taken from him. Henry Woodall came down the stairs to meet him with a smile which quickly faded when he saw the man's challenging stare and tight lips.

"Come into the study," he said. "We can talk in privacy there." Woodall closed the door and offered him a seat in front of his desk.

The stranger began: "Thank you, Sir. You are ....?"

"I am Henry Woodall, Mayor of Newcastle."

"I am Nicholas Knight, courier for Price and Petty, the London lawyers. I am here on behalf of a client in Bristol, who is eager to take possession of two farms which are part of the Nunburn Hall estate, owned by Mr. Alexander Woodall. I believe they are called Woodedge Farm and Hunter's Gap Farm. I shall be pleased to make an inventory of them both tomorrow, so that we can inform my client who is eager to assume the responsibility for them."

(Mistress Grant snatched her breath in horror down below and started to tremble, turning white as she pinched her hands tightly in front of her.)

In contrast, although equally aghast, Henry Woodall went red-faced with fury.

"To take possession of .... ?" he spluttered in disbelief. "Who and what can make your employers think this? There must be some mistake."

He strode towards the door and shouted for a servant. "Please find Master Lancelot and ask him to come here immediately."

A maid appeared and rushed off in response to the urgency in his voice. The search did not take long and within minutes Lancelot came into the study, sensing instinctively that a crisis had arisen.

"What does this gentleman want?" Lancelot enquired, his face tight with anxiety.

The explanation rendered him breathless. Gripping the edge of the desk till his knuckles were white, he almost shouted, speaking clearly and aggressively : "How can your client, as far away as Bristol, possibly think that he owns these two farms on our estate?"

"They were part of a wager which was taken at The Five Bells, near the quay at Bristol, between our client, Andrew Trelawney, and Alexander Woodall, the owner of Nunburn Hall," asserted the stranger equally aggressively.

Lancelot replied firmly: "Alexander Woodall is my younger brother and he does not own any property on this estate, or indeed anywhere. What was the form of this wager?"

"It was held in front of several witnesses, who are willing to verify it. The wager was in relation to two flies walking up the window of the inn. The fly that rose highest, inside a given time limit, won the bet. Our client was successful. I am here to see that Alexander Woodall pays his debt to the full."

His listeners were speechless with humiliation and rage. Lancelot turned round in despair to look out of the window, clasping his hands tightly behind his back and unable to speak. Henry Woodall was fidgeting in his seat and his hands were fretfully plucking at his wig as he worried about the legalities of the situation. His legal adviser was miles away in Newcastle and he felt confused and helpless. The effrontery of Alexander was too blatant to comprehend.

"The detail of this story is so striking that I find it credible, though my heart is revolted by the thought that my own son should betray his family in such a vile way," he sighed.

After a moment's thought, Lancelot decided that it was now important to find Alexander, and see if he could shed some light on the situation. While a search was instigated to find him, the three men sat in a pregnant silence.

Eventually Alexander appeared, smelling of fresh air and idleness.

"What's all this about?" he asked blithely.

Lancelot confronted him, behaving totally out of character, as he spat through his teeth: "This gentleman alleges that you used two farms on this estate as part of a wager in The Five Bells at Bristol. It concerns two flies on a window. Is this correct?"

Restraining himself from striking out in his fury, he said: "I find this unbelievable." He gritted his teeth with contempt and turned his back.

Nicholas Knight sat quietly observing the family, failing to suppress the sneer on his lips.

Alexander was quiet for a minute. "What a stupid story!" he faltered. "I did stay there but I can't remember this wager. I was weakened by a terrible fever."

The stranger glared at him. "You probably don't remember because most of your time there I understand was spent in a state of inebriation. Nevertheless you were capable of making a bet."

"But I don't own any farms. I'm penniless. Even if it was true, how could I possibly honour such a wager?" complained Alexander.

"Obviously our client in these special circumstances will expect a sum of money forthwith, equivalent to the value of the farms in question which you risked in the said wager. I am already assured that he is prepared to go to court over this issue," affirmed the stranger.

Alexander's eyes grew wild with fear as he assessed the angry countenances of his father and Lancelot, his face blanching with fright and remorse.The stranger drew closer to him, his steady hand holding out a document, and Alexander turned sick with apprehension. He could not take it. Before anyone could intervene he dashed from the room and raced out of the front door towards the stables. When Lancelot realised his destination he hurried after him, but his younger brother fled too quickly.

By a strange coincidence, Elizabeth had just arrived back at the stables, and the groom was about to unsaddle her horse when Alexander stormed in furiously, and, roughly ignoring the astonished Elizabeth, took over the reins of the horse. Before she could remonstrate he had dragged the horse outside, mounted quickly, and was off. Ignoring the shouts of disapproval, he set off into the countryside at a gallop. A few minutes later Lancelot seized the groom's horse and pursued his brother.

Alexander rode recklessly, half-blinded by the glaring sun, and the spirited Periculo responded to his slaps and heels, accelerating with great strength, its hooves drumming on the hard earth. Lancelot had no hope of catching him, but followed, hoping to keep him in view. Alexander was determined that nothing and nobody would impede his flight. The fugitive rode fast and furiously over the uneven stubble of the newly cut cornfield, and the horse obeyed without hesitation. At this frantic pace they thundered on, over the flat ground in a cloud of dust, leaping hedges without difficulty. It was not until they had reached the hedge at the edge of the third field that the poor animal in its crazy flight had the instinct to falter in alarm when it encountered an old tree trunk in front of the hedge over which it was expected to jump. Too late, it shied and crashed, its front leg snapping like a dry stick, and it rolled backwards, crushing the body of Alexander under its heavy frame. The poor animal writhed in agony and could not rise while Alexander lay motionless and silent.

When Lancelot reached them, it was obvious that both his brother and Periculo were in a dire condition. Blood issued from Alexander's mouth, his eyes were closed, and he appeared dead, his body trapped underneath the horse, which was breathing heavily and obviously in great pain. Lancelot flung himself down beside Alexander's body, but there was nothing he could do. He shook his head, hardly believing that a perfectly normal morning should end in such tragedy.

Help was already on its way from the Hall. Alerted by Woodall's cries resounding throughout the house, Robert Carr ran to the stables where he saw Elizabeth, still trembling with the violence of Alexander's seizure of her horse.

"Alexander has taken my poor horse," she spluttered. "Has he gone mad? He seemed to be hell-bent on riding away from here."

Robert replied tersely: "I'll tell you later. The master is beside himself, crying out and stumbling about. Please attend to him. We must catch Alexander before he does himself any harm."

"And what about my poor horse?" shouted Elizabeth after him in desperation, but in a moment he was on his own mount and away. Now distressed herself, she hurried towards the Hall to comfort her father and discover the cause of the alarm, still stung by Alexander's violence, and by Robert's brusqueness. She was also troubled by the regret that Robert had not wanted to collect her from Hackford..

It took the combined strength of Lancelot, Robert and two farm workers to pull Alexander from under the horse.They quickly realised that he was dead, and Lancelot fell weeping across the still body, bitterly regretting his recent harsh words. Robert offered to fetch a cart to convey the body home, and also a gun to put the horse out of its misery, as the hapless creature was thrashing about in a pitiable state.

Within half an hour a group of men from the Hall had reached the scene of the fatality. Alexander's body was lifted on to a stretcher, placed in the cart and taken back to the Hall, while Robert despatched the horse with a single shot and quickly overtook the silent party. As they approached the Hall they could see Henry Woodall, with Elizabeth supporting him, standing disconsolately at the front door. From their demeanour it could be deduced that they had heard the worst. The old man's shoulders drooped. He pulled away from Elizabeth and presented a pathetic sight, holding on to the doorpost for support as the cart creaked painfully to a rest in the courtyard.

To all the onlookers there seemed something unreal about the whole scene. Servants gathered silently near their master, looking bewildered. He hardly had the strength to stand as the body was carried slowly through the hall and Elizabeth looked up at his white face and felt guilty. She had never liked Alexander since the first day that she had met him, and perhaps even before, and she felt strong feelings of fear in his presence, but she had never once wished him dead. She shivered as she hoped her dark thoughts had not had an influence on his fate.

When the body had been taken upstairs Woodall returned to the stranger who had been hovering between hall and study.

Shattered with grief, he mumbled: "You can see the chaos you have caused in my household. I suggest that you return immediately from whence you came, before you suffer any injury.... and the Lord have mercy on your soul." Tears rolled down both of his cheeks, his face creased up in sorrow, and he had tremendous difficulty in speaking the words.

And so, sixty minutes after his arrival at the front door, the Angel of Death departed without ceremony, with sorrow and disaster in his wake. The deadly power of money had dealt its last blow at Alexander. Maybe he would have been happier if he had been brought up in more humble surroundings!

Chapter 25

The house was silent and only muffled steps could be heard along the corridors. The servants were already considering hanging black draperies in the principal rooms and wondering when they would be going into mourning themselves. Mistress Grant and Elizabeth tiptoed respectfully into Alexander's bedroom to prepare the corpse for burial. The former wept profusely. "I've been here for thirty years and this is the saddest day since the mistress died," she moaned.

They carefully removed all the stained clothes in readiness for washing the body and wrapping the corpse in the winding sheet. Elizabeth was sobbing uncontrollably as she remembered the fate of the fine stallion, which she would never ride again. Mistress Grant was unaware of this and joined her in mourning.

"It doesn't seem long since he was a baby. I don't know what his mother would have thought. She was always specially fond of Alexander. He could do no wrong in her eyes and he could wrap her round his little finger," she remembered fondly, tears running down her cheeks. "She was never able to leave the house, and little Alexander was her only consolation."

Elizabeth wiped the blood from Alexander's mouth. "I think he broke some teeth in the fall," she observed, examining his face very carefully. "The blood seems to have come solely from the front of the mouth. He feels cold, but his skin hasn't quite got the pallor of death." She spoke more slowly. "Let's see. But come here! I think he's not altogether....dead. Bring a glass!"

As she put the cold glass to his mouth she stiffened. She had seen a slight misting and she spoke urgently. "He must be breathing! I think there's some life left. Everything goes by opposites, so that if cold means death, then surely life is warmth. Quick! Let's have a fire lit in the bedroom, stoke up the kitchen oven and warm anything that will keep the heat. Anything like stones wrapped in cloths. Just anything that we can pack around him. Don't tell the master yet because we don't want him to be given false hope. Engage every servant in the household for as long as it takes to revive him."

Mistress Grant ran from the room as if the devil were at her heels. Within minutes all of Elizabeth's instructions were being carried out. Maids panted up the stairs with kindling and logs and hurried into the bedchamber. Two footmen bore piles of blankets from various rooms to the bedside and Elizabeth stroked Alexander's feet and hands as vigorously as she dared. He was soon packed around with warmth by the willing servants and a blazing fire crackled and spat in the hearth.

Elizabeth could not think what to do next. Alexander's breathing was so shallow that his heart must be working at a very low level. What would old Nancy have done? Did he have any internal injuries? Would a dose of spirits help? She was not sure.

Leaving a maid to watch Alexander, Elizabeth and Mistress Grant carried on their normal activities for the time being. The meal was a fraught occasion. Woodall could scarcely eat a mouthful and Lancelot kept his eyes down on the table in case he lost his laconic detachment.

Elizabeth watched the maids coming and going with the dishes, signalling with her eyes that they should on no account give the slightest glimmer of hope. No word that Alexander was struggling for life upstairs must be allowed to upset the master until the situation became clear. Lancelot, weighing his words carefully, broke the silence.

"I shall see Canon Ritschell tomorrow and beg him to come urgently to pray with us. He has known Alexander all his life and will intercede for him. Alexander seemed truly fond of him. I'm sure that there is no better comforter among the men of God."

Woodall still said nothing, but a faint moan escaped his lips, heard only by Elizabeth, who by this time was clenching her teeth to avoid blurting out her message of hope. Unable to endure the tension, she rose presently and excused herself, eagerly hurrying back to Alexander's room, where Mistress Grant had resumed her vigil.

"Is there any change?"

"No. But he is holding his own. His heart-beat seems to be regular, though weak, and we have continued to keep him warm, as you ordered."

The two women sat on chairs at each side of the bed looking tense. Elizabeth wet the invalid's lips with drops of water on her finger, and by and by improved on this by dropping the water directly on to his tongue.

"Please go and have your meal," she suggested to Mistress Grant, "and console the servants only very lightly, because we are still in doubt."

The older woman departed with a squeeze of Elizabeth's shoulder, and the bedchamber fell quiet. When a maid entered, Elizabeth asked her to fetch the books of plants and herbs from her own bedroom. Thus provided she feverishly thumbed through page after page, and her eyes fell on a page concerned with peppermint leaves. She wondered for a while, then asked the maid if she could procure some of these to make a simple medicine. By the time that Mistress Grant returned she had ground up a sweet-smelling infusion in her precious mortar and was testing it on her own tongue.

"This peppermint might help him, if only to bring up wind. We can but try."

Over the late hours they persisted with as many drops of water and trickles of peppermint as they could introduce into Alexander's mouth, with long pauses in between. Each woman took a turn while the other relaxed in her chair. Administering some sort of remedy seemed to reassure them. Any sort of activity was preferable to simply watching and waiting. Mistress Grant replaced the candle and used the old one to inspect Alexander's face more closely.

As it grew dark Elizabeth was still earnestly searching for further remedies. She turned the pages of her books in the dim light, desperate for the crucial plant to bring success, be it foxglove leaves, feverfew, even deadly nightshade or aconite. Yet she dared not experiment! Mistress Grant interrupted her reverie.

"He is still warm and breathing at a low level. If only we could see his eyes we might guess at his condition," she murmured.

Gradually of its own accord his skin seemed to become a healthier colour, though by candlelight this might have been an illusion. After midnight Mistress Grant thought she heard a hiccup coming from the body, but she could not be certain. In the small hours of the new day there was increasing evidence that he was breathing. His chest began to rise and fall, ever so gently. By dawn his heart seemed to be beating normally, though his breathing was still laboured. Apart from that, there was little sign of consciousness.

"Elizabeth, you have brought him back from the dead," Mistress Grant whispered, wide-eyed in wonder. Her tension was yielding to exhaustion.

"Every one in the household has played a part in keeping him warm, but he has not yet completely recovered. There is a long way to go. That fire must be kept going and we must keep him well wrapped up. Now I ought to warn father because we have kept him in misery for too long. He will be eager to hear this news."

She tripped along the corridor to her father's bedroom and crept in, finding him in a deep sleep. He looked old and worn after all the arguments and worries of the last few days. She was loath to waken him but she gently stroked his forehead and whispered: "Father, there is something that I want you to see. Alexander is alive and he is breathing again. The servants have been keeping him warm all night and they have done an excellent job."

Her father, newly raised from a troubled sleep and, remembering his tribulations, groaned: "What is it? Is that you, Elizabeth? Did you say Alexander? Oh, my poor boy!" He could hardly open his eyes.

"Yes. It's good news, father. Alexander is alive but not conscious. Come and see!"

Woodall could hardly believe what she was saying, and was led stumbling along the passage in a sleepy state. Mistress Grant, equally bleary-eyed with fatigue, rose as he entered the room. He stood over his son's bed and in a moment or two was able to discern the slight rise and fall of the chest, and the faint colour in the face. His face crumpled as tears ran down his cheeks. A flush of rejoicing filled his mind, and suddenly his alertness returned. He praised Elizabeth with all his heart: "Elizabeth, you have given me back my son." He bent forward and kissed Alexander on the cheek.

"We must be patient. He will need much nursing," whispered Elizabeth. She put her hands lovingly on her father's shoulders. "Come, I will take you back to bed. It's hardly daylight. We'll look after him for you."

Before he left the room Woodall sank painfully to his knees by the side of the bed, clasping his hands in front of him, and the women joined him in prayer. "Thank you, Lord, for once again giving me back my beloved son from the jaws of Death."

Mistress Grant wept tears of joy and sorrow, remembering all the varied troubles that the household had faced together over the years.

147

Chapter 26

Aunt Caroline came as soon as she was summoned. Arriving in the belief that Alexander was dead, she was amazed to discover the truth, and at her own undemonstrative level she rejoiced that the accident had not been fatal. Her immediate concern was to consult with Mistress Grant about the best course of action, in a tone engendered by many years of shared problems.

"There's nobody in the village, or even in Hexham who can deal with this. Would you agree that Nicholas Liddle must be sought from Newcastle?"

"Yes. Mr. Liddle has been very good many times in the past, when the boys were ill."

Woodall readily agreed and Lancelot rushed out to give Robert Carr this important mission. Robert, like the others, had been astonished at the turn of events, and was delighted that everyone was giving credit to Elizabeth for being so observant, so quick-thinking and so wise in medical matters. Her position in the family was fully reinstated.

He lost no time in saddling the horse, packed the food Mistress Grant had prepared for him and galloped off. In two hours he was talking to Nicholas Liddle in Newcastle, and in another three hours the pair had returned to Nunburn Hall, the surgeon on a hired horse, bearing his best surgical instruments.

They were met at the door of the great house by Woodall himself and were both invited into the shady hall, where jugs of ale were laid out for them.

"My dear Henry!" Liddle burst out. "I came as soon as I could. I am so sorry for your trouble. A riding accident, I hear. Let me see the lad at once."

"I appreciate your promptness," replied Woodall. "He's upstairs in his bedroom. Follow me. You too, Robert."

Robert was flattered by this unaccustomed attention and privilege, and he briskly followed the older men up the oak staircase. Lancelot, in charge of the comings and goings, greeted the newcomers briefly and opened the bedroom door. Robert looked first at Alexander, who lay on his back, pale and corpse-like. Then he saw to his dismay that Mistress Grant and Elizabeth were looking tired and worn, their faces displaying an extremely unhealthy pallor. Nobody spoke.

Liddle approached the bed, peeled back the blankets, and ran his hands lightly over the injured man's exposed upper body. After reflection he said: "Alexander is in a very grave condition. Concussion, broken ribs, and possible damage to the internal organs. The only hope we have is to bleed him."

Elizabeth was on the opposite side of the bed, occasionally allowing tiny drops of ale to fall into Alexander's mouth. With the exasperation of extreme tiredness she snapped: "Alexander has lost enough blood in the accident. Blood keeps the body warm, and I could see yesterday how his hands and feet changed colour as the blood seemed to flow into his limbs. I don't want him bled. But also I can't pretend that we are not at the end of our tether, and your presence is indeed most welcome," she added reconcilingly.

The barber surgeon was startled. Never before had his advice been questioned. He paused at first and glowered at her, scratching the balding pate under his wig. The girl who had gainsaid him was the most intelligent person he had ever met outside professional circles. She might have a reasonable point of view, but he had to appear sure of himself and resented her giving an opposing opinion. He dared not admit his own doubts before the present company, and he definitely had not anticipated coming all this way to be contradicted! She certainly created problems, wherever she was, he mused. In fact she was infuriating, but he could not help admiring her, and she might even be right.

"Well, I don't . . . . . ." he began to stutter.

Elizabeth, taking his hesitation for agreement, pressed on. "I know this by instinct. I feel so sure. However, my father should have the final decision."

Woodall, looking alarmed, was incapable of making such a momentous decision quickly. "I don't know what to think, Nicholas. What will be the result of not bleeding?"

"Much depends on the extent of internal bruising. Bleeding usually gets rid of congestion round the injured parts and allows the body to begin the mending process. Purging and bleeding prolong life, even in a healthy man."

Elizabeth, unconvinced, said nothing, but shook her head. Noting this her father said tremulously: "Since he is in such a grave condition let us leave him in peace for a while. Then we will consider the bleeding."

With that, the men withdrew from the bedside, leaving Aunt Caroline, Mistress Grant, Elizabeth and a maid huddled round the bed. Robert sneaked a last look at Elizabeth as she knelt at the side of the bed. There seemed to be no excuse to speak to her, but there was always another day coming. The men descended to the hall once more and Woodall explained to Liddle the whole chain of events, including Thomas Hubbach's account of the failure of

Alexander's colonial adventure, and the unsavoury gambling episode at Bristol. The barber surgeon was privately horrified by this catalogue of disasters, feeling glad that he was still a bachelor. He commiserated with his old friend but could not offer any advice. His own opinion was that Alexander was a hopeless case, and that this problem would soon be resolved, ... unless Elizabeth could work a miracle!

Leaving the maid to sit with Alexander, and Lancelot to read quietly near the door, Mistress Grant tripped off downstairs to supervise the meal with the help of Aunt Caroline, while Elizabeth took to her bed to catch up on lost sleep.

Robert was invited to dine with the family and the guests. Despite his fatigue he was pleased to accept, enjoying his new position within the favoured inner circle. He had longed to see Elizabeth again and his eyes strayed constantly to the stairs, hoping that she would come down. However, she was already sleeping like a log, too exhausted even to dream about him.

The barber surgeon accepted the offer to tarry longer at the Hall. He liked the country air, and his old friend's company, and did not find it difficult to yield to persuasion. Besides, he was intrigued by Elizabeth and genuinely wished her well with her patient. He admired the fact that she was so devoted to Alexander and stuck by her instincts, however misguided they might be. No wonder his old friend spent such a lot of time in his country seat. However, he had better warn him of the grumblings.

"You are much missed in Newcastle, Henry."

"I can well imagine, and I regret it, but I can't think of matters beyond my own family at this sad time. In due course I shall return to civic affairs, and to my own businesses. Can you tell me if Anthony ffarbrigge is still making progress in his search for fresh supplies of corn for Newcastle?"

"Yes. He is doing well. He was able to buy more wheat somewhere in North Yorkshire and steady supplies from Stockton are arriving weekly. But it wasn't cheap and the millers will be passing on the expense to the bakers, so the restless mob will still be going hungry."

Woodall passed his hand across his eyes. He was emotionally exhausted and felt he could not cope with any more problems. "At any rate I'm told that the present harvest is going to be good. That should ease our worries."

At dinner that evening the conversation centred round Elizabeth's discovery that Alexander had survived his horrible accident. Aunt Caroline was bubbling with the sense that she had brought him back from the dead.

"We had assumed his death," muttered the Mayor, as he picked at his meal, "because of the lack of any sign of life and he was so deathly pale and

150

unconscious."

"Yet these signs are often to be ignored," said the surgeon. "Men apparently killed in the Civil Wars could be revived, with brandy, or with massage. I have a soldier's leg in my store which was cut off a man who is still stumping around Newcastle, having been presumed dead."

To divert the talk from this grisly subject Aunt Caroline reminded them of St. John's story of Lazarus, raised from the dead by Jesus. "We must have faith in the Lord, who alone can decide on life and death," she reflected.

"And we must honour the servants of the Lord, who fulfil his mission," pointed out her brother. "For it was Elizabeth who alone realised that Alexander could be saved." Aunt Caroline nodded.

"Alexander must first be restored to full physical health and even to mental equilibrium," sighed Lancelot, his former anger returning. "He has been a burden to himself and to all of us since he came back from Barbados. At times his behaviour borders on insanity."

"You and Elizabeth must bear the brunt of caring for Alexander," cautioned their father. "I can sense the signs that it is time for me to return to my work in the town." Turning to his sister, he asked: "Could you stay a while longer, Caroline? We have so much to do and so little time to do it."

"I'll stay as long as I'm needed," she replied kindly. " I haven't forgotten that Lancelot's wedding plans have not even been discussed. There is a delightful sequence of arrangements to make, and I hope that I can be part of them. Poor Anne Shafto has no mother, and I may be able to help her."

With that she withdrew to keep an eye on Alexander and to arrange with Mistress Grant the rota of servants who would sit with him during the night.

Robert remembered that he had not yet mentioned to Elizabeth the matter of Ralph Stokoe's hand. If the man did not receive attention soon it might be too late. After the rescue of Alexander from death's door it was only fair to see what Elizabeth could do for their humble farm worker, who might be thought more deserving. He decided to ride across to the cottages where the sick man lived, to make enquiries, and he excused himself from the table.

A sad sight awaited him at the cottage. The burly invalid lay motionless on his poor palliasse of straw. His breathing was laboured and his neck was alarmingly red and swollen.

His wife stood wringing her hands, surprised at the visit and embarrassed by the way her little children crowded round the new arrival, staring up at him round-eyed. The smallest held his bowl of bread and milk, now almost empty, but he continued to scoop it up with his fingers as he watched Robert sit down next to the bed.

"He seems not to get any better, Sir," said the wife, "though we have tried all we know as remedies."

"I'll ask Miss Elizabeth to come to him tomorrow," rejoined Robert. "She has great knowledge of medical remedies, and in addition we have the help of a renowned surgeon from Newcastle who is at present staying with us. Tomorrow Ralph will have the best attention, do not fear."

Catherine Stokoe looked down and said nothing.

Avoiding the welter of little bare feet as he crossed the earth floor to the door of the cottage, he bade them goodnight and took his way home slowly and thoughtfully. Tomorrow he would press Elizabeth and Mr. Liddle to visit Ralph Stokoe, he would supervise the disposal of the dead horse, and he would attempt once more to visit the wheelwright. He looked up at the windows of the bedrooms over at Nunburn Hall, and as he stabled his own horse he saw the empty stall and said two little prayers, one sad and the other cheerful.

Chapter 27

The morning breezes from the sea blew cool across the Barbados plantation where Thomas and his band of men were hard at work clearing the land. His group of eight fellow-Northumbrians, enlarged by newly recruited Irishmen and African slaves, worked side by side, all poorly paid with only the addition of the food and drink required to keep them in a fit state to work. With Uncle Anthony's money he had bought back the four men sold by Alexander to the nearby plantation. To them Thomas was a God-sent benefactor, whose commonsense and kindness were in stark contrast to the lack of these qualities in Alexander Woodall. Although younger than most of the group he had soon earned their respect for his leadership and honesty. He was reliable and they felt safe with him.

"We prefer workin' for a man from Northumberland, that we can understand, to workin' for these greedy cavaliers, ready to abandon everythin' here and return to England at the first opportunity," said John Dinning, who had come from Woodedge Farm, near Nunburn Hall. "This island is bad enough, without being switched from place to place."

As far as adaptation to the tropical climate was concerned all the men had tried hard. They had learned how to avoid ants, cockroaches, chigger fleas, land crabs, snakes and lizards, as part of their survival techniques. William Askew used to have the others in fits of laughter as he joked about their plight.

"If we could get the snakes to eat the crabs and lizards, and the cockroaches to eat the fleas and ants, we could make a stew of all the snakes and cockroaches and be rid of the lot. Then the little men gnawing in my stomach would be happy, and Barbados might be a good place to live," he said stroking his stomach amid raucous laughter.

As the hungry men egged him on, he diversified into higher flights of fancy: "Soon there won't be a mosquito in sight, we'll have scoffed the lot!"

These diversions always ended in hysterical laughter, for they knew the realities of the tropics and did not want to dwell on them. Most of the men went barefoot and had been frequently bitten by both mosquitoes and fleas till their skin hardened to the texture of leather. Their only consolation was that they had missed the other pestilences - the 1661 infestation of chiggers and large poisonous worms, and the arrival in 1662 of hosts of caterpillars which, like locusts, stripped everything green - and they had heard of violent fevers, plague, and other malignant diseases which carried off dozens of people at a time. Rats and mice, swarming on the ships calling at Bridgetown, were blamed for much of this, and Thomas had warned the men to stay away from the town whenever there was an outbreak.

The smallest of the Tynedale men, Edward Buckham, had been the first of them to adapt to sleeping in a hammock, essential to avoid the insect menace on the floor of their fragile shack.

He had been in the first group which came with Alexander Woodall, and rough homemade hammocks were among their first acquisitions.

"It's only because you're little and skinny that you can fit into a hammock," said the others, who gave him no credit for being compact and athletic. Uriah Pattinson, with his broad shoulders and long legs, had found the hammock almost impossible to master, and it took several minutes for two of his companions to lift him in, accompanied by many groans and giggles before he got the hang of it.

"Don't break my leg," he complained. "You're twisting it the wrong way."

"Oh, you'll never miss it, if it comes off."

"No. And you'll never miss your head if I knock it off."

Latterly, he had tried to mount the beast himself, announcing as he was about to begin: "Hammocks are like horses. You sidle up to them, stare them in the eye and leap on them boldly before they can resist. If they think you're soft, they'll buck you off." Because he most often landed on the floor, his antics were a constant source of merriment.

Their only recent cause of grief had been the death of one of the overworked horses used to crush the cane in the gin-gang, and to transport sugar to the harbour at Bridgetown. The poor beast was no sooner dead than it had been cut up, cooked and eaten, with nothing wasted. The white men were given the best cuts and the negroes the rest. Uriah had sat for hours chewing and sucking the prime bones of the beast, for all the goodness he could extract from them.

"Now we're waiting for one of the oxen to drop dead," chuckled William Askew. "Perhaps we should work them harder? Or a nice bit of that little donkey might go down well." As he said this he smacked his lips hungrily.

"Don't wish that," retorted Thomas. "Do you know how much these beasts cost? Twice as much as a slave, that's what. We must be as careful as possible.

We must strive to make this the best plantation on Barbados."

"Have you been to see the plantation set up by Colonel Drax ?" asked Joseph Routledge, one of the more thoughtful men. "That must be the best plantation on the island. We heard that he had improved on the Brazilian method of refinin' sugar, but I don't know much about it."

"Yes," replied Thomas. "I had time to call there one Sunday after the church service. It's a really big undertakin', but Drax has returned to England and I hear that there is not the same drive amongst those in charge now."

"Well, he's not the only one to leave Barbados," commented Joseph. "Those last two Irishmen who joined us told me they had heard stories on the ship that fetched them here. The seamen reckoned that, since the price of sugar went down, hundreds of men have gone to Jamaica, Surinam and even Carolina and Virginia to grow tobacco."

"Aye, the tobacco here is not so good," said William Askew. "Soon there'll be only us left."

"That is, if the Dutch and the French allow us. I gather that we're in another war with the Dutch," observed Thomas. "But, if it's like the last Dutch war, everybody will just ignore it, and get on with the money-makin'."

Thomas had established friendships with several other small landowners in his locality, most of whom lived on the same level of hand-to-mouth existence, as they all strove hard to clear the land, keep the fields planted, and their men working. He had already learned that, over the thirty years since the British colony had been established, sugar had proved to be a more profitable crop, with cotton, and ginger as alternative cash crops. Indigo was much in demand in Europe, and though it yielded several crops a year, it required a considerable outlay for vats and labour.

"The owners of the really large estates are eager to buy out such as us, and they alone can grow enough crops like maize and potatoes to feed their men," said Thomas, "as well as a broad range of cash crops. We'll always be in debt to them until we can grow enough maize to feed the slaves."

"Aye," commented Joseph Routledge. "Only the rulin' clique grows rich and we have to sweat and take an early death."

Thomas remained optimistic. "At least we have benefited from the experience of the older planters."

"Even we were able to warn you from our hard-gotten experience."

Thomas continued: "Yes. The main lesson is that now at least we know that sugar cane is best planted horizontally in long shallow trenches, rather than in the small holes that were used at first. You remember how the high winds and heavy rains used to smash down all our canes ? Well, we should do better these days, with sprouts comin' out of every knot on the cane, and let's hope it still grows to eight feet tall."

In his first position of trust, Thomas had kept his head and remained immune to the temptations of rum drinking, which had ruined so many other sugar-planters, and his labourers appeared similarly abstemious. Their fervid wish for their families to join them, however, threatened the perfect peace of the plantation.

During a brief pause they sat in a circle sucking chopped pineapple. Thomas once more reassured the men: "I have written home to ask Mr. Woodall for permission for your womenfolk and children to be sent out here. I expect that he'll consider this matter when the corn harvest is over at home. If we work hard now it will be a happy place for them. We'll just have to wait."

John Dinning, the oldest of the Tynedale men, had become better adjusted to the new colonial life, but sorely missed his wife and sons.

"If only they might come out here in the next few months, I should be content. In black moments I feel that we have lost touch with our families forever. I just fear that Mr. Woodall might rely on us so much that he won't allow any of us to leave. Our labour is necessary here because you never know when those blacks are goin' to die, like those on our neighbours' plantations. They're strong but many of them are gone before their time. The poor souls have nothin' to live for because they miss their own country so much, and I've seen them tell with sign language what the dreadful voyage here is like, and how many of them die, and are thrown overboard for the fish."

Thomas replied: "At least we have hope. I'll send a letter to my cousin Elizabeth and see if she can persuade Mr. Woodall to send your families out here."

"That's just the start of our worries, when you think of the rough seas and pirates. Then when they arrive here, imagine how hard they will find it. Let's hope God will take care of them," said John. "None of us is gettin' younger, and we have no control over our fortunes. I wish we'd never come out here. I'd just love to feel the cool Northumbrian breezes from the moors and hear the sound of the pipes again. We all miss our family life, and I keep thinkin' of the fun at harvest time."

James Graham chimed in : "Aye, I'm missin' my little lads, I can tell you."

The others nodded. Thomas gave them a shrewd look. "Our success depends on how hard we work."

John resumed with some vehemence: "I used to think it was hard at Nunburn, but I'd give the rest of my life for just one year at home. Never mind, Thomas, it's been much better since you arrived. That Alexander is a demon and will destroy anythin' in his headlong rush to chaos. He's a child of the devil, and will carry anybody with him in his path to destruction. As far as I am concerned he should stay where he is. I dread him comin' anywhere near me. Let him rot in Hell!"

"Some things are better left unsaid," replied Thomas simply.

As they were resuming their back-breaking toil, a delivery waggon drawn by two horses pulled in to the edge of the sugar field and a shout came across from the driver's mate: "Package from England for Thomas Hubbach! Where shall I drop it?" Thomas walked over, holding out his hand. "Thank you," he said. Turning to the others he offered a glimmer of hope. "This might be the important message we're expectin'. I'll take it to Bridgetown to be read."

The men went on sharpening their blades as they tried hard to stifle their emotions. The letter might bring fresh hope, and things could scarcely become worse.

They were unaware of an ominous thin trail of cloud which had appeared high in the southern sky. It would change their lives.

Chapter 28

It was on a warm sunny morning when Elizabeth and the surgeon made their way to Ralph Stokoe's cottage, carrying the all-important bag of medical instruments. As soon as they were admitted to the cottage they could sense that things had taken a turn for the worse. Ralph's wife, Catherine, exhausted from her ministrations, had been angry with the children who were huddled in a corner, very subdued, and she was sitting distraught by the bedside.

"Thank you for comin', but I'm afraid Ralph is in a worse state now. He's had a restless night and has eaten nothin'. He has been shiverin' on and off all night and we have been coverin' him up with everythin' we can find." Rags covered the bed.

They examined the patient and found him perspiring heavily with fever, and the cut on his hand suppurating badly. The arm was inflamed along its length and his head lolled on the badly swollen neck. Elizabeth carefully put down her potion of feverfew.

"A clear case for bleeding! Bleeding reduces fever," pronounced Nicholas Liddle firmly, and immediately began to fish for the lancet in his waistcoat pocket, carefully removing the silver guard.

Elizabeth viewed Ralph thoughtfully. The poison from the wound was spreading around his body. Perhaps removing some of the bad blood might improve his condition, and indeed could make it no worse. Elizabeth nodded agreement, and the surgeon opened his bag, preparing to bleed the patient.

He directed Elizabeth: "Roll up his sleeve and bind his arm above the elbow with the cloth to stop the blood. That's it. Not too tight. Good." He took a bowl out of his bag to catch the blood. Grasping the blade between his thumb and forefinger, and steadying his hand with the other three fingers, he pierced the vein and the blood began to flow, staining the poor man's tattered shirt. Alas, with the first incision of the knife the patient moaned. The rest happened with shocking speed. All this seemed to be the last straw for Ralph's weakened body, and with a shudder he breathed his last. A chilling silence ensued and then, as reality dawned, his wife wailed in despair, pulling out her hair and rocking to and fro. Her worst fears had been confirmed and she was devastated that she had lost the family's sole bread-winner.

"My children! My poor bairns! Who will look after us now?" she choked.

Elizabeth was also worried about the fate of the little children, and desperately tried to reassure Catherine, hugging her around the shoulders.

"Mr. Woodall will see to your needs, you know that. Look after the children, Catherine. I'll fetch Martha Askew from next door to see to you."

They laid Ralph down on his bed and covered his face, packed their instruments and quietly let themselves out. Elizabeth went to the neighbouring cottage to seek help while Liddle waited on the track, occasionally turning to stare back at the cottages, trying to hide how depressed he felt. As they walked back towards Nunburn Hall, he tested her reaction.

"Well, our visit ended in disaster," he confessed.

"Yes. Nothing could be done for him. I've just recalled that Nancy sometimes used cobwebs on fresh wounds and reckoned they stopped the poison, but I fear that even with all her potions and salves, she couldn't have remedied his complaint. These accidents on the farm happen so easily, and if they aren't treated at once it's hopeless. We were powerless in the hands of the Lord."

"What! Cobwebs? Where is the potion made from spiders' webs that could cure a blood disease? I've never heard of such a thing," was the ill-natured retort.

They fell silent. Robert, on horseback, intercepted them when they had nearly reached the Hall.

"Any news?" he asked anxiously.

Elizabeth shook her head grimly without looking at him, and Robert understood.

"I'm sorry. We've lost a good man, and we'll have to help Catherine all we can. I'll call there at once."

He pressed on to the labourer's cottage to make the usual arrangements for a funeral. He would call on the parson in the village and pass on the tragic message.

As they walked up the steps to the Hall, Elizabeth muttered: "Perhaps we shouldn't even have tried."

Liddle, to whom death was no stranger, only humphed. He had despaired over too many cases of blood-poisoning to be long emotionally affected by this latest.

Back at the Hall, Elizabeth resumed her other tasks. She took her place by Alexander's bed and continued with the vigil, being joined shortly afterwards by the barber surgeon who peered closely at the patient.

"It looks as if there is no change. His vitality is still low, though he is maintaining his colour. Has he had anything to eat?"

"No. Mistress Grant says he will take only liquid, and that just in drops from the glass."

"Time will tell. Perhaps the smell of a tasty stew might revive his hunger?"

"A good idea. I'll have a word with Mistress Grant." Elizabeth was anxious to console the surgeon after his unsuccessful morning but still feared that he might suggest bleeding again.

It was not till evening that Elizabeth received a sign that Alexander did have a chance of survival. She had been dozing fitfully, curled up in the large chair by the bed, when she woke with a strange feeling. She looked towards Alexander and was alarmed to see two hostile eyes scrutinising her. She shivered and approached the bed, attempting to smile at him.

"At last you are awake, Alexander. Do you wish for a drink or shall I fetch your father?"

His voice was barely a croak but he indicated with his tongue that he needed a drink. Elizabeth felt strangely threatened as she catered to his needs and was relieved when a maid came in to replace her. She hastened out of the room to tell the news to the rest of the family who were gathered in the parlour.

Liddle was the first to congratulate her. " I must admit I didn't think he had much of a chance of recovery. He was lucky that he had you to look after him."

Her proud father hugged her, secretly awed by her success. "Elizabeth, you are my precious gem."

Straightaway the two men went up to see the patient, Liddle beginning to have prickling doubts about bleeding as a solution to every medical crisis. Here was one patient apparently recovering against all the odds without the help of bleeding or his ministrations, while the farm hand had perished at once when it was applied! He resolved to think hard about the matter.

"Well, Henry, I really think that Alexander has turned the corner and will make progress with patient nursing. My part here seems to be over and I am more than willing that Elizabeth should take charge of him. Her herbal remedies, plus good feeding, ought to meet his needs. If I ever want an assistant I may send for her, mark my words."

Chapter 29

A few days later Lancelot sought the help of Elizabeth now that they would be able to concentrate on his marriage arrangements.

"We'll have to send an invitation to Jeffery Shafto to bring Anne to stay with us. I'm sure that you and Aunt Caroline will make them feel thoroughly at home. What do you think?"

"That would be exciting. We'll all be able to get to know Anne better."

The prompt acceptance arrived, with a request that, as the bride's mother was deceased, they might be accompanied by Anne's younger sister, Maria.

Aunt Caroline was again preoccupied with making arrangements for this important visit. One morning she came into Alexander's room while Elizabeth was feeding him, asking her: "You don't mind sharing the room next door with me while we are entertaining the new company, and it will mean you are nearer to Alexander. Perhaps you can take more of the strain of looking after him as I will be busier during the visit."

Elizabeth paused, not relishing the increased contact with the disgruntled invalid, and then hastily assured her: "Of course I don't mind. I'm looking forward to helping to entertain the visitors and I'll do anything else I can to help."

She resumed the feeding process, but thought she had detected a malicious gleam in Alexander's eye. Maybe he had sensed that she was a little put out by the arrival of the future mistress of Nunburn Hall, and her own consequent inferior position.

By now the barber surgeon had left for Newcastle, and Elizabeth had full responsibility for her half-brother. As the weeks went by, there was a steady improvement in Alexander's health, and he was trying to walk, with help, but Elizabeth thought that he might be left with a limp. She also suspected that he could move round more freely than he pretended, because both Aunt Caroline and herself had been puzzled by strange noises from his room in the night.

Alexander's plight became of secondary importance as everyone awaited the new arrivals at the Hall. Even Lancelot showed signs of an unaccustomed apprehension when the day dawned that his designated bride, Anne Shafto, and her family were to visit Nunburn Hall for the first time since the ball. A groom was sent to the gates to give news of their arrival and everyone was alerted to attend the reception. The expectation spread throughout the house and was even communicated to Alexander in his bedroom.

The watching groom sounded his horn and within minutes a splendid coach followed by two smartly liveried horsemen, rolled majestically up the drive and all eyes were concentrated on the next mistress of Nunburn Hall as she alighted, to be warmly greeted by Lancelot and his father. The first impressions were good, and Elizabeth applauded Lancelot's choice. However, as she studied the new bride-to-be more closely, she noticed that there was nothing natural about her demeanour. Tall and gracious in the smallest movement that she made, it was immediately obvious that she possessed a calculated air of effortless authority that would not be gainsaid, and a charisma that commanded instant attention.

Her clothes were in tune with her rank and reflected her whole image. She wore a beautifully embroidered gold satin dress of an Elizabethan design, decorated with exquisite lace, which formed a collar that was raised at the back of the neck. A waistcoat of the same material emphasized her slim waist and dropped to a heart-shaped design at the front of the dress. The sleeves were ruched and full, narrowing at the elbow, and coming to a point at the wrist, also edged with the same beautiful lace, which was obviously of foreign manufacture. She expertly controlled a small train as she came up the steps to greet Elizabeth.

"Lancelot has told me all about you," she said enigmatically, greeting her with a smile. At close quarters Elizabeth was able to study her face, which was friendly in a formal way, but inscrutable. She was at that stage in a woman's life when her charms are at their height. Her forehead was high and smooth, with fair curls adorning her face in a naturally attractive way. Her skin, in sharp contrast, was treated with white cosmetics, emphasising the black velvet spots attached at well-chosen places on her face. She had high cheek bones and a prominent thin nose, which swelled at its tip, as if contrived, giving her a haughty appearance.

She swept on past Elizabeth into the hall, leaving the fragrant drift of lavender in her wake, and swiftly captivating Aunt Caroline with her charms. As Lancelot brushed past, following in Anne's wake, he exchanged a brief glance with Elizabeth, enquiring but inconclusive. Following him was Jeffery Shafto, the prospective father-in-law, who turned out to be a well-fed and jolly fellow, determined to enjoy the present occasion. He, too, was dressed a la mode, but in a more restrained way, as befitted his age. He wore ample black stockings just visible above high boots, and a well-cut black velvet coat, with great quantities of lace falling from the elbows. Every available pocket spilled over with white handkerchiefs, also edged with lace. His black hat, decorated with white feathers, was removed to reveal a wig of tightly curled black ringlets, its width being commensurate with his status as a wealthy landowner. His portly figure tottered up the steps, as best he could, on his high heeled boots which brandished huge buckles. He was followed by his younger daughter, who was well-dressed, but in a fashion not to rival the appearance of her sister. Maria's charms were poised to blossom as soon as her sister's marriage was finalised.

They were ushered into the drawing room, with Lancelot on tenterhooks, catering to everyone's needs, but he finally took his place in attendance behind Anne's chair. Anne had the air of one who expected to be entertained, rather than to please, and surveyed the company in a composed silence, effortlessly dominating the proceedings. All the members of the family felt obliged in turns to maintain the steady flow of the conversation, and even Elizabeth felt somewhat abashed in the shadow of this new society beauty.

Through all of this Anne kept a gracious and approving presence. Gradually the tension eased, and Jeffery Shafto proved to be a master of the comical anecdote, which, with his infectious grin, inspired a great deal of laughter.

"Upon my word, our schoolmaster was uncommonly keen on tormenting us with mental arithmetic. He gave me the old teaser about the times and distance involved in the journey of a coach from Newcastle to York. What was its average speed? When I estimated the speed at eighty miles per hour the rest of the class fell out of their desks with mirth. This was turned into hysteria when he told me I was a clever boy and should bring our horses to school to put them to the test."

Elizabeth's eyes sparkled at such stories, and even Woodall permitted himself a gentle smile. The atmosphere in the large room further improved with the arrival of tea, which at Nunburn was a new delicacy, but to the new arrivals seemed commonplace. Elizabeth noted that Robert was eager to discover the charms of the simpering Maria, and was very attentive, standing by the window and pointing to the far horizon, indicating with apparent pride and pleasure the direction of his family estates. Elizabeth heard him saying: "Yes, you can just see the road to the manor house on the horizon."

As he said this, Maria moved closer towards him, her startling blue eyes peering into the distance. Alone now, it occurred to Elizabeth that she had no lasting function at the Hall, so she made her excuses and withdrew upstairs, to relieve the maid who sat there and to find succour in her somewhat doubtful role as Alexander's nurse. She knew that Alexander would not appreciate her efforts. In fact she would not be surprised if in a very strange way he resented her. However, it was not long before Anne was again infringing her privacy as she was brought upstairs to view her bedroom and to be introduced to her future brother-in-law, Alexander. She treated him with the same cool detachment as she commiserated with him over his accident, and nothing seemed to affect her equilibrium.

"Hunting and riding accidents are so tiresome, and you were fortunate to survive. Horses are such unreliable creatures at times!" were her last words as she followed Lancelot out through the door.

"So that is to be the new mistress of Nunburn," Alexander sneered. "There will be no place for you here soon, or indeed myself. Father, I predict, will be captivated by her, and Lancelot will see no wrong. She will be mistress of all she surveys from here to Barbados, and nobody will be able to do a thing about it. Mark my words."

"Well, what do we want to do about it, Alexander? You speak as if you believe there is something wrong in your brother marrying. Fate rules our lives, and we must accept the new turn of events, and help as much as we can," protested Elizabeth, suppressing new fears within herself that there might be unsuspected changes which could affect her in a very tangible way. Her first impressions were that her own qualities, which had previously been so valued, would now be overlooked in a new and harsher regime, based on artificial concepts with which it was impossible for her to identify. She felt totally impotent in the face of breeding, wealth and education, which, she sensed, brought with them a hypocritical veneer of some consideration for others, while being totally motivated by selfish ends,

Mistress Grant fluttered here and there, showing Shafto to his room and his daughters to theirs, and ordering the footmen to deposit the visitors' luggage in the proper places. She returned at last to Elizabeth in Alexander's room.

"There will be extra work here for the duration of this visit, what with meals, laundry, and cleaning. Could you help me by asking some of the women on the farms to come in specially?"

"Yes," replied Elizabeth. "I was thinking of that myself. It's as well the harvest is behind us and the women have less to do. But I shall have a word with Robert as to which of the cottagers I should approach first."

Alexander asked them to help him out of bed to his chair, and, thus transferred, he proceeded to stare silently out of the window across the fields, his lips compressed in a sulky fury. Nothing had ever been right in his whole life. It was just his luck to have an invalid mother who was so very silly and absolutely useless, a clever brother who did not care for him, and who was going to inherit the huge family fortune, and a father who did not understand him. What a family to be born into!

Then, what about Elizabeth, a veritable witch! It was his further misfortune to choose a horse called Periculo that could not even jump a hedge and now, through him, he was left a cripple! He wished that he had not been brought back to life. What was his existence worth now if he could not even walk properly? He would make that self-satisfied Elizabeth pay the price for being so clever as to interfere with his life! He would find a way to get the better of all these cleversides. And he hated the Shaftos. They had not offered a drop of sympathy for his misfortune, and they were going to take away all his mother's money that had been promised to him. He did not believe that it had disappeared as his father had said. They were deceiving him because they wanted what was rightfully his.

Alexander had plenty of time to turn all of these grudges over and over in his mind as his condition improved. He would hide his gathering strength from that scheming bitch who looked after him. He could not stand Elizabeth pointing out how much better he was, as if he were her little wooden doll. A lot of people would have to pay for his misfortune, and he would have a great deal of pleasure in being the one to achieve it. "It is the will of God," his father had said yesterday. "You should remember the patience of Job."

Well, he would show them. Patience indeed! His scheme would confound those who had thrown him down. Let them beware the will of Alexander Woodall!

Chapter 30

The weather changed, and the trees, which for days had looked so exquisitely beautiful, clothed in their warm autumnal glow, were in a single night of frost transformed into stark black skeletons that presaged the coming of the icy tentacles of winter. However, even the breath of the colder air was welcome, as Elizabeth set out to visit the cottagers, thankful to be temporarily free. As the weeks passed she had become heartily sick of the monarch of the sickbed to whose welfare she was still obliged to attend.

Anne Shafto, having breakfasted early, was already in the parlour, and noticed Elizabeth as she set out on her short journey to the cottages. The two fathers had gone to Newcastle to consult Nicholas Hawden, the family lawyer. As Lancelot was abroad, supervising the estate, a whole day lay in front of her, with only her younger sister Maria to keep her company. What could she do that she had not done yesterday, and the day before, and the day before that, and the week before that? She could resume her needlework, stitching beautiful cushions that would grace her new home with Lancelot, but her eyes were feeling the strain and quickly became tired. She could continue her correspondence with her female cousins in Yorkshire, who were equally as bored as herself, but sometimes they gave her welcome glimpses of watering places that she had never visited.

She tapped her foot impatiently as she considered the possibilities. It was too cold now to exercise in the garden so she would patiently watch the sun's progress from the house as it moved slowly across the sky, defining her day. She would eat exactly at noon, and spend the whole afternoon in great boredom exchanging stories with Aunt Caroline. Then at sunset her eyes would be diverted to the fire, weaving wonderful tales from the pictures in the flames. There would be consolation in her world of dreams, nurtured by the many books she had read, and the tales recounted of strange faraway places, which she was never sure were real or imaginary.

She wondered what Elizabeth was doing that seemed so important to Lancelot and she longed to find out. She knew that her father would disapprove of her mixing with these village people, or indeed anyone below her own social standing. She even wondered about the situation with Elizabeth herself. Her new sister-in-law was delightful in her friendly acceptance of the Shafto family, in her lively conversation and her apparently inexhaustible energy. She was a skilled horse-rider, an able nurse, a learned herbalist and could read Latin. In addition she was so beautiful that Anne could not think of any lady of her acquaintance with whom she might be favourably compared. Yet her brother Lancelot was even more gifted!

How she looked forward to the prospect of marriage with the tall, dark, handsome, clever, concerned, rich, sensible, dashing and, above all, devoted Lancelot. He was always so meticulously dressed, he was thoughtful and considerate, yet firm and authoritative. She liked the way he looked everyone straight in the eye and in his reliability she felt safe with him. She looked forward to the prospect of having children like him to relieve her life of boredom. But what if they turned out like Alexander? She sighed, and with great deliberation flicked a piece of fluff from the armchair. How she longed to go to Newcastle in the coach and flaunt her beautiful clothes, to see, and be seen, and be a credit to her father, and soon to Lancelot. There she would have the freedom to mix more freely, away from the social constraints of the countryside.

She would love to ride a horse like the men, but had never had any practice, and, in truth, she was afraid to try it. Was it really ladylike to ride? Alas, soon the coach would be abandoned for the winter as the roads became dangerously impassable and all travel would be at an end. She was looking forward to Elizabeth coming back, to find out what was happening in the outside world. She could not herself break loose from her own restrictions, afraid that the social edifice on which her life had always depended, might collapse beneath her.

So she sat on her chair by the window, straightened her hair and her dress, and concentrated on looking composed, contented, beautiful, and detached, and above all, very happy. She was the perfect daughter, and would be the perfect wife. Yet all these matrimonial worries, she mused, were a bit disconcerting because, if her father were not as generous as the Woodalls expected him to be, it was possible that everything would fall through.

Then she remembered the poem which Lancelot had passed to her before he had set out on estate business that morning. Though it was in his own handwriting she wondered if it was of his own composition and, if so, it appeared that his mind was not altogether preoccupied with money. She read it again, cherishing every line.

The Song of Love

Come love, pass with me through life's long course
And feel the cloak of joy protecting with its robust force,
Our shelter from storms and fate's hard blows.

Rich treasures strew the way, like petals of the rose.
I speak not of gold or silver, but of those happy days
Which we will find at each turn of the maze.
Let devotion to each other shine from our eyes
As sun and moon beams bend down from the skies.
New delights arising day by day build up as common ground
While old memories seem as treasures freshly found.
Faith, love and hope are ours forever,
Nourishing the tender buds of our eager feeling,
And all our cherished vows of dedication sealing.
For it is true love that is the most precious treasure.
And true love that gives a complete measure.

Yes, they were Lancelot's own words. Anne refolded the message and carefully secreted it inside her bodice, safe there, for her eyes alone. She was aware that she was being watched with amusement by her inquisitive sister, who was pretending to be engrossed in her embroidery but furtively raising her eyes from time to time. If Lancelot felt like that then surely there would be a favourable outcome in Newcastle! She remembered how she had been warned: "Love is a friend, fire, heaven, hell." She was going to make sure that it was not the last.

Entombed in her own stifling boredom, she suddenly remembered the telescope that Lancelot had shown her. She would find it, and spend the time gazing at the cottages that Elizabeth found so fascinating. She had just taken up her stance at the window when Elizabeth returned and quietly let herself into the parlour. Elizabeth's dress and shoes bore traces of mud splashes and the whiff of cottage smells still hung on her clothing. The eyes and nose of the immaculate Maria were offended, and she gave a slight sniff of disapproval, but Elizabeth had already made a valiant attempt to clean up, so she ignored the implied criticism and approached Anne.

"You're looking through the wrong end of the telescope," she whispered in her ear.

"Oh dear, I'm sorry. I didn't realise it," said Anne, blushing.

"Now what is so interesting that you need a telescope to see it, and how on earth did you come by it? I haven't seen one since I was in Newcastle."

"It was something that Lancelot bought at the Stourbridge fair, near Cambridge. It makes life so interesting by bringing everything much nearer. He says it came originally from a ship."

"And what is it that you wish to study so carefully?"

"Well, it's the cottagers down yonder. You told me something of their history and I am eager to learn more about their lives." By now she had managed to focus successfully. "For example, take the people at this nearer end. It's like watching the actors in a living performance. They seem to be so busy, and even the children have their tasks. But why are they emptying buckets into holes near the trees?"

"Come on, Anne! Use your imagination," Elizabeth said, genuinely surprised.

"Really, I should think there are a lot of strong smells down there. Their carpets will be quite dirty."

Elizabeth raised her brows. "I'll take you down to them, if you wish. Perhaps you would like to talk to them?"

"No, I don't think father would approve, and I can see them well enough from here. There seem to be a lot of children around the third cottage. Who are they?"

"Those are Ralph Stokoe's lovely children. I told you about them. He died before you arrived."

"Oh, yes, I remember now! But who provides the money to feed them?"

"Their mother has been given a job at the Hall, and Mistress Grant sees that they get enough food and fuel. The neighbours help to look after the children, and though their mother makes a great effort to keep them happy, life is still very hard. They scarcely understand what has happened, but there will surely be dire times to come."

"You mentioned the eight families that have men in Barbados. Where do they live?" Anne enquired, turning the telescope in order to scrutinise the line of cottages.

"There are two houses together. One is having its heather thatching repaired. Can you see it? That's where two of them live, the Askews and the Pattinsons, and the others live on the outlying farms," explained Elizabeth. "I had a word with them yesterday. Although the wives are worried about taking the children on such a long sea voyage, Robert has explained to them that the climate is good, and the soil fertile, and I know that they are eager to see their husbands again."

"Good! Lancelot will be relieved, and it sounds as if his business will flourish."

She continued to peer intensely at her own personal theatre set.

"How exciting it must be to live in those houses and have the chance to sail off to Barbados! How I wish I lived there!"

"I wouldn't," retorted Elizabeth. "Yesterday they were all in tears at the thought of leaving the rest of their relations."

"All this squinting down the telescope tires my eyes!" complained Anne.

"Well, put it down," suggested Elizabeth. "Surely you have had enough by now."

"No! It's too interesting. Oh dear! One of the children is hitting Ralph Stokoe's smallest and he seems to be crying. See that they get something extra from the kitchen tomorrow. Now, I really can't stand anymore. I feel quite dizzy," protested Anne, and she gave up, fatigued.

She was growing to appreciate Elizabeth. She herself cultivated a rather detached attitude because she was very shy, and immediately retreated into herself when anyone tried to take her over in any way. She fiercely resisted control, but Elizabeth was too interested in other people to encroach, and she felt comfortable in hiding behind her.

"Sorry, I haven't asked after Alexander today. How is he?" Her concern sounded more genuine.

"We think that he is better than he pretends to be. He arranged for Canon Ritschell to visit him today. That's why I have some spare time. That reminds me. He has been a long time upstairs. We will have to call him down for tea."

The kitchen was informed, and soon the great scholar, comfortably ensconced in one of the ample chairs in the parlour, was charming Anne with his stories, in his delicious continental accent, and while they chatted Elizabeth was using the key to open the precious chest, to prepare the dishes of tea.

Ritschell leaned forward. "Alexander seems in a poor state of health at the moment, and he has turned to God in his distress. This afternoon he quoted the second coming of Christ: 'Old things shall be done away and behold all things shall become new.' I believe his affliction has purified him."

Elizabeth and Anne stopped drinking, looking at each other with raised eyebrows for a moment, as if transfixed.

"Yes," Canon Ritschell continued, "He wishes prayers to be said on his behalf by the whole family today in his bedroom, and makes a separate request for the servants to gather together to pray for him downstairs."

"He has never said this before," interrupted Elizabeth, rather puzzled.

"It was a great consolation to me to see Alexander's face beaming with the light of the Lord's salvation for poor sinners, and I was happy to assure him that all his sins had been forgiven. Then he wished everyone would share in his new birth as a Christian. He is a quite outstanding young man. I shall do anything in my power to lighten his heavy load and ensure his happy entry into eternity."

"You will soon have to set off for Hexham before it is too dark. We will have to arrange prayers at once," the practical Elizabeth suggested. The tea-drinking ended hurriedly.

Chapter 31

As Elizabeth and wise old Canon Ritschell walked up the stairs together, the latter took his companion by the arm. "As you grow older, Elizabeth, you will be increasingly aware that the way to Salvation is to see only people's good qualities and believe in the power of good. Many of my parishioners have not absorbed this simple truth. It is often jealousy of others, Satan's evil force, that stems progress and makes fools of us all. The common good is the only way forward. We must try to help Alexander as much as we can or we will all suffer. The world is surely a mirror of ourselves."

And so it was that the family found themselves in Alexander's bedroom. Alexander sat stiffly upright in bed, well padded with cushions, and indeed Canon Ritschell was right. There was a new flush in the young man's cheeks, and, as he beamed at everyone, he appeared strangely exhilarated. Maybe it was because he disliked them all so intensely.

Elizabeth, Anne, Lancelot, Maria, Robert, Mistress Grant, and Canon Ritschell crowded dutifully round the bed in the small airless room. The clergyman began with extremely long prayers for the sick, and thankfulness for the life of Ralph Stokoe. Then he continued: "Our dear brother, Alexander, has been struck down through no fault of his own in the first flush of his youth by his present affliction, owing to the dreadful accident that he has suffered."

Alexander looked on him benignly with a smug smile, secretly scorning the foolishness of the old devil. As the others were lifting their heads, expecting the long prayers to be over, another flood of exhortations started, asking them to pray for their beloved brother. Maria swayed towards Robert. Elizabeth could not have been concentrating on the proceedings because she grimaced.

When the canon had finished, Alexander himself began a set of requests for the salvation of sinners, detailing all the circumstances in which penitence should be sought, and then rambled on.

"Let us quietly consider the crimes by which humanity is ensnared. Preserve us, dear Lord from the pursuit of avarice in its various forms which, without restraint, could trap us in its deadly power; from selfishness, which can make us unaware of the needs of others, and also from the attitude of the ingrate who, surrounded in plenty, can be totally unaware of his good fortune. Above everything let us devote ourselves solely to the welfare of others. Yea, Lord, I see Thee coming through the darkness, coming like the morn, with healing on Thy wings."

His voice then seemed to slow to a cadence welcome to the listeners and, expecting an end to the oration, they relaxed slightly, but too soon. With renewed strength Alexander pronounced slowly: "So that we all shall reach the ultimate rest of sweet salvation". The last two words were spoken with such piety and emphasis that again everyone thought that he had reached the longed-for climax. With the resumption of the rambling, Canon Ritschell was almost convinced that Alexander could do better than himself at Hexham Abbey.

"I praise the Lord for the gift of man's best friend, the horse, usually a life-preserving helpmate who bears its burden so nobly. Yea, in battle and in peace time, an indispensable companion and willing servant. Such a noble horse has met its end in my service! Only last week, sitting at this very window, I had a vision of a strange portent in the clouds. Out of the midst of many rearing white steeds, and gradually growing as it appeared from the East, a great black horse galloped towards a group of angels, who, playing with stringed and wind instruments, produced the most melodious heavenly music that could be imagined. The black horse was immediately accepted into the portals of heaven and disappeared with the glory it deserved."

Alexander sighed with satisfaction, clasping his hands across his breast, while Elizabeth glared at him.

At this point the ladies were showing distinct signs of wilting and indeed the limbs of all that were assembled were weary and aching through having stood so long. They were further dismayed when Alexander requested that they kneel and bend their heads in silent prayer for his recovery, and future success. As they did so, there was a long silence, and Alexander surveyed his well-wishers with great amusement. He did not appreciate that the clergyman had over the years perfected the skill of seeing through the corner of his eye and was fully aware of the sad situation. Alexander recognised that nobody felt inclined to be the first to end these silent prayers, and simply gloated. Yet the restlessness of the company was about to end it all. Alexander's sly grin vanished as soon as the first daring head - Robert's - was raised. Even Robert's hair looked angry! How long could they all stand the strain! They were dancing to his tune as helplessly as those two flies desperate for freedom on the window pane.

"I shall be grateful, Mistress Grant, if you will now kindly lead the servants downstairs in prayers for my recovery," he asked solemnly, wishing to prolong the agony in every possible way. "It is such a small request for such great benefits." He sounded so saintly.

The housekeeper had not the slightest intention of granting this request and she exchanged a knowing look with Elizabeth as she left the room. Canon Ritschell appeared to beam with his customary benificence.

Alexander permitted them all to rise and, assuming the voice of a cleric, pontificated:

"Thank you all for your loving consideration, which will surely shorten my illness. I feel my strength returning already with your prayers and good wishes. I should be most grateful if you would come at least once a week, Canon Ritschell, to read these very same prayers and give these goodly people the benefit of your guidance. Yes, I do feel so much better already. God in his wisdom has helped me and I feel a great spiritual sense of redemption." The Canon nodded soberly.

"Oh, and send that widow woman up immediately. I have need of succour and she seems to have nothing to do."

There were smothered sighs from the rest of the company, varying from relief to indignation. Then, putting his hands together across his breast in the manner of a clergyman, Alexander sank back on his pillows, apparently exhausted, and closed his eyes with great contentment, making heroic attempts to prevent his lips from twitching. He was secretly thinking of the fun he had had at the expense of these clever fools! He rejoiced in the fact that he could bible-babble as well as the next.

As his audience filed soberly out of the room, all feeling extremely depresssed, nobody had anything to say, and only the Canon appeared happy with the outcome. He reflected that indeed, strange were the ways of the Lord, His wonders to perform, and Elizabeth was right. He should be off to Hexham. It was getting distinctly gloomy both inside and out.

Chapter 32

Late one morning Woodall and Shafto arrived back from Newcastle, congratulating themselves on having successfully thrashed out the complicated details of the marriage settlement, with the prudent assistance of their lawyers. It was a great relief to Anne and Lancelot, though Anne felt somewhat anxious now that their marriage was one step nearer. Woodall carried with him a letter from Barbados which he had not had time to open, and the family, along with the Shaftos and Robert, was asked to gather in the drawing room to hear Lancelot read out its contents. Only Alexander was excluded. The news was not what they had expected.

"Woodall Plantation, Barbados.

To Mr. Woodall at Nunburn Hall, Northumberland:

We received your letter offering to send out the families of our servants here and we thank you for your patent kindness. I have asked my friend, a merchant in Bridgetown, to help me write this letter, because circumstances have changed here dramatically since my last communication, which have very much altered our attitudes.

My latest news is bad. I am sorry to say that a hurricane struck the island a week ago, causing widespread devastation. Thirty vessels, carrying much-needed food, tools and other necessaries were wrecked in, and near, Bridgetown harbour. Our standing crops, and in particular the sugar cane, are now uprooted and ruined. The men's sleeping quarters, mere huts, constructed of four to six forks planted in the ground and covered with reeds and palms, were blown away, so we had no shelter from the tropical downpours till they were rebuilt. We have had to endure the discomfort of aggravating insects and hungry rats.

The slaves, who normally sleep on the ground without the protection of a hammock, are badly bitten by insects, and are in an even more dire state than usual. The hammocks have to be fortified with tarred strings, to stop the invasion of pests. You can imagine the protection we need against the scorching sun, and the relentless trade winds. What is worse, we are even hungrier than before and are in a terrible state.

I have tried to preserve the men's spirits but in truth I have myself had enough of these climes and heartily wish that I were at home in Northumberland, even if I had to endure the bleakest winter that could be imagined! Barbados has revealed itself as a place which no longer fits with my inclinations, and my patience is sorely tried. Only the black slaves, with their family groups, simple diet, and community spirit, seem to be able to survive here with any success. Faithful in pursuit of their traditions they even plant seeds here which they have brought in amulets and rear baobab trees in memory of their ancestors. Some of my men are now calling this island a white man's grave. In certain ways the black slaves are treated better and valued more than the white indentured servants, but the cruelty here can be indescribably sickening.

Last week I was passing through one of the plantations and I witnessed the whipping of one of the negroes, who was thought to have been slacking. When he was tied to the whipping post he smiled as his back was beaten until it was bloody. After his punishment, sugar syrup was smeared onto his wounds to attract the myriads of insects, including wasps, to further aggravate his wounds. All throughout this brutality he did not utter any cry of pain. Indeed I cannot bear to witness, let alone inflict, the cruelty that seems necessary for this island to prosper.

Our men think the Lord has forsaken us. I tell them that God's will is not to be questioned and that we are thrown down presently, to be raised up again in time. I hide my own desperation and try to keep them in good heart. We ourselves are without the means to return home, so I await your advice.

In truth there are fortunes to be made out here if estates are enlarged and negro labour employed. Sugar and cotton are the leading crops. Since the Dutch Wars started we have suffered from the effects of the Navigation Laws, and the withdrawal of Dutch trade from the island, although this has not altogether ceased. Due to the enforcement of trading with the Royal Adventurers the price of slaves has risen from seven pounds to seventeen. Many planters would welcome the return of free trade with the Dutch and lower labour prices.

Indian Bridge, as it was once called, or Bridgetown, is quite the main port of the Caribbean, though unremarkable except in its conduct of a thriving trade. Recently much of it has been destroyed but normally it is full of horse-drawn waggons and ox carts fetching and carrying goods to and from the plantations. I must confess that most of the planters are usually in debt to the merchants, and it is only by confining our expenditure to the least possible amount that we have remained out of debt ourselves.

The country is being rapidly opened up, with fresh roads into the interior to reach the new estates. Previously, clothes, Irish butter, cod from New England and such treats could not be delivered to the furthest settlements on the backs of animals, and on the heads of black slaves. The estates were developed around the coast, but now, due to much hard work, wide roads are being built, the widest where there are standing woods. Some of the bigger plantations have built stone windmills, which drive the cane-crushing rollers, and remove the need for oxen or horses.

There is no doubt that normally the startling beauty of the island would charm you, with its evergreen trees, the stunning green of the long lines of tobacco plants, the pale yellow of the ripe sugar canes with their dancing plumes against the darkest green of the ginger plants.

I have to be honest with you as to the above, but as for us Nunburn people, we long only for the opportunity to register with the Secretary's Office to procure a ticket marked "Time Out", and would be very ready to sail in three weeks. In seven to ten weeks, if preserved from the teeth of strong winds, heavy seas, and from pirates, we would be away from this dreadful "Little England", to our lasting pleasure. We are at your mercy and eagerly await your advice on the matter.

We send you our humblest respects and kindest regards to all at Nunburn.

Your Most Obedient Servant,

Thomas Hubbach."

Shocked and despairing at this dreadful news, Lancelot folded up the letter and sat down. There was a protracted silence that no one present was willing to break.

(Below, Mistress Grant took in her breath. She had a cousin in Barbados, one William Askew.)

Anne rose, and stood looking through the window, casting an occasional look in Lancelot's direction. Elizabeth opened her mouth and shut it again. Softly she whispered: "Poor Thomas!"

Shafto confessed: "I did not know that sugar brought such discomfort."

Embarrassed at the new turn of events, Woodall affirmed: "Something will have to be done soon. It seems that the plantation project was too ambitious in face of the natural forces at work. Fever, hunger and now hurricanes! There can be no success if the workmen are downcast."

Lancelot could not take his eyes away from Anne, guessing at her compassion.

"Yes, we will have to bring them all home, no matter what the expense, and either sell our land or instruct Thomas to appoint someone locally to represent our interests. We may have to divert our efforts into trade instead of leaving our men at the mercy of the tropics and as witnesses to these pernicious practices. The family must deliberate as to the best course."

Turning from the window, Anne relaxed and slowly raised her head to smile at him, impressed with his noble intentions.

Robert looked towards Elizabeth, having noted that she had remained throughout more discreet than he had ever seen her before. In truth since her return he had never been alone in her company and he wondered if the visit to Hackford had changed her attitude towards him. His thoughts were of her alone and he longed to speak to her and take her to Woodedge Manor, because he felt that her enthusiasm would surely inject life into the old building, and give him the confidence and purpose to forge ahead, but the more he had been away from her, the more distant he felt, and therefore the less bold he became. He longed to know if her father had plans for her and he was desperate with the present indecision.

Elizabeth, on the other hand, was equally insecure, tormented by the lack of contact. She had been longing for him to bring her back from Hackford, and what had he done? He had sent a groom for her instead. She had wanted to show him where she had been brought up and see her family, but he had not displayed the slightest interest. Then, when she had arrived back, he had not looked as pleased to see her as she had expected, but had galloped straight after Alexander without the merest word of greeting. Then she had resented his interest in Maria. She had seen him talking to her at every opportunity, and that sly little minx was always looking up at him with her bright blue eyes, tilting her head coquettishly.

Elizabeth had been feeling increasingly exhausted, looking after the detestable Alexander, yet in her anger she was able to summon up hidden strength. As for Robert, she felt nothing but puzzled resentment, and would make sure that she paid him no attention. Let him go off with Maria if he wanted! He had been standing beside her at Alexander's bedside during prayers and she had seen Maria leaning against him. She did not care, she did not care a groat, she did not care a snap of the fingers, in fact she did not care at all, and she would not even deign to look at him, except perhaps through the corner of her eye, when she thought he was not looking!

So the company broke up and prepared for dinner, each sad in their own particular way, and all equally trapped in their own little circle of misapprehension. In the privacy of her bedroom Elizabeth thought over a possible crumb of comfort in the attitude of Lancelot concerning the return of the Nunburn men from Barbados.

Chapter 33

Henry Woodall, Lancelot and Jeffery Shafto spent many hours, day after day, discussing the best ways to handle the withdrawal from the Barbados plantation. In the end it seemed to narrow down to only a few alternatives.

Shafto put forward his opinion first. "It would be regrettable if a potential source of income for Lancelot and Anne were just discarded. I see the point in fetching back your men but surely the plantation could be worked by the negro slaves under a white overseer."

A despondent Woodall interjected: "I feel like finishing the whole West Indian venture, selling the land and slaves, and evacuating the men, whatever the consequences."

Lancelot looked towards Shafto. "Perhaps we should think of the future and retain the land. If economic conditions improve we could always start again, using slaves or some of these Irishmen we hear so much about. Alternatively we could lease the plantation."

Shafto asked: "Do you suppose that Alexander, when he recovers, could make a second attempt to run the venture. He is still a young man."

Both the Woodalls' voices united in opposition. "I'm afraid not, Jeffery. The boy could not stand such a test of his physical endurance, and I doubt whether he has the business acumen to control either the agriculture or the trading."

Lancelot laughed sarcastically. "You don't know him, Sir. He lacks even self-control, let alone being responsible for men and commerce. Temptation is always the winner. We must leave him out of the arrangements completely."

"Well, what about appointing Thomas Hubbach to be in charge of the plantation, without the Nunburn men? He would still have the Irishmen and the black slaves. He seems to have done well so far, and his experience and his reliability are strong recommendations," urged Shafto, still intent on material profits.

Lancelot scrutinised his new father-in-law and abhorred the sight of a good man seduced by the lure of silver-edged lace and high-heeled boots.

"That would not be fair to him," replied Lancelot. "We sent him out only to help Alexander over a sticky patch. We know he has been reliable, and we were lucky to choose him, but at the same time we know that he has had more than he can endure out there, and is set on returning to his old life. I was agreeably surprised that without any experience he turned out to be a good manager, and it strikes me that if he returns we would do well to employ him as a steward to replace Robert Carr."

"Yes," agreed his father hastily. "I hadn't thought of that. Now that you mention it, we should include his appointment in our overall plan. After you and Anne are married you will not be at Nunburn all the time, Robert will concentrate on his own farms, and we shall need a replacement steward."

Lancelot commented wryly: "It is ironic that we have just persuaded the farmworkers' families to travel out to Barbados, and now we are cancelling the proposal."

"Business is like that, for everyone, I have found," said Henry, shaking his head with sadness. "Investment is always a risk. If it goes well then fortunes can be made. If badly, then the losses have to be written off to experience.This was a venture that was well recommended, but perhaps we embarked on it ten years too late, or even ten years too early. I feel that we have insufficient information on which to base a decision. I shall go to Newcastle to discuss the matter with some of my merchant colleagues who have contacts in London."

The discussion was terminated at this point and Lancelot went in search of Anne while the two older men took a short walk in the grounds.

It was a cold damp morning in tune with his mood when Woodall rode to his Newcastle house with two of his grooms as escorts. His clerk, noticing his dejection, welcomed him and heaped more coals on to the fire. Two piles of papers were neatly stacked on the large table.

"These items have accumulated since your last visit, Sir, but they are mainly routine stuff. Bills to check, agreements to sign, leases to renew, shipping returns, loans to be extended, colliery expenses, and so on."

"Yes. I'll deal with them later, Mr. Hogg. This morning I have more urgent business. The Barbados venture seems to be in deep trouble. Hand me the West Indies papers, please."

A bulky set of papers, tied in ribbon, was set before him and he opened it in excited haste. The topmost leaves dealt with the primary land sale in Barbados, and he gave these a lengthy perusal, nervously scratching his chin from time to time and adjusting his wig. Then he looked at receipts relating to the purchase of black slaves, timber, tools, corn, salt, clothing, and many other materials which the first expedition had been obliged to buy. He sighed, and felt deflated, guessing that the whole scale of his enterprise had been too small to be efficient, not forgetting Alexander's incompetence, the devastating hurricane and the vagaries of trade conducted against a background of Dutch and French wars.

He settled to dictating his letters to London and seemed mesmerised as he watched Mr. Hogg's quill scratching across the paper in his best flowery handwriting. A man was sent to the quayside to hand the letters to the captain of one of Woodall's own colliers, and Woodall himself hurried to the riverside office of Thomas Barnes, a wealthy merchant and property owner, who as usual greeted him warmly. When the clerk had taken his hat and heavy coat, Woodall stood looking out over the busy River Tyne musing on the earnest hopes of all who were engaged in the fragility of trade, and he despaired. He sighed. He was heartily sick of Newcastle and all his business enterprises. Worry and frustration were the price of a doubtful success.

The two men sat down to discuss the matter in hand. After he had recounted the brief history of his Barbados plantation, Woodall outlined what he believed were the alternative lines of action. Barnes was shocked by the story, and pulled an agonised face at each turn of the screw.

"I thought at the time that Barbados was a high risk, Henry. Too far away to exert the kind of close control which is possible with the coal trade and normal financial business. However, my advice is to sever all links with the sugar trade and cut your losses while they are minimal. Corn and coal may not pay the dizzy rewards of tropical ventures, but at least they are reasonably safe and satisfying."

"You see no future in keeping the land, leasing or renting it, and waiting for more propitious times then?" asked Woodall.

"Another hurricane or another war may be just around the corner. If you yourself are not there, you do not know at any moment what is going right or wrong. A ship takes many weeks to bring back news, by which time it is too late to affect the outcome. No, I believe that you would do well to abandon the enterprise. We are not young men any longer, and the fewer worries we have the better. We have lived through a rumbustious century, what with Scotch kings, religious bigots, civil wars, and even a regicide. We ourselves deserve some peace and quiet and it may be the lot of your grandsons to follow in your footsteps, at a time when all things have improved."

Woodall sat silent for a moment. He recognised that this was good advice. His family estates had luckily survived intact through all the civil strife, and none of the family had been killed, or even wounded. But he had lost his wife and was now saddled with a semi-invalid son who was weak, selfish, and unpredictable. Perhaps he had gone out on a limb in buying land in Barbados.

Was now the time to be content with what he had worked so hard to build up? He must spend more time on his civic duties and on his family. He might even be able to enjoy his beautiful estate in Tynedale, learning at first hand how the cottagers lived their lives, attending church more regularly, supporting the grammar school at Hexham, and other worthy causes.

"You can afford to withdraw, Henry," reasserted his friend, taking Woodall's silence for agreement. He got up and stood behind his friend patting his shoulder. "The vast balance of your funds lies here in Newcastle. Barbados was but an interesting sideshow."

"Yes. I am disposed to accept your advice, Thomas. I see now that I have over-reached myself, and created a good deal of misery for the folks who depend on me. I have written to London to learn the best way of extracting my capital from Barbados, and when that is clear I shall give instructions to my agent to expedite the matter."

After making kind enquiries concerning Barnes's family, Woodall stood up, and the clerk was summoned to bring his outer garments which had been warming in front of the fire in an adjoining chamber. Woodall carefully pushed his arms into the sleeves of his long black coat as the man held it up for him, put on his hat, and deep in his thoughts walked slowly down the stairs into the cold street, on his way to seek the consolation of his good old friend Anthony ffarbrigge.

Back in the office he had just left, Thomas Barnes rested his head thoughtfully between his hands. Then he shouted brusquely for the clerk: "Contact London immediately and bring me all the available information about Barbados."

The ffarbrigge establishment was warm and welcoming as usual which quickly put Woodall at his ease. Anthony, particularly anxious about the fate of Thomas, listened carefully to the latest episode of the tale of Barbados and did not interrupt once, painfully aware of his own unintentional role in the proceedings and anxious lest his old friend had been told his part in the whole story. None of this emerged, however, and at the end he tried to set Woodall's fears at rest.

Moving his chair closer towards him and taking his hand, he was reassuring.

"You have a clever son who is clearly going to be a far better man of business than either of us. It is not fitting to leave this Barbados millstone hanging round his neck just as he is about to start his career. The Shafto estate will undoubtedly add to his administrative duties and his forthcoming marriage with its extra social responsibilities will also take up more of his time. The sooner your

London agent makes the withdrawal, or sale, or lease, as you choose, the better."

"We have little news of the current situation in the West Indies. I still can't make up my mind between the options you have mentioned."

"All the more reason for returning Thomas and his men to England, then. He will give you the why and wherefore of the plantation business, and he is level-headed enough to give you practical advice."

"Yes, I agree. The men have been victims of a most unlucky chance, and I feel that I owe it to them to allow them to resume their old lives at Nunburn. We can delay the decision about the fate of the plantation until Thomas has had time to explain the situation fully."

Anthony was relieved for his kinsman but, as Woodall departed, his face darkened as he noted that his old colleague was looking more aged, worn down with all his worries. A furrowed brow was one thing, but was he also developing a limp?

Chapter 34

Meanwhile, through overheard conversation, and without really trying, Alexander could pick up a great deal of the family news at Nunburn Hall, and then he could easily fit in the connecting pieces with well chosen, apparently casual, questions. Mistress Grant could be particularly forthcoming in this respect, but that bitch Elizabeth had never disclosed a single piece of useful information. So the men in Barbados were to be brought back home and the family settlement had been finally approved? Those lazy good-for-nothings in Barbados would have no sympathy for him, and the family's financial arrangements would be of no immediate benefit either. That old crock, Aunt Caroline, looked as fit as a fiddle and might go on for years, so he might have to spend his precious youth just waiting for her death.

He wanted money - cash in the hand - to succeed as he deserved, and what he needed was to get by sea to London, now that the plague was over. He had gloated for weeks in planning the cunning preparations for his escape, disguising his recovery to put everyone off guard, sleeping in snatches all day and exercising at night. His lameness had almost gone, but he still flaunted it, and though his strength had recovered, he still hid it. He would have to take what was his, and soon. He had remembered the precious chest in his father's bedroom and he guessed that would be where his mother's family jewels were hidden, and, without doubt, a large amount of cash too. The next time his father left for Newcastle he would act, take what was truly his, and be away from this God-forsaken hole! His only possible helper would be that half-wit of a footman, Gerrard Rutter, who came in from time to time. He would talk him into bringing some tools to burst the locks on the chest, and two horses would stand by ready for his escape. He was now fully recovered and poised to act as soon as the time was favourable.

His carefully laid plans were ready for execution, so he was prepared when the long-awaited announcement came that his father was to go to Newcastle. The hours seemed to pass slowly as he rehearsed his plan and dressed for his journey. He waited until it was dark and allowed what he felt was sufficient time for all the household to be fast asleep. The house was deathly quiet when he crept into the corridor, and by the light of his candle successfully retrieved the tools which had been secreted in a cupboard for him. He stealthily opened his father's bedroom door and cringed as he had to endure the loud creaking from the hinges which he had never even noticed before. Yes! There before him was the old rickety chest lying in its familiar place. He examined the fastenings. God's wounds! What stupidity! The old wood was so rotten that a baby might have removed the outside hinges. The lid came off in his hands and now he rued the fact that he had asked the tame footman to bring the tools.

He tried to be quiet as he rummaged through the top layer of crisp old documents, taking out a small stout leather-bound book with parchment papers listing the monies collected from the estate. Flinging this aside, his feverish fingers dug deeper through the other papers. With relief he found underneath them a cask which surely would contain the jewels. He opened it without difficulty. Yes, there they were, shining brightly, precious in the light of the flickering candle. So far, so good. Then he examined some leather purses and heard with greedy pleasure the chink of coins within.

He put as many of them as he could carry into a sack, extinguished the candle, and slowly and noiselessly crept along the passage. He paused for a few moments outside Elizabeth's bedroom door and listened, eventually shaking his head. Not a sound. His heart was beating fast as he prepared to descend the stairs with the cask clutched tightly under his arm. On the landing, however, a horrible squelching creak brought his heart into his mouth, but nobody in the house stirred, and he softly padded down the rest of the stairs clinging on to his booty.

Having unbolted the main door he made his way to the stables, where the half-wit had saddled the two horses as arranged. He fastened the treasure on to the spare horse, and lithely mounted the other beast, then, with a gleam of exhilaration in his eye, he was off and away, to make his fortune! Success was now within his reach, and he looked back towards Nunburn Hall, theatrically kissing farewell to it and all its occupants with a sneer.

He was unaware that Gerrard Rutter saw his stealthy progress towards the stables. The footman, burly but usually inarticulate, had been content for most of his life to appear slow of understanding, sluggish in his movements and barely capable of performing the humble tasks set him by the household. Orphaned as a baby, he had been taken by the kindly Josiah Rutter and his wife who reared him as their own, and he had grown strong in his youth. The Woodalls had been glad to take on a man who demanded so little and who handled heavy work so easily. Now he watched as Alexander came out of the stables with the two horses Gerrard had saddled. The mystery of this bizarre adventure puzzled Gerrard, but he made no attempt to interfere. He was glad that Alexander seemed to be leaving in secret. Nobody in the household had a good word for him, with his surly behaviour and his undisguised contempt for the servants.

"I'd saddle a thousand horses to be rid of you, little rat," he reflected.

The night was cold and crisp but perfect for Alexander's intentions. In the moonlight he could make out the road quite clearly and he was lulled into a sense of security. He relaxed to the sound of the steady thuds of the horses' hoofs, as they picked their way through the muddy ruts and sloughs. The only other sounds breaking the silence were the familiar hoot of the owl, searching for his supper, and the sharp bark of the dog fox, similarly bent. It was not until they began the long climb up to a heavily wooded rise that the horses pricked their ears and communicated to him a certain uneasiness, which increased as they ascended. The light of the moon was cut off by the dense woodland and the darkness in the shadows was menacing. The hair stood out on the back of his neck, and in the gloom it was increasingly difficult to find the road.

The animals mysteriously slowed down and Alexander felt very tense. He could feel the thumping of his heart, and was almost ready to stop and dismount when it happened. The horses suddenly shied in front of a dark figure obstructing their passage, and a rough authoritative voice pronounced: "Stand and deliver!"

Shocked, as well as unarmed, Alexander had no alternative but to rein in the horses. Surely this was not to be the sorry end to all his carefully laid plans? Recollecting himself, he managed to croak: "I am just a poor man, travelling from Scotland to Newcastle. I have nothing of value."

"You expect me to believe that, travelling with two horses?" the other scornfully retorted. It was at this point that all Hell was let loose. Hardly discernible figures emerged from the gloom, and voices seemed to be coming from both sides of the road.

"Got you, Jack Preece, you rascal!" said one.

For a moment Alexander thought that he was being wrongly apprehended himself. There was a scuffle as two men attempted to seize the reins of the highwayman's horse. Prepared for such an emergency, the horse had been taught to rear and stamp. His powerful hoofs pounded the surprised attackers and were obviously finding their mark as they crunched down with heavy thuds. Men collapsed, shrieking in pain. A pistol shot rang out, accompanied by a strangled cry. More shots were fired and oaths, shouts, and screams pierced the night.

In the general confusion, Alexander saw his opportunity to escape. Roughly spurring on his horse, and dragging the other beast by the rein, he ignored the moans and thuds. They burst their way clear of the melee and he put his head down along his frightened mount's neck to gain some protection. Soon the shouts and cries of pain receded behind him. A few yards further on, the horses sensed others tethered by the roadside, and it was then that Alexander realised that he had blundered into an ambush laid for the highwayman. Just his luck again to choose this night!

As he gradually distanced himself from the fray he reckoned that it sounded as if his attacker had been apprehended, and he chuckled as he imagined the chain of events which would ensue. The court at Hexham would be swiftly vengeful and the punishment be noised abroad to discourage all others. Hanged for stealing! He wished that he could have stayed to watch that interfering rascal's legs dangling. The greedy nuisance of an upstart! But this was dreamland and he could not delay. He was off to his safe house in Newcastle where dwelt a very old acquaintance who would offer him the perfect shelter on the quayside until he could leave for London and where the rest of the family would be unable to detect his whereabouts. He laughed gleefully as he recollected that Lancelot would not have a clue about a place like that. It was all too unsavoury for that gentleman's finely educated palate! Soon he would be swallowed up in London, a place of fantasy, where he would forget his origins and be himself. He spurred his horse towards his refuge. Snow was beginning to fall softly and would cover his tracks, but it brooked no delay.

So we leave Alexander, beginning the most exciting and dastardly phase of his life, and we bid adieu to him with great relief, feeling that his present good luck was more than he deserved. No doubt as usual the bad coin would inevitably turn up again, and, indeed, he was already vowing to himself that when he was rich and successful he would enjoy flaunting before the rest of the family the bright world of Alexander Woodall.

Chapter 35

The morning at Nunburn began in the usual way, with the maids re-laying fires, making beds, and cleaning the hall and stairs. Alexander's breakfast was delivered and his absence from the bedroom was noted, but no one was unduly concerned. It was not until another maid entered her master's bedroom to do the normal cleaning duties that the damaged chest and scattered documents were discovered in the middle of the floor and Mistress Grant was summoned. She had observed herself that the house doors were unbolted and she told Lancelot that the grooms had reported two horses missing. It was then that the hue and cry began. Stifled whispers indicated that everyone was aghast at the implications. Lancelot paced the floor wondering what to do, embarrassed by the whole affair and despairing at being plunged into yet another emergency as a result of his wayward brother's selfish behaviour. He could confide only in Elizabeth.

"I'm reluctant to worry father with this but we've no alternative but to send a messenger to Newcastle to warn him about Alexander's disappearance. Robert and one of the grooms will have to look for signs of his possible route to try to track him down before he harms himself any further. All the staff must be told that since Alexander was bed-ridden he must have been abducted by the thief who stole the treasure and the two horses."

"I'm so sorry that you have been afflicted with even more trouble," sympathised Elizabeth as she disciplined herself to accept his explanation, but she was secretly concerned only with the safety of Robert. Why should the worthless Alexander be endangering the lives of those around him and always miraculously escaping himself? Large snowflakes were already blanketing the landscape, and as she watched Robert leaving for the stables, she felt guilty because she sincerely wished that he might not find Alexander and they would be rid of him for good. Lancelot in particular would be better without the worry of him, let alone their father, who was turning old and grey before his time.

The poor servants were reprimanded severely for not having alerted the household to the presence of the intruder because it was their responsibility to give the first warning. They in turn were equally resentful of Alexander and had their own ideas about what had transpired.

After hours of scouring the countryside and avoiding the deepening snow drifts, Robert and the groom abandoned the search. With their breath condensing and their throats pierced painfully by the wintry air, they returned without any news. There was no sign of Alexander or the horses anywhere. It seemed significant that in a few days there was a message from their father saying that he had decided to remain in Newcastle, ostensibly to look for his son, but Lancelot sensed that his father was at the end of his tether and felt that he could do nothing to remedy his troublesome son's wayward life-style. The worst affected was Anne who was secretly put out because the loss of the Woodall jewels meant that they would not be available to wear at her wedding.

Apart from that, life at the hall relaxed into a somewhat better atmosphere than had existed during Alexander's stay. The Shaftos had graciously accepted Lancelot's explanation of the robbery and Alexander's disappearance, and a week later when the snow had melted they set out for their own home, apparently not too bothered by the recent turn of events. Shafto stood at the bottom of the steps in the pale sunshine shaking hands warmly with everyone

"Thank you for your kindness. We have thoroughly enjoyed our visit. We will look forward to returning your hospitality soon."

Maria cast a sly look at Robert. Lancelot surreptitiously passed a note to Anne as she was about to climb into the carriage, and kissed her on the cheek. Of course everyone, including the servants, had noticed. She blushed, and smoothly slipped the note out of sight under her cloak. Inside the coach, Shafto sat back, beaming his approval, and continued to demonstrate his geniality to all and sundry. He was congratulating himself that everything had worked out as he had planned and that his estate would be in the hands of such a well-bred reliable son-in law. Young Maria leaned on Robert as he helped her into the coach and she could not take her admiring eyes away from him as she sat beside her father who patted her on the knees good-naturedly. Mistress Grant passed in the muffs and woollen rugs and then, with a crack of the whip, they were away. Elizabeth was sad to see Anne go because she had become in this very short time a treasured friend. Maria, however, was another matter.

Regretfully they watched the coach disappear from view as it crunched down the drive. Lancelot returned indoors last of all, slowly climbing the steps and swallowing his sadness at Anne's departure. He determined to switch his mind at once to his business affairs to avoid further pining. He attracted Robert's attention and together they entered the parlour, where they were quickly joined by Elizabeth, rubbing her hands vigorously to warm them.

"Robert, please warn the cottagers of the change of plans for Barbados. There is no need to give them any superfluous details, of course. Perhaps

Elizabeth will be able to help you."

Elizabeth appeared to accept this suggestion very coolly. Nevertheless she was secretly pleased to have the opportunity to accompany Robert alone across the miles of the estate. The cold weather and frost-bound tracks were no deterrent because they were both equally eager to set out. There were six farms to visit, since the Barbados men comprised volunteers from each separate farm on the Nunburn estate.

Mistress Grant came running out with a big bag of cakes just as they mounted the horses. At last they were together for the first time for months, as they jogged along through the deserted fields towards the furthest cottages at Woodedge Farm, and gradually a certain peace descended on them. At first they did not say a word to each other, because their innermost thoughts were identical, and too testing. Eventually Robert broke the silence.

"They will be pleased to hear the news of the return of their menfolk. This is one of the pleasantest jobs we could have been given."

"Yes. I know how eager I am to see Cousin Thomas again after all this time. Imagine the stories he will have to tell us." replied Elizabeth.

"I think you may be seeing a lot of him if he is offered a job on the estate when he returns. He is held in high esteem here."

"Isn't life strange? It wasn't long since we were persuading them to go to Barbados and now everything has changed. I feel deeply ashamed that I was involved, since we found out it was such a dreadful place. I wish I'd never heard about it."

"Life's full of surprises. At the time we thought it was best, but, as usual, experience has taught us better. We must take the rough with the smooth," replied Robert.

"But intelligent people have the ability to make their own luck with careful planning."

"And who planned Alexander? It was an unlucky night that he was brought into the world. I remember being taken to see the peaceful baby sleeping in his cradle and of course no one guessed then that he would be so much trouble," recalled Robert.

"And, if he hadn't been so much trouble to his mother, I may not have been here now. So the circle is closed. You see, I do have something to thank Alexander for. My very existence, here and now, past and present, and what's more important, the future. All due to Alexander," she laughed. "I like being here."

"I like you being here too," replied Robert. "Only because I have got this difficult job of explaining to the cottagers why the trip to Barbados is cancelled, and I am sure you will do it for me superbly," he teased.

"I thought that you had to do all the talking. Lancelot said that I wasn't to open my mouth, on pain of punishment," lied Elizabeth.

"I can't believe that, but I have noticed how quiet you have been recently."

"I've noticed how you have had a lot to say to Maria," pouted Elizabeth.

"Yes. I felt sorry for her. She's just a child after all, at a loss among the grown-ups. She deserved some attention."

Just at this point they had reached the bend in the road and they could clearly see Woodedge Manor standing on its low hill.

He pointed proudly towards the old building. "That is where our family lived before the Civil Wars. We owned Hunter's Gap and Woodedge Farm yonder and other acres besides."

She was intrigued by this fresh news. "Robert, it is sheer magic. I have never appreciated it before. Is that where you were born? How sad your parents must have been, to lose such a wonderful place. Can we see inside?"

"Perhaps, if we have the time," responded Robert casually, disguising the fact that the chance for which he had long dreamed had actually arrived, and it was his dearest wish to show her the home where he intended her to be mistress. "Let's consider these poor people first," he suggested.

Soon they were outside the cottages and the Graham children scampered in to warn their mother of the new arrivals. This time a gaggle of geese approached them aggressively but the woman with the floury hands shooed them aside and was once more welcoming Robert.

"Come in, Sir, and have a drink, and Miss Elizabeth too."

They entered the well-ordered cottage and sat down on the bench near the meagre fire. Elizabeth immediately endeared herself to the children.

"Hello, Tom and Richard. Look at what Mistress Grant has sent you from Nunburn!"

The boys were delighted at the sight of the cakes offered by the fine lady. Indeed the younger boy, Richard, was especially fascinated by everything to do with her. He sat down close beside her on the floor, the tip of one little outstretched finger secretly exploring and stroking her fine leather boots as he looked up at her, smiling innocently. Elizabeth edged more closely towards him. Proudly he brought out his most precious toys which he had been keeping in a corner: a dried stick in the shape of a horse, a large rusty nail and a few smooth rounded stones, all ready for a game. His handsome little face looked up at her mischievously and he beamed with happiness at his good fortune in possessing such treasures.

Robert smiled at Elizabeth, cleared his throat, and announced dramatically: "We have had another letter from Barbados, giving news of strong winds on the island that have destroyed all the crops."

"How are our men?" Mrs. Graham asked urgently.

"Don't worry. They are safe, but not very comfortable, because their shelters have been blown down. Master Lancelot has decided to bring them home as soon as possible," Robert announced dramatically at last. Mrs. Graham gasped in surprise.

The children stopped playing as they sensed the good news.

For a moment there was silence. "You mean we don't have to go to that faraway island?"

"That's right. It is no longer necessary," Robert assured her. "The business is to be transferred to others and the Nunburn men can return to their homes. Heaven knows, we can do with their help here."

"Thank God for that," blurted out Mrs. Graham. "They are sorely missed. Shall I tell the Dinnin's next door? They'll be over-joyed, because John went out with the first batch."

"No," said Robert. "It is my duty to give them this message. You are right to think of how pleased they'll be.Yet it will take a wearisome time before your menfolk reach home - probably in the spring, ready for the sowing of the corn."

Mistress Graham was now in tears, clasping her younger son to her, and rocking him in an anguish of delight, her mind far away from sowing corn. "Daddy's comin' back to us. God be praised!"

Elizabeth smiled. "I'm so pleased for you. It's a lovely present for the new year."

"Yes," sighed the wife. "Young Richard here has forgotten what his father is like, and Tom has only a dim idea. Ever since he left, all they can ask is when is their father comin' home, and my husband is never out of my own thoughts."

Robert and Elizabeth left the happy scene to knock on the Dinnings' door, which was opened immediately by John's wife, as she had been lurking at the window, alerted by the presence of the two tethered horses from Nunburn. The message was repeated and old Sam and Alice Dinning exploded with joy. With more tears and more shining eyes, Elizabeth almost wept herself to see these goodly servants showing their emotions so openly.

At length they were free to depart and crossed towards Woodedge Manor enjoying the sunshine from a clear blue sky. Frosty patches still sparkled in the old herb garden.

Elizabeth approached it in awe, as if in a dream, and time seemed to stand still as she savoured the atmosphere of the old building. It drew her with a compelling attraction, totally enveloping her, as if taking over her soul. As they stood in the Great Hall she seemed to hear the voice of the past beckoning and welcoming her.

Robert thrilled to see her in his old home and watched all the fleeting expressions that crossed her face. Neither of them spoke a word as he showed Elizabeth round the ground floor. She went from room to room, enthralled. She wandered into the tiny chapel and stood thoughtfully as she surveyed the beautiful stained glass window over the altar. Following the brightly coloured beams of sunlight, she noticed something on the floor and examined it with the tip of her toe. Excavating a book from the debris she blew away the dust to read an inscription in the front in beautiful handwriting, "Maria Carr, 1620." Elizabeth excitedly showed it to Robert. In hushed tones she said: "It's a Roman Catholic prayer book and must have lain there all these years. It was forbidden by law, Robert," she whispered, "but you must keep it because it's your mother's."

"That's all gone and forgotten," said Robert, quickly concealing it in his pocket.

By now Elizabeth was directing him towards the stairs.

"No, it isn't a good idea to go up there."

"Yes, I must. I want to see it all," she whispered, overcome with curiosity.

"But the stairs are rotten and dangerous," he protested.

"I must go."

Robert yielded to this pressure and went in front, testing all the stairs with his own weight and warning her where to put down her dainty feet. Elizabeth wandered through the upper rooms, stopping frequently, her eyes taking in every detail, as if she was already planning their revival. Robert followed closely behind her, his eyes for her alone. Her heart was gradually absorbing the spirit of the place and she felt at home.

To Robert she had already become its essence. Without her it would be nothing but a heap of mouldering old stones. He knew that only she could fulfil the role of mistress of his home. As words were unneeded they spoke very little,

193

and the few words that they did utter were hushed.

Eventually, when they came downstairs Elizabeth asked: "Do you think it possible to rebuild your old home, so that it is once again habitable?"

"Hmm ..... I would need a good reason for doing it. Anything does for an confirmed old bachelor like me."

Elizabeth stared at him. She could see through the facade of this bachelor act.

"Before this dampness penetrates your poor old bachelor's bones I think we must go out into the sunshine. Look at our breath condensing in the cold air."

As they stood in the garden, where, Elizabeth guessed, there had once been a spread of health-giving herbs, they surveyed the desolate building that had formerly been so full of love and life. There were the remains of a bower, built for Robert's mother who must have sat there on fine sunny days dreaming her dreams, and no doubt planning Robert's future. She loved that thought, and Elizabeth vowed that she would take on those dreams to herself and make his life happy and contented. She knew that she could do it, but would she have the opportunity?

Robert ushered her round into the back garden in the full glow of the wintry sunshine, and stood looking over the boundary wall into the fields beyond. Old rooks' nests, silhouetted in the tall bare trees, were now deserted, but soon they would again be the centre of activity, according to the natural cycle. She followed his gaze.

"Even the birds pair up in the spring, trilling their happy songs, and flit after each other, from one twig to another," said Robert tentatively.

"Yes, truly it is God's will that they do it, or else how should nature survive?" Elizabeth replied.

As he drew closer to her he whispered: "Just as all creatures attract each other, why should we not follow God's will? Faithful to each other to the end."

He took her into his arms and drew her towards him, and she felt a heightened thrill in a closeness that she had never experienced before but had so often imagined. Her heart began to pound and her senses were dizzy with antici-pation. She was like a child who had been hopelessly lost, and now was feeling safe and comforted, protected from the harsh blows of fortune. Robert was strong and loving and she knew he would care for her, and be an excellent father to their children. If she could not have Robert she would die an old maid.

Robert bent down low as if to find her lips, but instead kissed her on the cheek, arousing new feelings within her. She snuggled her nose into his neck and smelt the power of his masculinity for the first time, elevating her into the poetry of love. Then he kissed her neck and held her head in his hands, marvelling at the softness and silkiness of her hair. He thrilled to see her precious tresses glowing, as the low shafts of winter sunlight played round them. To Robert she was the most precious thing on God's earth, and now there was no need for him to tell her since she knew it herself. Such passion produced a togetherness that was something neither of them had ever known, and it was its very strength that at the same time both invigorated and calmed them. They were encircled in their own private heaven and they felt that the whole world was at their feet.

Feeling their one-ness nearly complete, he broke off, and whispered an extract from Proverbs: "There be three things that are too wonderful for me, yea, four which I know not: the way of an eagle in the air; the way of a serpent upon a rock; the way of a ship in the midst of the sea; and the way of a man with a maid."

Smiling down at her he asked: "Elizabeth, will you do me the honour of marrying me?"

This precious moment almost took Elizabeth by surprise, so affected had she been by his kisses.

"Subject to my father's approval, I shall not deny my true inclination," promised Elizabeth.

His brightest hopes now almost within his grasp, Robert heaved a sigh of relief. "When your father returns from Newcastle I will speak to him. Lancelot is already aware of my intentions, and gave me his blessing."

Then he kissed her on the lips so lovingly that she wished it would never end. Reluctantly they parted and left Woodedge Manor hand in hand, still in a dream.They had five more farms to visit but they were so elated that the time passed as if by magic. At every cottage their presence left a special happiness in their wake, beyond the good news being delivered. Excited children warmed to their mood and the women saw all they had to know in Elizabeth's bright eyes and Robert's tenderness. The couple leisurely wound their way back to Nunburn Hall, happy that they were now truly united in spirit.

Chapter 36

Lancelot appeared as soon as they arrived back at Nunburn Hall, anxious to know the outcome. He took one look at the couple and realised that all his hopes for them had been fulfilled. Tea was ordered in the parlour and Mistress Grant herself brought in some delicacies. Her eyes rested on Robert but he would not look at her, because he was savouring the occasion, and he did not let slip any indication of what had occurred between Elizabeth and himself.

Robert was talking to Lancelot about Woodedge Manor: "Walls have ears and we will have to make sure everything is sealed up."

Mistress Grant turned quickly on her heel and with a fling of her head walked out.

As soon as she had disappeared Robert turned to his lifelong friend and announced proudly: "If your father gives his approval, Elizabeth has promised to be my wife."

Lancelot was thrilled with the news and bent forward to kiss Elizabeth and shake hands with Robert.

"Two of the people I treasure most in all the world, united together! I am so happy for you. Anne will be very pleased to hear the news and father is so attached to you both that I can't imagine him offering any objection to the marriage."

"Both upstairs and downstairs, I guess, will be pleased with the news," predicted Robert with a twinkle in his eye as he tapped his foot. "For myself, I can't wait to be wed."

"You can stay on at the Dower House as long as you like, if you intend to renovate Woodedge Manor," offered Lancelot.

"You are very generous, Lancelot. I think that Elizabeth will be already forming plans for the old house." replied Robert.

Elizabeth had not spoken a word. In truth, now that she had time to recollect, she was rather astonished at the sudden turn of events, and was somewhat bemused by the fact that all her hopes had suddenly materialised, and she could not have the continued pleasure of nursing the anxiety of them. She had not yet been able to focus her mental energy as far as the refurbishment of Woodedge Manor.

Tea over, Mistress Grant came in again to clear up the dishes. She studiously ignored Robert but beamed on Elizabeth with obvious approval as loving smiles creased her thin face.

Elizabeth responded, rather puzzled at her excessive goodwill. The two men began to discuss the business affairs of the estate and Elizabeth had time to study them both. Lancelot she adored as the brother who was so dependable and Robert she loved without rhyme or reason. She felt like clay in his hands. Would she be able to cope with this relationship, however attractive? Only time would tell, but their cups were overflowing and they were so very fortunate. She guiltily remembered her family at Hackford and determined that as soon as her father had returned from Newcastle and had given them his blessing she would take Robert to see John and Joanna, and share this new happiness with them. Isabel would be so excited for her, and she would love to see Robert with the baby.

She came out of her reverie to hear Robert saying that he had to leave, as he had some important unfinished business. She was disappointed because she wished that this special day would last forever and wanted to savour every minute of it, desperately clinging on to the present in the fear that all this new happiness might evaporate forever into thin air like a dream. In the midst of her doubts she became aware of Robert kissing her lightly on the cheek, making her whole frame quiver with delight. Then he was gone.

In fact Robert felt obliged to visit Mistress Grant because he had teased her long enough. His riding boots clumped noisily in an exaggerated way along the short passage which separated the house from the kitchen, but, as he approached the housekeeper, she did not raise her head. With great deliberation she concentrated on a rabbit that she was jointing, and the butter, turnips and beans that were strewn around her on the bench.

"Nice day," he greeted her, but she did not reply.

He took a small piece of chopped turnip from her board and munched it slowly.

"Heard any good news recently?"

No reply.

"Cooking something good for dinner? Leave a little bit for me, a poor bachelor?" Robert said, like a little whining puppy, and then he went close to her side, twisting his head right in front of her face. "I love your food."

197

Silence ensued. He straightened his huge frame.

" I won't be a bachelor for long, because Elizabeth has promised to marry me !" he burst out, unable any longer to keep up his act.

Mistress Grant put down her knife and turned towards him, "Oh, Robert! I am so happy for you. My very best wishes to you both, you scoundrel."

"All owing to you keeping me alive over the years with your delicious food!" responded Robert.

"Indeed, you have taken a lot of feeding, and you've grown mightily," she said, as she stood back to admire him.

"Where do you intend to live with Elizabeth?" she inquired.

"Where else but Woodedge Manor?" replied Robert. "If you wish you can come and look after us. I'm sure Elizabeth would be delighted."

"That would be a full turn of the circle. That's where I started out as a kitchen maid, when I was eight years old. But, listen, you rascal, I would be very careful now of making such suggestions on your own, because Elizabeth will be the mistress of the house, and you will have to consult her on such matters."

The thought had not occurred to Robert.

"Any news of Alexander from Newcastle?" inquired Mistress Grant.

"No, he has just disappeared into thin air, and his loot with him," said Robert.

"That's another thing you're not supposed to say," warned Mistress Grant, looking round the empty room.

"Yes, walls have ears!" he said. "And so do floorboards."

Mistress Grant playfully pretended to box his ears.

"I'm letting out too many secrets. I'll have to go," apologised Robert.

She took him in her arms and whispered: "I'm so happy for you Robert. I couldn't love you more if you were my own son. You are aggravating, though."

Robert cuddled her and took his leave, too full of emotion to speak.

Mistress Grant sighed. How she loved her two boys. She was witnessing yet another turn of the wheel. She had often agonised over her other more important secret. Thankfully she would never have to confess. She thought of the dark night when Mrs. Woodall's dying baby had been exchanged for the newly born child of a poor woman from a neighbouring village, a relation of her own family. Both the ailing baby and the impoverished mother had died, but Lancelot had thrived in the Woodall household which had accepted the skilful switch in blissful ignorance. She had never regretted the deception. The dead mother had done sterling service at the Hall and it was common knowledge that Woodall had unwisely married into a family that had been tainted for generations. Woodall's wife herself had been deceived. There had been no questions. No suspicions. Mistress Grant alone harboured this precious secret which she had never needed to share. But ever since that day she had looked upon Lancelot as her own special treasure.

Robert, too, was finding his own secret oppressive. As soon as he saw Woodall arriving back at Nunburn Hall, he lost no time in crossing from the Dower House to the Hall to ask for Elizabeth's hand in marriage. Sitting in the kitchen till the master had been served with dinner, his face looked tense and severe. He nervously went over and over in his mind what he intended to say on this momentous occasion. Mistress Grant, returning from one of her many duties, sympathised with his plight.

"I would wait a while before you see the master," she said. "He and Lancelot have been picking the bones of the prodigal son, and working themselves into a pent-up savagery. The master was particularly worried by the presence of the Shaftos at the time of the escapade, though with Lancelot it is the loss of the jewels which weighs most heavily. If I were you I should see him tomorrow when a good night's sleep has allowed emotions to die down and his natural good temper has returned."

Robert mumbled: "This delay does my mental state no good. I am so anxious to have the answer to my request that every moment seems like a day. But I'm sure you are right. It is a matter which should not be tainted by the angry reactions to Alexander's crimes. Yes, I'll wait till tomorrow."

As the maids came in with the dirty dishes from the dining room Mistress Grant squeezed Robert's shoulder encouragingly and he departed for his lonely bachelor home, still flushed, and full of hope.

Meanwhile, when the servants had disappeared, his father was pleased to reassure Lancelot.

"Do you really think that I would be foolish enough to keep the family jewels in a decaying old box in my bedroom? For generations they have been hidden in a secret aperture in the wall of the library, so safe that no one could possibly guess that they were there. One day soon I will show you where it is. Alexander has gone off with mere sentimental baubles, and even the money from the rents was minimal because he didn't think to wait until the Lady Day collection. He will be furious when he finds out. However, it will be sensible to keep this to ourselves. I am appalled at his behaviour after all the love we have shown him. Perhaps if his mother had lived longer, things would have been different."

Thinking of Anne, Lancelot could only heave a sigh of relief.

Chapter 37

Next morning, as predicted, Woodall was overjoyed with Robert's good news and offered his blessing and as much help as was needed with the renovation of their house. He called Elizabeth and Lancelot into the parlour to toast the future happiness of the young couple. It was touching for Elizabeth to see smiles return to her father's face after all his recent troubles.

"When do you expect to solemnise this marriage?" he asked.

"As soon as possible," Robert replied, to Woodall's amusement.

"Three banns will have to be read in church," Woodall reminded them. "Before such an important event there are many preparations to make, and they will take time to complete. Besides, weddings are best celebrated in fine weather." Robert looked disappointed.

Elizabeth suggested: "We will have to go to Hackford to see John and Joanna, and we can call at Hexham to consult Canon Ritschell about the wedding."

"Yes, it is only proper that you take Robert to Hackford as soon as possible. All the other arrangements depend on that," Woodall pointed out.

A week later the two set out on horseback for Hexham in high spirits. They went straight to the abbey to find Canon Ritschell and tell him the good news. He nodded knowingly: "So you can't resist the charms of Elizabeth. What man could? I can remember you as a young lad at Hexham Grammar School. You have grown a lot since then," he said to Robert, looking up at him.

"Tempus fugit celeriter. You see, I haven't altogether forgotten my Latin," Robert replied.

"You were always a diligent pupil," Canon Ritschell recalled. "I had bright hopes for your future but Fate intervened. Now come with me. I must bless this coming together of two such fine people."

Long shafts of wintry sunshine shone through the abbey windows as they knelt in prayer. Canon Ritschell gave them his solemn blessing and marvelled at what a handsome couple they made.

He stood at the doors of the abbey and watched them mount their horses, relishing the thought that John and Joanna would be delighted with their news. For himself weddings were infinitely welcome, a special consolation to balance the more numerous funerals.

While they trotted along the stony track to Hackford, Elizabeth took a great delight in explaining to Robert details of the countryside, showing him where Thomas's family lived, and sharing with him her knowledge of each settlement as they passed along the Devil's Water towards the head of the valley. Elizabeth loved the smell of the moor, the timid rabbit who watched for danger and fled as soon as anything moved, and the wide-ranging crows who saw everything below from their laboured flights to the distant woods.

They reached the ffarbrigge farm as daylight was fading, just before the family sat down for their evening meal. Joanna quickly poured out piping hot vegetable broth for them and they all sat round the big table, feeling as if they had known each other for years. Robert and John were soon engrossed in farming talk, since Robert was eager to learn as much as he could from such an experienced yeoman and glean more of the lore of the countryside.

After they had finished a substantial meal and were sitting back comfortably in front of the crackling wood fire, John asked casually: "And what brings you to Hackford?"

Without hesitation Robert said: "We have come to seek your blessing on our forthcoming marriage."

There was a moment's silence.

"Can you look after her and love her as Joanna and I have done all these years?" asked John.

"Elizabeth has told me of her happy life here. I should try very much to follow in your footsteps," replied Robert.

Looking first at Joanna, who nodded happily, John said: "Then I give you our blessin' with the greatest pleasure and we both wish you every happiness. Where will you live?"

"In my parents' old manor house," replied Robert. The happy couple then went to great lengths to describe their new home, John and Joanna eagerly soaking up the information in wide-eyed amazement.

Elizabeth breathed a sigh of relief and kissed them both. " Before it is too late, we must go to see Cuthbert and Isabel and tell them the good news," she urged.

"Could you ask if Robert can stay with them tonight, because we are a bit crowded here," suggested Joanna, looking at John.

So the two of them wandered along the narrow lane which led for a short distance to Isabel's house, at Burntshieldhaugh, and caught them just finishing supper.

As soon as they entered the door Isabel screamed a welcome: "I knew it! I had a dream last night. I was showerin' you with grain and I just knew you would be comin'."

Cuthbert scorned her intuition: "That doesn't mean anythin'. She's always havin' dreams. Now why are you here? Are you two gettin' spliced?"

"Of course we are," said Elizabeth, blushing.

"I knew it," said Cuthbert, "As soon as you came through the door." He looked defiantly at Isabel, who smiled with a sniff of superiority.

All this time baby John was staggering round the room, eyeing the strangers. Elizabeth picked him up, talking to him softly, and handed him to Robert, in spite of the fact that he was somewhat wet.

Robert sat cradling him in his arms and endured the little fingers exploring his mouth. He looked up at Elizabeth with pleasure and she beamed.

"Mother hoped that you would let Robert stay here tonight. Will it be alright?" asked Elizabeth.

"Of course. A pleasure," said Isabel.

Cuthbert winked at Robert. "Mother-in-laws are all like that," he complained. "Sorry we will have to go to bed early because it will be a heavy day tomorrow."

"Suits us as well . We will be setting out early too because the sooner we get back, the quicker we get started on rebuilding my old family home. The house is in such a dilapidated state that there's precious little time before the wedding," said Robert.

"I could come and give you two days work," offered Cuthbert.

"No, it's very kind of you, but we have been offered plenty of help at the moment," replied Robert.

Isabel looked relieved. "Why not walk Elizabeth home? By the time you come back we'll have a bed ready for you."

They walked arm in arm, retracing their steps up the lane to the farm door in a comfortable silence and Robert kissed Elizabeth a tender goodnight.

"Do you love Hackford as much as I do?" Elizabeth whispered in his ear.

"More, because it was where you were raised. I like your family; they are just as I had imagined. They have made me so welcome that I feel I've known them all my life, and I have no one of my own left. Whatever was in your life now is mine and is infinitely precious," Robert replied.

Quietly lifting the sneck, he gently helped her into the house, and, once inside, she closed the rickety door and leaned back contented, listening fondly to every one of his receding footsteps. As she opened her eyes, she could just make out a figure in the light of the last embers of the fire. Joanna came out of the darkness towards her with open arms.

"I like your Robert. What a handsome young man! I'm sure you'll have a happy life together in your beautiful manor house. You have been so fortunate that I can hardly believe what has happened. Just remember us sometimes. We all love you so much and we are so proud of you." And she kissed her daughter goodnight to join John upstairs, who turned over and went to sleep, happy too in Elizabeth's good fortune.

Elizabeth settled snugly in the bed place below the stairs.

Chapter 38

Next morning everyone was up early, and George had saddled the horses ready for the return to Nunburn, long plumes of their steaming breath wreathing and rising in the cold air.

"You will come and stay with us when our home is ready," insisted Elizabeth earnestly.

"Of course," said Joanna, "we'd love to. Try and stop us."

There was laughter all round.

"Here, these will keep you warm on the journey," and she handed over two pairs of beautiful leather gloves, one large and one small, which she had herself stitched by hand. "There's nothing like Hexham tans on a cold winter's day."

They each tried them for size and they were an excellent fit. Robert was amazed, "How did you manage to guess such a perfect match?"

" A lifetime of experience in makin' gloves. I was studyin' your hands at supper last night when you weren't lookin'," laughed Joanna.

As they started their journey, everyone, including the baby, waved vigorously until the riders were out of sight, their enthusiasm easing the sadness of parting with their dearest ones. The frosty breeze which blew across the fells chapped their faces and made them eager to reach home. Elizabeth thought of her previous journey, when on that fatal day she had ridden her beautiful black stallion along this very road for the last time. She would never again own a horse like him, she thought sadly. To divert her mind she pointed out every landmark and enjoyed describing the legends of the countryside in great detail.

"See that distant hill? That is where Nancy lived."

"So that was the fount of all your knowledge and the spring of your scholarship," teased Robert.

"And a better one I couldn't have had if I'd gone to Thomas's London," she joked. Her face darkened a little and she mused: "I wonder where he is now."

Robert reassured her: "He'll be back soon and we'll be entertaining him at Woodedge. Then we'll all be together, just as you wish."

Elizabeth pointed to Blackhall Farm which was just coming into view. "Look! That's where the Swinburns live, relations of ours, and over there, near the West Dipton Burn, is the cave used as a hiding place by Queen Margaret and her small son after the battle of Hexham in 1464. Some local people showed her where to hide to save their lives before she fled to France."

With such conversation, and the joy of being together, they rode along the quiet roads contented. From time to time, as the horses swung closer together, their gloved hands touched lovingly. Entering Hexham, however, there was a marked contrast when they found themselves trapped among hundreds of people making their way towards the centre of the town, where a large crowd was gathering. There was a great deal of bustle in the market place with the stallholders hurriedly taking up their wares, and stacking them on carts. The windows of all the buildings were crowded with spectators, and the narrow streets were teeming with people as an excited stream of men, women and children pressed forward.

Elizabeth and Robert had no alternative but to go with the flow and followed the crowd blindly until they caught up with a cart, guarded by a squad of musketeers. Standing erect in it, and waving his long jewelled fingers to the bystanders, was a tall man, dressed very elegantly. He wore a long curled wig, which set off his fine-boned cheeks, and handsome aquiline nose. His black coat, of the very best material and cut, was adorned with silver buttons, which were twinkling with jewels and an excess of silver braid. The lace at his neck was full and edged with silver, while his breeches were of the finest doeskin, fitting tightly. As he was carried along he was cheered by the crowd and gaily waved his fine lace handkerchief, the silver of which flashed in the bright winter sunshine.

It appeared that he was being acknowledged by the populace as a sort of king, a king of knaves perhaps. In their dull lives, and dressed in their tatters and rags, which contrasted so sharply with the highwayman's finery, the mob had never before seen such a magnificent sight in Hexham. Indeed, thought Elizabeth, Charles II's entrance into London after exile could not have been more impressive, except perhaps in its much greater scale.

An excited bystander enthused: "That's Jack Preece, the rascal. He's been working the Newcastle road for years and nobody could catch him, but now he's robbed for the last time. Aye, but he could be very generous with his loot. They say he has kept alive many a poor widow. But this is the end of his reign of terror against the rich."

Robert gasped: " I remember hearing that a highwayman had been taken on the night that Alexander disappeared. It took a dozen men, one of whom was killed by a horse and two others shot and wounded. His trial must be over and now he is to be hanged for his villainy."

Elizabeth was shocked. "I don't want to see this, Robert. Is there any way that we can get out of the crush?"

"I'm afraid not. We are solidly packed in, and if we try to barge our way out, the horses may be injured or we may hurt someone. If you don't want to watch, then look elsewhere. It's too late to escape but we might just ease our way to the edge to join the other horsemen."

As he spoke he turned the head of Elizabeth's mount, and by dint of urgent requests to the people who were swarming around them, they were able to seek the company of those who had a similar vantage point on horseback.

The execution cart reached the gallows, where the prisoner, surrounded by armed soldiers, raised both of his arms aloft in a salute, and the crowd responded with cheers. He asked the captain of the guards if he might be permitted a few words before he met his end. Despite some brief opposition from the hangman who intimated that he was eager to get on with his work, his request was granted. Jack Preece stood to his full height and put his finger over his lips. The crowd immediately fell silent. The condemned man proceeded to address them clearly, confidently and with homespun eloquence.

"My friends, you think I am the prisoner, but indeed it is you that are prisoners, and have been shackled since the day you were born. You think that I meet death soon, but you have a living death every day of every year that you live. You are victimised by the wealthy, who waste the honest resources that you have earned with your hard toil. I have never taken from a poor man. In fact you all know how generous I have been. I have never killed except in self defence. I die as generous as I lived, and give my soul back to my Maker, knowing that I never to my knowledge stole from an honest man and never willingly transgressed the laws of God."

There was complete silence as the stunned crowd absorbed what he had said, then a cheer broke forth from the watchers, spasmodic at first, then swelling to a crescendo. The soldiers' grip on their weapons tightened as they realised the sympathy Preece had generated. Most of those present had never seen a public execution before. Some women were openly weeping, others were paralysed with the horror of the scene, while those filled with blood lust were relishing the spectacle. For her part Elizabeth gazed at the highwayman, fascinated by the vitality of the life that was about to be quenched. Looking anxiously towards Robert, she noted that he did not seem to show any sign of compassion. Indeed her own thoughts strayed out of control to the macabre display in the barber surgeon's hall.

The highwayman took off his periwig and threw it into the crowd, causing a commotion of outstretched arms eager to seize the prize. Ignoring the chill wind, he took off his coat and flung it as far as he could, with similar consequences, and then, with great care, he took the rings from his fingers and bent down to give them to two young men behind the cart. He was heard to say: "Do a good job, lads."

More cheers erupted as the crowd sensed that the end was near. The highwayman placed one foot on the front panel of the cart and raised his hand for silence.

"I leave you with this thought. When Adam delved and Eve span, who was then the gentleman? Now I reach out towards a welcome freedom," he announced, and took a step towards the dangling noose. The wary, stern-faced guards stiffened and menacingly levelled their muskets at the crowd. The hooded hangman climbed into the cart beside Jack Preece. He tied his hands behind his back and offered to put a scarf around his eyes, which was refused. Then he looped the swaying rope round his neck and dismounted. The silence was intense. Next moment, with a sharp crack of the whip, the cart was driven forward and everyone gasped. Jack Preece was jerked backwards and his legs swung wildly as he tried to resist the tightening rope. The two young men assigned for the gruesome task jumped up to grasp his ankles and under their combined weight the struggling soon ceased.

"What a waste of what could have been an honest soul," whispered Elizabeth. "I wish to go home now."

An emaciated ruffian nearby heard her. "And what sort of home is yours?" he sneered as he took hold of the horse's rein and looked at her menacingly.

Robert, alert to any threat, eyed him severely and in a flash struck him on the hand with the butt of his whip. Snatching her horse's rein he carefully steered them to the edge of the crowd which was already dispersing, clamorous after the excitement of the horror they had witnessed.

The ruffian yelped, wincing with the pain and eyed the musketeers, controlling his anger as he nursed his hand. "Who is that clever fellow who thinks he can put everybody right?" he asked his neighbours.

Someone replied: "I think it's Robert Carr, the steward at Nunburn Hall. I have seen him in Priestpopple Street on market days."

"I will never forget him," was the reply. "He's put my finger out of joint."

As they made their way through the throng Robert was worried that this had ruined their day. "You will have to put all of this out of your mind," he said. "We don't rule the world. Just a small patch around Woodedge Manor."

"Then let's make it a particular heaven for us and everyone," whispered Elizabeth.

"With you anywhere would be heaven, Elizabeth," Robert replied, gazing at her enraptured.

For the rest of the journey they travelled in silence. Robert felt threatened and was particularly concerned for their safety, but Elizabeth was wrapped in delicious dreams of their new home, planning their future together.

They were relieved to arrive safely back home and Robert described in great detail the recent events in Hexham to the alarmed Lancelot.

"We will have to be vigilant for a while. Rabble-rousing ideas can be dangerous, so see to your pistols, and keep the stables well locked at night. You'll have to keep an eye on Woodedge Manor, since it's empty," he said.

"Yes, I'll warn everyone. Do you mind if I spend some time at Woodedge Manor? There's so much to do, and I am eager to start on the work."

Elizabeth smiled. "I'll be there to help. You may be sure," she replied.

Robert frowned. "Steady on. It's no place for a woman. You'd just get in the way. See it when it's finished and I'll enjoy getting everything ready for you."

Elizabeth made a face.

Lancelot interceded: "I have been to inspect it recently and I could see that the old house will take months to restore. We can call in Aunt Caroline again to advise about the furnishings, and Elizabeth will have her hands full in that respect. You have a mighty task before you, but I'll give you all the time you need, and you are welcome to borrow some of the men."

In the ensuing months he was true to his word and each day some of the most skilled men were directed to the old house. Thankfully it was found that the roof was in good order and they were able to concentrate on the interior, removing the old plaster where necessary, cutting out rotten stairs and floor-boards, and dismantling damaged doors, doorposts and lintels. The discarded materials were either burnt in the hearth or carried out to a huge pile in the back garden, and the floors were constantly swept and surfaces regularly dusted. In time the carpenter was brought in from the village to make a list of every item which needed replacing, and the aged Christopher Charlton was delighted to be asked to accompany him. Robert sent a groom to Hexham to place an order for the timber required. He had saved money from his salary as steward for many years and now it was to be put to good use.

Chapter 39

When Robert visited Hexham to see the timber which had been ordered he carried a pistol. He had received a warning from the Charlton family that a kinsman of theirs had overheard a conversation in a tavern in which Robert's name had been mentioned, and a plot of some violence towards him. Old Christopher Charlton was sure that there was real mischief afoot.

"There are plenty of thugs in that town who resent any kind of gentry, especially those who are prospering. Take good care young master."

Robert laughed off the threats. "Why should anyone be bothered about me, when I live so far from Hexham?"

He would have realised that he had cause to worry if he had seen a group of ruffians that same evening, loitering at a corner in Priestpopple Street. The man with the disjointed finger, Matthew Milburn, spoke bitterly, holding up the injured hand.

"That's what I got from his high and mighty. And now he's putting right his manor house and preparing to marry that witch from Newcastle."

One of his companions was intrigued. "A witch, you say?"

"Yes. She was lucky to escape from hanging in Newcastle after her trial. If she hadn't put a spell on Woodall she'd have swung alright."

A third plotter, a cross-eyed man with dirty wild red hair, was full of vitriol. "That Lancelot Woodall is another cleversides. Both he and Robert Carr need to be taught a painful lesson. Jack Preece was right."

Milburn was energised by such talk. "Let's go and take them tomorrow night, when it's pitch dark. Carr gets it first."

The conversation was interrupted as the sullen sky, which had been darkening all evening, released a heavy rainstorm. The heavens opened and the threatened deluge cleared the street. In a matter of minutes torrential rain was flooding the road and the group hastily sought shelter in their familiar tavern. Their host brought ale and took a seat beside them. He was confidential as he leaned forward, speaking in little above a whisper.

"I have an interestin' guest tonight, no other than the young brother of Lancelot Woodall of Nunburn, just back from London He thinks I don't recognise him, and I'm not lettin' on, but he is very bitter against the Nunburn lot, and I told him that several of our townsmen feel the same, and are ready for action. He is anxious to meet you and to join your enterprise. It seems that he has a grudge against the family who have used him so ill and cast him adrift without a penny. He is meanin' to use us but we'll play the brat at his own game and use him. Shall I bring him down?"

The rogues were startled at this new development but Milburn's eyes glinted with excitement. "Yes. He can help us no end. He'll know all the buildings, the family routine and the possible risks. If we need to burn down the place he'll tell us where to find the wherewithal. Bring him here now."

Alexander Woodall entered. He looked ill-fed and was as dirty as any of the conspirators. He sat down beside them and addressed his eager audience in a voice which throbbed with malevolence.

"Gentlemen. You are kind enough to ask me to help in your endeavours, which may be made easier by what I can tell you. But I have old scores to settle at Nunburn and I'd be grateful if you will allow me to accompany you when you go there."

Milburn nudged his nearest companion. He pretended to scrutinise Alexander very carefully, and after due consideration said: "Good! You are very welcome. Let us talk."

They decided to carry out their mission on the following evening, taking advantage of the dark nights and what promised to be a drier day.

They set off next day as planned. Milburn was armed with a dagger and the others with heavy cudgels, hidden under their coats. Alexander guided them along by-ways which he had known since his boyhood and no human eye detected their steady northward progress. By late evening they had passed Humshaugh and continued through damp meadows adjoining the river. They rested for a while in a grove of trees and ate a meagre bite of bread and cheese, washed down with ale.

"We have only a short distance to travel. Let us go over the plan once more so that each man knows his part," said Alexander, taking charge.

Ignoring him, Milburn growled: "We wait for Carr to do his final rounds and retire to the Dower House. Then Peter, Dick and I catch up with him just before he secures the door. What can you do?"

"I'll keep watch on the house and warn you if there is any danger," replied Alexander, "And once Carr is dealt with leave the witch to me. She won't even be recognisable when I have finished with her. I'll get straw from the stables and heap it in the best places. You return to me and between us we set fire to the ring of straw piles. But remember, leave the witch to me. I'll enjoy taming her cleverness. Is that agreed? Then we head back to Hexham and tomorrow we'll hear of the dreadful accident which has befallen the famous Woodall stronghold."

Milburn chuckled evilly as he ran his thumb along the blade of his knife. "I may just have time to cut off his fingers, to remind him of his mistake in injuring mine. And if you make any mistake I'll take one of yours."

Alexander was unable to stop a shiver running down his spine as he heard the threat, but he gave no sign of his unease and stood up to continue the final fatal furlong towards his erstwhile home.

The gloom stood them in good stead and they were able to take up positions behind the Dower House, where they lay concealed till Robert Carr should return to his bachelor quarters.

Chapter 40

That night Robert had stayed late at Woodedge Manor, talking with old Christopher Charlton. By the time he took his leave it was pitch black outside and he began to regret that he had stayed so long. His horse, however, knew the road well and kept to the track in that strange instinctive way possessed by animals.

He passed the Hunter's Gap cottages where he could hear a man and woman bickering angrily and the voices of sobbing children. His neck prickled with apprehension as they neared Nunburn, where the track skirted a line of trees, their outlines lost against the starless sky. Then the horse's hoofs crunched on the gravel as it turned into the grounds of the Hall.

In the stables he found one of the footmen trimming lanterns. It was Gerrard, the silent young man, sent out by Mistress Grant, who jumped as he entered.

"Oh! Mr. Carr! You gave me a fright there. It must have been you who made the horses uneasy. They've been restless for the last ten minutes."

"Sorry, Gerrard! I didn't know anybody would be in here now. I'm straight off to bed, anyway. It's such a dark night that I'll take one of your lanterns across the yard. Goodnight."

After stabling the horse he chose a lantern and crossed to the Dower House. The Hexham men watched intently and silently closed in, ready to launch their assault. Inside, Robert stooped to pick up the oak bar which secured the door at night, and was just about to drop it into its twin sockets when the door was hurled open by the combined force of the three intruders. Robert was swept aside and fell to the floor, still clutching the heavy bar. The lantern was knocked over and the light went out. Now the initiative of the intruders was lost. Robert sprang to his feet, swinging the bar at head-height, and had the satisfaction of feeling it impact on something hard but yielding. The man who had been caught by the immense blow grunted sharply and collapsed. One of the others tripped over the prone figure and went sprawling. Robert could only guess at the odds he now faced, and chose to make the most of his knowledge of the Dower House.

If only he could climb the wooden ladder to the living quarters above he would be safe from attack and have access to his pistols. A few warning shots might rouse the Nunburn Hall household and bring much-needed help.

Meanwhile Gerrard was disturbed by the renewed agitation of the horses. He seized a pitchfork and carefully opened the stable door. Then he heard shouts coming from the Dower House. He bent double and scuttled across the pitch-black yard towards the noises.

Robert's heart was pounding as he tried to establish if the way to the steps was clear. His life probably depended on it. He listened intently as feet scuffled about the floor space, and heard the oaths as the intruders blundered into sacks of straw. He found a piece of wood in his pocket and cunningly threw it into the corner most remote from the intruders, who paused and then made a rush towards the sound as the wood rebounded from the wall.

In the same instant Robert groped for the ladder and at last came to it without interference. So often had he climbed these steps that he knew every rung and angle. Just as he thought he had safely reached the trapdoor a vibration through the ladder warned that someone was following him. His frantic leap up the last few steps took him to the level of the living quarters and he thrust open the trapdoor, just avoiding a clutching hand which sought to pull him back.

Once safely up on the floor of his living quarters Robert slammed down the heavy trapdoor, pinioning the hand which could not be withdrawn, but which prevented the heavy bolts from being secured. Robert placed his whole weight on the trapdoor and the man below screamed in pain. When Robert judged that the hand was sufficiently crushed he stepped aside from the door and the man fell down the ladder in a series of uneven bounces. Quick as a flash Robert slipped home the bolts and sat on the boards, panting for breath.

As he lit a rush-light he could hear voices below snarling threats. "Let's smoke him out."

"You'll have to do it. My hand is crushed and useless. I can't rouse Peter. I think he's dead. But get young Woodall. He knows where everything is."

At this Robert became very alert. Who could they mean? Surely Alexander was not one of their number? And yet they seemed to have planned very accurately the details of the ambush and were knowledgeable regarding the layout of the Dower House. It all pointed to the renegade having made a vengeful return, in his cowardice recruiting thugs to make the physical assault.

He took out a pistol, checked that it was primed, and fired off a single shot through one of the slit-like windows. The sound cracked sharply across the darkness and roosting birds took off in fright. In the Hall several sleepers awoke and peered through their windows, seeing nothing. A second report shattered the silence. Men tucked their night-shirts into their breeches and headed for the nearest doors.

Alexander, hastily summoned by Dick, entered the Dower House where Matthew Milburn was nursing his broken hand.

"Quick! Set fire to these bags of straw, then we'll run for it."

Alexander, incompetent as ever, was all thumbs. He dropped his tinder box and could not locate it in the darkness. By now his courage was failing and he blamed his companions for their failure to deal with Robert Carr. His usual luck, he thought. Retiring to the doorway through which a cool breeze blew, he stumbled over Peter's inert form. As he recovered his balance he turned left through the doorway and skirted the Dower House wall. He had covered about ten feet when a strong arm drove the sharp pitchfork clean through his neck, and he fell with a stifled scream, choking on the blood which spurted into his throat from the dreadful wound. Gerrard, the footman reputed to be a half-wit, had been his downfall. A lack of so-called wit had never diminished the strength of his arm. Alexander's body was dragged into the bushes.

Matthew Milburn and his crony peeped out of the doorway. Lights were appearing in numbers across at the Hall but a confusion of voices indicated that there was no conception of what was happening. All they knew was that the pistol shots probably came from Robert's gun, since he was the sole pistol owner apart from the Woodalls. Lancelot held back the little band of retainers till he could ascertain Robert's circumstances.

"Robert! Where are you?"

An answering cry came from the slit window where Robert stood.

"I am safe on the first level. But take care. There are three or four of these villains. I may have disabled one or two of them, but they are desperate. They're trying to set fire to the house."

Lancelot bravely advanced, pistol in hand, and as he did so the two assassins slipped quietly round to the back of the Dower House. But they, too, had not reckoned on the resourcefulness of the slow-witted footman. He had hidden close to the massive wall, crouching low, and when he heard the furtive footsteps and heavy breathing of the fugitives he held his trusty pitchfork tightly, ready to impale an unsuspecting enemy. Matthew Milburn was the unlucky one this time. While only a foot away from his doom the pitchfork speared out and cut short his career of villainy. Dick took to his heels and ran completely in the wrong direction. Another body was concealed in the bushes.

Silence ensued. Lancelot's group were sufficiently emboldened to approach the Dower House and their lanterns revealed Peter's body, half of his face stoved in where Robert's mighty blow with the oak bar had caught him. Abandoned cudgels and a knife lay on the floor.

"Robert! You can come down safely. The gang has run off."

Robert unbolted the trapdoor and descended the ladder at a more leisurely speed than that of his frantic ascent.

"Thank God you came so promptly. They were going to set fire to this place. See that tinder-box on the floor! I was on the verge of shooting my way out when they lost their nerve."

"All seems to be clear, now," announced Lancelot. "The rascals have fled, but as soon as it is light we'll scour the district on horseback, and with a little luck we'll catch them."

As the throng, buzzing with excitement, discussed the surprise attack, Gerrard secured a lantern and was eager to look at his victims, just in case a fat purse was going begging. He walked to and fro, as if looking for the intruders. When safely among the bushes he found the bodies where he had left them. He did not recognise Milburn but was more than alarmed when he saw Alexander's haggard face with its gingery bristles. Panic gripped his heart. It would never do to be held responsible for the death of Mr. Woodall's son, even in self-defence.

Dousing his lantern, he hastily threw Alexander's body over his shoulder and headed for the river. With luck it might never be discovered, and a flood-stream could even carry the evidence down beyond Hexham. He returned to the scene of the attack and mingled unnoticed with the excited crowd of domestics, who knew that they would have a topic of conversation for many years, stories enriched by fertile imaginations to chill the hearts of listeners around the winter hearth. But his part in that story would never be told and Robert had already chosen to stifle his darkest thoughts. The blood-stained pitchfork was wiped clean and restored to its stand, ready for more mundane tasks.

Chapter 41

The search next day yielded only the body of Milburn in the bushes near the Dower House. It was assumed that he had been stabbed in error by a blundering associate. Lancelot informed the magistrates at Hexham and for a few days armed soldiers combed the area, but found nothing to report. The heavy rains had given the swollen river such power that a body went swirling head downwards at great speed past villages and towns. Little did Henry Woodall realise it, but, as he watched the busy river at the Newcastle quayside, his ill-fated son was being carried by in the heavy depth of the out-flowing tide, vanishing forever under the pall of salt-works steam, smoke and coal dust.

Over the succeeding weeks memories of the gang's intrusion faded, and confidence returned to the Woodall establishment. For a while no great improvement was seen at Woodedge Manor, but in due course the place suddenly seemed to look habitable, and Robert could breathe again with a sense of relief. Indeed it was possible to breathe more easily in the house itself as the damp parts had been cut away and a beautiful aroma of freshly-sawn wood replaced the musty smell.

Aunt Caroline became very useful at this stage, because she could remember visiting Robert's parents, and had a clear idea of what the manor had been like in its heyday.

"The Great Hall had pale blue walls above the panelling and the oriel room was mainly gold and pink. Its window seat was upholstered in dark red which matched the rugs on the floor. The parlour was largely panelled but its upper walls were coloured in a pale yellow or primrose, and, as I remember vaguely, the chapel was of bare stonework with a single dark red rug. We weren't allowed in there very often."

She was eager to help Elizabeth with the restoration, and arrived once more to stay at Nunburn. Their first task was to visit the manor and take measurements for curtains, with the help of two of the maids. More than once they enjoyed the excitement of being driven into Newcastle to visit Uncle Anthony and inspect the rich variety of materials which were readily available at the mercers' shops. A couple of seamstresses were brought to Nunburn Hall to help with the making of curtains and hangings. The Hall was again a centre of constructive activity and the two rooms used as workrooms were in constant use.

When she saw what was involved Elizabeth anxiously questioned: "How are all these to be paid for, Aunt Caroline?"

"Oh, don't worry. Uncle Anthony told me to tell you that his ship has come in. That's all! Don't give it a second thought." However, Elizabeth ruefully remembered her uncle's own faded curtains.

For a long period Aunt Caroline and Elizabeth spent many happy days making beautiful cushion covers and quilted bedcovers. Elizabeth was well on the way to becoming a skilled embroideress, a craft which had previously been beyond her experience. She was delighted to see the accumulation of new furnishings growing daily.

"This is going to be such a happy surprise for Robert. He is so fully occupied between his duties as steward and his rebuilding tasks that we see little of each other, except at mealtimes."

"Well, that means that you don't have the opportunity to fall out," chuckled her aunt.

However, the one person who bridged the gap was Aunt Caroline herself, and she would often be missing for hours, driven up to Woodedge in a little cart pulled by Merrilegs.

She confessed: "I need to refresh my memory on the details of the manor, such as which rooms receive the full sun and which are shady. The positioning of the furniture is also important, so I'll need measurements for that."

She checked the progress of the work, took the important measurements, and made little lists on her slate. She even had time to visit the cottagers at both Woodedge Farm and Hunter's Gap Farm, after which the slate was covered on both sides. Elizabeth visited her new home less frequently. She was hounded by the idea that so many things would not be ready by the date of the wedding and was alarmed that so much seemed to depend on guess-work. Nevertheless she trusted Aunt Caroline completely and therefore did not interfere. She knew how important it was to listen to experience, and relied on her in all matters of taste.

After the prolonged activity the seamstresses were nearly finished and thoughts were turned to the bride's gown.

"Elizabeth, your father will want to have you dressed like a princess. You so deserve it," enthused her aunt, "And your uncle has promised you the best material that money can buy."

"No, Aunt Caroline. Robert and I have decided that a quiet wedding would be more fitting in our circumstances and we will have only our closest relations to return with us to the Dower House."

Aunt Caroline looked surprised.

"I am going to send to Hackford for my sister Isabel's wedding dress and bonnet because I want to be dressed exactly like her. Hers was such a happy wedding day," said Elizabeth. " I wish for everything to be just like the wedding at Hackford."

Aunt Caroline paused, deep in thought. "Every bride should have what she wishes on her special day, and I'm sure you'll be very beautiful, whatever you wear," she predicted, with tears in her eyes, her secret feelings being full of reservations.

And so the wedding arrangements were easily completed, not perhaps as Aunt Caroline had wished, but to the satisfaction of the bride. The improvements at the manor house were abruptly terminated a week before the ceremony and Woodall insisted that the labour was to be withdrawn, much to Robert's annoyance and disappointment. As Robert had neglected his work on the Nunburn estate he was required to perform many other duties and after this time it was mysterious how no one was ever available and all was so quiet at the Hall. Uncle Anthony arrived one day in a rush and had no time to talk to anyone except Aunt Caroline. Even Mistress Grant was too preoccupied to be of any use. However, time seemed to fly as the important day came close. Elizabeth was nervous now, hoping that all the guests would be able to come, yet anxious that they would get on well together, their backgrounds being so widely different.

It was a relief to Elizabeth when she learnt that Anne Shafto and her family had committed themselves to a sojourn with their relations in Yorkshire and could not attend the wedding.

Chapter 42

At last the wedding day came. The dull May morning was turning into a bright sunny day as the bride's party looked out of the window and spied Robert and Lancelot setting out from the Dower House for Hexham. A groom trailed behind with extra horses. Elizabeth was dressed in Isabel's wedding dress, which looked stunning in its simple elegance. Her father stood back to survey her and said: "I couldn't have been happier on my own wedding day than I am now. Robert is a fine fellow and I am very proud of my clever beautiful daughter."

He put his hand in his pocket and showed Elizabeth the most exquisite necklace she had ever seen.

"This is your grandmother's, and I know she would wish you to have it on this special day."

With tears in her eyes Elizabeth allowed him to place it round her neck, in spite of the fact that the sparkling diamonds and emeralds were totally out of keeping with her simple homemade dress.

The servants lined up as the bride, her father and Aunt Caroline descended the steps towards the decorated coach which was to convey them to Hexham, and clapped them all the way down. Aunt Caroline, who was beautifully dressed in a simple blue gown and bonnet, was brimming over with happiness and she paused briefly to watch Elizabeth as she was being helped up the coach step. She wished that she too could be young again and that she had not been robbed of her husband so early, with the chance of having children. However, she consoled herself that she had played an important part in this wedding. With a knowing look she said to her brother: "Thank goodness everything is ready now."

"So all the preparations are complete?" he inquired.

"Yes. All is ready, nothing is left to chance," she replied mysteriously, looking away from him.

They were finally installed inside the coach and four horses moved forward as one at the driver's command. Elizabeth was wrapped in her own thoughts as she swayed in the jolting carriage, watching the passing countryside. She wondered what her companions were thinking. She need not have bothered because at present their minds were almost blank.

Now that the great day had come she distinctly lacked something to worry about. She thought hard. This was the last day that she would be a maid, and she would soon be under what could be the stern authority of Robert. Alas, even as a child, when pretending not to be listening, in the company of other women her ears had pricked up as she watched the wagging heads warning that no one could ever tell what a man was like until the door was locked behind them. Her eyes narrowed. Was Robert to be the caring husband that she and everyone else took him for? Surely she was not like a lamb going to the slaughter! She had longed for this day and she knew that she could not help herself, so why worry?

Better to worry about John and Joanna and her friends from Hackford. How would they be able to mix with the Woodall circle? She hoped that they would enjoy themselves. It was an important day for them too, and they deserved some happiness after their early setbacks and for their kindness in looking after her. She rejoiced as she thought of all her life, past and future, spreading out before her. She felt an inner glow as she imagined Canon Ritschell waiting for them in Hexham Abbey, just as he had done when he had married John and her mother, then John and Joanna, and then Cuthbert and Isabel; Canon Ritschell, who had baptised her and educated her and watched over her all her life. All were ever-turning circles of love and understanding, and all linked inextricably together. Such were her varied thoughts as they drew up outside the abbey.

With her happiness and confidence restored Elizabeth radiated beauty and elegance. The coachmen, perched on their high seats and constantly alert, surveyed the crowd and patted their pistols.

Waiting for them in eager anticipation and covered in smiles, were John and Joanna, and Cuthbert and Isabel holding the baby. When Woodall helped her to alight from the carriage he took Elizabeth's hand and gave it to John.

"John, this is your special day. You must take her to the church."

John was touched and Joanna put her hand on his back, looking up at him proudly. He bent down to Elizabeth and kissed her and Elizabeth hugged him affectionately. They led the party to the heavy doors, past the wide stairs, and entered the nave. Robert was waiting with Canon Ritschell and Lancelot and he nodded to John. The service was simple and the voices clear as they made their vows. When Robert slipped the ring on Elizabeth's finger he whispered: "This is my mother's ring and it was never taken from her finger till the day she died."

"Then it will be the same for me," Elizabeth vowed, looking up at him intently.

The couple appeared strikingly handsome as they walked down the aisle and through the churchyard to climb into the first of the two waiting carriages. In the second carriage were Joanna, Isabel with the baby and Aunt Caroline, followed by the men on horseback. The journey to Nunburn Hall was sheer delight and Robert held Elizabeth's hand. Mesmerised by his good fortune he kept spinning the wedding ring continuously round her finger. It seemed no time before they came to the gates at Nunburn Hall to take the expected path to the Dower House. However, the coachman missed the turn and continued on the road to Hunter's Gap. Robert urgently tapped on the roof and they came sharply to a halt, blocking the coach behind. An annoyed Robert popped his head out of the door, shouting loudly: "How on earth have you missed the way to the Dower House?"

Woodall's firm voice came from behind: "You must go straight to Woodedge Manor."

Hardly had he spoken before the coaches resumed the journey and Robert was thrown back into the carriage, puzzled and very annoyed. His lips began to twitch furiously as he transferred his gaze from one side of the road to the other.

"I didn't want you to see the manor house until it was properly finished. It was an untidy mess, with little furniture, when I left it last week. I can't think why on our wedding day your father is doing this to us. Mistress Grant will have prepared a good spread for us at the Dower House. I thought that at least now I would be in full control of my life."

He was perturbed and Elizabeth felt her heart fluttering, but she remained silent, diverting her attention to the passing countryside. The sway of the coach was making her feel sick and she thought it was surprising how their mood could change so quickly. Despite their irritation they found the good grace to wave back at the Hunter's Gap tenants who were lining the road dressed in their Sunday best. The cottagers trooped along behind the coaches, following in great glee.

When they came close to Woodedge Manor, they could see that a crowd had gathered. The coaches came to a halt at the front entrance and Robert helped Elizabeth from the carriage, hardly stifling a glower in the direction of his new father-in-law who was dismounting.

An unexpected guard of honour of eight deeply bronzed men was ranged up in front of the main doorway, their arms raised to form an arch of crossed hay rakes. Behind them on both sides were the families from the cottages, clapping and cheering loudly. Laughter filled the air as the couple first stood and looked at them in astonished silence, and then Robert moved forward and exclaimed: "John Dinning! And so brown!"

Elizabeth recognised the women and immediately realised that these must be the men from Barbados. The tenants shouted: "Under the Guard of Honour," and, holding hands, the bridal pair bent their heads low to pass beneath. The young brothers, Tom and Richard Graham, darted in front of them, scattering flower petals in their path. At the last they had to duck even lower as little Edward Buckham was there, grinning broadly, with his arms outstretched, and standing on tiptoe to make himself taller.

As they reached the garlanded door it swung open mysteriously of its own accord. Shouts of : "Carry the bride over the threshold!" came from all around. Robert bent low to sweep up Elizabeth's graceful frame into his arms and proudly carried her inside their home, amid a shower of grain, cheering, and shrieks of laughter. They had now entered the screens passage, and as Robert put Elizabeth down on the flagged floor, a tall handsome figure emerged from the shadows to greet them. It was cousin Thomas, his blond hair bleached into flaxen streaks by the tropical sun, his skin browner than she had ever seen, and there he was, waiting for them with his arms outstretched. Elizabeth ran forward, and, in floods of tears, kissed him again and again and again. All she could say was: "Thomas, oh, Thomas, you're safely back," as the tension was broken with sobs.

Lancelot and Robert were motioning to the other guests to come inside, and Woodall strode out and indicated to all the gathered tenants that they too were welcome to join in the feast and celebrations.

A piper was pumping up his pipes in the kitchen recess, and he took up his position in front of the couple to lead them into the hall. Elizabeth would not release her hold of Thomas so he entered the hall with his arms round both of them, but took a step backwards as they stopped before a most astonishing sight.

The hall had been lavishly prepared for the wedding. Bright curtains and wallhangings were all in place, crisp and clean. A large oak table laden with food ran down the middle, and unlit candles were standing ready everywhere. A fire was crackling in the huge hearth and there sitting by the fireplace was none other than Uncle Anthony. He beamed with happiness at their surprise, rubbing his hand round and round his red bulbous nose, completely unaware of what he was doing, and from time to time snorting with uncontrollable laughter, accompanied from behind by Francis Hall's characteristic high pitched "Hee-hee-hee". Anthony rose and pointed to the table. "Charles's wedding present for you!" he cried above the din of the revellers. The milling throng moved in and the excited voices swelled as the locals viewed the transformation.

"So this is the reason why I was being kept out of the way! The house is exactly as I remembered it," gasped Robert in amazement, as his bright eyes flashed around the room. Elizabeth appreciated all the carefully made furnishings that had been keeping them busy for so many long hours. By now Aunt Caroline was standing close to them, eagerly watching their reactions and her brother was lingering nearby, nervously flicking the stiff curls of his brand new wig. Elizabeth spotted them and nudged Robert to get his attention. The older woman kissed them fondly.

"So this is why you've been mysteriously disappearing all these days and keeping us away! Thank you. This is the most wonderful wedding present ever."

"You haven't seen half of the presents yet," said Aunt Caroline, and gently ushered them to the side of the hall.

Standing beside the furniture, which was arranged exactly as it had been years ago, were the tenants in their best finery, grinning at the newly married couple. Robert immediately recognised the well-loved furniture of his childhood, with the familiar plate ranged on top.

Almost choking with joy, Aunt Caroline explained: "These good people came into the Hall before the Parliamentary Commissioners arrived, and hid your parents' possessions in barns and in their houses until they felt it was the right time to hand them over to you."

Robert surveyed everything in amazed rapture and went round the room shaking hands and thanking them over and over again for their kindness. Then he returned to the centre of the hall and proclaimed in a loud voice: "My wife and I ..." to good-natured cheers of approval, and continued proudly.... "bid you a warm welcome. Now let us all feast!" This was exactly as his father had said it so many years ago.

Mistress Grant, Dolly Askew and other helpers stood behind the table and distributed the wedding fare with an amiable mixture of kindness and deftness. The table was spread with boiled and roast meats, enhanced with fancy pickles and sauces. An excited Isabel quickly found the white manchet bread which she had never seen in her life. She called Cuthbert across to see how baby John was enjoying it in his mouth. "Look, I don't have to chew it for him. He can manage it himself! He won't want oat-bread after this."

The little one stretched out his arm, opening and shutting his palms, eager for more. John and Joanna were the first to congratulate the housekeeper on the sumptuous feast and wandered all round the newly refurbished manor with some incredulity, marvelling at their daughter's good fortune. The barber surgeon smiled at them, brandishing a tankard of ale in one hand and a tasty leg of chicken in the other.

When the tables were empty and the candles lit, the fiddler started playing well-known melodies, and the hall was cleared for dancing. An elated Robert and Elizabeth led off at a brisk pace, the latter high-stepping with great energy, and the rafters of the old hall again resounded to music and merriment. Baby John screeched with excitement as Cuthbert whirled him round and round at head-height, his fist still holding on to the precious bread.

Later, John found time to whisper to Elizabeth: "George asked me to tell you that he'll soon have the best possible weddin' present ever for you."

Elizabeth was intrigued: "Come on. Tell me what it is."

"I can't. It's goin' to be a surprise," said John resolutely, and he pulled her chin ever so gently.

Old William was there to provide a quiet time with songs and stories, allowing the dancers to recover their strength. Woodall stood with his hand on John's shoulder, listening intently to the traditional tales which he had never heard before. William had everybody under his spell, changing his voice to suit each character that he portrayed. It is doubtful whether he even knew of the existence of Shakespeare but he would have been enthralled with his plays, and would obviously have been in his element as an actor. His final story was the old ballad, "The Faire Flower of Northumberland."

His listeners were enthralled to hear the tale of the liberation of a Scottish prisoner by the beautiful daughter of the Earl of Northumberland, their flight to Scotland, and her pitiful return home after hearing from the faithless knight's own lips that he already had a wife and five children. William concluded with great passion:

"Scots were never true, nor never will be

To lord nor lady nor faire England."

Some of the female listeners were in tears and there followed a short silence broken only by Dolly Askew who failed to stifle a sob and was immediately given a sharp nudge by Mistress Grant.

Woodall took this opportunity to shout out: "King Louis' Dance" and Uncle Anthony stoutly echoed the request. Straightaway the fiddler was able to strike up the well rehearsed tune and the floor was cleared. Elizabeth and Lancelot had no alternative but to take up their positions and to the amazement of the rustic company performed the sophisticated gyrations with a studied elegance that amused even themselves. At the end there was loud applause and the simple peasants marvelled at the elegance of the French court, though finding it somewhat quaint.

Mistress Grant beamed with pleasure as she shook her head. "My little

Lancelot was forever forward."

"What do you mean?" asked Dolly.

"God be praised you will never know," said Mistress Grant quietly.

Still at Woodall's side John whispered to him, "You have made Elizabeth very happy."

Deeply touched, he replied: "She has made me even happier. I've never felt as close to anyone in my life, except perhaps my mother."

Aunt Caroline observed their familiarity as she was sitting beside Uncle Anthony, and, when the country music resumed, both tapped their feet with great gusto, and were having a wonderful time, watching the tenants enjoying themselves. Uncle Anthony whispered in her ear: "It's lonely, being alone." Aunt Caroline looked at him intensely and nodded. A tear formed in her eye.

After hours of merriment, the guests' energy and enthusiasm dwindled, and after shaking hands with the newly-weds they began to disperse, except for the Hackford family who had been invited to stay overnight. Cuthbert and Isabel had found a nook in the hall in which baby John was already tucked up, fast asleep. Cuthbert was among those who pushed the protesting Robert up the stairs and there was no gainsaying them.

"We are going back to the Dower House!" protested Robert repeatedly, looking behind him but he could not resist the pressure of the following pack of well-wishers and his words were lost in the din.

Thomas followed, carrying Elizabeth. Next came Lancelot who whispered to Elizabeth over Thomas' shoulder: "To have a sister and brother-in-law like you is a God-given treasure!"

Elizabeth was so happy, then. She whispered to Thomas: "It'll be your turn next."

Thomas was emphatic in reply. "No. I'm a one-woman man!"

When Robert arrived at the top of the stairs his suspicions were confirmed. The bedroom was already prepared for them. The bed curtains shimmered in the firelight and the walls were hung with old tapestries which for many years had been carefully preserved at the Dower House. A log fire crackled cheerfully in the ample hearth while friends and relations took a great delight in preparing the bride and groom for the nuptial bed. The bride-men took Robert away to be dressed in a crisp white night-shirt.

Elizabeth was installed in the most sumptuous standbed imaginable, enveloped in expensive green curtains embroidered with scrolls and flowers in silver thread. The bride had hardly the opportunity to examine her beautiful night gown but she could feel the embroidery on its high neck and ran her eyes down the sleeve seams which had matching decorations, and held out her arm to admire the careful gathering at the wrist which flared out in a characteristic design which surely revealed Aunt Caroline's skill.

As the bridegroom was brought forth with a flourish by Lancelot and his rollicking friends, she peered at him from behind the curtains, looking curious but apprehensive. The bridegroom leapt into bed. Lancelot and Thomas took up their places, sitting crosslegged at the bottom of the bed, and their winks and mischievous grins embarrassed the couple. Then the tousled head of a red-faced Edward Buckham popped cheekily round the doorpost.

"Watch out! Jiggers and snakes on the march!" he cried.

Conditioned to the dangers of the tropics, Thomas stiffened with fright, and then relaxed as he recognised the joker, who immediately fled down the stairs.

Lancelot and Thomas flamboyantly threw the stockings backwards to the anxious contenders, to be greeted with screams of delight. A smiling Isabel caught Elizabeth's eye as she retrieved from the bedside the bridal gown and the hair combs which her mother had used to adjust Elizabeth's curls. With no further excuse to dawdle the inebriated revellers tumbled down the stairs with parting shots of rustic advice. With the voices fading away the couple relaxed as they thought that they were alone for the first time that day.

Robert surveyed Elizabeth with admiration. He could hardly believe all the wonderful things that had happened. Elizabeth whispered to him: "How lucky we are to have such good friends and relations. I feel we are encircled with silver and golden threads binding us to them for the rest of our lives."

Robert looked up at the expensive curtains. "I hope so."

Elizabeth considered a moment and then, looking as innocent as a newly hatched chick in a nest, said teasingly: "There are three things, nay, four, that are wonderful to me. The flight of the eagle....."

With his finger Robert gently pressed her lips closed. "No more than the serpent on the rock." He took hold of Elizabeth's ring and made to slide it off her finger.

"No, never do that," she remonstrated, " It will stay there to my dying day."

"I wish to show you the two interlocking rings and how they come apart."

"But it's a bit too late for that!" Elizabeth insisted.

"Trust me," said Robert. He took Elizabeth's finger and firmly keeping the ring over the end, gently slid the interlocking rings sideways and read out the inscription hidden between the two halves. "That which God has joined let no man divide." Elizabeth put her head down to hide the tears in her eyes, quickly closed the lock and replaced the ring.

Robert stretched over to the bedside chair and took from his coat pocket the little wooden horse that he had once retrieved from the dusty floor. He held it out with great pride.

"This wooden horse is our lucky token. I spent many long hours playing with it as a child. It could tell better and more exciting adventures than even old William. Perhaps it will be a symbol of the happy change in our affairs and it will always remain here as a memory of the day when our own good fortune began."

He rose and with great deliberation placed it centrally on the mantelpiece. Elizabeth watched him closely because she was afraid that the flames from a log might reach his night-shirt, and she was relieved when he came back to bed. The horse fell on to its nose, but remained unnoticed. Robert carefully closed the bed curtains.

Totally wrapped up in each other they were completely unaware of a someone in the form of Dolly Askew creeping stealthily across the bedroom floor, slowing down and cringing at every creak of the boards and pinch of her skirt. She was genuinely trying not to show an interest in the bedroom talk, but could not help hearing and being puzzled by what she had heard. Why had the master been babbling on about his toy horse and now the mistress about the flight of an eagle? What could possibly be the meaning of the serpent on the rock? George Madgen, thank the Lord, was definitely not like that. Were all rich people so queer?

Dolly in her present position would have reminded anyone of a rabbit with her prominent buck teeth and bulging dark eyes. Much of the time she relied on the disarming innocence of a vacant expression, except when her curiosity was engaged, and then she could not disguise that she was remarkably focussed. She had come upstairs during the dancing because she could not resist having an inquisitive look round the unfamiliar rooms.Throughout the whole day she had concentrated on making sure that her behaviour had been impeccable, because she badly wanted a permanent position here at the manor. However, she was horror-stricken at the arrival of the bedding party, when she found herself trapped in the little room adjoining the bedchamber. In a panic she had spent the rest of the time leaning against the inner wall, chewing her finger nails and saying to herself: "I shouldn't be here - I shouldn't be here," and wondering how she would get out of this latest pickle.

When at last all was quiet she had decided to make a slow bolt for it on hands and knees. Her curiosity was more than satisfied by now, but she still could not help marvelling at the couple's conversation. She kept bravely on and then stopped when she heard Elizabeth say: "What about the way of a ship in the midst of the sea?"

To which Robert replied: "At the moment the fourth is my only concern."

Dolly definitely did not want to hear any more and reckoned that she must hasten away forthwith on all fours. She crept on so quickly that she did not even stand up when she reached the landing, but continued to creep down the stairs, exercising such control that she did not emit a single "Ouch." When she reached the bottom she came face to toe with Mistress Grant, who, in a tired voice said: "What on earth are you doing, girl? To think that I'm trying to groom you to be a fine upright housekeeper!"

Dolly was crestfallen. She quickly stood up, rubbing her sore knees, gulped painfully, pulled up her skirts, and fled to the kitchen in case she was further chastised, mumbling that on no account should they wake the baby. Besides, she was anxious to set out for the safety of the Home Farm immediately, hoping to meet George on the way. And so the big day ended with Mistress Grant sitting alone by the dying embers of the fire, sipping bride ale. She could not have been happier with the wedding if she had been Lady of the Manor.

~ ~ ~ ~ ~ ~ ~ ~

A junior doctor, Melissa Carr, was resting in a room at the Woodall Hospital at Newcastle. She snapped the book shut. Yes, she had enjoyed it, and it had come to a happy conclusion, but was it not just the beginning? It tantalised her, leaving a long list of unanswered questions. What would Elizabeth be like as a wife? She had no idea, but she congratulated herself that she had not lived in those hard times. How she wished that she could have done something to help them!

She put out the light and lay down to sleep, her auburn locks spread across the pillow. At last she would have some rest, and all she wanted to do was to sleep and sleep. She grimaced as her pager buzzed and she hastily dressed. Hurrying into the corridor, her white coat-tails flying, she almost collided with James, a colleague, who jumped smartly aside to avoid the bump.

Before she could escape he whispered in her ear: "Melissa Carr, you looked bewitching at the disco last night."

"I haven't got time. I must see my patient before his nibs comes round."

"You're joking," he gasped.

"Oh, no. I understand her much better than he does. You see, I feel for her."

Proof positive that the wheel indeed had turned, and will, we hope, continue to turn successfully for ever, and anon.